PLAIN FEAR
FORSAKEN

A NOVEL

PLAIN FEAR
FORSAKEN

A NOVEL

LEANNA ELLIS

sourcebooks
landmark

Published by Sourcebooks Landmark, an imprint of Sourcebooks, Inc.
P.O. Box 4410, Naperville, Illinois 60567-4410
(630) 961-3900
Fax: (630) 961-2168
www.sourcebooks.com

Library of Congress Cataloging-in-Publication Data

Ellis, Leanna.
  Plain fear : forsaken / Leanna Ellis.
      p. cm.
  1. Amish—Fiction. 2. Vampires—Fiction. I. Title.
  PS3605.L4677P57 2011
   813'.6—dc22
                              2011017398

Printed and bound in the United States of America.
VP 10 9 8 7 6 5 4 3 2 1

For Reita,
Rest peacefully, my sweet friend.

There is no fear in love. But perfect love drives out fear...

1 JOHN 4:18

PROLOGUE

JACOB FISHER SHOVED THE metal door, banging it against the warehouse, and the hollow sound reverberated in the awaiting stillness. *Don't look back. Not one glance.*

As he bolted into the sticky heat, darkness devoured him, but he continued into it, grateful for his only cover. The damp pavement made his tennis shoes skid, and his arms flailed wide as he regained his balance and pushed himself faster, harder, further. A shaft of light injected hope into him. *How far?*

Lungs burning, he risked one glance over his shoulder. Just one.

The warehouse door remained open, the alley empty. He was alone. For now. But how much longer? Whispers encircled him. Was it the wind? Or was it *them*?

"*Angels and ministers of grace defend us,*" Jacob whispered the Shakespearean words like a prayer.

Or had he gone crazy?

> *Be thou a spirit of health or goblin damn'd,*
> *Bring with thee airs from heaven or blasts from hell,*
> *Be thy intents wicked or charitable...*

No, *they* weren't a fabrication of his imagination or a half-baked fantasy. *They* were real, far too real. The blood, the bodies, and the evil permeating every crevice were authentic. Trolls of the night. Visitors from the bowels of hell. Their purpose was heinous, reflected in those black eyes that were void of feeling. And *they* chased after him now.

Misty rain surrounded him, not falling and yet always there, disorienting and confusing him. In those few seconds, he lived a century before he reached the end of the alley and skidded to a stop. Streetlamps provided halos of golden light, illuminating cars and storefronts, and yet at the same time created shadowy exiles. Where was everyone? An hour earlier—or had more time passed than he realized?—the street had teemed with people. Cars had honked, sirens screamed, and traffic lights blinked green, yellow, and red in quick succession. Both young and old had jockeyed for place along the crowded sidewalks, eager to get home after a long workweek.

But now, not one soul. Not one person to help. Not a single witness.

Fear gnawed at him. He'd only felt that kind of fear once before, when he had knelt beside Hannah's too still body. But his mind had stormed the barricade of fear then, frantic and frenzied. *Do something! Quick!* His heart had pounded out doubt. *How could he save her?*

Now what could he do to save himself? This fear continued to chase him, snapping at his heels. He bolted ahead of it, keeping just out of its chilling reach.

He kept to the sidewalk's edge, pressed his body flat along the brick building, pausing before each darkened doorway. *Glance left. Right. Go.* Shoot through the pale lamplight. Stop in the dark. Chest heaving. Check—front, back, then go again.

Metal bars covered the windows of the shops. Someone had warned him this part of New Orleans wasn't safe. What part was? But wasn't the possibility of danger why he'd come to the Big Easy?

His whole life he'd played with danger like a child's toy, running further, climbing higher, pushing farther than any of his friends dared. Maybe that's why he'd read books with their forbidden, dark views that had given him a glimpse of another world, a world set apart from what he'd known and experienced in his home of Promise, Pennsylvania, and made him question, wonder, and imagine. All his life he'd yearned to walk on the sinister edge, teetering on the brink of uncertainty.

But not anymore. God help him! Not anymore.

He imagined his father clad in plain, black clothes with his straw, flat-brimmed hat, his stern, sullen expression accompanying the slight disapproving shake of the head that made his long beard dust the front of his shirt. Jacob had seen that look too many times, and he could almost hear his father say the usual, "*Ach*, Jacob…"

Then something solid snagged Jacob's foot, and he stumbled out of his memory and righted himself with a steadying hand on the brick wall of a pawnshop. He glanced back at the shadows—a dirt-crusted shoe…a shabby coat…grizzled face. The old man's watery eyes swayed drunkenly, unable to focus, and he clutched a nearly empty bottle.

Could this old drunk be a sacrificial lamb? His salvation? Could he serve as a decoy? The decision came easily. Too easily. Jacob took one step away. Then another. Rationalizations paved his escape. Who would miss this drunk? No one would blame Jacob for abandoning him, leaving him in the path of those who were coming.

But one last glance at the old man slowed his footsteps. Guilt clawed at him, ripped through the fear. More of his father's words came back to him: *Doing right is often doing that which is hardest.* Cursing his own stupidity, Jacob jerked around, brushed at the sweat on his forehead, and retraced his path. "Hey! Hey, mister?"

The old man's head bobbled as if it might roll off his shoulders.

"Is there somewhere you can go?" Months in New Orleans had shaved off most of the Pennsylvania Dutch accent from Jacob's speech.

The drunk mumbled something unintelligible.

Jacob hesitated. Should he sacrifice himself for an old drunk? *If it be God's will.* Right was right, no matter if it was in Promise or New Orleans. He grasped the old man's dark brown coat. The smell of urine, sweat, and rancid wine made his nostrils flare.

The drunk yanked back, protecting his bottle, and the liquid sloshed. "Mine."

"I don't want your booze, old man." Reaching into his jean pocket, Jacob pulled out a folded twenty. The way he'd once offered a carrot to an obstinate workhorse on Daniel Schmidt's farm back home, he waved the money in front of the drunk. "Look, here. I'll buy you more booze. Whatever you want."

The weak, bloodshot brown gaze locked onto the bill, and the old man swiped a hand outward in a slow, klutzy effort to gain the twenty. His legs twitched as if trying to stand but were limp and disjointed. Jacob fisted the money and grasped the man around the middle. He weighed less than a couple sacks of feed.

Jacob dragged the drunk past a darkened drug store and cleaners. *Now what?* He kept moving forward, glancing behind each time he thought he heard a footfall, the sound of a distant siren, or whispers.

"Thirsty." The man's voice sounded condensed by the thick, moist air. Fog rose from the pavement like tidewaters.

"Just a little further," Jacob coaxed. But where would they go? And how long till *they* found him?

Neon lights from a liquor store flashed red across the pavement, and an electric sign in the window buzzed and popped. He pulled the old man toward the light and propped him near the door. Metal mesh curled from the outer door and scraped Jacob's arm, drawing blood. Flinching, Jacob jerked open the door and twisted the knob of the inner one.

Liquor bottles lined the shelves behind a counter, and a black man glared at him, his brow furrowing over thick brows and suspicious eyes. "We're closed."

Jacob pressed the twenty in the old man's hands and shoved him forward. "Stay here. Until it's safe. And"—he met the irritated gaze of the clerk—"lock the door."

Without waiting for a reply, Jacob searched the shadows along the street. Nothing stirred. Silence constricted all sounds. But he sensed *them*. He heard their whispers, circling, clouding out all reason, disorienting him. They stalked him. Hunted him like prey. They *were* coming. Would nothing stop them? With all the time in the world, it was a game to them, and they would toy with him first.

He pushed through the fog and rain, the drops thickening and falling in earnest, plastering his shirt to his chest. Through the silvery haze, a statue glowed ghostlike; its smooth face calmed him, drew him toward it, and he stumbled forward, crossing a street. The whispers fell away as he crouched low and found refuge beneath the shadow of its angelic wing. From that vantage point, he squinted up at the soft curve of the cheek, the full lower lip. His heart thudded heavily. The smooth marble reminded him of *her* face. He should have never left her. Why had he? Tears blurred his vision and the stone angel wavered before him. The words of an old poem came back to him: "*But we loved with a love that was more than love—*"

If he lived through this night, he would go home. To Hannah.

CHAPTER ONE

TWO YEARS LATER

HANNAH.

Her heart leapt, fluttering and gaining strength at the whisper of her name. Hannah Schmidt shifted and stirred under her quilt. "Jacob?" His name came to her lips like a repeated prayer. "Jacob."

She sat up and looked around the small, unadorned room. Shadows hung like curtains, heavy and oppressive, leaving the room dark as the soul. She held her breath, waiting to hear the voice again, but it didn't come.

After a few minutes, she shoved off the quilt and sat on the edge of her single, narrow bed, her back rigid as she listened to the house settling around her. Dat's snores rose upward through the floorboards in a low, rhythmic rumbling from her parents' downstairs bedroom. Her little sister, Katie, slept down the hallway, and in the next bed Rachel, her older sister by two years, slept peacefully, her dreams probably filled with details of her upcoming wedding. The thought twisted in Hannah's stomach like a knife, the smooth edge slicing away at her own unrealized dreams.

Lifting the green shade covering the window, Hannah stared out at the night blanketing the countryside, the frost forming along the rows of dried corn stalks and empty fields. Its coolness seeped through her nightclothes and raised chill bumps along her skin.

Hannah. The voice whispered in her head again. *Come to me.*

The tightness in her chest eased at the sound of the now familiar voice. The first time she'd heard the whispering, she'd jumped, looked around, searched for the source. Was it on the wind or in her head? Was it her imagination or something more? Someone calling to her…maybe even from the grave? *Jacob.*

Now, the voice called, and she obeyed.

She dressed quickly, her fingers fastening the straight pins with practiced precision, and she moved across the room and knelt in front of the cedar hope chest. Lifting the lid, she pushed aside a quilt she'd begun making when Jacob left on his cross-country trek, every stitch purposed with the belief that they would lay beneath it together as husband and wife, but the seams remained unfinished, the quilt squares unattached. At the bottom of the chest was a flashlight and a slim, hardcover book, both of which she laid in her lap and tucked her apron around in a makeshift pocket, securing the ends of the apron in the waist, then she closed the lid without a sound and slipped out of the room.

Careful on the stairs, she avoided each step that creaked and groaned. Dat's snores grew louder as she descended. Stealing through the kitchen past the wooden slab table, the lone calendar on the wall set to October, the propane-fueled refrigerator, she came to a drawer and hesitated only a moment before tugging it open slowly and quietly. She selected a carving knife, the blade sharp, which pricked her dress material as it clinked against the flashlight in her apron, the heavy handle knocking against her belly.

When she stepped outside onto the back porch, the coolness of the night made her shiver, but she tiptoed down the steps, careful not to make a sound and awaken her grandfather, who lived in the smaller attached house. The ruts of the gravel drive guided her toward Slow Gait Road, and her footsteps crunched too loudly in the stillness. The cooling air brushed her face like a caress. She should have worn her coat, but it was too late to go back. She didn't want to be late in case he was waiting for her.

Darkness shadowed her and with it came uneasiness. On her father's farm, she felt safe, but stepping beyond its boundaries gave her an eerie uncertainty. But nothing would hold her back. At the end of the lane, she pulled the small flashlight from her apron and continued down the dirt road, the beam of yellow light arcing over the bits of dried grass and buggy wheel tracks. Overhead an abundance of stars, like angelic hosts, peeked through the parting clouds to watch over her.

At the juncture in the road, she detoured across a field, passing a giant oak and three small bushes that, come next summer, would produce blueberries, and she took a path she'd traveled often. She came to a wooden fence and hoisted herself over its rails. The knife, still buried in her apron, clunked against the wood and the point jabbed her hip. Hooking her leg around the top rail, she grabbed the knife and held it with one hand while she clambered down the other side.

She had never felt more alive, her heart palpitating, every nerve vibrating, her ears sensitive to every crunch of footstep, every rattle of leaf in the wind. She listened fiercely for his voice, his direction. She watched for any shadow, shift, or sudden appearance.

The circle of light from the flashlight bounced jerkily with each step, then settled on the solid granite tombstones, small and plain and jutting out of the field, many leaning from the weight of years. She walked among them as if those buried there were only sleeping and whispered hello to friends and relatives, even Grandma Ruth, sliding her finger along the top of the stone as a gentle greeting.

When she was a young girl, she had come here for her friend Grace's grandfather's funeral and wondered what it would be like to speak to these souls now that they had moved on from this life. Was their pain gone as the Bible promised? Every tear wiped away by the hand of God? Or were they only asleep, nestled in their caskets, awaiting a holy touch or a sacred trumpet blast?

She had imagined lying several feet under the topsoil, nestled inside her own casket in the dark, hearing the footsteps of friends and loved ones overhead, hearing their whispered prayers, their questions and confessions. Of course, Dat said all of those buried here were not really in this place because their souls had moved on. And yet...still...even now, she wondered.

One day after Jacob had returned from his journey to New Orleans, his determination to be baptized fierce, his devotion equal, she had mentioned these wonderings to him. He hadn't dismissed her questions exactly but had only said, "There's much we don't understand, Hannah."

A week later, he had joined the company of the dearly departed.

Now, with her path direct and certain, she moved toward his grave.

But a noise from behind stopped her. Was it a cricket lamenting the end of warm weather? Surely by this time of year the crickets were long gone. Had she heard something else? Her ears strained, her heart yearned. She glanced back and swung the light around, arcing it over the grave markers. The emptiness of the field beyond proved her foolishness. Of course, Jacob wasn't here. It was impossible. But maybe… just maybe she'd hear his voice again.

She knelt beside the granite in the thick, dry grass and planted the butt of the flashlight at the base of the marker. Pale yellow light slanted upward across the carved name: Jacob Fisher.

Leaning against the stone slab, she pulled the small book from her apron. Jacob had given it to her years ago and had often read to her as they sat in the barn's loft or beneath the shade of an elm or along the creek, their feet submerged in cool water. The cover was worn, the edges slightly frayed, and her hand trembled as she turned the thick pages. The poems spoke of love and loss and echoed what was in her heart. She began reading aloud the words that had become so familiar to her: "*Of the sweet years, the dear and wished-for years, Who each one in a gracious hand appears To bear a gift for mortals, old or young…*"

Her throat tightened, and she paused. Living without Jacob made her life feel empty and incomplete, like a well gone dry— no longer useful, no longer worth anything. A wind stirred the brittle grass and the hair at her nape, drying the sweat from her vigorous walk and giving her a shivering chill. Again, she glanced over her shoulder, not from fear but hope. One day she would turn around and find him standing there, watching her, smiling at her. He would somehow come for her.

Oh, come, Jacob. Come back to me.

She didn't know how, but if it was possible, he would.

This was not something she could share with her closest

friends or even Rachel or Mamm. She tucked her hopes and dreams inside her, buried them deep inside a crevice of her heart.

It was in this old cemetery where she felt most at home, finding comfort in the words of Elizabeth Barrett Browning's poem, which Jacob had read to her, and she whispered the words to the night. *"And, as I mused it in his antique tongue, I saw, in gradual vision, through my tears, The sweet, sad years, the melancholy years…"*

She laid aside the book and pulled the knife from her apron. She couldn't explain why she had brought it. Had the voice told her or was it her own heart? What was it for? She didn't know, but it felt good against the palm of her hand. The words flowed from her heart: *"Those of my own life, who by turns had flung A shadow across me. Straightway I was 'ware, So weeping, how a mystic shape did move, Behind me, and drew me backward by the hair; And a voice said in mastery, while I strove—"*

Her voice broke and she laid the knife's blade flat against her wrist. She felt the cool metal and, with the slightest tilt, the bite of the blade. A bead of blood appeared on her white skin, but she felt no pain, no regrets, no fear.

Was death friend or foe? It had coupled her to Jacob, the solid ties wrapping around them, securing them together, holding them close when he had saved her from nearly drowning, and his bravery had easily won her love. But she had failed to save him in return, and death had separated them in its retribution, stolen their hopes and dreams of a future together. Did it now demand a sacrifice? Would her death bring their hearts once more back together?

This time, her voice stronger and bolder, she spoke the words of the poem: *"'Guess now who holds thee!'—'Death,' I said. But there The silver answer rang, 'Not Death, but Love.'"*

Hannah.

Her hand stilled once more at the whisper of her name. Her breath caught in her throat. Her heart hammered. Was he calling her to come to him with one quick, bold slice of the knife? Or was he calling her to wait? She raised her head, tilted it, and listened for that voice again. The rustle of the remnant leaves in nearby trees was all she heard, except the heady beat of her own heart. Laying the blade flat against her wrist, she drew it through the blood, and a red stain smeared across her skin and along the tiny green vein running the length of her arm. She imagined her heart pumping, yearning for something forever lost. If she cut deeper, could her heart have its desire? Would she once again be with Jacob? Was that the only way? Was that why the voice called to her? Maybe he couldn't come to her. Maybe she had to go to him.

But something invisible stayed her hand, something she couldn't understand or explain, and she trembled with the force of the battle raging inside. Tears stung her eyes, burning with the acid of her trapped emotions.

"*Not Death, but Love.*" Pain choked off any more words. She squeezed her eyes closed, her hands shaking, and the knife fell to the ground. She grabbed the cold stone marker for support, splayed her hands across its front as a sob wrenched free from her chest. Then her fingers began tracing the letters etched in the rough, gray granite, following the curve of the letter *a* as if following the curve of his jaw. Over and over again, she fingered the same letter. Was Jacob now an angel watching over her?

"Oh, Jacob…Could I trade my soul for your love?" She flattened her palm across the granite slab as if it were his chest, as if it held the very beat of his heart. "If it were but possible…"

CHAPTER TWO

*B*EING DEAD WASN'T SO *bad*.

Roc Girouard felt nothing—nothing at all—which was how he always imagined death: a sea of nothingness that you floated, bobbed, drifted along on, like the lazy current of the mighty Mississippi. Now he was like an empty bottle riding along the river of afterlives, toward a delta swollen with other lost and forgotten souls, like one of New Orleans' crowded and flooded cemeteries, its caskets bobbing and swaying. But his body felt weighted with the iron chain of inabilities, anchored by his failures, his soul dragging the bottom, lodging on a rock of regret buried beneath the silt and sludge of his past.

It was that bone of thought, hard and angular, that caused the first sensation, a throbbing pulse near his lower left rib—his heart—proof he wasn't actually in the hereafter. He wanted only to lose himself, the memories, the pain, in the abyss of not knowing, not feeling, not wanting. He longed for that sea of aching souls, for then he wouldn't be alone, and he kicked outward.

Instead of freedom or sweet release, water slurped around him, surged up his nostrils. Sputtering and coughing, he grabbed the side of the enamel bathtub and knocked over one of Emma's candles, which thunked on the tile floor. Sitting up, he felt pain jab his eye socket, and he pressed the heel of his hand to the bridge of his nose and sunk back into the tepid water. He groped for the bottle on the edge and drank down the bourbon in solid, greedy, desperate gulps until his empty belly burned and the pain inside his head and heart dulled.

He forced open his eyelids and peered around the now darkened bathroom. Dozens of tiny flames flickered along the edge of the tub, casting eerie shadows and wiggling light on the walls. The exotic smells of magnolias and musk, vanilla and honeysuckle levitated around him, reminding him of her. This was Emma's haven, her escape from the stresses of long work hours, the sorrow of losing a patient, and life in general, but he hadn't found comfort here the way she once had. Fact was, there was no solace, no reassurance, no absolution to be found anywhere. Here in her sanctuary, the wisps of smoke acted like prayers he was incapable of uttering.

The tiny rectangular window above the showerhead revealed the night sky. It was much later than when he'd climbed inside the warm bath with his memories to drown his pain. Now the water had grown cold, his toes and fingers and other body parts wrinkled. He'd probably missed his shift at work again. But who cared? He tossed the empty brown bottle over his shoulder and it crashed against the corner, scattering slivers of glass over the white tile. *Okay, maybe that wasn't a smart move.*

A tap-tap-tapping came from the other room. Roc ignored it—probably another trick-or-treater. He stared at one faint flame that dipped and wavered, until the tapping became a pounding. *A demanding ghoul, huh?* If he didn't answer it old lady Reynolds downstairs would tromp up the rickety wooden stairwell and complain of the noise. Finally, huffing and muttering to himself, Roc stepped out of the tub, water pouring off him, extinguishing candles and soaking the floor mat. It wasn't until his third step that he felt the sharp jab in his heel. He cursed himself for throwing the bottle and hobbled toward the door, dripping water and leaving a trail of blood. Halloween in New Orleans could be just as wild as Mardi Gras. He twisted the lock, jerked the knob. Night air rushed in, chilling his bare skin.

"What kind of treats are you offering?" This was no costumed ghoul. His ex-partner gave him a once-over. "You could get arrested."

"You can do the honors."

Without so much as a smile, Brody Wynne strode past Roc. Inches shorter and thicker through the chest and abdomen, Brody was nearly ten years his senior. "Get dressed."

"I'm busy."

Brody made a face, his gaze drifting downward. "Not interested in your love life. You still working nights at that daiquiri drive-thru place?"

Roc plopped down on the sofa. "That illegal now?"

"Oh, it's legal." Brody shut the door. "Long as you're not drinking on the job."

"I don't need AA if that's why you're here."

Brody's brow furrowed. "What do you need?"

Roc shoved old pizza boxes out of the way to prop up his bleeding foot on the coffee table. "What do you want?"

Brody stared down at him, crossing his arms over his chest. "This is work related."

"Not my line of work anymore. Or have you forgotten?"

"Don't play hard to get."

Roc turned the bottom of his foot toward himself and poked around on his heel, hissing as he felt the sliver of glass push deeper into his flesh.

"Look, Roc, things got...crazy for a while. You don't owe me or nothin' but..."

Roc yanked the glass sliver out of his foot and tossed it onto a grease-stained cardboard box. Then a cold finger trailed his spine. He glanced up at Brody. "If you've got my old man in the drunk tank or deep freeze, then that's your problem. I washed my hands of Remy Girouard—"

"Only if your old man was twenty-something and looked a helluva lot like Emma."

Most cops had seen enough not to be shaken by the sight of a corpse. Some used humor to shield themselves, while others kept their gazes on the crime tape, the concrete, the faces of witnesses. Roc had always focused on the details—dirt beneath broken nails, blood-matted blond hair, fixed blue eyes. But this time, the details ripped through that protective barrier and rattled him to the core.

It was precisely the blond hair and blue eyes that grabbed him. So like Emma. Too much like Emma. And yet not. But it was the gaping death wound that shook him like a limp rabbit in the jaws of a wolf.

A trembling started deep within, creeping up on him, threatening him, overwhelming him. Yeah, he'd seen his share of dead bodies but only *one* had been his complete undoing.

Brody stamped his feet and chafed his hands together. He stood next to Roc, studying him, not the corpse. Around them were majestic antebellum homes, gleaming white and polished during the day, but at night they darkened into shadowy mansions and creepy enclaves. "Somebody walking their dog found her. No purse. No ID."

An older detective walked the corpse's perimeter. "I say

she croaked, choking on a chicken wing or something, may-be an asthma attack, then a gator tore into her."

Brody tipped his head in the older guy's direction. "This is Al Smith. We call him Smittie." Then he rolled his eyes, dismissing the older man's comments. "Could be a voo-doo ritual," Brody offered. "We thought that back when Emma—" But he stopped himself. "Roc?"

He heard his name but it sounded far off, like Brody was calling him from Lake Pontchartrain. His chest tightened with each breath. The wound in the woman's neck looked like someone had a hankering for a midnight snack. That part was just like Emma.

Smittie frowned. "You that Roc Girouard I heard about?"

"How would he know what you've heard?" Brody cut between them and turned Roc back toward the police and emergency vehicles. The pulsing blue light hit Roc's optic nerve and made him squint and stare at the ground. Brody clapped him on the shoulder. "We're gonna get this SOB. I promise."

Anger burned deep down inside of Roc, and the flame licked outward, spreading, blazing, devouring the shakiness in its smoky wake. He wanted to walk away, forget he'd seen her. But he couldn't. Someone else had died. Someone like his Emma. This girl had a name, a life, a family, loved ones who would mourn her, weep at her funeral, some even drinking to calm the shaking. Now, someone had to pay. "I'm gonna find 'em." Roc ground the words out through clenched teeth. "Then I'm gonna—"

"Detective!" A young female officer jogged toward them, her dark hair pinned back in a slick, professional manner. "We found this just a few feet away from…her." She held out a plastic evidence bag.

"What the—?" Brody held the bag up and examined the object inside the plastic sleeve. "A bonnet?"

"Yes, sir." The female officer sounded breathless with excitement. "Looks Amish or Mennonite or something like that."

Brody quirked an eyebrow at Roc. "Now ain't that interesting?"

This time the details, so different than before, created a new shield, and Roc studied them, focused on them. The victim wore a plain blue dress, white apron, and black sneakers. No makeup. No earrings. Details. Not the typical Cajun woman.

"My wife reads them Amish romances," Smittie said, hitching up the waist of his brown slacks. "She tells me all about them folks."

Brody stepped toward the body. "What's an Amish gal doing here?"

"Vacation?" the policewoman suggested.

"Running around," Smittie said with authority.

Brody, Roc, and the female officer stared at him as if his mind had taken a leave of absence.

"No, really. That's what they do—Amish young folks— they go runnin' around until they commit to God...or whatever it is they do. But before that...anything...and I mean *anything* is allowed. Not all leave home though. That's somewhat unusual. Why, I bet this gal knew a thing or two—"

Something inside Roc snapped and he lunged, slamming Al up against the side of the antebellum home. They were standing up to their waists in prickly bushes. Roc paid no attention to anything but his arm pressed against the older man's throat.

Al's eyes bulged, his jowls turning red.

"Whoa there, Roc." Brody tugged on his shoulders, tried to pull him back.

"Did you know her?" Roc demanded.

Al shook his head. "No, no. Didn't mean—"

"You don't know squat." Roc shoved Smittie aside.

The older detective slumped sideways into the bushes, gagging and coughing. "I. Know. You. You're that crazy—"

"The Amish," Brody cut him off, "don't they live up in Pennsylvania?"

"Nah." Al braced his fat hands against his knees and gulped in a few breaths. "My wife…she says they live all over. Ran out of land in Lancaster County seems. And they all gots big ol' honkin' families. So they buy up land in other places."

Roc's brain clicked into gear. "Mike Peters lives in Philadelphia now."

Brody peered at Roc over the top of his reading glasses. "That right?"

"You can borrow my wife's books," Al offered as he straightened.

Roc stared at the body once more, taking in the details, every tiny detail. For the first time in sixteen months and seven days, he had a reason to draw his next breath.

Roc packed his ammo first.

Mike Peters, it turned out, knew about the Amish, and he also knew about a series of dead animals and a missing teenager from Lancaster County. *Was the missing Amish teen the same as the dead one in New Orleans?* Unofficially, Roc was now on NOPD's bankroll and about to head north.

Next to the ammo, Roc shoved T-shirts, underwear, and jeans into the bag, tossing in his toothbrush before zipping it. He'd already packed what few things he still cared about into a box—his mother's rosary, Emma's wedding ring, a few books and pictures, and whatever clothes he wasn't taking. He'd quit his job, broken his apartment's lease, and canceled his subscriptions, because he didn't know if or when he would be coming back.

He shoved his box and his duffle bag into the trunk of his 1969 Mustang, which had been one of his pop's unfinished renovation jobs. When Remy disappeared on one of his drinking binges almost ten years ago, Roc kept the car and completed the project, not understanding why he fixed it, other than the Mustang was cool—when it ran.

Ten minutes later, he pulled up next to a small church, where dark-red brick formed the walls, a barrier Roc had more than once accused Father Anthony of hiding behind. A statue of the Virgin Mother stared at him, her accusations soft but apparent, and Roc carried the box toward the rectory at the back of the property.

Church and Roc went together about as well as whiskey chasing beer; the mix guaranteed a headache or worse come morning. But he had no choice. He needed to see the priest, which would have made Brody laugh his ass off. But the priest wasn't just Father Anthony. Roc knew him as Tony. They'd played kick-the-can as kids, spin-the-bottle as teens, and beer-pong as college freshman. Eventually their paths had diverged. Anthony had gone a spiritual direction of right versus wrong, following after salvation and hope, and Roc had taken a more practical approach and served the law as a police officer. He'd believed he could do some good, but he'd seen a lot wrong and not much right. And he'd failed in his pursuit of justice.

Maybe it was the foolishness they'd shared as gawky teens

that made Anthony feel brave to share with Roc some of his non-traditional and out-of-the-church-box beliefs, things that other priests and even the Pope might be shocked by. It was with that same freedom and unconditional love that Roc often felt comfortable saying, "You're full of crap, Tony." But he wasn't here today to debate Bible doctrine or Tony's beyond-the-pale beliefs.

After a quick knock, the door opened. Anthony's gray eyes widened, then the door did the same. The young priest's skin was as pale as his white collar. In spite of his youthful face, his tall, thin frame gave the impression that he was feeble, but Roc knew the man's fortitude was as strong as one of the Navy ships in harbor and came from his staunch beliefs. "Come in, come in. I've been doing some studying."

"Anne Rice again?"

Dark circles shadowed the priest's eyes as if he'd stayed up too many nights. "No, these are ancient texts."

Roc plopped down on the sofa. "Bram Stoker then?"

Anthony sat on the edge of the chair next to Roc, his gaze intense with a fiery passion. "Look"—he dug into his pocket and pulled out a folded piece of paper—"it's from the Book of Enoch." The paper whispered as he opened it. Written with precise penmanship in black ink, the paper read: "*And all the others together with them took unto themselves wives, and each chose for himself one, and they began to go in unto them—*"

Roc crossed his arms over his chest. "This is risqué stuff for a priest."

"*—and to defile themselves with them, and they taught them charms and enchantments and the cutting of roots, and made them acquainted with plants.*"

"Like cucumbers?"

"*And they became pregnant, and they bare great giants, whose height was three thousand ells: Who consumed all the acquisitions of men. And when men could no longer—"*

"What exactly is an 'ell'? Does that translate to inches?"

Anthony's fingers tightened on the paper but he kept reading. "*—when men could no longer sustain them, the giants turned against them and devoured mankind.*" He paused long enough to swallow. "*And they began to sin against birds, and beasts, and reptiles, and fish, and to devour one another's flesh, and drink the blood.*'" He looked up then. "*And drink the blood. Blood.* Are you listening, Roc?" His gaze lowered to the paper again. "*Then the earth laid accusation against the lawless ones.*"

"I'm not a cop anymore." Roc knew if things didn't go well in Amish country, Brody would cut him loose and he'd be on his own. Without a safety net.

"Which is why you are perfect. A cop is hampered by—"

"The law?" Roc laughed so hard he coughed. "If you're dealing with voodoo vampires and things that go bite in the night, then maybe you don't need reality either." Then he handed over the cardboard box to his childhood friend.

Anthony's features elongated. "What's this?"

Roc stood. "If I don't come back, then toss it in the trash."

"Not come back? What's going on? Roc, giving up is not the solution. Let's talk about this."

"I'm not gonna eat a bullet, Anthony. I'm going to Pennsylvania, chasing after whoever killed Emma."

Relief relaxed Anthony's features. "The monster."

"Call him whatever you like: monster, psychopath… whatever. I'm going to put him down like a rabid dog."

Anthony held up a hand, his fingers splayed. "You need to take something."

"Garlic won't help."

Anthony jerked his chin back, making his Adam's apple more prominent in his long Ichabod Crane neck. "Of course not."

Roc watched his friend rush from the room. From down the hall came rustling and thudding, and in a short time Anthony returned, brandishing a piece of wood over two feet long and intricately carved. One end was as solid as a man's fist, but the other culminated in a wicked point. "I was given this by a priest in Mexico City. There have been… disturbances there as well."

Roc chuckled and rubbed the back of his own neck. "Man, I'm not going to Transylvania. I'm not chasing after a vampire or werewolf or any other voodoo creature. Just a man." He flashed his Glock nestled under his jacket. "This will do the trick."

But Anthony placed the spike in Roc's left hand. "Take it."

"What else do I need? A bucket of water?"

Anthony's mouth twitched with half a smile that disappeared just as quickly, and his gray eyes hardened and turned cold. "There's only way to kill a vampire, Roc."

"Yeah, yeah, shove this through the heart, right?" Roc brandished the stake, flipping it in the air and catching it again. The pointed end was stained a darker color than the rest, which gave him a sudden chill. "And something about sunlight?"

Anthony shook his head. "That was a play on words. The truth has been twisted by literature, and I suspect by the very ones who need to protect themselves."

"So you're saying Bram Stoker was a vampire?"

Anthony's shoulder lifted in an awkward gesture. "It could have been the editor or publisher just as easily. Even today…they've turned vampires into the good guys."

Roc waggled the stake and tried not to roll his eyes. "Really, Anthony, and you thought *I* needed help."

"You do. You can't do this alone. When you get to Pennsylvania, look up my friend, Father Roberto Hellman. He's in—"

"Hell-man? You've got to be kidding, right?"

"He's in Philadelphia. Retired now from serving the church, but he serves God in other capacities."

Roc stuck his Glock in his hidden shoulder holster and the stake through the belt loop of his jeans. "Take care, Anthony."

"I'll be praying for you, Roc."

"Prayers won't help me, Father. Not anymore."

CHAPTER THREE

Hannah's stomach shifted and stirred the same way wheat swayed and sighed in the fields, but instead of a sky-blue summer day she faced a hazy autumn dawn, her mood drifting toward gloom as the clouds shrouded the first rays of daylight. This day should have been much brighter. *May it be so, for Rachel's sake.* After all, this was a good change, happy in its trappings, and yet this day awakened emotions lurking deep within, feelings dark and forbidding.

A match flared with a tiny whoosh and pushed the darkness in the room aside as Hannah touched the flaming tip to the wick inside the kerosene lamp. Light wavered over the whitewashed walls of her bedroom. She lifted the green shade, then raised the window a notch and in blew a cool, gentle breeze, which stirred wisps of hair around her face. The sun peeked over the horizon and cast an array of pinks and reds upon the immense trees, the pint-sized shed, and the stalwart barn.

She bowed her head and whispered, "Dear Lord, forgive me this selfishness."

When she stepped toward the bed, a sharp pain bolted through her foot. She jerked her toes back and turned her leg to look at the bottom of her foot, where a straight pin stabbed the pad between her first two toes. With girls in the house, there were bound to be stray straight pins, and this wasn't the first time she'd stepped on one. With a quick yank, she removed it. The wound was of no consequence, yet a tiny red dot welled up with blood. She swiped it with her thumb but moved more cautiously to the side of the twin bed, placing a hand on her older sister's shoulder.

Rachel's eyes opened at once, and for a brief second she seemed far away, her pupils dilating with fear then contracting with awareness. "Hannah?"

"Come on, sleepyhead." Hannah smiled. "You don't want to keep your bridegroom waiting."

Rachel tossed back the thin quilt and sheet. "Josef is already here?"

"No, not yet." Hannah moved across the room and smoothed a hand over the plain dress hanging on the wall. "But there is much to be done before he arrives."

The bride-to-be shoved her hair out of her face, rubbed a hand over her eyes, and pinched the bridge of her nose as if trying to push away the last bits of sleep or the fading remnants of a dream.

Hannah poured water into a bowl. "How do you feel on this, your wedding day?

"Happy." Rachel's pink lips curved upward, her eyes sparkling with secrets, and she hugged her knees. "Nervous too."

"As nervous as you were for your baptism?"

"Josef isn't as serious as Bishop Stoltzfus." She covered her mouth and hid another smile.

Hannah joined her sister on the edge of the bed, smiling with her, and pressed her forehead to Rachel's, her blue eyes looming large. Hannah's heart swelled within her chest. She would miss her sister, but she would also rejoice, for Rachel loved Josef as no other. A pinch of jealousy she didn't want to acknowledge pressed in upon her, and she pushed away before Rachel could see it too.

But Rachel reached for her.

Hannah kept moving, rising from the bed. "You must hurry."

"What about you, Hannah?"

"Me?" She forced a laugh. "I'm already dressed." Her hand fluttered against her stomach, mimicking the feeling inside and ignoring what her sister meant.

The soft tread of bare feet on the wooden planks alerted Hannah to Rachel's approach. "I meant, what about *you*? It's *your* time to step out. Past time."

"I don't need *rumschpringe* to show me what I want."

Rachel touched Hannah's shoulder, turning her around. "Is it Levi then? Is he the one?"

Hannah's heart thrummed, but she managed to keep her voice steady as her gaze drifted away from Rachel's, toward the window and the barn below. Already he would be feeding the livestock and going about the chores her father laid out for him. "Levi is a good man, I reckon."

"Is that where you went last night?" Rachel smiled, no judgmental shadow darkening her eyes. "Off to meet him?"

Hannah's throat thickened.

"I heard you get up after midnight." Rachel dipped her chin in that encouraging way of hers but it felt to Hannah like a tool shoved into her side, attempting to pry loose all that remained private and secret. "It is all right if you did, Hannah. Your secret is safe with me."

Hannah's lips compressed and her teeth clipped down on her tongue. Guilt chewed at her insides. She turned away and gathered the plain, unadorned, lavender dress and thrust it toward Rachel. "Hurry. An Amish wife can't laze about, not even on her wedding day."

It took only a few minutes for Rachel to slide the straight pins through the material and hold her apron in place. She looked much as she did every day, for an Amish wedding dress was no different than ordinary clothing, but this one was newly sewn and today a peaceful calm radiated from her.

Hannah stepped behind her and placed her hands on Rachel's slim shoulders, wanting to make amends for not confiding in her, the way Rachel often shared of her stolen moments with Josef. Rachel patted Hannah's hand, and their gazes locked momentarily. Words were unnecessary, and the love Hannah harbored for her sister welled up inside her. Smiling, Rachel reached for the white *kapp* on the bed. Hannah placed the thin organdy material at the back of Rachel's head, then carefully pinned it in place. Her fingers traced the ties downward and linked with her sister's.

"Are you ready?" Hannah's voice sounded husky.

"Even so much more than when I was baptized. Is that awful bad? May the good Lord forgive me, but it feels as if *this* is what I was meant for." Her fingers smoothed out the long tie of her *kapp*. "There's something comforting in knowing what lies ahead. That I will one day wear this *kapp* when I am placed in my coffin."

Hannah's fingers tightened on Rachel's. She couldn't think about losing more loved ones, not after losing Jacob, even if it was life's way—the cycling of the seasons. A daisy sprouted, budded, bloomed, and faded until it fell apart, becoming part of the ground from which it came. Death was as much a part of everyday life as living and breathing. Death brought her love once. Could it again?

Rachel's fingers tightened on Hannah's and her gaze intensified, her pupils narrowing to pinpricks of black. "There's security in knowing that much of our lives, isn't there?"

The harsh reality was: there was no security, no knowing how their lives would play out. Hannah once had hoped she would be Jacob's wife, have his children, stand alongside him as they grew old through their years together along with the turning of the seasons, but now her hope had turned brown and crusty, like a fallen leaf waiting to be trampled. She had once felt the same as Rachel, having known she was meant to be with Jacob. Now what was she meant for? Doubts rose inside her, but she swept them into a hidden place before they overwhelmed her and eclipsed the day.

For Rachel's sake, she wanted today to be special. "You look lovely, Rachel. Josef is blessed."

For today at least. For no one knew what tomorrow would bring.

Levi Fisher hefted the long wooden plank out of the wagon. The Stoltzfus family stored the benches in their barn and had brought them over last night. Levi's chore first thing that morning was to carry them into the Schmidt house for the wedding. He paused briefly, leaning his arm on the wagon's side, and his gaze flicked upward to the brightening sky then toward the window on the second story.

The green shade was still pulled low, though by this time of morning it was usually rolled to the top of the frame. But he could see the window was raised only slightly and the shade wavered in the breeze. It was getting late and soon the guests would be arriving, so Hannah couldn't still be in bed. She would be helping Rachel. But he hadn't yet seen Hannah this morning, and he always felt a coil of tension in his belly until he saw her. This day was no different.

Especially since the Yoder girl had gone missing. Of

course her parents were worried. What parent wouldn't be on their knees praying for their child to come home? It was the prayer of every Amish parent that their children would make quick work of their running around years and decide to be baptized and take their place in the community. Some in the district thought Ruby Yoder had gone off with an English boyfriend. Some said she had decided not to join the church and ran away rather than face her parents. Others thought she'd come to harm. Levi prayed nothing had happened to her. The good Lord would have to watch over her wherever she was. But the mystery of Ruby Yoder's disappearance had caused an unsettling feeling to sweep over him. It only reaffirmed his commitment to keep an eye on Hannah. And keep her safe.

"Levi!" Daniel Schmidt called to him. The older man stood on the wraparound porch of his house, carrying a rocking chair and looking as nervous as if he were the bridegroom. Levi supposed seeing your oldest daughter married was not an easy task for any father. "When you've finished unloading, Levi, go out to the road and help the guests with their buggies."

Levi nodded and gave a wave to signal he'd heard. He'd worked for Daniel for almost two years now and would gladly keep right on working for him if it meant he could be near Daniel's daughter Hannah and possibly marry her someday.

"Don't worry yourself, Levi. I'll help with the buggies." Ephraim Hershberger hooked a suspender over his shoulder and came bounding down the steps, sprier than a man half his seventy years. Daniel nodded a greeting to his father-in-law, who lived in the small house attached to the back of his own, and hurried back inside to finish readying for the benches to be brought inside.

It would be an awful busy day, but Levi assured himself he'd catch sight of Hannah sooner or later.

CHAPTER FOUR

ROC DIDN'T HAVE TIME for this. A normal traffic jam would be bad enough, and he'd sat through his share in New Orleans, but one with horses and buggies was just plain bizarre—like he'd suddenly been transported to some long forgotten time and place.

He slammed a hand against the steering wheel of his black Mustang but it did nothing to ease the tension knotting his shoulders or his impatience, the fuse of which was firing down to its natural conclusion. What was it with the buggy? Couldn't it pick up the pace? Or at least move over? Get out of his way?

He swerved into the oncoming lane, ready to gas it, but realized he was fourth in line to three other horse and buggies. And coming toward him was another. *What is it with these people? Wake up and smell the gas fumes and smog of the twenty-first century!*

He'd hit Philadelphia late yesterday, checked in with Mike, slept on his couch a couple of hours, and was now headed for the hometown of the missing Amish teen. Now here he was in Intercourse, PA, at the crack of dawn, which he figured wasn't a bad time for intercourse. Was there ever a *bad* time for that particular recreation? Not if he'd had time or the inclination or a warm and willing lady. Still, maybe he'd check the map later to see if just past Promise, PA, there was Foreplay.

Ahead, one of the buggies turned down a gravel drive. Followed by another. Was this some kind of a parade? If so it didn't compare to Mardi Gras. No green and purple beads. No bared breasts. No booze. Did these folks know how to party? Maybe they were going to a funeral.

The thought slammed into him. *A funeral.* Or prayer meeting. Any kind of gathering meant tongues would be wagging. If a missing teen caused news in these parts, then these folks would be talking. And he should be there.

He leaned forward over the steering wheel, peered out the windshield at the somber black and gray buggies inching along, and caught a glimpse of a driver—a sour-faced, somber-looking man. Roc had crashed events from funerals to wedding receptions in his time as a cop, managing to blend in with the mourners, but that might be more difficult considering the circumstances. His T-shirt, jeans, and leather jacket weren't exactly Amish attire, not to mention his set of wheels.

During his time as a cop, he'd learned to trust his gut instinct, never knowing where it would lead, which was often down schizo bunny trails. But then again sometimes… those trails led to a clue or a motive or a suspect. Or even a monster. Could one be lurking in this seemingly innocent farming community?

The picture-postcard farmlands looked as peaceful as a Currier and Ives' Christmas card, minus the snow. Oh, man, he hoped there wouldn't be snow. But peace, Roc had learned, was a façade when you didn't know what lurked in the shadows. According to Mike, the Amish lived in their own little world, protected by their freedom of religion and their fear of all things current or containing an electric current, oblivious of the prowling danger.

But Roc knew. This monster left no obvious trail. No

fingerprints. No footprints. Only the trail of blood. And the dead. He suspected this monster was on the move and that the trail led right into the heart of Amish country.

The black and gray buggy turned down a narrower road, this one with only one lane, which led toward a farmhouse. The plain two-story, with limestone rocks at the base of white clapboards, had a rambling construction as if the original structure had been added onto over the years. With its white paint, the house looked pristine yet functional. A laundry line ran from one side of the house to a white pole. Green shades covered each window, kept nosy outsiders like him from peeking inside.

Could something sinister be hidden behind those shades? He'd learned in the NOPD to take appearances at face value. Some of the wealthiest families had the worst problems; some of the most abusive husbands or fathers had the widest smiles; some of the most devout hid the worst sins. Could the Amish cover evil as easily as wood slats with white paint? A porch embraced the entire structure and gave the place a homey feel, but it resembled something dreamed up by Hollywood more than any reality he'd ever known. Suspicion rose up like a serpent inside him.

The buggies pulled into a row at a diagonal slant, all seeming to know where to go without the benefit of painted lines on the dry, winter grass. Roc parked next to the one in front of him and killed the engine. An older man with a gray, scraggly beard—not a normal beard, but one without a mustache—wearing a black coat and trousers waved to the drivers. With what seemed like a practiced hand, the man patted the horse standing next to Roc's car and eyed the slick machine as if it might bite.

Roc pulled his Glock out of the glove compartment and

slid it into his shoulder holster, tugging his jacket over it. With one flick of his wrist, he opened the Mustang's door. A frigid gust of wind blasted him and tossed his hair, which whipped at his face. In self-defense, he slicked it back, fastening it at the base of his neck with a rubber band, which he kept on the dash.

He hadn't been in Pennsylvania long and already the cold had burrowed deep into his bones. November sure wasn't the same up north. He was convinced hell wasn't hot like the parish priests warned. Roc's own father had laughed at that and boasted, "If I can live through a New Orleans summer, I reckon I'll do okay in hell." But Roc suspected God would punish Remy Girouard, so hell must be cold, cold as ice—maybe as cold as Intercourse, PA.

Several of the other men moved on past him, hollering greetings to one another in what sounded like German, giving him a passing glance. Mike had told him the Amish spoke Pennsylvania Dutch but that they could also speak English. Chin down, Roc peered over his shades at the Amish man and gave what he hoped would be considered a friendly gesture. The elderly gentleman nodded and waved at those he was familiar with but kept a steady eye on Roc, finally returning Roc's gesture and moving toward him. They sized each other up, like two Wild West gunmen not looking for a fight but not backing down either.

"Hello there. Can I be helping you?"

"Maybe." Roc held out a hand. "Roc Girouard."

"Ephraim Hershberger." His handshake was solid—the man's hands knew hard work—but Roc could feel age settling into the enlarged knuckles.

"This your place?" Roc nodded toward the house and beyond that the matching white barn.

"My son-in-law's." Hershberger's gaze veered toward the chrome bumper behind Roc.

He stepped aside, giving the older man full view of the Mustang. "You like?"

"Haven't seen anything like this. Doesn't much go with the line of buggies, *ja*?"

"Guess not. But the colors coordinate."

A hint of a smile emerged, just a hint. "They do at that. What is an *Englisher* such as yourself doing out this way so early in the morning?"

Not exactly sure where to begin, Roc crossed his arms over his chest, but before he could answer a yellow lab trotted up to investigate. Ephraim put a hand out, which the dog nosed before sitting and staring at Roc with mild curiosity. "Nice dog."

"Toby is awful good." His words had a clipped yet melodic sound to them. "He is accustomed to strangers getting lost here. Is that what you are, Roc Girouard? Lost?"

"Wouldn't be much Promise in that. But then there's Intercourse." Roc offered a friendly grin, hoping his little joke would break the ice, but it was met with a slow, perplexing blink. Roc coughed and rubbed the back of his neck. "Thing is, I got caught in the tide."

The man remained silent, watchful, wary.

Roc glanced around, searching for some common ground, something to extend the conversation. "How do you folks tell all these buggies apart? Or do you just swap them out?"

"We know our own, just as the good Lord knows his children."

"Can't say I know about that." Roc peered inside one of the buggies, which had a black side and gray top. The inside was a solid bench seat and a window open to the elements. The whole thing looked to be made out of wood. Roc could just imagine the buggy as a splintered mess if it ever got rammed by a car or truck. He bent down looking underneath the buggy and at all the wheels. "They look the same."

"Similar, *ja*, but not twins, more like you and me. Men, the same, are we not? But they look different."

Roc could see a lot more differences between Ephraim and himself than just their clothes. A long pause weighed between them, not too heavy but weighted nonetheless, as if the man was deciding what to do or say with the outsider standing in his yard, but Roc had learned to wait out silence. Folks, in their discomfort, always started talking, and that's when things got interesting. But maybe this man wasn't in a hurry either and had the patience of a croc.

"Some of the youngsters," Ephraim admitted, finally breaking the silence, "sneak around and put radios in the back of their buggies."

"Guess teenagers are the same in your world as well as mine." Growing up a marginal Catholic, he was well versed in the Ten Commandments and such, but he didn't remember anything about radios or music being bad. "So radios are considered a sin?"

"Not a sin. But not allowed by the *Ordnung*."

"Not allowed?"

But Ephraim offered no explanations.

Roc wasn't here for a treatise on Amish culture, even if his curiosity was piqued about why radios weren't allowed and yet teens had them. But he'd gotten way off track. This place had a lulling effect, the façade of security and safety. Still, Roc knew better. No place was safe.

"Amish and *English* teens make their parents hair turn gray."

The older man glanced at Roc's dark brown hair. "You don't speak from experience."

"No."

Ephraim stroked his wiry, gray-streaked beard that came down to the middle of his chest. "Children are a blessing from the Lord."

"Even those that go missing?"

Not a muscle in the old man's wrinkled face twitched, but his gaze shuttered like the windows on the farmhouse.

"A girl went missing hereabouts," Roc prompted.

"Are you an *English* policeman? Or a reporter?"

"Neither. Just trying to find out what happened to her."

Ephraim shrugged. "Young folks go off during *rum-schpringe*. Sometimes further than their parents would like. And they usually come home after a time."

"Rum...?" Roc attempted the unfamiliar word then waited for a translation.

"Before baptism, before they become members of the church, young folks are not held by the same rules. *Rumschpringe* is their running around years. So for the most part, teens in your world are the same as in mine." Ephraim placed a hand on the buggy then his chest. "You and me, *English* and Amish, our buggies even, yours and mine, are the same. *Ja*?"

"More than we realize. Guess that's my problem then." He winked and the man's eyes widened. "I'm still in my running around years. Explains a lot actually." He looked toward the barn where a group of men were unloading long planks from a wagon and carrying them into the house. "The men here run around earlier in the morning than where I come from."

Ephraim gave a tolerant smile. "It is our way." His gaze

followed Roc's to the group of men working together. "They are here to help a friend. Can I help you find your way then?"

"Find my way? Gotcha, see…" Roc rubbed his jaw and the bristles of not shaving for over a day scraped his hand. "I'm not really lost. I'll just check my GPS, thanks."

"GPS?" The old man's forehead creased beneath the brim of his black felt hat.

"Sure. I'll show you." He slid into the Mustang, cranked the engine, which made a horse nearby bob its head, but he motioned for the old man to peer in through the open window. "See." He pointed to the screen's map. "Here we are. Right here."

Someone hollered something incomprehensible, and Hershberger knocked his hat on the window's opening and juggled it in his hands, then placed it back on his head as he stepped away. Ephraim turned toward the Amish fellow walking his horse past them, the hooves clomping on the gravel with a metallic sound. The younger Amish man's gaze strayed toward the black Mustang that was as out of place there as drive-thru daiquiris would be.

Ephraim Hershberger raised a hand. "I will be along shortly."

"I apologize for intruding on your"—Roc searched for a word—"gathering here. I'll be—"

The black clad shoulders squared. His jacket looked homemade. No lapels. But the old guy wore a plain, store-bought dress shirt. A smile creased his face. "It is my grand-daughter's wedding this day."

"Well, then, congratulations. So a party's brewing, eh?"

"*Ja*! It is a good day. Would be better if my Ruth was still with us." He rubbed his jaw and shook his head, his tired eyes looking moist.

Roc knew that pain and looked away.

"I would invite you to stay but—"

"No, no." Roc cleared his throat. He was focused on death when others were going about living. "I understand. Sorry I intruded. It's a bit on the cold side, but I reckon the happy couple can keep themselves warm."

Ephraim rocked back on his heels and laughed. The contrast of the man's somber exterior and his robust sense of humor intrigued Roc. "I won't keep you as I'm sure you're busy with wedding stuff."

Nodding, Ephraim waved and walked in the direction of the house, his shoulders stooped to combat the wind, the yellow dog following along beside him.

Roc ran his hands over the steering wheel, stared at the GPS screen, and contemplated his next move.

"How many horsepower?" A deep male voice intruded on Roc's thoughts. It was a young man with the same bowl-shaped cut and clean-shaven jaw as all the other younger Amish men he'd seen so far. This man's German heritage was obvious in his curious blue eyes, blond hair, square jaw, broad shoulders, and long limbs. Roc always appraised folks he met by whether he could take them down if the need arose, and he hoped the need wouldn't arise with this fellow because he looked as strapping and sturdy as…well, as a horse.

"Three hundred hp," Roc answered.

The younger man's eyes widened, and he gave a low whistle.

Maybe Ephraim was right. Maybe *English* and Amish were more alike than Roc had realized. After all, what man didn't want a fast horse…or a fast car? Roc alighted from the car again and backed away, giving room for the man to peer inside at the tan seats. "You wanna take a closer look?"

But the man remained where he was as if not even tempted. "You were speaking with Ephraim, no?"

Roc introduced himself and they shook hands.

"Levi Fisher." The man was close to his own age, maybe two or three years younger, and didn't seem to feel the
need to impress with a Rocky-style handshake like most
guys would; still, his grip was solid and strong without a hint
of weakness and Roc got the impression his strength came
from within.

"Nice fellow, Ephraim. Is he your grandpappy?"

"No. I work here for Daniel Schmidt. You know Josef
and Rachel?"

"Josef and Rachel?" Must be the bride and groom Roc
figured. "Can't say I've had the pleasure. Hear it's their
big day."

"*Ja*, 'tis."

Together, they stared at the car. Had Ephraim sent Levi to
make sure Roc left? "You and your buddies like cars?"

"Some."

"You're not"—what was the word?—"in rum...rum—"
Rum might be a diversion for the teens if they were ever
introduced to it, as many in New Orleans often were.

"Of running around age?" the Amish man asked. "No."

"I see." Sort of. He wondered if it was looked down
upon to even show an interest in a car, since they weren't
allowed to drive one, so he suggested, "If y'all have a hang-
out...ya know, somewhere you kick back with a cold one,
I could swing by sometime while I'm in the area, give you
a look-see."

"The others might take a shine to your fancy car. Looks
like it cost much."

"More than one of your horses, I'd bet."

"*Ja*. Horses are cheaper. But provide fertilizer."

Roc laughed. "Keep that under your hat, will ya? If all the 'green' folks hear you, they'll have us riding around like y'all."

A wisp of a smile crossed Levi's features, crinkling the corners of his eyes. "If you've a mind to, you might try Straight Edge Road late tonight. Some of the young folks…hang out"—his use of the *English* phrase broadened his smile—"that a way."

Roc gave a thank-you nod.

"You know any good places to stay while I'm here in Intercourse…or is it Promise?"

"Promise. But Intercourse isn't far."

"Prayer answered."

Levi tilted his head but continued, "There's a bed and breakfast not far. On I-30. Bender's B&B, I believe it is called. Run by a nice family."

With a tip on where the young and reckless rebelled and a name of a place to stay, Roc slid inside the Mustang and fired the engine. A horse shied, prancing a bit and nodding its head. Levi walked over and helped calm the animal and assisted Roc in backing out and avoiding horse poop, ruts in the drive, and buggy bumpers. Tonight, he'd find out what young Amish kids did for fun and if they knew of any strangers in the area. Strangers with a penchant for blood.

CHAPTER FIVE

HANNAH'S STOMACH KNOTTED.

The wedding was over, the happy couple joined, and now the dinner, of roasted chicken, noodles, and creamed celery, along with potato casseroles, cherry pies, relishes, and all sorts of breads, was ready. Succulent smells of the simmering meats, sugary pies, and yeasty loaves drifted along on the cool autumn air. It was a perfect evening for an outdoor feast, which was good since the family and friends gathered were too numerous to all fit inside the house.

But one thing remained to be decided: Rachel and Josef had not yet chosen which of the single male guests would be paired with which available maids. This wedding tradition in their district of Promise involved matchmaking and wishful thinking, and the idea of being paired with a young man of her sister's choosing made Hannah's stomach harden like a lump of clay left in the sun.

From the porch, she watched the future bridegrooms-to-be (or so the community hoped) follow the wedding couple out of the barn and toward the tables set up outside. Some of the men chatted amiably amongst themselves, their eagerness apparent. Others looked somber; maybe they were just as nervous as she was. As the sister of the bride, she doubted she could get away with not being paired for the evening meal or allowed to hide in the chicken coop.

She looked toward the barn for an escape route. A cow called out from the paddock as its calf thrust its head against her milk bag. Children chased after the lamb, Snowflake, which Katie had nursed with a bottle last spring.

"Careful!" Hannah called to Noah Hostetler, who grabbed for the lamb's tail, but Snowflake scampered into the barn for refuge.

"Whoa!" Levi Fisher stepped out of the wide open doors, caught the running Noah, and swung the young boy high into the air. A smile broke across his tanned cheeks, and his teeth flashed white in the waning sunlight. Noah squealed and squirmed, but Levi's grip was strong and sure. The other children looked up at the tall, broad-shouldered man as he spoke to them quietly, and they scurried back toward the house. As if Noah weighed nothing, Levi swung him upside down then set him back on his feet. As Noah rushed after his friends, Levi straightened his wide-brimmed hat until his gaze met Hannah's, and he held it steady as he walked toward her with purposeful strides.

His clean-shaven jaw, the sure sign of an unmarried man, clenched. Cut from the same cloth as his brother, Jacob— Levi being the eldest—the two brothers resembled each other with Fisher family characteristics—broad foreheads, broader shoulders—but they were boldest in their differences. Jacob had taken after their father with his dark hair and eyes, whereas Levi resembled their mother with fair hair and deep blue eyes. Levi was quiet where Jacob was boisterous and full of life. Or had been. Jacob's curiosity made him adventurous and searching, whereas Levi seemed…content with all that was and never seemed to questions things the way Jacob had.

There had been moments over the past two years, while

Levi apprenticed with her father, when she'd hoped Levi would flash a light beneath her window. The trouble was she compared every man with the one she had loved and lost, but her occasional weakness—an attraction to Levi—had been swallowed up by the voice that spoke straight into her heart.

As Levi approached now, striding up the back steps, the intensity of his gaze made her insides shift and stir. "Hannah." His voice was as deep as the roots of a pine tree. "It is time for supper. Would you care to sit with me?"

His polite question showed he didn't take her acceptance of their pairing as a guarantee and she appreciated his courtesy. Her cheeks grew warm in spite of the coolness of the day, and she dropped her gaze to the wooden floorboards. "*Danke*, Levi."

"Rachel requested we follow her and Josef."

Hannah glanced toward her sister, who smiled, her hand on Josef's arm, and Hannah suspected they were discussing the successful pairing. She gave a brief nod to Levi and walked beside him toward the wedding couple. A procession of the newly formed couples began, trailing through the gathered guests until they reached a table designated for the wedding party. Even though Hannah suspected everyone was searching out their own daughters or cousins or nephews, she still felt as if all eyes were on her and Levi, and her heart galloped in her chest.

After a quiet moment of prayer, Levi leaned toward her, his shoulder grazing hers. "It was a fine day for a wedding, *ja*?"

She nodded, her throat tight.

"Josef is a good man."

"Yes. Rachel is blessed."

He nodded and sampled the chicken.

Hannah eyed the other couples around them chatting with each other, eating, and laughing. All seemed to be enjoying themselves, even her friend, Grace Wagler, who had been seated beside Amos Borntreger, a pairing Hannah knew Grace would never be pleased with, as Amos had a tendency to wipe his nose on his sleeve. Still, Grace smiled and spoke amiably about the day's events.

Levi seemed comfortable eating and not conversing, which suited Hannah well too. She was thankful he at least had good manners but felt guilty for the silence between them, so she said, "I heard there was an *Englisher* here this morning."

Levi swallowed and nodded. "*Ja*, drove up with the *newe-hockers'* buggies in a fancy car. Thought Adam Smucker would trip over his jaw staring at the fancy rig."

"Did you speak to him? The *Englisher*?"

"Your grandfather did first. But *ja*, I did too. Seemed a nice fellow. Just lost."

"Were you like the others who ached to ride in the fancy rig?"

He paused, his arm resting on the table's edge. "Nah, Hannah. The *English* world holds no interest for me. There are other things more fascinating to me now."

Her stomach shifted as his intense gaze bore into her. Embarrassment churned inside her with a steady paddle of heartache. "But Jacob…he yearned for *English* ways."

Levi's mouth compressed and he stared for a long moment at his plate.

How careless of her to mention his brother! Hard as it was for her to endure her own heartache, a brother must find it equally painful if not worse. She placed a tentative hand on Levi's elbow. "I'm sorry, Levi. I shouldn't have said—"

"It's all right. I know you loved him too." He leaned toward her, just a slight inclination, but she felt the heat of him pressing against her. "Would that I could make you smile again."

Never before had he referred to the changes Jacob's death had brought. Never had he dared. But it was her fault for speaking his name, and she glanced away, tears prickling her eyes, then stared at her own plate full of tempting foods that she could not seem to eat. Mamm would think she was sick. Rachel would think she was in love.

She'd learned over the last two years that Levi's features closed up tight and became unreadable when his brother was mentioned. If Hannah said his name at home, Mamm said, "You must move on, Hannah." If she whispered his name around Grace, her friend patted her arm, hugged her quickly, then directed her attention to Amos or Levi or any of the other available men—anything to distract and discourage looking back, wishing, or regretting.

It's the Lord's will. That was the Amish way. And she believed it too. Or had. Until Jacob died.

Children romped around the front porch, their clomping and laughter a good interruption. A couple of the older girls rushed toward the kids to quiet them and help them with their plates. Noah's little sister, Esther, who had just learned to walk, teetered forward, but an older girl's quick hand pulled her back from the edge.

Grace murmured something to the others at the end of the table about Ruby Yoder. Ruby had once shared with Hannah about an *English* boy she'd met, and Hannah suspected Ruby had run away to be with him. The district would not have shunned her, as she was not yet baptized, but it would have caused an uproar in her family and her parents much pain. Still, Hannah admired Ruby for following her heart and wished she too had gone away with Jacob.

"Hannah?" Levi's hand touched hers beneath the table. Just a brief encounter but it caused a fluttering in her belly, like a new butterfly taking flight for the first time.

Hannah blinked and lifted her gaze to meet his. Something about this Fisher brother made her feel unsure. Would she have ever felt this way about him if Jacob had lived? Guilt acted on her like a splash of ice water in the face.

"Are you okay? I didn't mean to upset you."

"I'm fine, Levi."

He studied her for what felt like a full minute before he accepted her words. "Are you going to the barn singing tonight?"

She shook her head, lifted a fork, and forced down a bite of buttery noodles. "No, I…uh…think not."

Tonight, she would go see Jacob.

CHAPTER SIX

H OURS AFTER ARRIVING IN Promise, Pennsylvania, Roc drove around the area, speaking with Mike on the phone, who said there were no leads on the missing Pennsylvania teenager other than she was blond, blue-eyed, and Amish. But the Amish didn't take photographs so no pictures could be compared to the body in New Orleans. The parents had provided hair samples from Ruby Yoder's brush for DNA testing. Still, the girl could be off having the time of her life or regretting her decision to leave home.

Animals discovered by police or citizens on the side of the road or in ditches with their throats chewed convinced Roc he was in the right place and on the trail of whoever had killed Emma.

Roc unpacked his car and carried his bag toward the room at the back of the B&B, passing through a small courtyard, which had a hot tub and gazebo. A Chihuahua sat on the lap of a red-headed teenage girl, yapping until she shushed it. But the girl never looked up, just kept her nose in a book. She was surrounded by wilted, brown plants, which didn't seem any better suited to the cold weather than Roc, but the teen seemed impervious to the chill in her furry jacket. Even her disgruntled lap dog wore a coat, like it was attempting to be Paris Hilton's dog. Whatever the teen was reading caused a smile to curl her lips. A glance at the dark-covered book made Roc shake his head. Anthony should have a talk with this one and compare notes.

"You know," he said to her in passing, "vampires don't shimmer in sunlight."

"How do you know? Oh, never mind." She went back to reading.

According to Anthony there was a lot of misinformation in literature, not that Roc believed in any of that vampire crap. Who would want to read about such nonsense anyway?

He walked on. When he reached the steps that led to the second-story room he'd rented, the girl called to him, "You really should read this." She waved the book at him. "You might end up a vampire fan."

"Doubt it." He doubted he'd be a believer either. Not the way Anthony was. But Roc wondered why such a vile creature had become a superhero. That bothered the judicial side of him, like putting Ted Bundy on a pedestal. "Are you a fan?"

"Oh yeah!" She sat forward, a gleam brightening her eyes. "Why?"

"They're cool." Her innocence worried him. Shouldn't evil be called evil? She lifted the book. "They're vegetarians and nice."

What if they were behind this latest misinformation? He pinched the bridge of his nose. Obviously he'd been driving too much over the last two days. He needed to get some sleep. Still, he hated that this teen—and so many like her—just accepted what they heard as if it were truth.

"So, what...they eat carrots?"

"Are you crazy?"

Probably so for engaging in this conversation. "Didn't you ever hear you can't squeeze blood from a turnip?" The teen stared at him like his head had just popped off. "These vampires of yours…what do they do? Drink Vulcan blood?" He chuckled at his own joke.

But he was the only one with a sense of humor as the girl rolled her eyes. "They eat *animals*."

"Like your little Fifi there?"

The girl hugged her persnickety dog tight. "Her name is Bonita."

"Uh-huh." Roc wasn't a biologist or anything, but something with teeth and fur wasn't for vegetarians. "Still carnivorous."

"Whatever."

And he shrugged off his own foolishness. Why did he bother trying to make sense of something nonsensical?

CHAPTER SEVEN

LEVI STOOD IN THE cleft of darkness, his body relaxing against the slats of the barn wall, his eyelids drooping closed. He'd been awake since four that morning, which was not unusual considering the work he did for Daniel Schmidt, but staying up this late, keeping an eye on things at the barn singing, was. He wished the voices would quiet and the playing would end. It was obvious Hannah was not coming.

She'd stayed away again. He'd watched and waited and hoped that, despite her words, she would be lured by the fun. Disappointment weighted his chest like a hefty sack of feed had been plopped on it, a sensation he should have been used to.

The first time he'd really noticed Hannah, she couldn't have been more than twelve, with those wide brown eyes, humor making them the color of autumn leaves. He knew then he would have done anything for her.

It was foolishness, for she'd only ever had eyes for Jacob.

But Levi hadn't been able to help himself. He had studied the way she carried herself, never hesitating to help someone, never quibbling about obeying her mamm. And when her laugh rang out, sounding like the angels, Levi had thought he'd landed in heaven. Jacob had known how to make her laugh—dangling upside down from a tree branch, balancing a bucket on his head, or whispering something in her ear.

But Levi had rarely coaxed a smile from her and now the task seemed impossible.

But at night he dreamed of Hannah smiling for him. Only him.

The soft click of a door closing made him tense. His eyes opened and blinked against the darkness, but he remained still, as unmoving as when he and his friends went hunting in the hills for deer. He eyed the barn, the Schmidt front porch, the back door. A slight figure crept among the shadows.

He straightened. His heart kicked hard against his breastbone. *Hannah*.

She was coming. Finally. Hope bloomed inside him. He took one step out of the dark crevice but then laughter erupted behind him from inside the barn.

Hannah stopped, turned. A slant of moonlight glinted on her pale face. Fear widened her eyes. But why fear?

When she scampered down the steps, the hem of her skirt snagged on a gardenia bush, which she jerked loose before rushing forward, her footsteps light and quick as she moved away from the barn, and he understood. Her destination was the reason for her fear—fear of discovery. What she didn't know was that he had followed her before.

With the moon veiled by thick clouds, darkness made it difficult for him to follow her, but he knew the way. Why did she feel compelled to go? Had it become a ritual with her? Love was a river that had to run its course, shifting and turning, slowing and tapering down to an eventual stream. He hoped there would be a moment, a boulder plunked in the middle of her defenses, a dead end to her resolve, and he would jump in and chart a new course for them, open a new current for a new love to flow open and unrestrained.

Until then, he would watch and wait.

CHAPTER EIGHT

CARRYING A THIRTY-PACK OF Keystone Light, iced as cold as the weather, Roc located Straight Edge Road. It sure wasn't Bourbon Street, but he remembered his own surprise at what New Orleans offered. What would these boys do if a stream of floats with partiers came dancing down one of their gravel roads, tossing about bright purple and green beaded necklaces and flashing body parts?

Then again, the teens couldn't be strangers to the baser needs of life with places nearby like Intercourse. Virginville had to be a main attraction, right? These young Amish men were still men, bursting with hormones, and they couldn't be naïve about the birds or the bees or any other farm animal for that matter. Why else would they marry so young? Mike had told him they were plagued by ordinary teen problems, just like any other part of America, from drug abuse to the occasional teen pregnancy. Hadn't the Amish fellow he'd met earlier—*Evan…Ethan…Ephraim?*—admitted as much?

Still, how much did they really know of the darker side of evil and depravity? Of that, these healthy, young men were probably completely ignorant. And Roc was glad of it; he'd grown tired of the weary looks in twelve-year-old eyes back in New Orleans, from some kid who'd spent too much time and too many nights on the streets. These young Amish folks had healthy appetites, appetites for discovering life, experiencing the forbidden—appetites that any red-blooded American boy would have.

Even now, some ate out of red-and-white striped buckets; others scarfed down pizza, while he supplied the perfect beer to wash it all down. They eyed him skeptically when he first walked up, but they gladly accepted the offered beer. Roc handed out the cans, then popped open one for himself, and poured it down his throat, giving the kids time to get used to him being there.

Less wholesome activities—kids groping in cars and buggies, bottles of whiskey passed around a bonfire, and joints passed from hand to hand—were also prominent. Roc helped himself to a few blood-warming gulps of whiskey since nothing else beat the cold. *Nothin' wrong with that.* He doubted these unseasoned kids knew many of the things he'd seen over the course of his life—both in his career as a cop and since.

The teens stared at him oddly, timidly at first. They didn't know he might be the only thing standing between them and pure evil.

He warmed himself at the blazing bonfire the young men had started in the middle of a cleared field. Eventually they began to loosen up; whether it was the beer or simply acceptance of him he wasn't sure, but their boisterous laughter rang out in the night. Just as Ephraim had told him, they all sported jacked-up buggies with state-of-the-art stereos and high-def speakers. Hard-edged rock music poured out, an electric guitar wailing, the music pulsing and throbbing through him. It was like a 1950s movie, minus Elvis—just kids being kids.

He'd brought the beer as bribery to barrel through any defenses they might have about strangers, but the young men seemed more open than their elders. The clincher was the

Mustang. Several of the lanky teens circled the bumper, and Roc felt obliged to leave the warmth of the fire and answer their questions.

"How many horsepower?"

"How fast can it go?"

Speed was the same in any language or culture. Roc lifted the hood and showed them the engine, the muffler, the rims, and tires.

"It looks like it has aftermarket headers."

Roc grinned. They had quick minds and didn't come close to the dumb "Jethro" he'd thought they might be. They were curious and, even inebriated, somewhat naïve.

Finally, getting a sense he wasn't going to get back to the warmth of the fire, he took a different track. "Wanna take a ride?"

"Really?" One kid's pupils were already dilated, and his skin flushed. "*Ja!*"

"All right then." Roc shooed them back from the car. "Hop in."

"Which one?" one of the boys asked.

"Me!" The eager kid held out his hand. "Gonna let me drive?"

"No way. Only I drive this baby."

With a no-big-deal shrug, the kid climbed into the passenger seat, grinning from ear to ear.

"What's your name?"

"Adam."

"All right, Adam. Buckle up."

So began a line of eager young men—Joshua, Luke, Zachariah, James, Caleb—who wanted a taste of life in the fast zone. It was hard to differentiate between the boys at first as they all had similar haircuts: straight across the brow line, then longer and cut straight across the back. Either they all had the same barber or this was another one of their many rules; he'd learned they went by what their leadership, the *Ordnung*, told them. But he gave them credit: they didn't scare easily. Instead, they whooped and hollered as Roc pushed the edge. They won his respect as he won their confidence.

After punching the accelerator and turning deserted roads into a local drag, he U-turned like James Bond on a high-stakes pursuit, then took it slow on the way back to the field, put-putting along Sunflower and Stone Haven Roads, half afraid of running into a buggy in the dark. They steered clear of Slow Gait, where he'd been earlier in the day, before the wedding, although the name sorely tempted him to give it a taste of the Autobahn. The boys showed him Hallelujah Creek, which bisected the community, winding past the local cemetery and an old, broken-down mill.

By the time he'd given them all rides, he'd learned much of the Amish lifestyle, how they used propane to fuel refrigerators as well as farm equipment, how they would probably each abandon their running around and join the church and community through baptism, and how they only went to school through the eighth grade. If he'd been a teen again, he'd have gladly given up school for this lifestyle. At least temporarily.

Holding a beer and pocketing his keys, Roc leaned back against the driver's door, watching the boys still admiring every aspect of the Mustang. "I hear an Amish teen went missing not too long ago."

One of the teens still looked under the hood and said, "Ruby Yoder. I don't think she's missing at all."

Roc started to ask why he thought that but another broke in with: "Heard today the Yoders gave something of Ruby's to the *English* police. Some kind of test." His voice lowered. "They're thinking they found a body might be hers."

Another poked a tire with his foot. "Nah, don't believe it. She done run off with the *English* boyfriend she fancied."

"You know his name?" Roc asked.

The first teen snapped down the hood of the Mustang. "Can't remember it now. He ain't from around here. But I reckon she'll be back. Iffen he tires of her, or she tires of the *English* ways."

"So you get many strangers around here?"

"Not many, no," Caleb, an extra tall boy who had a fuzzy upper lip, answered.

"Occasionally though." Adam rubbed his jaw, and his skin turned a deep shade of red. "Remember that fancy gal?"

"Oh *ja!*" Zachariah clapped a hand against his thigh. He had more freckles than Louisiana had crawfish. "I know the one you mean."

Luke said something in Pennsylvania Dutch, and Roc shook his head. "What?"

Joshua let out a low, slow whistle, while James waved his hands in the air in that timeless shape that all men instinctively recognized as purely feminine.

"Her car broke down over toward the cemetery one night." Joshua crossed his arms over his chest. "Said she wanted some action."

Roc grinned. "Uh-huh, I bet you boys gave her some, huh?"

Caleb shook his head. "She was into some crazy stuff."

"Oh yeah?" Roc didn't move a muscle. He imagined all sorts of sexual deviations that might curl the hair on these boys' chests. "Like what?"

Adam glanced over his shoulder before whispering, "Drinking blood."

Roc's pulse jolted.

Caleb backhanded Adam's arm. "It was chicken's blood, you imbecile."

Adam shrugged, his lip curling. "Don't matter. Blood's blood."

"There are those that believe in the power of blood," Joshua whispered, sliding into the passenger seat.

Adam's face looked paler. "Still, it wasn't right."

"Would you recognize this woman again?" Roc asked, casually eyeing his thumb.

The boys nodded and gave their usual, "*Ja*."

"Good." Roc made it sound like "*goot*" as in their dialect, which tugged a few smiles from them as he slid behind the steering wheel and punched the gas.

Music pulsed around them, accented by the thrum of the powerful engine, pushing him on, pushing him further and faster. But it wasn't really the music. The music only stirred up the rage and resentment inside him. He was in this peaceful, bucolic place for one purpose, which was the same reason Brody had sent him away from New Orleans. But Roc sensed he was on the right trail for something else—revenge.

CHAPTER NINE

Y OU SCARED OF THE devil?"

Hannah wiped her hands on her apron and turned toward the customer at the bakery where she worked three days a week. "Excuse me?"

"You all here seem so scared of worldly influences, like thinking buttons are sinful and all. And I seen some of them hex signs…" The woman leaned close and her cloying scent made Hannah's nose twitch. "I just thought, ya know, that you're scared of the devil himself."

Hannah fingered the straight pin at her waist. Why didn't these *Englishers* realize some of their questions jabbed harder than a pinprick? "We aren't afraid of buttons or modern conveniences." She went back to stacking jars of chow-chow and jams on the shelf. "We simply choose not to use them."

"Why?" The woman's nose was straight and long and sticking into things that were none of her business.

"It is attachments to worldly things we avoid. Not the things themselves."

"Like cars?" A short, stocky man joined them, and it looked as if he could use a little restraint in sampling the pretzel rolls.

Hannah separated out the blackberry and blueberry jams and put them in their proper places. "Yes."

"And electricity," the woman added.

"But ain't you using electricity with all this baking here?" The man nodded at the woman like he'd caught Hannah in hypocrisy.

"You are right that Old Order Amish districts do not allow electricity, but we can use generators and gas-powered machines. The Raber family is allowed to run this bakery because they don't own the building. They lease from a Mennonite family. Mennonites do not have restrictions about electricity."

"Seems like just a lot of hairsplitting to me."

"Hannah!" Grace called from the kitchen.

"If you'll excuse me…" Grateful for the excuse to leave, Hannah lifted the box of jam jars and carried them toward the back. After putting away the remainder of the jars, she peered toward the front of the store where the man and woman added more goodies to their carts. She nudged Grace and gave her a relieved smile. "Thanks."

"Anytime." Grace pinched the edges of a piecrust.

English customers poured into Lancaster County to gawk at the horse and buggies, plain clothes, quilts, and fields. They asked about the straight pins in her apron, her white prayer *kapp*, and why she didn't believe in buttons and telephones. They drove on Amish farms and snapped away with their little cameras or even videotaped Amish children at play.

"Need help?" Hannah asked Grace.

"Sure. You can stir up the filling for the shoo-fly pie. So, have you decided to go tonight?"

Hannah grabbed the large metal spoon and began to stir the thick batter. "Where?"

Grace swiped her forearm across her forehead, leaving a trace of flour. "There's a gathering, just some of us hanging out."

Hannah shook her head, making the ties of her *kapp* waggle back and forth. "I don't think so."

"You should come. It'll be fun. Here." Grace handed Hannah one of the four piecrusts, laid out smooth in a pie pan, the edges neatly crimped. While Grace poured in the dark, thick batter, Hannah turned the pan in her hands until it was evenly distributed, then helped place the pies into the oversized oven.

Hannah wiped her hands on her apron and carried the empty bowl to the sink where an older woman, Marnie Raber, washed. She was a sister-in-law of the owner and had worked in the kitchen every day, except Sundays, since her husband had passed away a few years back. Glancing over her shoulder at the tourists browsing in the shop, Marnie said, "You should help the customers now."

Grace sent her a sorrowful look and Hannah went back to the front of the shop, steering clear of a woman who looked a bit harried as her two children jostled through the shop, pretending to shoot each other and knocking a package of jellybeans off a shelf. Hannah picked up the candy and went back to realigning the jars along the shelves, adding more jars of apple butter and chow-chow. The couple who had pestered her with questions earlier had left, but others had taken their place, gawking at Hannah as if she were on display with the gift items.

"Are these organic?" an older woman asked, indicating the shelves of jars.

"No." Hannah pointed out a separate section to her. "But these over here are."

The woman's gaze narrowed on Hannah, scanning her from prayer *kapp* to worn tennis shoes. Finally, she nodded, settled reading glasses across the bridge of her nose, and studied a jar label.

Easing herself toward the display of freshly baked pies, cookies, and breads, Hannah spotted a man who seemed more intent on studying the customers and Amish behind the counters than the apple dumplings and whoopie pies. He had dark hair pulled back and fastened with a rubber band. His dark complexion only made his scowl more menacing. "May I help you?"

He turned serious brown eyes upon her. "I'm looking for someone."

Someone, not something? His statement surprised her. "Where are you from?"

"New Orleans. Have you been there?"

He might as well have asked her if she'd been to the moon. She shook her head but said, "I know someone who went there once." Suddenly she wanted to change the conversation's direction. "Do they have apple dumplings in Louisiana?"

The skin between his dark brows furrowed, then he glanced toward the display case where snickerdoodle cookies were wrapped in Saran Wrap, along with tiny loaves of pumpkin bread and gingerbread and cherry crumb. "I don't know. Maybe. Maybe not. Did you make these?"

"Some."

"Show me something you made."

"This chocolate shoo-fly pie."

"Is it good?"

She gave a shy smile. "Of course."

He laughed. "All right then. I'll take it."

Hannah scooped it up and gave it to him, his fingers brushing her hand, and she pulled back abruptly. Gesturing toward the cash register, Hannah said, "You can pay over there."

"Thanks, *ma cherie*. And…"

Hannah turned back when she would have turned away. "Yes?"

"Have you seen a stranger hereabouts?"

She glanced around the shop, busy with tourists perusing the Amish quilted potholders, aprons in bright fabrics that no Amish woman would ever wear, postcards and books telling about life in Lancaster County. "Like you?"

A burst of laughter erupted from him. "You're quick. And yes, exactly. Someone like me. From far away. But more dangerous." His words gave her an odd prickly sensation at the back of her neck. "What's your name?"

She hesitated only a second. His gaze, though brazen, had a trustworthy glimmer. "Hannah."

"I'm Roc." He took a step toward her. "Do you know Ruby Yoder?"

"Sure."

"She's missing."

Hannah glanced down at her hands, twisted her fingers together. "She ran off with her boyfriend."

"That's not necessarily true." Roc touched her forearm with one finger, just a glancing contact, not even something anyone else would notice. "You be careful. All right, Hannah? I wouldn't want anything to happen to you."

She met his concerned gaze. "Nothing can happen to me that isn't the Lord's will."

Those words came back to her like a belch while she rode her red scooter home later that afternoon. Her hypocrisy nettled inside her like a sticker burr. She'd once believed in God's will whole-heartedly, but now…How could she have believed God wanted her to marry Jacob and yet God took him? Why would He do that?

A cold rain began to fall, slowly at first and then gaining

strength. Thankful for her coat, she tucked her chin and hurried, pushing off the road with one foot and pressing into the handles of the scooter with her hands. The clippity-clop of hooves behind alerted her, and she glanced back through the slant of rain and saw a horse moving toward her. She scooted onto the side of the road so as not to be sprayed by the wheels rolling through puddles. But instead of passing her, the buggy pulled over and came to a stop. A dark figure swung down from the buggy and Hannah caught a glimpse of Levi's face beneath the rim of his hat.

"Hurry into the buggy." Levi reached for the scooter. "I'll take care of this."

Nodding and full of gratitude, Hannah hurried ahead and climbed into Levi's buggy. A minute later, he joined her, his strong muscles rippling beneath his white shirt and black coat, his actions fluid and assured. Even though they were both wet and shivering in the cold, he shared a warm smile with her that started a flicker of a flame inside her that could have melted a marshmallow.

"Saw the clouds approaching and thought I'd pick you up and give you a ride home, spare you the wet, but I missed you at work."

"Thank you. That was kind of you, Levi. Marnie told me to leave early when we saw the rain coming. But I suppose I wasn't quick enough."

He nodded and clicked the horse back into motion. "Wouldn't be such a bad walk if not for the weather. You'll not take a cold, will you?"

"I'll be fine." But she felt her skin contract and a shiver pass through her.

"And how was work today?" he asked.

"Busy. But that is good, *ja*?"

"*Ja.* 'Tis."

The swoosh of the wheels and the clopping of the hooves filled the space and silence between them. It was already getting late, and Mamm would have supper on the table. Usually Levi left the farm by this time to go to the small house he rented from the Huffstetlers. When Levi's father sold his carpentry shop, which included their home above the showroom, and moved the rest of his family to Ohio, Levi took over Jacob's job with her father and moved in with the Huffstetlers.

Did he miss his dat and mamm something awful? She couldn't imagine being far away from her own parents for any length of time. He had told her once when he worked late in the fields during harvest and ended up eating supper with her family, "These rolls are near as good as my mamm's."

His compliment made her smile and gave her a warm, gooey feeling inside, like a melted chocolate chip. "Oh, no one could make potato rolls like Sally Fisher."

"Just to be sure," he'd said, "let me try another." He'd taken a roll out of the basket. "*Ja,*" he mumbled, "just as good."

Mamm's gaze had shifted toward her, and Hannah knew what she was thinking and it erased the smile she had felt blossom from Levi's compliment. But was he really interested in her?

Now, his steady gaze settled on her, not with the weight of a heavy hand but like the feather brush of a finger against her cheek. With her skin tingling, she tucked her chin downward.

"There was a man in the store today," she said, not knowing why she was talking, babbling like a crazy, overflowing brook, "from New Orleans."

"Hmm."

"It made me think of…" her voice drifted, her throat

closed and she stared out at the gray sky and falling rain.
"I'm sorry."

"Nothing to be sorry for. Jacob went to Louisiana."

"And he came home."

"Hannah," Levi's voice dipped lower, "I know your
feelings for Jacob ran deep but—"

"You're going to miss the turn."

His gaze shifted back to the road and he pulled back on
the reins, slowing the horse and turning into the lane that led
toward her house.

She stared down at her clasped hands and wished he
would hurry. She felt a shivering start deep down inside of
her, the quaking spreading through her limbs.

Levi didn't speak again until he pulled to a stop in front of
her house. "Hannah…"

She didn't move, but her heart fluttered like an injured
bird unable to flee.

"I know you cared for Jacob. So did I. He was my brother." Levi rubbed his thumb along the leather reins. "I loved
him." He too stared straight ahead, not looking in her direction. "I don't know if he made you any promises, but he's
gone now."

Her fingers clamped hold and she squeezed until her nails
bit into her palms.

"And we all have to move on. This is the way of life. This
is our—"

"*Danke*, Levi, for carrying me home." She scrambled out
of the buggy, tripping on her skirt and practically leaping
for the waterlogged ground. She didn't look back, didn't
stop to help with the scooter, but simply ran for the safety
of her room.

CHAPTER TEN

BLOOD SPURTED LIKE AN oil well gone amok.

Roc rolled his eyes and scrunched down in his seat, arms crossed over his chest. When would this movie end? Surrounded by the Amish teens he'd met a week ago, he laughed inwardly at their grunts and groans when axes split heads like melons—*Hollywood probably used cantaloupe and honeydew*—but Roc had seen blood as thick as Log Cabin syrup, smelled death where the rotting odors forced him to smoke a cigar to counter its effect, and tasted the coppery tang of fear. This horror flick didn't come close.

His cell phone vibrated in his hip pocket, and he reached for it as he slid out of his seat and up the aisle, jogging through the swinging theater door and into the bright lights of the lobby with its orange and purple carpet. "Roc here."

"Have the Amish converted you yet?" Mike's voice came over the line extra loud and Roc turned down the volume.

Roc paced in front of a row of gaming machines with *Star Wars* lasers and *Terminator* weaponry. "Yeah, I'm at church right now."

"Well, say a prayer."

"What's up? Too early for the DNA test on the New Orleans Amish gal."

"A body was found. South of Promise."

Roc went as still as a predator on the hunt. "The missing teen? Ruby—"

"It's not official yet but looks like it. Don't say anything."

"Who am I going to tell? Jesus?"

"He knows."

"So who was the gal in New Orleans?"

Mike cleared his throat. "Brody thinks it's a local girl out having fun on Halloween."

"You mean trick-or-treating as an Amish?"

"Yep. Just a costume."

Roc laid a hand against the wall to steady himself. So he'd been sent here on some wild monster chase? He had to see this new body, see if there were any signs the two murders (three counting Emma) were related. Otherwise, he'd head back to Louisiana tonight. "Where are you, Mike? Still at the scene?"

"Not my jurisdiction. I'm just passing along the information."

"I need to see the body."

"Look, I saw the pictures. They're similar to the ones you sent of the trick-or-treater. Like Little Red Riding Hood, the Grimm's version, ya know what I mean?"

Unfortunately.

"Man, you missed it." Caleb Esch veered away from the group of teens emerging from the theater and headed toward Roc, who pocketed his cell phone. The teen had a relaxed, loose-limbed gait and hair like a thatch of hay on the top of his head.

Roc nodded toward the theater where the pounding music poured out through the doorway. "How'd it end?"

"More blood."

The popcorn hardened in Roc's belly as he looked at the teens gathered around him—young and innocent, even in their rebellion. "I'm going to have to get going."

"You got a hot date?" The words came from the teen, Zachariah, who looked from the neck up like he belonged in the eighteenth century and from the neck down like he could be on MTV, which only made Roc's grin broaden.

"Something like that." He palmed his keys.

With the lingering scent of popcorn and manufactured butter clinging to them, they pushed out into the crisp evening air. The cinema was sandwiched between a Wal-Mart and a hardware store. As they moved into the parking lot, the boys heading toward an *English* friend's truck and Roc toward his Mustang, Luke shouldered him. "We'll be on Straight Edge Road this weekend. Will we see you then?"

"If I'm still in town." He sensed he was on the right trail, but if the trail led elsewhere he'd be out of there.

"That your date?" Caleb gave a nod, his gaze fixed on something in the distance.

Roc followed the trajectory to a sleek red Ferrari. The woman inside had long, black hair, straight and gleaming as if polished. She wore dark shades, even though the sun was no longer a threat this evening. She was definitely looking in their direction, and she gave them a slow smile, her lipstick-red lips parting in a seductive invitation.

Adam laughed. "Roc would have to upgrade from Keystone Light."

"You better watch out!" Zachariah turned his back on her. "She's the one that drinks chicken blood."

His comment turned Roc's blood to ice. He brushed past his Amish friends and began walking toward the sleek car, his stride long and determined, but as he got within twenty feet, the tinted window raised and the Ferrari took off, tires squealing, engine roaring as it swerved out of the parking lot. Roc's pace quickened as he launched into a run and cut through the parking lot toward his Mustang, keeping his gaze on the rear of the Ferrari, trying to catch a glimpse of the license plate.

"Go get her, Roc!" one of the teen's hollered to the accompaniment of cheers, whistles, and laughs behind him.

By the time he jumped into the driver's seat, sweat prickled his forehead. He cranked the engine, but it stalled, and Roc slammed a hand against the steering wheel. He tried twice more before the engine caught, and he peeled out of the parking lot. But the red-hot Ferrari was gone. Roc stomped on the pedal, jerking the wheel as he whipped around cars that seemed bent on getting in his way. He leaned over the steering wheel, sweat trickling down his spine, as he frantically searched the streets—why, he wasn't exactly sure, other than the lady had a reputation for exotic drinks. But at this point she was his only lead, and so he punched the gas and flew through a succession of yellow lights before he caught sight of the Ferrari cruising in the opposite direction.

He slammed on his brakes and wheeled the Mustang around until he came even with the high-priced sports car. That tinted window slowly descended and revealed the woman, laughing now. Laughing at him? She flicked a curtain of hair off her shoulder, and he could see her smooth mahogany skin. Was she toying with him? Playing some kind of game? Her expensive car slowed and came to a sudden stop. Roc glanced up in time to see the red light and slammed on his brakes, jerking to a stop beside her.

He reached for the door handle, with a plan to confront her, but the woman motioned with her forefinger for him to roll down his passenger window. He cursed the age of his car and leaned over to palm the lever, pumping his arm as the window descended.

"You are one determined man." She had an exotic voice, low and sexy, with a lilt that reminded him of the tropics, something like Jamaican or maybe Creole.

"I can be."

With her mahogany skin and fine bone structure, beautiful seemed too easy a word to define her, and yet it missed its mark. She was stunning, striking, with her dark hair and skin that looked as silky as satin sheets and instantly brought to mind images of lingerie. She gave a slow smile, her lips closed and pulling sideways in a seductive leer. "I like that in a man."

"You're from Louisiana?" he said, having noticed her license plate earlier.

"New Orleans," she said in that rolling cadence only one born in the Big Easy could manage, "and you?"

"Same."

"And we had to come all this way north to meet, did we? Or are you following me?"

"Would I have reason to?"

She winked. "Many men would say so." Her finger trailed the line of her collarbone to the deep cleft between her breasts. "But you tell me."

He had to speak to this woman, other than the ping-pong of flirtatious comments. He had to know if what the Amish teens said—that she drank blood—was true, but sitting at a red light was not the right place. Not knowing what else to say, Roc asked, "You want to have a drink somewhere?"

She lowered her shades and peered at him over the dark rims. Her eyes were black, like what he'd heard described as a hole in space, and he had the sensation that he was falling into her gaze, falling and unable to stop or retreat. "I have already had a drink this evening, and one is my limit. But I will take you up on your offer soon, *ma cherie,* very soon I am thinking."

Minutes melted into what felt like seconds. A spell of some sort wrapped around Roc, thin threads holding him fast, and then the blast of a horn jolted him, snapped the threads and released him from wherever he had been taken captive. Her smile spread wide, dazzling and beguiling, as she flashed her white teeth at him. Then at the most leisurely pace, the Ferrari rolled forward with lethal grace.

He followed, letting cars edge between them but still keeping that tantalizing red rear in view. She ended up doubling back, crisscrossing her path, and he suspected she was trying to lose him. Or maybe she was toying with him again.

The thought struck him in that hypersensitive area at the back of the neck and made those tiny hairs stand upright. It was the same feeling he got when he instinctively knew something was being held back during a suspect interview, and it only made him dig deeper, push harder.

The red Ferrari turned into a brick parking garage, and when Roc reached the gated arm a minute later, he grabbed a ticket from the machine and inched forward, heading up the ramp. He scanned the parked vehicles on either side of him, but in his rearview mirror, something snagged his attention and he saw *her* walking along the sidewalk. *How'd she park so fast? And where?* But it didn't matter. He needed to follow her.

He jerked the wheel and pulled into the nearest space, which wasn't actually a parking spot. He jumped out, noticing the Mustang was crooked, then he ran back down the steep concrete and out onto the street. He paused for a minute, his breath coming hard and fast, telling him he'd ignored his workout regimen for too long. He waited to spot her again, but when he didn't, he walked toward the corner of a traffic-congested street.

There he waited, watched the cars passing, horns blaring, and his muscles tensed. The chill of the evening wafted over. He was more out of practice in tailing a suspect than he realized. What had been second nature to him when he was on the force now took more effort. He'd grown lax serving daiquiris.

After a few minutes of standing on the curb like an idiot, he headed back to the parking garage. He'd find the Ferrari, search it if possible, and then wait for her to return.

But then he saw her.

She was walking along the street in spiky high heels and a dress constructed with one thing in mind—sex, hot and steamy with easy access. Not exactly fall evening attire here in Pennsylvania, but she didn't seem to be bothered by the crisp air. She had an elegant, graceful way of moving. But she wasn't alone. A man walked beside her. Even though he was a head taller, they matched strides. He had dark hair, pale skin—a walking contradiction—and he wore a black leather jacket that had a custom fit.

Roc kept his gaze bonded to them and jogged across the street, dodging a car and then an Amish girl puttering along on a red scooter. The couple, looking as exotic as a palm tree growing in Pennsylvania, moved together, the woman talking, emphasizing her words with flowing hand motions, the man staring straight ahead, without a glance in her direction or responding to her in any way, as if he didn't care what she was saying. Roc couldn't imagine too many men ignored this woman. Or that she allowed it.

In between two brick buildings, they turned left into what appeared to be an alleyway. A dumpster overflowed with waste and the smell rolled out of it, creeping toward the street. Roc followed, and as he entered the alley, whispers teased his ears. He glanced up above him, searching the windows of the buildings, the fire escapes, the doorways. When halfway along the narrow passageway that held a battery of closed doors that led to restaurant kitchens and storage rooms, he realized it was a dead end. His footsteps slowed but never faltered. *Never reveal a weakness.* He took two more deliberate steps, then whirled around.

There they were—standing casually apart, the woman with one hip cocked, the man with feet spread and arms at his side. It was a non-threatening stance, and yet Roc sensed the threat like a rabbit senses a wolf on the prowl. Danger pervaded the air. The inside of his arm flexed, and he felt the solidness of his Glock in its holster.

The woman's lips curled in a seductive smile. "You want something, *ma cherie?*"

"You." His answer surprised him.

She slid a hand along her thigh. "It is no surprise." She lifted her sunglasses to the crown of her head, hooking her hair behind her ears and giving a glimpse of the long column of her neck. "But this desire comes with a price, no?"

"Does it?"

She looked at the man beside her. "You tell him, Akiva. You have paid this price."

The man named Akiva scowled at her. "You would know about that, wouldn't you? But you'll never know the exact cost."

She shrugged as if it didn't matter.

Roc noted the man's accent, not quite the clipped Pennsylvania enunciation he'd been hearing all week and nothing at all like the woman's. His gaze shifted between them. It's then he realized they had the same eyes, dark and fathomless, and the sensation that he was falling unbalanced him.

"This isn't my concern. Do what you wish with him." A note of boredom made Akiva's voice flat.

"Are you sure?" she cooed. "You won't be jealous? You won't interfere?"

"Is that what you're doing?" Akiva gave a sputtering, mocking laugh and took a step back as if to show he was disengaged.

The woman turned her gaze away from Akiva then and onto Roc. "So, tell me, Roc Girouard…"

His name on her tongue shocked him. "How do you know—?"

"I know many things about you. This is true." She walked toward him, those eyes holding him in place, faint whispers filling his head. "I know about your father; how long it has been since you've been with a woman"—her voice embraced him like a heavy cloud of perfume and muddled his thinking—"even what happened to the one you loved."

Each step brought her closer and closer to him, her high heels clicking against the concrete like the tapping of a long, glossy fingernail. She seemed unhurried, like a tiger, sleek and lethal, toying with its dinner. Her curves mesmerized him. She had no weapon, and yet a cold knot twisted and tightened in Roc's belly. Her eyes, heavy-lidded in that just-had-the-best-sex-ever slant, glittered with intensity. Slowly, she reached toward him, dragging a nail down his chest to his belly and leaving goosebumps in her wake. "I even know what brought you here to Pennsylvania…to Promise. In time, Roc, you will know many things about me too."

"Most you'll wish you didn't know." Akiva's words were hard and cold.

Her smile spread wide but she kept her gaze on Roc. "Ah, you are jealous, Akiva."

"You'd like that, wouldn't you?"

A low-rumbling laugh escaped her lips. "You know I would. It's intoxicating, isn't it?" she asked Roc, leaning toward him. "To know each action you make stirs something in another." Her lips parted and released a sultry breath. "Not tonight, *ma cherie*, but soon, I promise you, Roc. Hmm." Her tongue flicked out to lick her lips. "Soon."

Then she stepped back from Roc, and in less than a blink, she disappeared. Just simply vanished. One second she was standing in front of him and the next she was gone.

Roc shook his head as if to unclutter his thoughts and fell back a step, then another. "What the—?" His heart pummeled his ribcage. He stared at Akiva. "What just happened here?"

"If you are smart, you will go home...before you cannot."

Roc wasn't sure what happened first: him pulling his Glock or Akiva crouching low in an attack stance. "Who the hell are you people?"

Akiva's mouth pulled to one side and a rumble of laughter rolled out of him and filled up the alleyway, vibrating inside Roc's head, shaking him to his core. "You do not want to know."

Then he too disappeared. But the laughter remained. Roc swung around, pointing the Glock right, left, at the windows staring blankly down upon him, at the entrance to the alley. But Akiva was gone.

CHAPTER ELEVEN

S UNLIGHT SLANTED ONTO THE plain cloth, and Hannah traced the curve of a cross-stitched letter *a* in the word March, the threads smooth against the pad of her finger. "Is this your *best* work, Katie?"

Her younger sister nodded, her narrow throat working as she swallowed. Her sparkling blue eyes glanced from the stitching to Hannah, anxiety etched in their corners. How easily Hannah remembered what it was like to have Mamm critique her own work when she was but ten.

"Your work is greatly improved. The stitches are even and neat."

A smile, like the dawn, emerged across the younger girl's face, brightening her cheeks to a healthy shade of pink. "*Danke.*"

The rumble of a car engine and the crunching of tires on the drive erased the smile, and Katie rushed toward the window, leaning over Dat's chair to see out. "*Englishers.*" Her tone rose with excitement. "What do you think they want?"

"If it's the milk truck, then it is late."

"No, it's a car."

Hannah carefully folded the cross-stitched material. "Dat will see to the *Englishers*. Come—"

"But what do you think they want?"

"To take pictures or some such. You know how they can be." *Englishers* often wanted to use a camera to capture their image. Some called them names. Others honked and whipped past them on the roadways, making the horses shy and the buggy pull sideways. "Or maybe," Hannah suggested, "they're lost. Come, Katie, let's set the table."

But she remained rooted at the window. "What kind of a car is that?"

Hannah peered over Katie's shoulder. Toby trotted from the barn toward the car to greet the visitors; the yellow lab rarely barked, treating strangers with polite curiosity. The windows of the car were as dark as the metal sides. "A black one."

"Have you ever driven one?"

"You know, the *Ordnung* forbids such."

"Timothy Borntreger used to own a car."

"That was before he was baptized."

"I wanna drive one, make it go faster than the buggy."

"Why not just ride in a car then? That's allowed by the bishop."

Katie sighed longingly, then placed her fisted hands in front of her like she was steering the wheel. "But wouldn't it be fun to make it go? Just once."

Hannah grasped her younger sister's arm and tugged at her to come away from the window. "It would give me a fright for sure." She picked up Katie's doll and waggled the floppy arms and legs. It had no face, just a blank plumpness. "It would scare your baby doll too."

Katie laughed and clasped her doll to her chest. "I think it would be fun."

"And what would Bishop Stoltzfus say?"

"Maybe if there is a reason."

"What reason would you have for owning one when you could hire a driver?"

"I don't know." Katie's forehead creased. "Just once wouldn't hurt." Then she brightened, her blue eyes lighting from within. "Do you think the *Englisher* will stay for supper? Where do you think they're going? Where did they come from?"

Hannah held out a hand for Katie to join her. With a heavy sigh, the little girl relinquished her perch and moved toward Hannah. She braided their fingers together. "You have too many questions, Katie." The little girl reminded her in a small way of Jacob, and her heart swelled with love and patience. "Come now."

CHAPTER TWELVE

I T WAS JUST ANOTHER Amish farm. After a while, they all looked the same with white-washed sides and green-shaded windows, like eyelids closed, blocking anyone from getting a glimpse of what was going on inside. The shades on this house, however, were raised and the windows open. Laundry hung on a line, legs and sleeves, socks and sheets, waving a greeting in the late autumn breeze.

Roc let the Mustang idle a few minutes, enjoying the last few seconds of heat before he killed the engine. *Might as well get this over with.*

Everything seemed in its place—neat, tidy, yet weathered a bit around the edges. *What would life be like in such a place as this? Boring, for sure.* Not as lively as the house he'd grown up in, where the sun popped the paint right off the wood and mosquitoes grew as big as bats. Nothing about his childhood home had been neat or clean, certainly not orderly or peaceful. His old man had kept clunkers on the driveway along with worn-out batteries, crunched bumpers, and bald tires. His mother had bought statues of saints, her Cajun and Catholic roots running deep, and planted them in the yard as if each one would banish his daddy's sins. Remembering she'd named Roc after a saint never failed to make him laugh.

A crunch on the gravel alerted him, and Roc spun around, his hand automatically reaching beneath his jacket for his gun. Old habits died hard. Still, Roc left the gun where it was and watched a slim woman walk toward him. Her cheeks and nose were pink in the cold weather, making her blue eyes even bluer. Wide-eyed innocence took on a whole new meaning for him when he looked at her. Like all the other women he'd seen in plain Amish attire, she wore a solid blue dress and white apron with a white bonnet covering her brown hair, which was pulled back in some traditional style he'd seen all over Promise—but it was her eyes that captured his attention.

"Good day to you." Her voice sounded warm.

Roc stuck out a hand automatically. "Roc Girouard."

She stared at it then slowly reached forward and clasped his hand. Her grip was strong and sure, her hands reddened from hard work, and her brief touch startled him in its perfunctory frankness. "Rachel Schmidt."

In spite of the cold, her hand was as warm as toast, the skin soft as butter. Noting her unexpected last name, he released her hand quickly, crossed his arms over his chest, and cocked his head sideways. "This another Schmidt farm? I thought I was just there." He thumbed over his shoulder eastward. "I met one of your neighbors, maybe a relative of yours then. Daniel…"

A thin veil of pink rose up along her neck and covered her face. "*Ja*, you're right. That is the Schmidt place just yonder. I am Rachel *Nussbaum*. I am not used to my name just yet."

"You're newly married then?"

Her cheeks brightened even more. "My husband, Josef… this is his family's farm. Did my father, Daniel Schmidt, send you here?"

"Not exactly."

She only blinked, waiting for him to explain. These Amish seemed comfortable with silence and his old trick backfired on him as he shifted in the cold and searched for something to say.

The wind bit at his neck, and he cursed, belatedly chomping down hard on the word. "Sorry." Her blue eyes frosted around the edges, and he stamped his feet. "Is it always this cold here?"

"You're not from around here."

"That's right."

The woman sniffed at the air as if dissecting it. "Wait till winter arrives."

"This isn't winter?" Roc glanced at the fields that should be blanketed in snow according to his southern thermometer.

"Oh no. 'Tis fall."

"Great." His tone held anything but enthusiasm. His gaze scanned the laundry on the line, the barn area, and the silo, which he'd learned held grain and corn for winter. "Nice place you have here, though. Real nice. If it weren't so..."

"Cold." Rachel Nussbaum offered a soft, unapologetic smile.

The frigidity of the temperatures was suddenly upped a notch or two. Roc cleared his throat and jammed his hands in his front pockets. "I'll come right to the point, Mrs. Nussbaum." He rocked forward onto the balls of his feet. "I'm looking for someone."

"Amish?"

"I don't think so. But I don't know really." The woman with the black eyes and Casper the ghost's disappearing abilities hadn't been Amish. But the man...well, he wasn't sure what he was either.

"Then I would not know him. Or was it a woman you are searching for?"

"A man and a woman actually." He wasn't handling this well. His rehearsed lines jumbled in his brain, and he tried to block out Rachel Nussbaum's blue gaze and focus, remembering those dark, black, fathomless eyes and the fear that accompanied them.

"If they aren't Amish, then I doubt I can be of any help."

Apparently around here, the distinction between *English* and Amish, or normal and plain, mattered. "Maybe they used to be. I'm not sure what the connection is. Yet."

"What is their name?"

"Akiva. That's the man's name. But the woman…I don't know."

"That does not sound Amish. Is that a common *Englisher* name?"

"Not so much. Not where I come from anyway."

"And where is that?"

"Louisiana…New Orleans to be exact."

Only the slightest change in her features alerted Roc. Her skin turned a shade paler. Her eyes widened. Her mouth tightened.

"Have you been there?"

She blinked several times then wiped her hands on her apron, crossing her arms over her middle. "Wh-what does this *Englisher* look like?"

Roc's smile disappeared at her insistence that the one he was hunting wasn't Amish. "I don't have a photo. He has dark hair, pale skin, and"—Anthony's insistence about vampires came back to him and he almost laughed—"dark…very dark eyes."

Rachel glanced at the ground, rocked back slightly on her heels as if thinking about the description. "How do you know they are in Promise?"

"I saw them yesterday not far from here."

She tilted her head sideways and one of the long ties of her bonnet lifted in the breeze.

"Look, I know none of this makes any sense, but it is important. If you know anything"—he pulled out a paper from his pocket and scribbled his cell phone number on it with a pen—"don't hesitate to call me. Okay?"

"We don't have a telephone."

"You have access, right?" He'd heard this excuse, but he'd also learned the Amish often had a neighbor or business phone in the barn for emergencies. Or sometimes a teen in the family had a cell phone. "With a neighbor maybe?" When she gave a quick nod, he continued, "If you see a stranger, be wary. You have a nice family, I'm sure. You want to keep them safe. Yes? *Ja!*" He'd heard that often enough this week that he wasn't sure if he was being sarcastic or adopting the Pennsylvania-Dutch dialect. "These folks I'm searching for are dangerous."

At least until proven otherwise.

"Are you a policeman?"

Was. Past tense. Not anymore. But he couldn't say that, so he tempered it with, "You might say I'm sorta like a private detective."

"And this couple has broken the *English* laws?"

"If they did what I think, then it's one of God's laws too. Murder, that is."

Rachel's gaze widened and her face paled decidedly this time. Suddenly he had an odd desire to protect this woman. Or maybe he simply wanted to protect her community. The folks he'd met were kind and thoughtful, and although they might be plain in speech and manner, they seemed rich in other ways—ways he'd never imagined possible with their close-knit community and bulging families that actually seemed to like each member. He didn't want them hurt in anyway. But before he could figure out his thoughts, he watched this small woman shift, straighten her spine, and steeliness deepened the blue of her eyes. "We are not afraid of strangers. Or of God's will here. *Em Gott Sei Friede.*"

That phrase got around. Each farmer in this district of Promise liked to bandy it about like children playing with a balloon. But this was no harmless toy. Their balloon, the security of their district, could easily be burst. Roc snagged Rachel's arm. "You'll need God's peace for what is coming. Believe you me."

CHAPTER THIRTEEN

DUSK SWOOPED DOWN LIKE a hawk on its prey, and the last blood-red rays soaked into the land. Akiva relaxed in the shadows, but his keen gaze bore into the lit window.

Hannah stirred something on the stove and turned toward her little sister—what was her name? Kim? Kate? Katie? But his gaze latched onto Hannah, tracing her every movement, straining to catch a glimpse of her as she moved about the kitchen, memorizing each hand gesture and smile. A longing welled up in him to feel the warmth of her smile aimed in his direction. It had been too long, and he drank in the sight of her like a man traipsing through the Sahara devours water.

"*I see my beauty in you.*" He whispered the words of the ancient mystic that welled up inside him like spring water burbling out of the ground, unable to be contained.

She wore a dark purple dress; that color had always been his favorite. Tiny wisps of blond hair escaped the traditional Amish way her hair was twisted and tied up. His chest tightened and his throat convulsed, the longing that had lain dormant for so long awoke within him, stretched, and made every fiber come alive with an inner heat. It spread throughout his body and his skin tingled.

She was poetry in motion, a sonnet begging to be written, and snippets of words and verses from wordsmiths far beyond his skill came to mind.

She was a phantom of delight
When first she gleamed upon my sight;
A lovely apparition, sent
To be a moment's ornament;
Her eyes as stars of twilight fair.

Then the green shade slid downward, covering the window, blocking his view, and his longing hardened into a cold knot in his chest. He'd waited so long to be near her, to see her. Would she still smell of flour and sunshine, rain and cedar? Did she taste of strawberries? Would she once again soften in his arms?

But before he could touch or taste her again, how could he approach her?

Would she even recognize him?

Fear him?

Or rush to meet him?

The last stanza of the Wordsworth poem said what he couldn't manage: "*A perfect Woman, nobly planned, To warn, to comfort, and command; and yet a spirit still, and bright with something of angelic light.*"

It was always the same being near Hannah—his tongue tangled, his throat closed, and poetry loosened the words from within him and allowed him to reveal his heart. If there was a beating muscle inside him after all of this time, it was collapsing and folding in on itself, the weight of grief heavy and unrelenting. Love, like a beacon guiding him, had brought him all this way to find her, to be with her once more. And yet now that he was here, doubts and fears poisoned his hope.

The back door of the house opened, and a wedge of lantern light slanted across the porch. Akiva whirled away, bolted over the porch railing, and vanished into the barn. The earthy smells of hay and manure surrounded him, and he paced before the stalls. A horse stamped its foot and whinnied. The animal's nervous agitation seemed contagious and soon the other animals acted restless and uneasy, shifting and snorting, backing away from the openings as he passed. He moved over to one stall, stared at a gray mare who ducked her head, a muscle along her neck twitching.

Then something lying on the ground caught Akiva's eye. He turned away from the stall, bent, and retrieved the faceless rag doll. Dressed like an Amish girl, the doll reminded him of one Hannah had carried long ago. He placed it against his chest, the place where his heart could no longer beat without her.

She was the reason he had returned.

She was his only reason for his existence.

And she would be his salvation.

Then it became clear what he must do. He would risk his last hope, all his love, even what life he had left. *Everything*. His hand tightened on the doll, crushing it with the strength of his determination.

> *Out of the night that covers me,*
> *Black as the Pit from pole to pole,*
> *I thank whatever gods may be*
> *For my unconquerable soul…*
>
> *It matters not how strait the gate,*
> *How charged with punishments the scroll,*
> *I am the master of my fate:*
> *I am the captain of my soul.*

CHAPTER FOURTEEN

MAYBE IT WAS SIMPLY Hannah's mood of late, the gloom slithering over her as night approached, like dark fingers snuffing out the lamp of daylight. Time should have made missing Jacob easier, and yet it seemed harder, the sorrow darker.

From the kitchen window, she watched Levi climb into his buggy, readjust his hat, and flick the reins to get his horse moving. Only to herself did she admit she felt a stirring around him, more than a passing interest, and yet her heart seemed shackled to the past and she was unable to step forward. Were the shackles fear? Plain old fear of once more losing her heart? Or was her love for Jacob so strong that it bound her to the past forever? Would she never be free? Free to love someone again…someone like Levi?

"Hannah?" Mamm called.

She released the edge of the green shade, and it flopped back against the window. Then she hurried to take the platter of roasted chicken to the table. Dat sat at one end, Grandpa Ephraim at the other; Katie and Hannah looked at each other across the honeyed bread and buttered potatoes; Mamm perched cattycorner to her girls. The large wooden table seemed almost empty now with Rachel and Grandma Ruth gone. Sadness swelled inside Hannah's chest as her family nest seemed to be dwindling, which Mamm said was a new season for their lives. She bowed her head and silently thanked the Lord for His bounty and prayed for no more losses.

As soon as Dat cleared his throat, the signal for the food to be passed, Katie looked toward him expectantly. "The *English* man didn't want to stay for dinner?"

Mamm paused, holding the bowl of beets. "What *English* man?"

Dat took the beets then potatoes, scooping hefty helpings onto his plate, and the beet juice bled into the fluffy, white mound. "A stranger stopped earlier while you were at Molly's. He was not looking for a meal, Katie. He was lost. That is all."

"Easy to do out here." Mamm passed the acorn squash, buttered in the center and sprinkled with brown sugar.

With a heavy sigh, Katie rested her cheek against the back of her hand. "I wish he would have stayed."

"Pass the butter." Dat broke off one end of the sourdough loaf and mopped up gravy with it.

"Did you see the inside of his car?"

Dat made a disgruntled sound. "Why would I do that?"

"Curiosity is not evil," Grandpa Ephraim said, "but it is pride that leads to destruction."

Katie opened her mouth, but Mamm pressed a hand against Katie's arm to shush her. She glanced from Mamm to Dat and then stuffed her mouth with potatoes.

There was no other news, other than the weather forecast and how Molly Esh was readying her household for Sunday services, nothing of interest to discuss, and so they chewed in silence. Hannah stared at the calendar nailed to the wall, waiting for the meal to end, her thoughts lost in confusion. Her feelings were all jumbled, and she stared at those blank squares until her mind felt equally vacant.

After Dat scraped the last spoonful of potatoes onto his plate, the women waited for him to finish eating. Hannah's hands remained folded in her lap. Finally, he pushed back from the table, muttered, "*Gut,*" and stood.

Katie and Hannah cleaned off the table, scraping plates and bowls and covering the leftover bread.

"Mamm," Katie said as she took a plate from Hannah and began drying it, "I left my doll in the barn. Can I go and get her?"

"When you finish with your chores."

Katie nodded and worked hard to finish the dishes, scrubbing and washing the pots and pans and dishes. When Hannah folded the dishtowel at last, she smiled at her little sister, noticing how her summer freckles were starting to fade. "Go on now. I'll finish up."

With a big grin, Katie skipped toward the back door.

"Hannah," Dat called from his chair in the main room as Katie opened the back door, "go with her."

"But…?" She stopped immediately at the frown slanting Mamm's eyebrows downward as Mamm took a plate from her. Worry darkened her mother's eyes and made Hannah's stomach clench tight. Why would Dat want her to go? Did he want to speak to Mamm privately? Was there something wrong? She ducked her chin and folded the rag.

Mamm took the rag from her too. "Go on. I will wipe the counters."

As Hannah walked out the door, just before the latch caught, she heard Mamm ask, "Is everything all right, Daniel?"

He grunted. "And why wouldn't it be?"

But a minute later, he followed Hannah outside and stood on the porch, hands on his waist as he looked beyond the railing. She felt his gaze on her as she caught up with her younger sister and they walked toward the barn together. It was an easy walk, the ground smooth, and only fifty yards. Dat and Levi kept the area neat and cleared, as the milk truck pulled through here each morning to collect the milk and needed enough space to turn around. To one side of the barn was a paddock, and to the left was the spring house, the chicken coop, and the shed where the buggy was stored. On the backside of the barn was the silo, more paddocks, and where feed and hay were stacked. Fields stretched out beyond, which were now put to bed for the winter but in spring would be plowed and planted.

With Katie at her side, Hannah slid open the barn door. It was heavy and resisted, but she pushed hard. Waning light made the inside dark and shadowy, and Hannah wished she'd brought her flashlight. Katie ran ahead down the row of stalls. "You left your doll in here?"

"I thought so." Walking back toward Hannah, Katie shook her head. "Maybe I left it in the loft." With a shrug, she climbed up the wooden ladder into the rafters where a momma cat and her kittens lived.

Hannah walked along the stalls, peering inside each one and searching the shadowy corners for the doll that often seemed permanently attached to Katie. Sometimes her sister would steal away in the afternoons and play with the kittens or lamb, her doll always in her hand or under her arm.

A breath of a breeze drifted across the back of her neck, and chill bumps rose along her arms. She turned, glanced around. It felt as if someone was here. Her gaze drifted toward the boards above and she heard Katie rummaging around. Of course, she wasn't alone. But where was Toby? Wouldn't the lab bark if there was something dangerous? Then she heard the voice, the whisper of her name.

Hannah.

Her heart battered her insides. A sudden flush made her skin prickle.

"Katie?" Her voice quavered.

"It's not here either." Katie's voice was muffled but Hannah could hear the disappointment.

Hannah. I'm here. Don't be afraid.

She turned in a circle, searching for the source of the voice, her gaze frantic, her heartbeat frenzied. An icy chill flowed over her from head to toe and seeped into as if her bones were sponges, and she began to quake.

"Katie?"

Her little sister poked her head out of the opening above. "What?"

"Did you hear that?"

"What?"

Hannah shook her head. "Nothing. Must have been the wind."

"Maybe my doll is in the spring house." Katie climbed back down the ladder, cuddling a kitten that bolted out of her arms, obviously eager for freedom. "I played in there earlier."

"All right." Hannah rubbed the chill from her arms. "We'll try there." She took Katie's hand in hers, glanced over her shoulder, and hurried her out of the barn.

Together, they walked across the small patch of dirt. Even in the short time they'd been in the barn, darkness had stolen over the farm, but the moon and stars lit the way to the small building on the side of the barn that housed the diesel engines required for refrigerating the milk, and the air compressors, which pumped water to the house. Toby came around the corner and nudged the back of her skirt then wandered off, nose to ground. When Hannah finally unhinged the rusty lock and pushed inside, Katie followed closely behind. The wind slammed the door shut and buried them in darkness.

Katie gasped and clung tighter to Hannah's hand.

"It's all right." Hannah's voice sounded odd and tiny in the small building, as if all sound was absorbed in the darkness. Even though her heart was pumping harder and faster than the machines, it had no effect on banishing the cold fear that burrowed into her belly. She blinked hard, trying to see, but the black was deep and complete.

"Should I get the lantern?" Katie's voice sounded timid.

Hannah patted their joined hands, as much to comfort her little sister as herself. "Just give your eyes a minute to adjust."

In that length of time, she could make out shadows and shapes of the machinery, but the corners were lost in shadows so black they must have been able to soak up all light. "Why were you playing in here? Dat doesn't want you in here."

"I forgot. I won't do it again." Katie started forward then stopped and tugged on Hannah's hand. "Will you come with me to the back?"

"Sure, Katie."

They picked their way over power lines and cords. The air pump hissed and popped in a steady rhythm, but the usually familiar sound seemed louder in the darkness and made Hannah's skin contract. They moved along the back wall, inching forward, feeling their way along the wooden planks until Hannah saw a small, dark lump. "Is that it?"

Katie rushed forward and scooped up her baby doll, which used to be Hannah's and before that Mamm's. She smoothed out the doll's rumpled skirt and squashed bonnet. "Toby's gonna be in trouble. I think he stole it."

Hannah laughed with relief. "At least she's all right now. Let's go back to the house."

"Where have you been?" Katie scolded her doll. "You shouldn't go wandering off alone like that. I didn't know where you were. Come along, it's almost time for bed."

CHAPTER FIFTEEN

ANOTHER BODY WAS FOUND." Mike's voice came through the cell phone.

"Amish again?" Roc steered the Mustang with one hand, keeping his eyes on the dark road and the swath of light the headlights provided. He'd taken to patrolling the farms and small businesses located in Lancaster County, moving through Bird-in-Hand, Intercourse, and Promise.

"A homeless guy in Philadelphia. Same MO. Neck wound. And—"

"Do you think the perp is on the move?"

"How the hell should I know?"

Roc didn't have a clue either. He'd had a composite sketch drawn up on the couple he'd met in the alley, but he wasn't sure why. What would be the charge if he managed to find them? Drinking chicken's blood? Not that he had proof. Strange behavior? He was an eyewitness. Something didn't sit well with Roc. Something had happened that night in the alley, and he wasn't sure what. Had to be some mind trick, some illusion, but Roc was at a loss as to know what exactly had happened.

With few clues except a mad dog run amok, or so it seemed, someone who liked to take a bite—actually a chunk—out of necks, Roc powered up his determination. "Let me know if anything else happens or turns up."

"You staying in Promise?"

"Until I have reason to move on."

Roc tossed the cell phone in the passenger seat and continued to drive down the narrow back roads, his gaze scanning left and right for anything that might alert him. But there wasn't much to see. It was pitch dark. The Amish appeared to be abed and a-snooze or else working on expanding their families. It was after all, close to Intercourse.

Other than the Mustang's headlights catching an opossum, which froze in the middle of the road, making Roc steer around it, he hadn't come across anything suspicious. Without any lamps or traffic lights on these back roads, the moon and stars provided the only illumination. Thankfully, the moon was full and bright and the stars plentiful tonight.

For several nights, he'd driven through the farm country, past the Amish homes, businesses, and farms, hoping he'd see something and yet hoping he wouldn't. The folks here deserved to have the peace they so desired. And for some crazy reason, he felt protective of them. Even though the latest body wasn't Amish, Roc sensed there was a connection. And that gut instinct of his that had served him well in his cop days was throbbing like a red alarm.

He drove through Bird-in-Hand and Intercourse until he came to Promise, driving extra slow as no one seemed to be on the roads this late. The houses he passed were dark, the shades drawn, and, he hoped, the doors locked. These folks didn't have security alarms; most had dogs, though they were more the friendly type than the sound-the-alarm barking kind. These folks' security came from an undying faith in the Almighty to protect them. Roc preferred the nine-millimeter solid steel kind of faith that he could hold in his hand.

A flash of a light off to his right grabbed his attention, and he slowed the Mustang even more, leaning over the steering wheel, trying to peer across the dark field where moonbeams slanted downward. Sure enough, what looked like a disembodied light bobbed and weaved like a drunken firefly. It had to be a flashlight or lantern of some kind. *Who would be out this late? In this cold? And why?*

Roc pulled the Mustang to the side of the road and parked, grabbing his Glock as he sprang out of the car, and closed the door quietly. Rather than following the path of the light, he gauged where he anticipated the light was headed and ran along the road, his boots cushioned by dry, fallen grass, and then he cut across a field to bisect its potential path. He crouched low beside a fence and the light came toward him from the right, not directly but about fifty yards south. At that angle, he would catch sight of who was out here. For several minutes, he remained still, silent, searching. It was so quiet. Where were the crickets? The hum of business and traffic? Maybe the cold had frozen everything. Roc felt the cold tunnel deep into his bones, but his heart pumped hard and fast in anticipation of a chase.

A rustling noise to his left startled him, and Roc's head snapped in the direction of the noise. The bobbing light froze. With the faint moonlight behind him, he could make out a dark shape, but it wasn't a tree or pole. It had bulges and bumps, not the smooth line of something artificial. But was this man or beast? When the shape moved, he knew it was a man. The shape shifted forward then halted. Roc reached for his gun. He transferred his weight from one foot to the other, just enough to prepare to spring forward, then the shape whirled away and made a crashing sound as the man's footsteps pounded through the dry brittle grass and brush.

Instantly, Roc was on his feet and giving chase before he could even formulate a thought. He ran a good hundred yards, leaping over fallen trees, tripping on something and scrambling back to his feet, across a mushy patch of ground and into a stand of trees. A branch grabbed at him, and dry, brittle leaves scratched his face when he came to a stop beneath a covering of trees that the moonlight couldn't penetrate. The darkness became denser, the shadows deepened.

The only sound was Roc's breath, as he sucked it in through his teeth. Not even a breath of a breeze stirred the patches of dry grass or bare branches and withered leaves. His sides heaved and a muscle pinched just above his lower rib. Then the whispers seemed to coil about him, as if the leaves were chattering among themselves. A bad feeling sunk into him. Was this a trap? Like in the alley? Roc made a slow turn, his gaze darting forward, back, right, left, frisking brush and trees, searching shadows.

"Are you following me?" the voice came from behind Roc.

He whirled around, aiming his Glock. The man stood in a leafy shaft of moonlight but Roc recognized him. "Akiva."

"The question is: *who* are you?" But before Roc could answer, the man continued, "Roc Girouard." He tilted his head sideways. Shadows and moonlight played across the man's face, distorting his features. "But who is Roc Girouard? No longer a police officer, are you? More a drunk than anything else. So why such a keen interest in the Amish?"

Roc gritted his teeth. His trigger finger itched to tighten. It would only take a fraction more of tension to fire a bullet straight at Akiva. "What's your interest here?"

"Are you playing at police detective work again?" Akiva shook his head and tsked. "Didn't you learn anything? Did you not understand my warning? You cannot stop us. Wasn't Emma's death proof of that?"

The words felt like a punch straight into Roc's chest, and he fell back a step. His heart stopped then began to pound with a fierceness that pumped molten anger through him and tightened his grip on the Glock. "You have a death wish?"

Akiva tipped his head back and laughed. "If that were but possible."

"It's very possible." Roc took a step forward, then another.

The laughter stopped and those dark eyes bore into him with an intensity that made sweat emerge on Roc's brow. Akiva took a step in Roc's direction, then another.

"Don't move," Roc said. "I *will* shoot."

The man's lip curled with disdain, and he took another step, then another.

Roc squeezed the trigger. It was a simple reflexive move, one he'd done a thousand times on the shooting range and only occasionally aimed at a perp on the run, never straight at man's chest. The second the bullet hit Akiva, the man's body crumpled forward, folded in on itself. It seemed to shrink and collapse inward and then, with a flutter, took flight and disappeared before Roc could fire again.

CHAPTER SIXTEEN

HANNAH'S NERVES STRETCHED TIGHT like the clothesline. Every skipping leaf and creature stirring in the brush made her pause and listen, turn and peer into the darkness. She swung the flashlight, the yellow eye searching trees, bushes, fence posts, and hay bales. Her breathing sounded loud in her own ears.

But there was nothing out there. She was alone. The moon shone brightly until a cloudbank swept over it. Now it was darker, colder.

When she reached the fence rail, she stuck the flashlight back in her apron and climbed the slats. Her foot caught in the folds of her skirt, twisted, and she wobbled at the top, turning awkwardly, careful to keep the ball of her foot on the thin, narrow board. She managed to hike a leg over the top rail, then the next, as she turned to face the way she'd come, and pushed off, jumping to the ground. Her skirt billowed outward, and the dry grass and fallen leaves softened her landing and tickled her calves and ankles.

It was then, facing the way she had come, that she saw a shape, not twenty steps away, just a shadowy form in the weak, scattered moonlight that resembled man more than tree or beast. Clouds shifted, moving over the moon. Her heart thumped feebly in her chest, the sound pulsing in her ears. The knife she sometimes brought was home in the safety of its drawer. She yanked the flashlight from her apron and swung the light around, arcing the yellow beam across the shape then jerking it backward until it hit pale blue eyes.

"Levi Fisher!"

He squinted, raising his arm to ward off the intrusive light. "Hannah. 'Tis all right. It's only me."

He moved toward her like it was perfectly normal for them to run into each other in a cemetery in the middle of the night. His footsteps made crashing sounds through the dry brush.

Hannah planted a fist on her hip, her heart settling back into a normal cadence but her temper sparking. "What are you doing here?"

"I could ask the same of you."

"You were following me, *ja*?"

He stopped at the fence, not climbing over, simply hooking an arm over the top rail. "I'm protecting you."

"From what?" She turned her back on him, huffed out a breath, then faced him again, her heel digging deeper into the dirt. "Why? There is nothing here."

"Nor is Jacob." His broad brimmed hat shadowed his face and she could not make out his expression, not that she could have read him anyway. "Go ahead and do what you came to do." A weariness sank into his voice that she didn't usually detect. "I'll wait. Then I will see you home."

"I don't need you out here, Levi. Go home. I want to be alone." Her body tightened with anger. This was *her* place, the only place she had to grieve. Jacob might not be here physically, but she felt him nonetheless. In a more reasonable moment, she might have seen the absurdity of her reaction, but she couldn't seem to contain herself.

Levi ducked his head and started to climb the fence. "Hannah—"

"I am not yours, Levi Fisher." Her words hung in the air like a wintry frost.

"A memory cannot warm you, Hannah."

"Maybe. Maybe not."

A moment of silence passed between them. The moon emerged from behind the clouds, and she wished it would disappear and douse her in darkness. "Well then," Levi muttered, "if that's the way of it."

"It is. You can go home, Levi. Do you hear me?" Her voice gained strength.

She watched him walk away, his shoulders squared, his back straight, until his shadow merged with the night. Guilt stalked her but she refused to give in to it. Levi had no right coming here, following her. She'd never given him any indication that she was interested or wanted his protection. When she could no longer hear his footsteps, she knew she was alone again.

But now the solitude she once knew in this place felt shattered, the jagged pieces of her security and grief fractured into tiny slivers and shards. She felt exposed. How long had Levi been following her here? Had he heard the poems she read? Seen the tears she shed?

She moved through the tombstones, her footsteps halting. Levi was not a rebel; he wouldn't stay where he wasn't wanted, not like Jacob. Yet a tingling plucked at the nerves along her spine, just like they had in the barn earlier. It felt as if someone watched her, a sensation she couldn't erase even as she rubbed the back of her neck to dismiss the chill bumps.

Then she came to his grave and settled at the side of the stone, tucking her legs beneath her and spreading her skirt and cape over her to ward off the coolness of the night. She positioned the flashlight at the base of the granite, and a shaft of light sprayed upward, bathing Jacob's name. Words lodged in her throat and she covered his name with her hand—her way of greeting him. The cold stone was as hard, as determined, and as eternal as her love.

The air bit her skin, and she curled her fingers inward, tucking her hand in her sleeve. Memories nipped at her but she could do nothing to shield herself from them. At times they comforted, wrapping around and strengthening her, but lately the memories sank into her like sharp teeth. Jacob's contagious smile, mischievous and playful, caused her heart to ache. It was the kind of ache that came when her toes thawed after being outside in the wintry elements—a pulsing throb.

It had been a warm day in late summer, two years ago. Changed, different, and more serious than ever before, Jacob had returned the month prior, from his journey traveling to New Orleans to pay homage to his favorite authors. In a way, he had aged, not with gray streaked in his hair or sudden lines on his forehead, but with a weary tension coiled in him. He had purpose and was ready to be baptized. Actually, he had been in a hurry to make his commitment to God and the community, asking the bishop to move the district's baptism up by a few weeks, but it always came in late fall, after harvest was over, and there was no moving the bishop. And so he'd waited.

Beneath the warmth of the sun, her heart had felt light with the knowledge that everything she did took her one day closer to being with Jacob for the rest of their lives. That particular day, she was busy with the wash, hanging it out on the line for drying, when a buggy approached the house and she recognized it as the bishop's. Dat met Will Stoltzfus on the drive. Nothing seemed out of the ordinary. The sun still shone. Her heart continued beating. And yet, her world changed. She simply hadn't known it yet.

When the bishop climbed back into his buggy and turned his horse down the drive, Dat stood for a few minutes before slowly turning and walking, not toward the house or the barn, but toward Hannah. It was her first inkling that something was wrong. Very wrong.

"Hannah." Dat's tone sounded deep and rough.

She stood still, a wet shirt dangling from her hands.

He placed a steadying hand on her shoulder. Was it for her or for him? Whatever the exact reason, a tremor took hold of her and shook her with such force she thought her knees might buckle. With a slow, heavy thumping, her heart pummeled her breastbone. "Jacob…"

The second Dat said his name she knew. Maybe it was the dip of his voice or the crackling sound in his throat like that of splintering glass, or maybe her heart sensed it was about to break. Did she actually hear the word "died"? It was all blurry now, those next few minutes…hours, days, weeks, and months spun around her. All else that Dat added was drowned beneath the roar in her ears, and then her knees dipped.

Dat grabbed her arm, keeping her upright, and murmured comforting words she couldn't even remember. Somehow, together, they made it to the house. Mamm was there, fussing, hugging, and crying as if she had lost one of her own. Hannah laid her head on the kitchen table, feeling like her purpose and hope had drained out of her fingers and toes, and a heavy weight descended on her. Numbness spread through her limbs. But there were no tears. Not from her. Not yet.

"We must go to the Fishers," Mamm said from what seemed like far away.

"No." Dat's voice sounded curt. "They have already had the burial."

Unable to lift her head from the table, she swerved her gaze toward Mamm, who asked the questions that couldn't form on her own tongue.

"Already? So soon? But when did the accident occur?"

The accident.

Jacob's father was a carpenter, making chairs, tables, swings, and birdhouses; his oldest son, Levi, was to inherit the business, but all three of the Fisher boys helped with the family business. Jacob had been using some piece of equipment when something went wrong. Terribly wrong. The details were sketchy, but in her dreams Hannah had seen Jacob lying on the sawdust-crusted floor covered in blood. His eyes—once full of life and fun—stared vacantly.

And those darkened eyes crept into her dreams time and again.

For a long time it seemed as if she would never cry. Tears piled up inside of her like logs in a beaver's dam, but she knew they couldn't stay trapped and stagnate forever. The first night she climbed out of bed and wandered outside—an attempt to run from those haunting eyes in her dreams… or run toward them, her footsteps becoming more determined and purposed the further she went—she ended up at the cemetery alone, and the dam inside her broke open and the tears flowed. More nights than she could count, she sat snuffling and sobbing, her face wet, her clothes damp. The gravestone became her pillow, the soft mound of dirt, then grass, her bed. The flow of tears would cleanse the pain welled in her heart. Or that's what she had hoped.

But her head, then heart, couldn't accept what had happened, how Jacob had been snatched out of her life. It didn't seem real. Mamm said, "You never saw his body in death, never touched his shoulder and felt the hard, cold reality." But would that have made any difference?

Eventually, the tears that once streamed down her face so easily slowed until they quit flowing. She sensed they had frozen in her heart like tiny, glittering icicles. The poetry book Jacob had given her secretly before he left on his travels became a comfort. She began reading to him as he'd once read for her, and she hoped he would hear the words to build a bridge between the here and the beyond, or maybe open the barrier to her heart once more, because tears seemed better than the bitterness trapped inside of her.

The millstones of pain became like the Israelites' remembrance stones from the Old Testament, and the poems reminded her of tender moments she had shared with Jacob or hoped to share one day. Hannah took the now worn poetry book out of her apron and found the page she wanted easily.

"One of us...that was God...and laid the curse so darkly—"

A rustling nearby stopped her reading. She glanced up. The wind stirred. The grass around her swayed, and the shadows danced beneath a sliver of moonlight. Thick clouds moved in, overtaking the stars. Opening the book where she kept her thumb as a mark, she found where she had left off. *"...the curse so darkly—"*

Hannah.

Her heart leapt a single, solitary beat. Was that her name on the wind? Had someone called? She lifted her chin and whispered back, "Jacob?"

"I carry your heart with me..."

CHAPTER SEVENTEEN

T HE WORDS HANNAH READ aloud poured over Akiva like a waterfall, and memories of simpler and sweeter times, when he had spoken those words to Hannah, flooded him. To hear them from her now, to watch her place a loving hand upon the stone that bore what once was his name gave him a jolt of confidence.

She hadn't forgotten him.

She remembered.

More than that, she hadn't let go of the love she once had for him.

Boldly, Akiva stepped out of the darkness, his gaze sharp on her, his mind pouring words straight into her heart. Seeing her again was like drinking in cool, refreshing water. He could drown watching her. *If* he could drown.

The words took shape in his mouth and he spoke them aloud: "*One of us…*"

Hannah gasped and jerked the flashlight from off the ground, swung it around, and the book tumbled onto the grave. Her long skirt tangling around her legs, she fell backward but scrambled back to her feet. Panic darkened her eyes, sharpened the edge of her jaw. The light struck him squarely in the face, but he didn't flinch or recoil. He stood as still as the headstones surrounding him. *It's me, Hannah. I'm home.*

But the words stuck in his throat, and he could only speak

them with his mind and hope she heard…recognized him… came to him. As so often in the past, her nearness tied his tongue into knots, and he could barely breathe. So he resorted to the words of the poet, who could say what he couldn't: "*…that was God…and laid the curse so darkly on my eyelids, as to amerce.*"

His voice, supple and melodious, was his greatest weapon. Whether spoken aloud or into the silent spaces of her mind, it lulled and lured. Slowly, her hand lowered and the light followed, just as the sun arced in its descent.

"*…my sight from seeing thee,—that if I had died…*" His voice rasped raw with the strain of self-control. If he had died, he would not have had this moment. *This* moment that made the last two years almost bearable.

He watched emotions flicker across her face in quick succession—shock, disbelief, recognition. That tiny glimmer dawned in the chestnut depths and gave him hope. Hope of what would be. Her hand went limp and the flashlight fell to the ground and rolled, the light slanting across his own grave, oblique and forlorn.

He drew the Elizabeth Barrett Browning poem from memory—"*Men could not part us…nor the seas change us…our hands would touch…and, heaven being rolled between us at the end, we should but vow the faster for the stars.*"

Her eyes dilated, looking dark and soulful, and she took a step toward him, the words pulling her nearer. One tiny step—but a step. Which gave him hope, a soaring hope of promise.

"Hannah…" His voice deepened with a rash need. It was in the nuances of his voice that her soul recognized him. He held a hand out toward her. "Come to me."

"Jacob." Her perfect mouth formed his name but her

voice was no more than a whisper. Her hand lifted toward him, mirroring his movement.

Then a cry split the night, an owl dove for a kill.

Hannah blinked. She gave her head a tiny shake and withdrew her hand as if she'd inadvertently touched a flame. Confusion clouded her eyes.

Akiva sniffed the air, tilted his head toward the fresh kill, the scent of blood, which saturated the night and awakened a fire within him.

Her gaze searched his face. The light of recognition vanished and the spiky talons of fear took its place, stabbing a hole in his heart. "W-who are you?" She glanced and took a step back. "How did you know my—"

Feeling the crushing blow of her fear, Akiva dipped his chin low, focusing on her eyes, holding her captive. She swayed as if the wind buffeted her. A strong will resisted his skills, but only for so long. But he couldn't make her see him for who he was. Immediately his tactics changed. He would need a new plan, something that would keep her near him, show her he really hadn't changed so much and remind her of their love. It would take time, but time was on his side. He'd have to take the risk he'd most feared. "You do not know me."

It was a statement, raw with disappointment, not a question. He'd hoped despite the changes in him that she would somehow see the boy she'd once loved, a piece of him, a desperate part that yearned to be loved again.

"You're *English*?" Her voice sounded cold.

He felt the shield he'd built around his heart rise like a thick wall. "Would that be good or bad?"

Her gaze skimmed over him, resting on his chest, and his followed. A dark stain covered the front of his shirt and he tugged the zipper of his leather jacket upward.

"You're hurt." Concern erased the defensiveness and fear in her voice.

"I will be all right. Given time." He moved back a step, giving her space but not too much, and sat on the top edge of a gravestone. "Forgive me, but I had to see you."

"Me?" Her gaze remained steadfastly fastened to the wound in his chest.

It did not hurt, not anymore, as the healing had already begun. Nourishment would speed the process, and his need pulsed within him, exacerbated by the scent of blood on the night air. But he resisted. Waited.

"Do I know you?" She squinted, searched his face. "Why did you come here?"

"I'm sorry, Hannah." He rested his hands on his knees, locking his elbows, bowing his back slightly.

A pinch of concern creased her brow, as he'd known it would. The tenderness in her heart was always easily stoked.

"I didn't mean to startle you earlier. I do know you. Or so it seems." His voice sounded heavy with regret and sorrow. It was too soon to reveal himself; too many questions would stir up fear. So he tossed out the temptation, like a line in the river—bait—"Because of Jacob."

Her breath caught. "Jacob. You knew Jacob?"

He gave a slight nod. "He told me about you."

"How? When?"

He leaned forward easing the pressure in his chest and puffed out an icy breath. "We met in New Orleans. Two years ago. He told me of you, of the poems you read together, of your plans...of his love for you."

Her eyes softened with tears, and she stepped toward him, this time of her own accord. "How can I help you? Let me go for some help." She touched him first, a brush of her hand against his, and sucked in a breath. "You're cold. You've lost a lot of blood."

The warmth of her skin was almost his undoing. He closed a hand over her arm, entrapping her, and her pulse tapped his palm with urgency, pulling him, calling to him. His breath snagged on his windpipe. "No one can know I am here."

"But you need help."

"I will not die, if that is your worry." But instantly his heart contracted, as he stared into her trusting face and remembered the pain of that day when his life had changed irrevocably. A line from some poem bobbed into his consciousness. Was it Shakespeare? No, Lord Byron:

> *She walks in beauty, like the night*
> *Of cloudless climes and starry skies;*
> *And all that's best of dark and bright*
> *Meet in her aspect and her eyes;*

"What happened to you?" Her quiet question pulled him back.

"It would not be good for your reputation for others to know we met here. Jacob told me what it is like—the Amish community." Slowly, he lifted his gaze toward hers. "What would you tell your family? They would not understand or approve."

Her mouth set in a firm line, then she dipped her shoulder beneath his and lifted him to his feet, her arm slipping around his waist to offer support. "Come. I know of a place you can stay."

Hannah. No longer a phantom of his dreams or apparition in his desperate imagination, she was real and so close. So very close. Her nearness weakened his resolve. He breathed in the scent of her—grass, wind, milk, and moonlight. It surrounded him, penetrated his defenses, enticed him to abandon his plan and take her. His soul cried out for her. He yearned to tell her it was him, to make her his. Right now. This minute. *Now.*

But if he wasn't careful, she could die. And then they would be parted forever. Right now, a fragile line held them together and if he wasn't careful it would be severed for eternity.

If not for this blasted wound, if he wasn't so weak from hunger already, he might be able to fight it off, not give in.

My love is as a fever longing still...

And frantic-mad with evermore unrest...

Shakespeare. Definitely Shakespeare—a man who must have known love and loss and all-consuming longing.

But no. He wouldn't take what had been taken from him. He wouldn't frighten her. She couldn't understand, not yet anyway, and he needed time to prepare her.

A shudder of resistance rocked through him and he clenched his teeth.

"You're in pain. Let me get you some help."

"No, I'll be fine." He should have pushed away from her. He should have run, to protect her, to protect them, but he could not. Instead, he rested his head against Hannah's shoulder, which was padded by her cape, and rolled the back of his skull against the soft curve, brushing her long, sleek neck with the tip of his nose. He drew in a slow breath of her intoxicating warmth. Her pulse was strong. Powerful. Intoxicating. He heard the ebb and flow, the rush of blood through her veins. The invigorating scent pulsed, called to him. He was torturing himself but he couldn't help it. It was the sweetest torture knowing she would be his one day.

Clenching his teeth, he resisted what had become second nature to him.

Not now. *Not yet.* There would be a time though, but not to satisfy a physical thirst. It would be to gratify his soul. They would be together, Hannah and him, forever. Because being near her again was as close as he would ever come to heaven.

CHAPTER EIGHTEEN

"Y ou look like hell."

"Yeah, well, feel like I've been there." Roc fell into the chair. The glare of a lamp made him squint, and he bent forward, shoving his fingers through his hair, and held his head in case it fell off like the headless horseman's and started rolling around on the floor. After what he'd seen tonight, it could have been a possibility. "Or maybe I'm still there."

Mike shut the door to his apartment and gave the chair a wide berth, as if anticipating Roc might hurl or worse. He had, after all, come banging on his friend's door some time after three in the morning after he'd driven the hour from Lancaster County and then cruised the lonely, mostly empty streets of Philadelphia, letting the night's events churn in his mind.

Mike had the thick neck and bulging biceps of a workout guru, but it was the eyes, the been-there-seen-it look, and the constantly shifting and measuring gaze that said he was either a bouncer or a cop. He was most often the latter, but occasionally he worked late night hours in a bar downtown. With a practiced eye, he gave Roc the once-over. "You been drinking?"

"Not yet, but I'm ready if you have something."

Mike clicked off the radio that he'd been known to play all night—classical music chased away the demons of his own past, memories that lurked in his dreams. Roc knew a few of the nightmares that chased Mike, the same that nipped at his own heels, and after tonight Roc figured he'd have a few more giving chase.

"So what's up? I'll let you know if it warrants a drink or not."

"What am I, on probation or something?"

Mike watched him for an elongated second, a tight line forming between his brows. Then he went to the kitchen and brought back two beers. "So what gives?"

Roc twisted off the cap and tossed it on the nearest table. He took two long swallows and clunked the beer down next to the cap. How could he explain? What would he say without sounding like he needed to take up permanent residence in a psych ward? Digging his elbows into his knees, he peered at his friend through stringy hair that had flopped forward. "Tell me about the body. Better yet"—he grabbed the chair's arms—"let's go see the homeless guy."

"Can't."

That single word halted Roc's rise out of the chair and he fell back against the pillowy frame.

"Already been claimed and cremated."

"Was it really like—" His throat closed up shop.

"Yeah. Too much like Emma." Mike leaned back, holding the beer he'd yet to take a drink of, and stared at the blank television.

Roc wouldn't allow that image to spring to life in his mind, or else he'd find himself listening to strings or making some Three Stooges sounds. In self-defense, he shifted his gaze toward the radio then to Mike. "That why you've got Chopin going?"

"Mozart."

"Whatever. That why?"

Mike shrugged a shoulder. "So what's going on here, Roc? You show up and suddenly folks are disappearing…dying."

Roc's belly knotted. "You accusing me of something?"

"If I thought you were guilty, you'd already be locked up."

"So you must've checked with Brody when I was last in New Orleans. Confirmed my alibi."

Without any sign of remorse, Mike tipped his head sideways as if he suspected Roc would have done the same. "Ruby Yoder was already missing before you left New Orleans."

He reached for the beer. It would wash away the nightmares, the craziness he'd seen tonight. But without taking even a sip, he set it back down. "Okay then, so tell me."

"There's nothing. No fingerprints. No nothin'. Like some phantom with big teeth. Explain that to me. The coroner said if it was an animal, which I never thought for a second, there'd be saliva. And there should be something."

"Just like when Emma…."

"Yeah. And the coroner said something else."

Roc waited, his heart contracting.

"There wasn't enough blood."

"What do you mean?"

"There should have been more at the scene. The wound hit an artery, for Christ's sake. So there should have been more blood. Everywhere. But where did it go?"

"Maybe something blocked it. So it stayed in the body."

Mike shook his head. "That's the other thing…there should have been more blood in the body but it was damn near drained."

Roc felt the blood drain out of his head, and his heart went into overdrive to handle the excess.

"An Amish kid and now a bum on the streets." Mike finally drank some of his beer. "So what's the connection?"

"Don't forget Em." Roc's voice sounded as if it was not coming from him, as if someone else was speaking...thinking. He swallowed hard. "And the teen dressed in an Amish costume in New Orleans."

"Some fetish for plain folks? Or bad timing? In the wrong place?"

"Emma wasn't plain."

"No, but she was wearing scrubs that night. Plain blue scrubs, remember? Plain."

Roc rubbed the heel of one hand with his other thumb, back and forth over the deep lines. "I have a suspect."

Mike's hand paused midair, beer poised for his mouth. "What? Who?"

"I don't know much more." He explained about the Amish kids and the woman known for drinking blood—chicken blood—and how he ran into her and Akiva.

"What kind of a name is that?"

"Hell if I know." He stood, paced a few steps. Did he really want to confess this? What would Mike say? Think? If Roc actually said aloud what he was beginning to believe, would it make it all the more real or scatter the delusion? Mike was waiting. Watching. Roc felt his gaze on him, studying, analyzing, dissecting. Drawing a shaky breath, he admitted, "Thing is, I saw him...Akiva tonight, following an Amish woman through a field."

"And?"

"He ran. I chased him."

The tension in the room shifted a notch. Mike leaned forward.

Roc faced him, like he was on a lineup. "And I shot him."

Mike jerked back slightly then his eyes narrowed. "You're not gonna tell me you have a body in the trunk of that Mustang, are you?"

"I wish."

"So what happened? Where is he?"

"I shot him. Square in the chest."

Mike didn't blink or move. He waited.

Roc wished there was a different ending to the story. He wished there was a body. Anything to disprove what he was about to say. "And then—" Roc looked down, stared at his boots. Dried grass and mud from the field still stuck to the soles, which made the night real—too real. "He disappeared."

Mike blinked. "Excuse me?"

"I shot him. Here." Roc splayed a hand across his own chest, smack in the middle.

"You sure?"

"I know how to shoot."

Mike gave a clipped nod of agreement. How many times in years gone by had they stood side by side at the shooting range and then compared bullet holes in their outlines? Roc's accuracy was gold-medal worthy.

"So he ran away. Maybe he was on crack. That happens. Perps' bodies all pumped up on speed or some other drug and nothing but a Mac truck will stop 'em." Mike reached for his cell phone lying on the table. "I'll call for—"

"No. I'm telling you, the sonofabitch crumpled forward and...I don't know. It was like he folded inward. And... Poof!" He couldn't meet Mike's gaze. "He disappeared. Zippedeedoodah. Just like that. *Sayonara*. Gone. Like he flew away."

"Flew?" Mike dipped his chin and stared at Roc,

suspicion darkening those jaded eyes that had seen his share of the bizarre. "You have been drinking, haven't you? Or smoking something."

Roc shook his head, wishing he could explain and knowing he couldn't. He rubbed his face with his palms. It had been a mistake to come here. He'd hoped in some way that saying it out loud would make it seem ridiculous—and it certainly sounded that way—but speaking the words had the opposite effect on Roc and somehow made the incident more real. His shoulders tensed in defensiveness—trying to turn the irrational into the rational was hopeless—and he turned toward the door.

"Where are you going?"

He fished in his pocket and pulled out a piece of paper Anthony had given him. "I'm gonna talk with a priest."

"A priest. You think you need forgiveness for something?"

With his hand on the doorknob, he looked back at Mike. "I need help. And not the kind you're thinking of: a doc with a notepad of prescriptions ready to hand out. I have a bad feeling Anthony was right."

"Anthony?" Mike was on his feet. "Who's Anthony? And right about what?"

"That we're not dealing with your ordinary serial killer. More the *Twilight* kind. And this one isn't a vegetarian."

CHAPTER NINETEEN

THE NIGHT WAS STILL, and the cold air frosted Hannah's breath. A dark head shadowed her shoulder, his skull pressing against her bone, but it was not painful; her discomfort remained deep inside. This strange man, an *Englisher*, leaned into her, and she was grateful for her wrap forming a thin protective barrier between them. His breathing sounded ragged, his footsteps halting, his weight heavy. *What was she doing?*

Dat would not be angry for her helping an injured man; helping others was their way of life, but he would disapprove of her going to the cemetery. Not because she was alone, not because it was night, but he would not understand her need to be near Jacob. This unending grief was *not* their way. God's will was not to be questioned or doubted or even resisted. No matter what happened, they moved on to the next season obediently, without question. But questions and doubts churned inside Hannah, as they once had Jacob. Maybe she'd learned that from him.

Her wickedness surely exceeded the actions of her friends who had thrust themselves whole-heartedly into their running around season, for she could not accept God's will concerning Jacob. How could Jacob's death be good for anyone? How could she be sure God's will was for her to marry Jacob and then he died before that could be? God's will didn't make sense. Maybe it wasn't God's will after all. She resisted it. Resented it. Hated it. It was to her disgrace and to her shame, but it was the truth.

She was all alone in her grief. No one would understand. Not her parents. Not Rachel. Not even her close friend, Grace. Even Levi seemed to have moved beyond his own brother's death as easily as the seasons shifted into each other. The Lord must surely look upon her with disappointment, but what greater displeasure if she abandoned this man in need too?

And yet she knew her motive wasn't entirely charitable: this man *knew* Jacob. And even for a second, it made her somehow feel closer to her beloved, especially because this was an area of his life that she had never known.

But there was something else…something about this man felt familiar. And yet everything about him seemed strange to her. Was it simply that the poem he quoted was the one etched on her own heart? Or was it the cleft of his shoulder that felt as if she'd nestled her head there once before? She couldn't make sense of it.

So she would hide this stranger as she had hidden her resistance to God's will, her unwillingness to let Jacob go. For to bring this stranger out in the open would require answers, answers she didn't have, answers best left in secret. She prayed he would not die. She prayed he would be healed, that she too would one day feel whole again. She prayed God still listened to her prayers.

Her back ached from shouldering the man's weight, her muscles cramped under the strain. His breathing was labored, harsh, and ragged, too much so for conversation. There was a slight rattle when he exhaled, which reminded Hannah of her grandmother's breathing before she succumbed to the pneumonia. But this man didn't cough. He didn't even speak. He plodded forward, one labored foot at a time.

Questions churned and frothed in her head, but she could see this stranger was in no shape to answer her questions about Jacob.

When she saw the post, which held the mailbox at the end of her family's drive, she gratefully turned toward the house. It wasn't far now. Thankfully, it was still dark. But for how long? Dat awakened at four. Levi arrived by four-thirty. It could not be much earlier than that now. And what about Toby? Could she sneak this man past the doghouse? There was but one place she could think to hide him, and she veered toward the spring house. The moon still rode in the sky, high enough and full enough to offer light, so she snapped off the flashlight, dousing them in darkness, so that no one would see their approach.

The man came to a sudden halt, and Hannah realized she too was breathing hard and through her mouth. His gaze settled on her, unsettled her. A fine sheen of sweat covered her skin from the long, arduous walk. Moonlight reflected off his pale features. "Are you all right?"

He nodded, but he didn't look all right. He looked pale, deathly pale. His eyes were sunken into his skull and appeared as dark as a pit.

He opened his mouth to speak but at first no sound emerged, just that raspy breath, then he managed to speak. "I must not be discovered."

Hannah glanced toward the house, where the windows were dark. It had taken much longer to walk back from the cemetery than it usually did. "We should hurry."

With a backward glance at the house and keeping a wary eye out for Toby, she unhinged the rusted lock, swung open the wooden door, and urged the man inside. Clicking the button on the flashlight, she shone the pale yellow light toward the back. "It's all right," she said more for her benefit than his. In the dim light, his face was pale but passive, unconcerned, like granite. "You'll be safe here."

He took a few steps forward, stumbled over a cord, and made his way toward the back, sitting hard on the ground and leaning his head back against the wall, his legs splayed outward. One of his hands rested near his heart.

Hannah breathed easier to have at least made it here safely, without incident. Now as he lay sheltered from the chilly temperature, she should check his wound. Zippers were not allowed under the *Ordnung*, but she had seen them before on friends' *English* clothes, which they had begun to buy during their running around time. Carefully, so as not to disturb his rest, she knelt beside him and tugged downward on the metal tab, the zipper trailing in parallel tracks, like teeth opening, exposing the dark stain on his white shirt.

But he covered her hand with his own, his touch ice cold, and fear shot through her. She remembered helping Mamm when Grandma Ruth got sick last year, her skin growing cool as she neared the end of her life, her breathing labored and ragged—and then when she lay in her casket, her skin shrunk on her skeleton, her cheeks sunken, her form hard and cold.

What if this man died? What would Hannah do? How would she explain? Would she be at fault for not getting him help soon enough? Her heart pounded in her chest. Should she tell Dat? Have him call for a doctor? She stared into those black eyes. She'd known others with dark brown eyes but these…there was no distinguishing the pupil from the iris, just solid black. Something about those eyes compelled her to lean closer and her hand moved to cup his jaw. He rezipped the metal contraption on his leather jacket, all the while watching her with those impossibly dark eyes as if gauging her response.

"You should leave, Hannah." His voice sounded cold too.

"I didn't mean to startle you." Her voice sounded calmer than her heart felt. She didn't want to panic him or confess her concerns. "You need blankets." She stood. "They'll warm you."

He shuttered his gaze. "I'm going to be fine." His voice wavered. "I just need nourishment."

"I can get you something." She backed away, stepping over the cords and wires, her heart beating in the frantic rhythm of the pump. The flashlight's pale glow moved along with her, bouncing, shifting, leaving the man in tempering darkness. "Maybe some bandages too. And salve." She was thinking out loud more than speaking to him, her mind skipping in different directions. What could have caused such a wound? Could he be in trouble? She paused at the doorway. "What happened to you?"

Even in shadow, she could make out his frame. He leaned his head back against the wood-planked wall. Were those dark eyes closed or was he still watching her? She sensed the heat of his gaze and her skin felt warm in spite of the coolness outside. "You would not understand."

With distance between them, she felt somewhat braver than normal. She'd seen similar wounds in deer, which Dat and Levi shot in the winter. "Were you shot? W-with a gun?"

He didn't answer. Again, she longed to ask about Jacob. What was Jacob doing with a dangerous man such as this? How did they meet? After a minute, his breathing became deep and even, but at least he was breathing. He needed sleep, so she carefully backed through the doorway.

"Will you come back, Hannah?" His voice remained soft, yet there was an urgency lining his words, a need. Or was it fear? Did he realize how ill he was? Was he afraid of being alone?

Her answer was a whisper in her head before she spoke: "Yes."

CHAPTER TWENTY

Once upon a midnight dreary, while I pondered,
weak and weary,
Over many a quaint and curious volume of forgotten
lore…

AKIVA'S BELLY BURNED WITH a hungry ache, but re-membering the Poe poem drew an ironic smile from him over his ravenous state. His integral system of arteries, veins, and capillaries constricted with need, and he grew colder and stiffer, his usual beyond-natural strength waning, and no amount of blankets could warm him. Only lifeblood, hot and pulsing, could fill him, warm him, heal him.

Ah, distinctly I remember, it was in the bleak
December,
And each separate dying ember wrought its ghost
upon the floor.

In his mind, he watched Hannah enter her family's house and knew she would be out of his way and safe for a few minutes, leaving him time to find nourishment. With great effort, he pushed to his feet, leaned against the inside wall, and drew deep gulps of air. Then he sniffed, his senses much keener and sharper than they were in his other life. A light, delicate scent called to him, and he followed, his foot-steps quickening as the sweet aroma became more potent and intoxicating. The fragrance swirled around his head, muddled his thinking, and stirred the raw need building inside him. Food, such as it was, would make the wound heal that much faster.

At one time, he'd been the one afraid, sensing fear, running. But no longer. Being on the prowl, the one hunting rather than being hunted, strengthened him, filled him with a surge of power. Fear, the tangy, pungent scent of others' fear, was invigorating. It fed something inside of him, a raw and urgent need, which came over him gradually, then built until he could no longer deny its fierceness. And it drove him.

> *Tyger! Tyger! burning bright*
> *In the forests of the night,*
> *What immortal hand or eye*
> *Could frame thy fearful symmetry?*
>
> *In what distant deeps or skies*
> *Burnt the fire of thine eyes?*
> *On what wings dare he aspire?*
> *What the hand dare seize the fire?*
>
> *And what shoulder, and what art,*
> *Could twist the sinews of thy heart?*
> *And when thy heart began to beat,*
> *What dread hand? and what dread feet?*

In his former life, when he was running around, drinking alcohol had been fairly new for him, and he enjoyed the escape it provided, the heat it generated, the confidence it induced, real or false didn't matter. But now he thirsted for something more stimulating than shots of bourbon or bottles of beer, something that truly imbued him with a power he had never known existed.

What the hammer? what the chain?
In what furnace was thy brain?
What the anvil? what dread grasp
Dare its deadly terrors clasp?

Crouched low, he stalked into the cold night. Surely there was an animal nearby that could slacken his thirst. But a powerfully sweet scent filled his mind with a swirling red haze. It had the heady strength of youth and seduced him into following. He stumbled forward, chasing the alluring scent, which stripped him of all reason. His urgency made him rash and foolhardy, but his desperation drove him onward as he took the corner of the house and came to the back—a solid wall of wooden slats, punctured by the occasional window. He stared up at a darkened, shaded window.

When the stars threw down their spears,
And watered heaven with their tears,
Did He smile His work to see?
Did He who made the Lamb make thee?

He rested a moment, catching his breath, and that tiny amount of time allowed doubts to intrude. Some small part of his conscience from his past life gnawed at him. Guilt was a human emotion, beneath him now, and yet...it was Hannah who stirred it in him. *She would be the one to suffer if we pursued this tempting blood. She would weep for her loss, for the loss of something so pure and good.* But it was that pureness that made the sacrifice so powerful.

If God made all things, then Akiva, even in his new form, was a part of that creation, and in this life where good battled evil, some sacrifices had to be made. God never required the sacrifice of something old and worn, something injured and diseased. He demanded something young and pure, without blemish.

In the past two years, Akiva had learned more about death than he'd ever understood before. Life did not end here. This would not be the end of purpose and hope but the beginning of something more wonderful. Those that mourned over a death would one day understand. Maybe that's simply what God meant in the Garden of Eden when He spoke of the fruit revealing the truth—gaining God's perspective on this life as but a second—and Akiva had been given that privilege.

This day, this sacrifice, Hannah would not understand, but someday she would. Someday she would embrace it and understand the purpose. Even today, she would not deny him to save a loved one. He knew her heart so well. She would come to understand that this small sacrifice would empower them to be together, to love each other and live forever. How could that be wrong?

The tender life force calling to him was strong, the heartbeat arousing, and his focus became a laser, blocking all reason, all thought, the why's and why not's banished to another time, another life. He braced himself at the base of the house, gauging the height to the window. It would be an easy jump under different circumstances, but wounded, he had to garner his strength, concentrate more, and will himself beyond his waning abilities. With a hard push, he leapt, clutched the frame, his nails biting into the wood, and crouched on the ledge that only provided inches for the toes of his shoes. The window was unlocked, and he gained entrance quickly, though not as smoothly as he might when not injured. Still, he stood in the deep shadows of the room waiting, watching, wavering with need.

The young girl slept soundly, her face pale and delicate, her features soft and similar to Hannah's. Her long hair billowed around her, yellow with the light of heaven. Her breath remained steady and even, undisturbed by his presence. Her dreams stayed plain, simple, uncluttered with fear or stress or dread. He siphoned through her thoughts as her scent whirled around him, tantalizing, enflaming, provoking. *Katie.* One so young had strong powers for healing; too young would have the opposite effect, but still this one would do very nicely. He concentrated on taming her thoughts, injecting the desire to please, to offer herself without regard or restraint, and he took a step toward the bed.

But another presence in the room emerged from the shadows, revealing herself, eyes blazing, and despite her diminutive size, she emitted a stalwart sense of power and strength. The old woman rose from a rocking chair beside the bed, the wood creaking, and Akiva recognized Hannah's Grandma Ruth, who glared at him, her eyes keen and alert in her ancient face. She gave a slight shake of her head as if to say, *This one is not yours.*

With a guttural growl of frustration, Akiva lunged for the window, the green shade slapping the window frame, and retreated into the night. He landed hard on the ground, the wound in his chest throbbing, and he gulped in air as if that could save him. He searched the darkness, sniffed, then with a last glance back up at the window, he rushed toward the barn, his footsteps light and swift.

He made no sound—the perfect predator. A phrase came to mind—*prowls around like a roaring lion, seeking someone to devour*—and he smiled to himself. *Precisely*. His gaze pierced the darkness. He didn't have long. Dawn was near.

Hooves scuffed the dirt and hay-strewn floor, and an animal snuffled. The dusty scent of hay and the raw, earthy smells of dung filled him with memories, some good, some not so good. He rarely thought of his family anymore, those he had known drifted far from his mind, but being here, among the Amish again, memories crept up on him, and for a moment a sentimental longing welled up in him to be near his family and part of a community again. But that was impossible.

He was separated now.

Isolated.

Forgotten.

Forsaken.

Vampires did not live in packs as wolves did, moving, hunting, living together. They were more like grizzly bears—loners, finding their own kills, defending their own turf. Some paired up, but many kept to themselves, distrusting all. The bloods he had met over the past two years, he did not trust either. After all, one had stolen his life from him, changed him without regard, her desires outweighing his.

With stealthy movements, he crept toward the far stall. He didn't much like animal blood, which lacked something vital humans carried, but it would have to do. For now.

A lamb, young and tender, lay on its side. When he entered the enclosed space, it raised its head. The warm, brown eyes were soft and innocent and expectant. It knew no fear. Not yet.

Before it could rise to its feet, before it could make a

protesting noise, before it could bolt, Akiva sprung forward and swooped down on the blameless animal, sinking his fingers into the thick, soft wool and restraining the head, arching the neck. A leg kicked outward, but the struggle for life finished before it really began. Warmth spread through Akiva, pooling in his chest and spreading outward to his limbs. Blood filled him, restored him, rebuilt his strength. He became like new.

His father had attributed rebirth to another source, but Akiva knew another life now, another birth, another salvation. He shoved the limp animal back on the strewn hay, its neck flopping lifelessly sideways, revealing a gaping red hole.

> Tyger! Tyger! burning bright
> In the forests of the night,
> What immortal hand or eye
> Dare frame thy fearful symmetry?

CHAPTER TWENTY-ONE

I T WAS QUIET. Too quiet.

With arms laden with woolen blanket, pillow, and bread from supper, Hannah returned to the spring house. "Mister?"

There was no answer. Where was he? Had he left? Or expired?

Her heart pounding, she tiptoed toward the back of the spring house, past the old well her grandfather had used, following the circle of light from her flashlight as it slid around the edge of the room and scattered shadows. There, along the back wall, the stranger slept. Hannah kept the flashlight aimed at the ground, but even so she saw the man's color had brightened and he looked better.

She made a pallet, stretching out the blanket and folding the top back. Whispering, soft and mysterious, teased her ears, and the hair at the back of her neck prickled. She glanced back at her guest. Was he awake? Watching her? But he had not moved. His face looked as if it were carved from stone. His chest appeared still. Too still. An icy chill of fear wafted through her. What if he wasn't asleep? What if he were actually dead?

She edged toward him. Slapping her hem out of her way, Hannah knelt and reached toward him, hesitant, and yet when he didn't move she grew bolder and touched the backs of her fingers to his forehead. Heat radiated off him. In that instant, his eyes opened.

Hannah gasped, the sound filling the inside of the spring house, and she pulled her fingers away.

"I am still here, Hannah."

Her heart thumped crazily in her chest. She attempted a smile and folded her hand against her skirt. "I am glad."

"No need to fear, Hannah, I won't die."

Her brow furrowed, and she pressed her hand to his forehead again. "You have a fever. I could..."

The muscles along his jaw flexed with what she imagined was discomfort, and he shifted, breaking contact with her, but his gaze remained, burning into her, making her insides shift and squirm.

She cleared her throat, rubbed her hand against her apron. "I could, uh, arrange to call someone...a hospital...someone better equipped to help you."

"No, I'm better." He sat up, his motions quick and fluid, proving the truth of his words. He closed a hand over her wrist, his touch like a fiery poker. "I do not want to put you in danger or you to get in trouble over me."

"I will not be in trouble for offering aid to someone in need. We believe in helping others."

"And that God is in control of it all. His will, right?" His mocking tone caused her eyebrow to lift but she felt the internal poke of truth in the sensitive area of her own doubts.

She unrolled cotton bandages that she'd brought in her apron. "Are you an unbeliever then? Not simply an *Englisher*?"

He chuckled in a derisive way. "Oh, I believe God exists. It is He who has rejected me."

"God forgives. All you have to do is ask."

His expression softened. "Sweet Hannah. So innocent."

She felt a jolt straight through her at the familiar use of her name. Her insides quavered at the way he said *Sweet*

Hannah, the way it reminded her of the texture of Jacob's voice, Jacob's hand cupping her chin, Jacob's mouth covering her own.

But this stranger didn't seem to notice her distress. "Some things," he said in a contemplative tone, "can't be forgiven. But, you wouldn't know about that, would you?"

Her spine stiffened, and she wasn't sure if her irritation stemmed from his words or her chaotic emotions. "I may be plain but that doesn't mean I don't know the different types of sin."

He leaned closer, his breath bathing the skin along her neck and causing a tingle along her spine. "So you know all types of sin, do you?" A smile played about his lips, curling them, making something curl inside her. Was he toying with her or simply amused with what he considered to be her innocence? "Tell me, Hannah, of this sin you know so well."

Heat rose inside her and seared her cheeks. Images flashed in her mind of stolen kisses, intimate touches, whispered promises, and forbidden thoughts. "I do not have to commit a sin to recognize it as such."

And yet she had sinned. She knew that as well as her own name.

"And do you see the sin in me, sweet Hannah?"

Sweet Hannah. That part of her heart that had been closed, locked up tight as the chicken coop, was suddenly pried open. It was as if she recognized Jacob in the voice of this stranger. But he wasn't Jacob. He was a stranger. His eyes were black and dark and not her beloved's. His use of that endearment scraped along her nerves. "Do not call me such."

"You are though. Sweet as the honeysuckle. Tender as—"

"No!" The forcefulness of her own voice startled her. She blinked as if her eyelids were keeping the rhythm of her heart, and she pressed a hand over her chest to quiet the erratic beat, surging to her feet. "I'm sorry." Shaking her head, she backed away. "Jacob." His name snagged on her vocal chords and her voice sounded huskier than usual. "He called me that."

This stranger's playful smile vanished and something akin to satisfaction lurked in those eyes, but maybe she was reading something that wasn't there. How could he see what she felt? And why would that please him? "Ah"—his tone dipped low—"you are not over Jacob yet, are you?"

Her peace of mind or what was left of it wrenched loose. To cover her fraying emotions, she reached for a blanket, unfolded it, and settled it over his legs. "I will come and check on you later."

"You are young still, Hannah." He swept a twig off the floor, rolled it between his long, lean fingers. "You are in the time of *rumschpringe*?"

His use of Pennsylvania Dutch unnerved her even more. "How did you know…? Jacob?" Then she shook her head. "I am ready to take my vows."

"Are you now?" His gaze brushed over her, lingering here and there and causing a shift inside her. "A faith untested…" He bent the fragile twig until it snapped.

She bristled. "I know what the Bible teaches. It does not take sinning to test a faith."

"Is that what you think *rumschpringe* is all about?"

Her gaze fled the intensity of his, and she clasped her hands together, her fingers reddened from diligent work. "What do you know of this? Of running around? Of our faith?"

Her ire surprised her, and she drew a steadying breath. She should probably apologize, but instead she lifted her chin a notch and met his gaze solidly with her own challenge.

"More than you can fathom. But you explain it to me, Hannah." He gave a confident smirk. "What does it take then?"

"Plain living. Obedience. Discipline." Inside her chest, she felt the prickle of heat, her own awareness that she had already failed the test.

"And has your faith been tested, Hannah?"

She nodded. Tears sprang to the surface and she squeezed them back.

"You can't force it, you know. You can't make yourself have faith."

Opening her eyes again, she studied him, wondered about his life, where he had come from, what he had seen and done. He looked young, not older than twenty, and yet he seemed as old as a rock with a hard, crusty edge of bitterness or disappointment.

"Don't you think there comes a point in someone's life when it's just too late? They've gone too far?"

A trembling started down inside her. She wasn't sure if the fear that welled up was for her or for this stranger. Maybe it was for both of them. "No."

He sighed and closed his eyes, rested his hands over the wound in his chest. "If it's okay with you, I may hold on to your belief. It sounds better than what I know to be true."

"Maybe you do not know the truth." For a long moment, she watched him, wondered what had made him that way. The life of an *Englisher* was so far removed from her own, she could not even imagine what it must be like to not grow up with a faith, which seemed like a leaf falling from a tree, nothing to anchor it, nothing to hold it in place, nobody to care where it fell, and then it was tossed and tumbled about midair by every wind, then finally trampled under foot. Even when she had her doubts and the wind blew and made her shiver and quake, she was still secured to the root of her faith. She must pray for this man. But then she realized—"I don't know your name."

"It's not important."

"It will help me to pray for you."

"You would do such for me?" A smile tugged at his firm lips and a ripple passed through her abdomen.

"Of course."

"You may call me Akiva."

"Akiva." She tested the name on her tongue. Somehow it suited him, different and exotic. "Is that foreign? Are you from some faraway place?"

He laughed. "You could say that."

"It's an interesting name, Akiva." She watched him as he closed his eyes again and seemed to drift to sleep. Hannah's brow crinkled with concern not only for his wound but also for his soul. "I will pray for you to believe." She clasped her hands together for affirmation. "I'm not sure at all who you are. But I will pray. For you."

She rushed out the door, closed it firmly behind her, and leaned against the wooden planks, giving her pulse time to calm. "And I will pray for me too."

CHAPTER TWENTY-TWO

THE NUN WAS DRESSED in pink.

Fog curled around the edges of St. Joseph's and crept over the grounds, giving the Philadelphia neighborhood an otherworldly charm. The nun seemed to float out of the mist like an angel rising from a cloud, as she walked at a slow, reverent pace along the stone steps from one building to the next. The white head-covering hid most of her face in the gray dawn hour.

Mesmerized by the sleepy and sepia quality of the early morning scene, Roc leaned against the Mustang parked along the curb and watched her for a moment, remembering back to his childhood when nuns were his teachers, his tormentors, his conscience, their black and white habits a reflection of their staunch views. But what manifested pink? He supposed if nuns could wear pink then the existence of vampires might not be so outrageous.

Before "Mother Theresa's" pink shadow could disappear through the doorway, he called out, "Excuse me!"

The nun's footsteps halted, and she turned toward him, waiting patiently as he jogged across the grounds.

"Hello. Sorry." He crammed his hands in his pockets in a feeble attempt to stay warm. "Didn't mean to startle you or anything." The nun's youthful features looked calm and serene as if she'd just come from a spa treatment rather than prayers. "I'm looking for Father Roberto."

"He is usually in the garden at this early hour."

"The garden?"

She gave a slight nod and inclined her head to Roc's right. "Around the back."

"Great. Thanks." He took a step in that direction and then paused. "You're wearing pink, right?"

She gave a tolerant smile. "Yes."

"Good. Thought I'd really lost it there. Thanks." Then he headed off in the opposite direction of the pink nun and rounded what looked like the main building. If his parochial school nuns had worn pink instead of black, maybe they would have looked like this one instead of just old and cranky. His breath puffed out before him as he strode along the edge of the stone cathedral, the domes, arches, and spires above looking bleak in the weak light. This early in the morning, the streets were deserted and empty, save for an occasional garbage truck rumbling along, but those inside the spiritual sanctuary were already bustling about the day in their do-good mode.

Passing the small rectory and then the school building, which still looked asleep, Roc came to an inner courtyard where several benches were strategically placed around a drained fountain, creating quiet spots for meditation and contemplation. As with everything else in Philadelphia, the grass was dormant, but some of the plants in the beds managed to remain green, exhibiting an optimism Roc had long lost; he sided with the withering, shriveled plants—realists— and huddled inside his leather jacket.

Along one flowerbed, where pansies braved the chilly breeze, a stooped gentleman crouched down. He looked frail; even through the black cloth, his bones protruded at jutting angles. But his hearing must have been acute because at Roc's approach, the priest turned. Even though he wore a white cleric's collar, he also wore tan trousers and a blue pullover sweater beneath his black jacket. He had piercing blue eyes that went from sharp and pointed like bits of glass to a softening shade of curiosity.

"Father Roberto?"

"Yes." He remained in a kneeling position and Roc noticed how his gnarled hand curled around a trowel's handle. Beside him, plastic bubbled over several plants, at the base of which were strips of cloth wrapped like scarves, but the priest didn't seem in need of any such wrap himself. He held out his other hand for Roc's assistance in standing.

Roc clasped the frail hand but felt strength in the older man's grip. Bracing his other hand beneath the priest's elbow, Roc lifted. Father Roberto was light and his feet were unsteady until he had fully straightened and met Roc's gaze straight on.

"Should I know you?"

"I don't think so. Father Anthony suggested I come talk to you."

"Father—"

"Anthony Daly…from New Orleans."

The priest's eyes widened only slightly. "You must come inside then. Quickly. Please."

Leaving all the gardening tools but the trowel behind, the priest shuffled along the sidewalk toward the rectory. Roc wasn't sure if the priest had forgotten that he carried the small pointed tool or if he did so on purpose. The older man did not take Roc through the front door but instead showed him a side entrance where Father Roberto pulled a set of keys from his pocket, a slight tremor shaking his hands, and he unlocked the first lock, the bolt sliding and clicking. But still he did not open the door.

He turned his attention to Roc, and those blue eyes looked suddenly weary. "How long have you known Anthony?"

"We went to kindergarten together."

"Ah, that is a long time. And why did he send you to me?"

"He said you knew how to help me."

The beeping of a garbage truck disturbed the quiet but didn't dissuade the priest's inquiry. "And what kind of help are you seeking?"

Roc always believed in the direct approach, which usually saved time. With a heavy sigh and shoving aside a hefty amount of lingering disbelief, he forced himself to say, "Killing vampires."

The crepe paper skin around the priest's eyes tightened and his eyes darkened. He flipped his collar inside out and retrieved another key from a hidden pocket. This one opened the last lock. Turning the knob, he pushed the door open and whispered, "Hurry."

The inside was like a gaping hole with stone steps leading down into total blackness. Was this the stairway to hell? Would he end up with a trowel stabbed between his shoulder blades? Never keen on walking into a dark, unknown place, Roc hesitated and glanced first at the priest, then pulled his Glock.

The priest shook his head. "Darkness is not what you should fear. And that gun will do you no good. No good at all. Now hurry. I will close the door behind us."

Disregarding the priest's advice, Roc kept his Glock poised as he took a cautious step down first one step then another and another. The door closed with a *thunk* and darkness swallowed him whole. The priest's breathing had a whistling quality and reverberated off the walls of the narrow stairwell as he clicked and bolted the locks. Roc kept blinking, trying to see an outline, a shape, something, but it was like he'd walked into a black hole, one he hoped held the answers he desperately needed. At the moment though, he might be lucky to escape this one.

"Hold on a minute." The priest's hand fluttered about Roc's shoulder, then patted him as if confirming Roc was still there. "Just a minute now."

Irritation tightened the muscles along Roc's neck. Who was this priest that Anthony had recommended?

"Okay. There." The priest acted like walking into total darkness and discussing vampires was a regular occurrence.

A light snapped on and the beam shot through Roc's retina, blinding him again. He squinted and raised his arm to block the flashlight's high beam.

"Oh, sorry." Father Roberto slanted the light toward the steps. "Now if you'll just head down that way."

With the path somewhat illuminated, except for the momentary spots in Roc's vision, he made his way down the stone steps. The uneven surface made him worry for the Father's safety, but the older man kept a hand on the wall and didn't seem bothered by the steep incline. A musty odor crept toward them as they descended. At the bottom, the stairwell opened into a small, cave-like room made even smaller by the shelves of books and haphazard stacks piled high on the floor and on a tiny rectangular table. In the corner was a small cot with still more books taking up space.

Father Roberto pulled out a rickety chair from the table, causing a stack to tilt and slide. He righted the tower and turned the chair to face the cot, where he backed up and sat down, the springs of the cot protesting and another stack of papers tilting precariously. "Please have a seat."

Roc eyed the chair dubiously but then took a leap of faith that the chair's loose hinges would hang together long enough to support his weight. Still, he kept his gun securely in his hand. "Let me say first off, Father, that I don't believe in that vampire crap. Sorry. I don't mean to offend. But I don't. And…and…" His gaze snagged on a stack of books and their titles: *Vampire Lore*, *The Power of Blood*, and *Dark Angels*. "Uh…well, I just thought you should know that."

Father Roberto did not seem offended, but he merely blinked and clasped his hands in his lap. "Then why are you here? Just because Anthony sent you?"

"Yes…no. Okay, look." Roc stood. He shoved a hand through his hair. "I saw something…a few things…that I can't explain. And even though I don't believe in…all of this"—he waved toward a shelves of books—"I don't really know what to think…or believe."

"Maybe you should start at the beginning and tell me what you have seen. Or what you think you have seen?"

"So you think I'm crazy?" He blew out a breath. "Because I'm thinking that."

"You are not crazy, Roc Girouard."

Something inside Roc hardened like an icicle and he felt the point jabbing him in the gut. "How'd you know my name?"

"Anthony called me. I'm not accustomed to strangers approaching me about vampires and, considering my beliefs, well, you can imagine the precautions I must take for the safety of those here at the St. Joseph's." The priest had a slight accent, a rolling of the syllables in a way that made Roc wonder if he was a foreigner or had lived overseas for a time. He set the trowel on the bed as if deciding all was safe, that Roc wouldn't harm him. Not that a tiny gardening tool would stop a bullet or assault. "Anthony knows all of this about me. He did not want you wounded in any way."

"Wounded?" This old man thought he could hurt him? Roc almost laughed but caught himself.

The priest slapped his forearms. "This old body may look weak and frail but I know how to take care of myself. I have been fighting vampires for almost fifty years. And their strength is far superior to yours or mine."

"Uh-huh." This had been a bad idea.

"Have there been killings?" he asked matter-of-factly.

That snagged Roc's attention. "What do you know?"

The priest shook his head. "Nothing. Nothing at all. But wherever there are vampires, there is death. That is a certainty I have come to know."

"Uh-huh." The nerves along Roc's spine quivered. "Have you seen a body killed by…you know…one of those?"

"Many times."

Roc laid his gun carefully along the top of his thigh. Was this guy a loon? Or could he be something more? Maybe even a suspect?

"Each vampire has their own method, their own way of killing. Some like to break the neck before they drain the body of blood. But others like the fight, the fresh kill, the thrashing of the body as they subdue it."

"And…?"

"It is not as Hollywood would make you believe, is it? The movies make it seem so romantic, two little piercings in the neck, neat and precise, like a rattlesnake bite or some such. But in reality, it is violent. Animalistic. As if a wild animal were set on a human…an animal that had not eaten in a long while."

Roc swallowed hard. What exactly did this mild-mannered

priest know? Roc's gaze shifted and he looked around the confines of the small room, up at the watermarked ceiling. Way down here, beneath the rectory, no one would hear a young girl scream.

"In South America, so many bodies disappear without the authorities knowing. The bodies decompose in the jungle or vanish in rivers. And in many places where wild animals roam, only the animals are suspected of such crimes. This is how vampires remain in one place for so long."

"And you've been to South America?"

"Oh, yes, many times. Europe is more difficult with so many cities, which may be why the vampire colonies have dispersed to other parts of the globe. But they can still be found…if one is willing to look hard enough."

"Uh-huh, yeah. I understand. Sure." Roc stood and turned away from the priest, his fingers curling around the butt of the gun and his trigger finger sliding into place, while he scanned the bookshelves, the walls, the table, searching for any evidence. "That's all very interesting. Very interesting. And where else have you traveled?"

"On mission trips to the Far East and Africa to…I tell you this: I can go someplace and almost instantly know if there is vampirism in the area. It is a special sense I have developed over the years. I can sense evil deep in my bones like one who senses a storm approaching."

"Have you been to New Orleans?"

Father Roberto did not answer.

Roc glanced over his shoulder, a paranoid glance. Father Roberto remained on the cot, his hands folded neatly together. Roc then walked a few steps toward a bookshelf near the stone steps. "You said you knew Anthony…I just thought maybe…."

"I met Anthony in Florida."

"So you haven't been to Louisiana?"

"New Orleans is a place of much activity, a stronghold, if you will."

Still not exactly an answer. Roc lifted a book—*Dark Days*—then set it down again. Over his shoulder, he slanted his gaze toward Father Roberto. "So how many have you killed?"

"Pardon me?"

"The vampires…how many have you…?"

"Oh, of course, thirty-one to date."

Roc's heart set a heady pace, and his breathing became shallow, erratic. He fingered the Glock's trigger, eased off the safety. On the shelf sat Bram Stoker's *Dracula,* which almost made him laugh. Had all those books of vampires and evil stirred something in this man, made him a predator. No matter; this was the closest he'd ever get to a confession, and it would have to do. "Not a great track record, considering you've been at this…what did you say? Fifty years? And you feel—"

In one motion, Roc whirled around and took aim at the priest. But the old man no longer sat on the cot.

CHAPTER TWENTY-THREE

SOMETHING WAS WRONG.

It wasn't something obvious that Levi could point toward. The sun had not yet appeared on the horizon and the usual lamplight shone around the edges of the green shade in the kitchen window. All appeared normal, the way he'd left the Schmidt farm yesterday evening. The barn door remained closed, the farm equipment in place, but as soon as he stepped inside the barn, he sensed it, as surely as he could smell when a skunk came inspecting the exterior.

Usually the farm animals were quiet, just starting to stir when Levi arrived, but today, Ash, a stout, gray mare, moved about her stall, restless and uneasy. When her wide brown eyes lit on him, she pulled her thick lips back over her teeth and nodded her head up and down, up and down, up and down.

"Easy." Levi reached out a hand to comfort her, but she shied away and moved to the far side of the stall.

For a moment, he watched her, intent on checking her thick legs, her flat feet, her rounded belly. All seemed as it should. And yet...

He started to move away when something tripped him. A high-pitched screech made his skin contract. A kitten, the tiny black and white fur ball scurried out of the way. The mother cat, a tri-colored tabby, came from behind a crate and rubbed against his leg, her tail curling into a question mark. He smoothed a hand along her back as his heart slowed to a normal pace.

Nothing seemed wrong at all this morning; maybe it was simply his imagination or lack of sleep. With a shrug, he went about his chores and filled a bucket of oats and feed and poured it into Ash's trough. The mare, usually eager to eat, didn't come close. Could she have colic? He walked toward her, laid a hand under her nose, spoke soothingly, and rubbed her side and belly. A muscle twitched along her neck and her tail flicked, but she stood still, showing no signs of discomfort.

Under the stall door, Toby, the yellow lab, crawled on his belly and came to greet Levi. "Where have you been hiding this morning? Or were you sleeping late?"

The dog wagged its thick tail but he was panting, his ears pulled back, giving the usual friendly face an anxious look. Toby nosed Levi's hand, and Levi gave him a good rubbing, as the dog's hind leg lifted as if to scratch its belly. "Feel good, eh?"

"Morning, Levi."

Levi turned and greeted Hannah's father. "Morning, Daniel. I've been looking after Ash. She's off her feed this morning."

Daniel leaned his elbows on the stall door. "Maybe she ate too much of that alfalfa yesterday."

"Could be. I'll be keeping an eye on her, I reckon."

Daniel nodded and headed toward the Holsteins, the clanking of pails and machinery followed. Accompanied by Toby and his thumping tail, Levi filled the troughs for the rest of the livestock, then readied the pellets for the lamb that Katie had bottle-fed last spring. The lamb had been given free rein until she got into the hay a few weeks back and made a mess. Since then, she'd been kept in a stall at the far end of the barn during the night. When he reached the wood slatted entrance, he waited for her black nose and brown eyes to greet him. But they didn't. He peered into the stall and felt a catch in his throat.

The lamb lay on its side, head away from him. Even from a few feet distance, he knew the animal was dead. Dead animals he'd seen before. One didn't work a farm without witnessing the beginning of life and the end, sometimes in too-quick succession. Could something have been internally wrong with the little lamb? Is that why its mother rejected it at birth? Animals often had a sense that humans did not. He'd known momma cats to eat their kittens if something was wrong at birth.

He set the bucket at his feet and swung open the half door. Poor Katie. She would not understand. She would cry over this little lamb of hers. And Hannah. How would she handle this—one more loss?

With a weariness born of dealing with the hard facts of life, he pushed open the wooden gate and approached the lamb. That's when he saw the blood.

Chapter Twenty-four

Dat and Mamm were awake already.

Hannah could see the kerosene lights flickering in the windows. She clutched the folds of the cape over her clothes, as the icy fingers of the morning crawled beneath her clothes and along her skin, and she felt the weight of a sleepless night. Keeping to the shadow of the barn and moving toward the house, hopeful to get inside without anyone seeing her or asking questions, she heard Dat's voice and came to a quick halt.

Her heart leapfrogged into her throat, then beat its way back into place as she realized he was not speaking to her but to another. His tone was too deep to register what he was actually saying, the murmurs curt and crisp, but then his words penetrated the fog that seemed to fill her brain and ears.

"Let us not speak of this to the women."

"Shouldn't they know?" Levi's voice stood out with more certainty than question. "So they can be more careful?"

"Of what? A wild animal?"

"Exactly. Or whatever..." Levi paused awkwardly, "...did this thing."

"There is nothing to fear."

Fear what? Levi's words caused an icy blade that had nothing to do with the weather to skate along Hannah's spine. *Fear of what?* She glanced over her shoulder toward the spring house. Had they discovered Akiva? His hiding place? No, that wasn't possible. She'd just come from there, and the door was closed, the latch in place. Besides, why would they fear an injured man? She pressed her face against the wooden slats of the barn to better hear her father's words.

"I will keep a lookout tonight. We should double-check the chicken coop and make sure nothing can get in."

"The barn door was closed as always when I arrived this morning. Daniel, this isn't—"

"You might have been mistaken. It was a fox or a wild dog maybe."

"Daniel…" Something in Levi's tone, the way it seemed to unravel when he spoke her father's name unnerved Hannah. "It could be something else—"

"What? What else could it be?"

There was a long pause. Levi's silence made the seconds tick by slowly, measured by the heavy thud of her heart. The morning sounds of buckets rattling and footsteps scraping against the dirt floor, along with the snuffling of noses that pushed pellets around the bottom of wooden troughs and metal pales, intruded and lulled her into a calm. But was it false?

Concern crinkled her brow. She should not be eavesdropping. She should hurry, as Mamm would be needing her help in the kitchen. She took a hesitant step away.

"You must be right." Levi finally spoke, but his tone held a heavy dose of doubt. "It was a wild dog or predator of some kind."

She froze in place, even holding her breath, afraid of being discovered yet needing to find out what had happened.

"I haven't known of wolves in these parts." Dat's voice had more confidence. "Must be a wild dog, *ja*. Never seen anything like this, have you?"

Levi's answer was slow but definite. "Once."

What are they talking about? What had happened? And what are they trying to convince themselves of? Hannah inched closer.

"A wild animal," Dat said, "kills because it's hungry. Nothing more. It is nature's way. But we should lock the barn from now on at night."

"The barn door *was* secure."

Dat did not respond to Levi, and her ears strained.

"Katie will grieve the lamb."

She sucked in a breath. Her heart quickened, racing and staggering and lurching, in an uneven rhythm.

"It was her favorite." Levi spoke again, heavily. "She bottle-fed it all spring and summer. Hannah will grieve too." His understanding of her heart could not soothe the sudden ache.

She thought of Snowflake gallivanting across the barn-yard, kicking up its heels, rubbing its head against her hip. A cold numbness swept over her. Then a furry lump at the end of the barn snagged her attention. She hadn't seen it there before, as shadows had darkened it, but now as the first light rose, the ghost of a moon still visible in the pale blue sky, the soft wooly coat became clearer as the wind stirred it. The back leg was bent, the tail limp. A sob caught in her throat, and she covered her mouth.

"Some lessons are hard. Death is one. It is but a picture of the Lord's Passover, *ja*?" Dat's voice remained steady and calm, yet it only caused a trembling deep inside her. "They will both mourn, as we all should for the loss of something innocent. But acceptance is what makes our faith grow."

CHAPTER TWENTY-FIVE

THE KICK CAME FROM Roc's left, slammed into his hip, and sent him crashing against the table, which succumbed to the weight. Roc, along with stacks of books, hit the stone floor hard, but immediately he rolled onto his back. He once more aimed his gun at the priest, who now stood over him and kicked the gun out of his hand. The Glock sailed through the room and skittered across the floor.

"I told you not to underestimate me." Father Roberto aimed a weapon right back at Roc. It was a wooden stake, dark and intricately carved, and bearing a close resemblance to the one Anthony had given him in New Orleans. "Now, before I let you up, let's get this straight. I didn't kill any young Amish woman, vagrant, or teen in Louisiana or even JFK. I kill vampires. That's it. And I have no remorse about that whatsoever. As far as I'm concerned, one less vampire in the world is a good thing.

"And if you're wondering how I know about those already dead...I have my own network of informants around the city and in the police department."

"Why should I believe you? Maybe you cracked your lid and think the ones you killed are vampires when they're not."

The priest's chin dipped, and he gave Roc a cutting look. "You *shouldn't* believe me. Don't believe *anyone*. Don't trust anyone. Your blinders have not been removed; if they were, you would see there is evil in this world—more evil than you ever thought possible. So rule number one: don't trust anyone. Because vampires will say anything, do anything. They have no souls. Haven't you seen that in their eyes? The eye is the window to the soul. Theirs are black, am I right?"

In his mind, Roc could see those black eyes of the one called Akiva…and the equally black eyes of the woman, and he remembered their chilling effect on him. Reluctantly, Roc gave a slight, grudging nod.

"The bodies discovered…and I'm warning you there are probably more…didn't have much blood left, did they?"

Roc simply stared at this strange priest brandishing a stake like a Samurai warrior wielded a sword.

"All right then." He held out a hand toward Roc. "Truce?"

With another unenthusiastic nod, Roc grabbed hold of the older man and felt himself hauled to his feet with more strength than he would have believed the priest had stored in his scrawny muscles.

The priest flipped the stake in the air, caught it in the middle, aimed the sharp end at himself, and offered the thick handle to Roc. "Now, sit down and tell me what you have seen."

Roc weighed the stake in his hand, a solid weapon that could do much damage, as he weighed his options. Father Roberto could be crazy, but then again so could he. Hell, he was insane for even considering vampires as a possibility. But how else could he explain what he'd seen? Picking up his wayward Glock and sliding it into his holster, he then righted the rickety chair and settled his bruised bones onto the wooden seat and began telling Roberto everything from the dead trick-or-treater to the Amish teens who'd met a woman who drank blood, to the incident in the alleyway, and finally the woods where Akiva had disappeared.

The priest listened as if Roc were performing the Eucharist, leaning forward on the edge of the cot, hands clasped between his knees, shoulders hunched with concentration and acceptance. When Roc had finished and was still holding the stake, Roberto bowed his head and Roc wondered if he was praying or about to swing into action again. Finally, the older man looked up and met Roc's gaze squarely. "Why do you care so much about all of this?"

The question took Roc by surprise. He was a cop, and dead bodies didn't set well with him, but he knew it was more than that. "What do you mean?"

"You are not a police officer anymore, are you?"

"No."

"Then why? Did you witness something? Know one of the victims?"

Roc swallowed hard and he felt his heart form a solid stone in his chest. "What does it matter?"

"It matters a lot. It is the line in the sand between trust and suspicion." Roberto braced his hands against his knees and stood, no longer appearing as frail as he once had, but Roc could still see the weight of age on his shoulders and in the corner's of his eyes. The priest paced in front of the cot, his hands clasped behind his back, and glanced at Roc, then back to the floor as if trying to decide. "My older sister… she was my connection to this evil. She was killed by one of *them*."

Silence wrapped around them, bound Roc to this man in a way he never could have imagined. Grief hung in the air like a noose, tightening about Roc's throat.

The priest met Roc's gaze and gave a slightly awkward

shrug as if he too were uncomfortable with the admission or memory. "This was a long time ago—fifty-seven years. I was but a boy. Maria was like a mother to me. We lived in Guatemala in a small village. That was my first encounter with these demonic creatures."

The man's eyes held his family's burden, and yet there was more in those depths, more than simple revenge, burning like a blue, electric flame.

Roc swallowed back his reservation in asking the bizarre question that popped into his mind. "Was she...*changed*?"

"You mean did she become one of them?" Roberto shook his head. "Blessed Mother of God, Maria died before my very eyes." The tension around his mouth eased. "For that I am grateful. Even though it took me many years to come to that realization."

For the first time, Roc understood there might have been something worse than Emma's death. He'd never imagined it possible, and he couldn't say he was at this moment grateful...more relieved that there wasn't some other horror he had to face and deal with. "So you saw it...your sister's death...or did you see her after the fact?"

The older man's gaze drifted as if replaying the vision in his head. "I witnessed it all." The old man's throat contracted, and Roc couldn't contain the emotions building inside him as once more the images of Emma assaulted him—the fear on her face, her shoe she'd kicked off in the struggle cast to the side, the blood on her hospital ID.

"I could do nothing." A strange tone entered Roberto's voice, as if he were once again a child, trying to explain. "The beast...was too strong. After he flung me off, I cowered behind a kapok tree. And to this day, I do not understand why he did not kill me too." The priest turned away from Roc.

It felt as if he were in a confessional with all the guilt and pain surging to the surface, because this was expected, required, needed. "My wife…Emma…she was killed." Roc stared at the frayed edge of an ancient textbook, the pages yellowed, the cover as scarred as his soul. "The same way."

"Recently?" Roberto's tone turned practical and helped Roc suppress the painful memories and turbulent emotions beneath an icy demeanor.

"Almost two years now."

"I am sorry." Roberto sounded as if he had uttered those words many times for others to find comfort. But comfort was not what Roc was seeking. "So you are here for revenge. It is understandable. I must confess that is how I began too, but I believe the Lord will show you a new path for your life, Roc Girouard. A new way. A new hope."

"I don't know about that. But I'm ready to kill the SOBs." He shifted his gaze toward Roberto to prove his intent. "Just show me how."

"It is not so easy, I'm afraid. But I believe in this case, the one you are hunting has some connection with the Amish community. I do not know why, but if we discover the reason, then maybe we can track this one and kill it. Before it kills any more."

CHAPTER TWENTY-SIX

THE KITCHEN SMELLED OF frying eggs and sizzling bacon, buttermilk biscuits and melting butter, tangy orange juice and hot coffee. The calendar nailed to the wall had already been turned to December. *To every thing there is a season, and a time to every purpose under heaven.* The Amish adhered to the seasons, the changes, the life cycles that the Lord had prepared for them, planting and plucking up that which was planted in due course, and yet Hannah felt a resistance in her very soul concerning *the time to mourn and a time to dance.* Was it her time, as Rachel and Grace and Beth Ann had suggested to her so often? But to Hannah, the reasons to mourn kept piling up inside her, from Jacob to Grandma Ruth to this confusing loss of an innocent lamb, and moving beyond those reasons seemed an impossible task.

She slipped off her cape and hung it on the peg beside the back door, averting her gaze from Mamm and Katie who were already bustling about the kitchen.

"You were up early, Hannah." Mamm cracked an egg into the frying pan. "Did you rest well last night?"

Hannah nodded, slipping into the morning routine as quickly as possible, as she checked the puffy biscuits in the oven that were just beginning to brown.

Katie walked into the kitchen from the pantry, her bare feet scuffing the wooden floor. "I made the biscuits all by myself."

"Looks like you did a fine job."

"You weren't in your room when I searched for you." An accusatory tone took hold of Katie's voice.

"I woke early." Hannah set the metal pastry cutter into the sink. "I couldn't sleep."

"Me either. I got cold in the night."

"That's because you left your window open." Mamm shook her head at Katie then flipped an egg.

Katie wrapped her arms around Hannah, forcing her to turn, and pressed her face against Hannah's chest. "You're cold now."

"Yes, silly. It's cold outside." Hannah rubbed a hand along her sister's back, held her longer than usual. Today would not be easy when Katie learned of Snowflake, and she wished she could spare her the pain of grief. Finally, the younger girl squirmed away, and Hannah blinked back tears that threatened to spill over.

"What's wrong?" Katie stared up at her. "Are you crying?"

Hannah fought for control over her emotions, blinked back the tears, and focused on cleaning the mess Katie had left on the counter from rolling out the biscuit dough. "I'm fine. Katie, can you fetch the butter and honey for the table?"

Reluctantly, Katie went to the propane-powered refrigerator and retrieved the stick of butter. Hannah felt Mamm's heavy gaze settle on her, but she focused on the window that looked out toward the barn, where she saw Dat and Levi headed her way, their cheeks bright red from the cold. Dat spoke to Levi, who then turned back toward the barn. Dat called out Levi's name but to no avail.

"You certainly had fun with all the flour this morning." Hannah smiled at her little sister and scraped a patch of dried dough off the counter.

The worry tightening Katie's features relaxed into a smile, and she picked up a lump of dough and kneaded it in the palm of her hand, bits of flour sifting through her fingers onto the floor. Hannah wiped up a puddle of milk and rubbed, rubbed, rubbed at the crusty dough until Mamm came alongside Hannah and placed a hand on hers, stilled her movements. "Are you all right?" She touched Hannah's cheek. "Are you feeling well?"

She wanted to lean into Mamm's warm hand, throw herself into her mother's arms as she once did when she was Katie's age. But no one could take away the grief or give her the answers she so desperately needed. "I'm fine, Mamm. Really." But Katie soon wouldn't be, and yet Hannah couldn't tell her. It was something Dat would have to do. Pinpricks of tears stung the backs of her eyes. "I am well."

"Maybe she saw Levi last night." Katie's voice had a sing-song quality.

Mamm looked toward Katie, and Hannah took the opportunity to move across the kitchen and set the table, shuttering her gaze as she gathered fig and cherry preserves from the pantry. But she heard Mamm scold Katie quietly.

"Did you and Levi quarrel?" Mamm's sudden closeness startled Hannah, but not as much as the question.

She clunked the glass jars on the table. Did Mamm know she slipped out at night? Did she suspect it was to meet Levi? Other girls her age, Grace and Beth Ann, both went running around with their boyfriends; relationships of that sort were usually discreet and private. Feeling the pressure of Mamm's presence, her question, Hannah gave a quick shake of the head.

The back door opened, ending the questions, and a blast of cold swirled through the kitchen's warmth. Dat stamped his feet and removed his outer coat.

"Breakfast is nearly ready." Mamm hurried to check the biscuits in the oven. "Daniel, the water is no longer hot. Is something wrong with the generator?"

Hannah's stomach flipped, and she moved quickly toward the back door. "I'll go check the line."

But Dat blocked her path. Slowly, he hung his hat on the peg beside the door. "I'll take care of it after breakfast."

"Dat!" Katie ran toward her father. "I made the biscuits today."

His gaze landed on his youngest daughter. Where there was usually a smile, today a tightness pinched the corners of his mouth. "You are a good helper."

Mamm's smile was for her youngest, but worry darkened her gaze that trailed Hannah. "Idle hands are the devil's play ground. Better be calling Levi."

"He'll be along after his chores." Dat's voice sounded gruff.

"The eggs and biscuits will be cold." Mamm eyed me and tilted her head toward the door. "Let Hannah go hurry him along."

Before Dat could protest, Hannah rushed out the door.

Hannah ducked her chin against the blustery wind and hurried toward the barn. The cold pricked her cheeks and made her nose run. She sniffed as she entered the barn, and the warmth of the animals embraced her. A cow lowed, then went back to munching hay. Hannah searched each stall, but it wasn't until she came to the end where the tack hung on the wall that she came to a sudden halt.

Levi stood shirtless, his torso bare. With his back partially turned, he didn't notice her as he hung a shovel on a wall peg, then wrapped something up, making the muscles in his arms and back ripple beneath his skin. Despite the chill in the air, a sheen of sweat covered his back. Hannah's breath sounded harsh in her own ears, and she felt her heart tripping over itself.

Then Levi turned around fast. Had she startled him? Heat rose up from her center, along her chest and neck, and seared her face. She caught only a wide expanse of skin, blond hair, flat-muscled stomach, which stirred another memory, before she shoved her gaze toward the floor. This was the body of a man, his strength obvious in the play of muscles, but Jacob, when she had seen him without a shirt, had been thinner, lankier, younger. Dark hairs had only just begun to sprout across his chest; the starkness of dark hair against pale skin had always intrigued her. But Levi…she felt a rush of heat as she'd never felt before.

"Hannah? Is something wrong?"

She shook her head but then nodded. Her gaze slid back toward him then skittered away. He didn't rush to cover himself but held his shirt balled up in his hand and finally chucked it behind him. As the seconds stretched out, he reached for one of Dat's coats and with slow deliberation, he tugged first one sleeve then the other on. But the coat had no button or fastening and so it gaped open, revealing his chest and belly, his muscles firm and toned.

He moved toward her, and she dropped her gaze to his shoes. "What is it?"

Something in his voice tugged at her and she glanced up and met his gaze. "Something happened here."

The corner of his mouth pinched and his lips flattened. "Snowflake died."

She blinked slowly, absorbing the news that she already had heard. "But what happened?"

"An animal. A…predator of some sort." His features twisted, and this time his gaze shifted sideways. She glimpsed pain in his eyes.

"A predator?" She repeated as if she did not understand, yet she did.

"Did your father tell Katie?"

"No, not yet."

His gaze drifted away from her as if he was troubled by something else.

"Levi." She took a hesitant step toward him. "I need to know…what are you…have you said anything to Dat about last night?" Which seemed years ago.

His gaze was solid and sure and his jaw hardened. "Why would I?"

"I…well, I didn't know. I needed to be sure is all."

"Your secret is safe with me, Hannah."

My secret. Is that what it was? It seemed worse than a secret; it seemed like a betrayal in some way. She waited for Levi to lecture her, to tell her it wasn't safe, it wasn't proper for her to go off at night to a deserted cemetery. But he said nothing of the sort. To fill the silence, she said, "Breakfast is ready."

"I'll be along."

When she turned, Levi called her name, and once again she faced him.

"Have you seen—" His lips tightened until he shook his head. "Do not trouble yourself."

Perplexed by the concern in his eyes, the tension in his stance, the unspoken question, she retraced her steps out of the barn, her heart beating faster than her footsteps could carry her. Hannah's friends whispered about the different shapes of the boys they knew—who was built strong like an ox, who was thin as a twig, and who was husky from too much strudel—but Hannah had rarely purposefully looked, not since Jacob. He had been beautiful. But after this morning, she had to admit that Levi was rather pleasing to behold, and with the memory of him now tucked in a safe place inside her mind she felt her face once more grow warm.

With her thoughts dragging behind, she rushed toward the spring house. She paused at the door, glanced over her shoulder to be sure Levi wasn't following, then pulled it open and blinked against the darkness. It took a moment for her eyes to adjust as slivers of morning light cut through the boarded walls and slanted across the dirt floor. Picking her way through the wires, cords, and machinery, she moved toward the back.

She needed to warn Akiva that her father would be coming soon. He would have to leave. He couldn't linger. He couldn't stay.

But when she reached the back, the pallet she'd made was empty, and the space he'd occupied only a short while ago was vacant, the bedding neatly folded in a pile. Disappointment and relief swirled through her because now she wouldn't have anything to explain. But where had Akiva gone? Would he be all right?

Then behind her something scuffed the dirt. She whirled around. Her heart leapt into her throat, pounded, and extinguished her air supply.

"What are you doing?" Katie stepped out of the shadows.

Hannah's hand covered the spot her heart should have occupied, and she took shallow breaths until it dropped back down into place. "You startled me, you goose."

"I'm not a goose." She leaned to one side to look behind Hannah, who pulled her skirt sideways to hide the blanket. Still, Katie's eyes widened. "Is Levi in here?"

"Levi?" Hannah's heart faltered.

Katie laughed and shook her head. "Mamm sent me after you." She stepped sideways and pointed toward the stack of blankets and pillows. "What's that for?"

Hannah gave an indifferent shrug. "I was going to take it back to the house. You can do it for me."

"Were you out here with Levi last night?"

"Take the bedding to the house, all right?"

With a decided pout, Katie picked up the blankets and pillow, and backed her way through the door. She let the door slap closed behind her, leaving Hannah alone in the darkness again.

A fluttering overhead made her dart sideways, her heartbeat became more of a flurry than steady, rhythmic beats, and then she heard the decided flap of a wing, felt a sudden brush of air on her cheek, and ducked. When she pushed the door ajar and light poured in, she realized it was only a trapped bird.

CHAPTER TWENTY-SEVEN

"Blood is powerful."

Roc listened intently to Father Roberto about his research and experience with vampires. Together, they had left the priest's little room with his research books, taken a turn about St. Joseph's, and ended up walking around the neighborhood past rundown houses and businesses that had metal bars covering the windows. This was an elderly part of Philadelphia, and its age spots were showing not only in the dated architecture and decrepit row houses but also in the ancient oaks, hackberries, and maples, their bare branches spindly, gnarled, and arthritic.

"But the blood"—the priest spoke as if discussing the weather—"which these foul creatures feed on, only offers temporary life. It's counterfeit to the sanctity of the blood of Christ, don't you see?" His eyes glittered, like a professor discussing his own dissertation. "That is why *they* must feed often."

Obviously Father Roberto filtered this vampire theory through his religious ideology, but Roc hadn't swallowed the murky Kool-Aid yet. Still it was all he had to go on. For him, all that mattered was that a dead body, or two, demanded someone had to pay, and compensation came through simple judicial accounting. This meant the perp had to be caught, and the best way to do that was to know everything there was about him…or her. And if that meant learning about bloodsuckers then that's what he'd do.

But that didn't mean he felt comfortable with the subject, and he crossed his arms over his chest to ward off the chill that seemed to permeate his bones, though he wasn't sure it was simply the weather at fault. "How often do they have to…you know…uh, drink?"

"Every few days. When they feed, they grow warm, even hot, to the touch. But when they are hungry and on the hunt, their body temperature drops and they're cold, cold as a dead body. They move a bit slower then." A smile lurked at the corner of the priest's mouth. "It's a good time to kill them. And yet, you must be careful because when they are hunting they are also desperate, and therefore extremely dangerous."

Roc rubbed the back of his neck. The cold he felt inside had nothing to do with the weather. If he thought of what Father Roberto was saying logically, he began to doubt his own sanity, for listening to this nonsense or even considering it. But nothing rational could explain the things he'd seen. Illogical as the vampire premise was, it didn't mean it wasn't true. Still, he tried to focus on the words, excluding all thoughts and doubts, and simply absorb the information.

"And is it possible to kill them?"

"Of course, but it isn't easy. They have to bleed out entirely. You must keep your distance because if they latch onto you, bite into you, they will only grow stronger. And then your chance will be lost. And you will end up dead. Or worse."

Death no longer frightened Roc, but allowing these… creatures to get away with killing made him burn. "Akiva…I wounded him. I'm sure of it. When he disappeared, could he have bled out somewhere?"

"Unlikely." Roberto clasped both his hands and raised his forefingers toward his chin like a steeple. "One thing you must do is bind them. I keep a leather strap for this purpose." From his hip pocket he produced a thick leather strap that looked as if it could hold Samson. "But a rope would work just as well. Handcuffs even. If they are bound then they cannot change or vanish."

Roc cast an uncertain sideways glance at the priest. "Change?"

"They morph into other creatures, bats mostly, but anything will do. I saw one morph into a snake and slither away. But they usually choose something that can fly so they can escape more easily and get where they want more quickly."

Roc stopped walking and a part of him wanted to bust out laughing. *Come on!* This was like a sorry B-movie. But the priest's serious demeanor kept Roc in check. The whole premise was absurd...and even more impossible to imagine a vampire could be killed at all. It was like playing a game where the rules kept changing in favor of your opponent. "So what you're really saying is that it's impossible to kill one."

"It isn't easy, I'll grant you that. It has to be done fast. Bind, kill. Like a one-two punch. It's the binding that does the trick. You must wrap something around them, an ankle, a wrist...but it can't be anything flimsy because they are fiercely strong." He tugged on both ends of the leather strap, then slapped it against his thigh, making a *thwap*. "But you must not hesitate. No second thoughts. No vacillation. Remember, they will not falter at striking, at killing. Did you hesitate when you shot this one called Akiva?"

Roc shook his head. "I gave him a warning." Years of training had kicked in. "But I shot him, square in the chest."

"But it wasn't a kill. You must destroy them."

"Even a mortal wound in the chest wouldn't kill one?"

"Not if they have the opportunity to kill and revive themselves with blood. What is mortal to you and me is not mortal to *them*."

Roc remained in place, unable to move forward into the world of dark toothy tales but unable to back away from all of the insanity. "Then there's probably another victim. Is that what you're saying?"

The priest gave the sign of the cross. "God forbid. Akiva may have found an animal to feed on, but if not…then most likely you are correct."

Why didn't that make Roc feel better? "Okay so how does one become a…you know"—he swallowed back his reservations—"vampire?"

"*They* choose someone. Who knows why some are chosen and others killed. They have their reasons, I'm sure, they just don't divulge those motivations to us lowly humans. And that's how they think of us. We're inferior in every way: physically, mentally, and, in the worst way, according to them: we have a conscience. They don't seem to be hindered by that. Anyway, I have known vampires to choose someone as a mate and then change him or her.

"It's a delicate procedure though. Their feeding can get out of control and become frenzied. If *they* are hungry then they will not have the self-control to be careful and they'll end up killing instead of changing the person."

"So what happens exactly?"

"It is somewhat conjecture on my part, of course, as no one has lived to…" Father Roberto's voice played out.

"Tell about it?" Roc finished for him but no smile emerged as a result of the cliché. Anyone changed was no longer alive. Not the way Roc or Father Roberto saw life.

The priest nodded. "Once a vampire, well, they are good at keeping their secrets. In fact, they release false information, which then helps protect them. But after much study, I believe what happens is the vampire bites the human, drains blood from them until they are weak and barely alive, then they must sacrifice another victim. The vampire offers the chosen one this so-called sacrificial blood. When the human drinks the blood of another, the change takes place. It is a delicate process, and I imagine it sometimes ends in death for all concerned."

Father Roberto clapped a hand on Roc's back. "Think you'd like to take over my mission some day?"

Roc laughed. "You've got to be crazy."

The priest's gaze was steady and unwavering. "Not at all. I can't do this forever."

"You seem pretty strong and capable." Roc touched his side, which still felt tender from the priest's strong kick.

"You should have seen me in my prime." His gaze raked over Roc. "You must work on your own strength, because this task will not be easy. It will demand every ounce of strength you possess…and maybe more. You have been ill for a while?"

Roc sniffed. "In a way."

"You will be strong now. I will pray for you."

Somehow Roc knew it was going to take more than that.

"*For such a time as this…*" the priest whispered, looking off as if seeing something Roc could not.

"Excuse me?"

Father Roberto waved a hand, dismissing what he had said and began to walk forward, waving his hand for Roc to catch up. "You are named after a saint, yes?"

An invisible hand tightened around the base of Roc's

spine. "How'd…" But his question died on his lips, because, of course, a priest would have studied the saints.

"It was either that or Rocky Balboa." Father Roberto smiled. "Do you know about this Saint Roch?"

Roc rubbed the back of his neck and looked up at the brightening sky. "My mother spoke of him some."

"He is sometimes referred to as Rocco." The priest shoved his hands into his pant's pockets. "But that is neither here nor there. He did great things, healing many from the plague. That scourge disappeared under his sign of the cross. And this new pestilence will be destroyed with *your* help."

What was the priest saying? That all Roc had to do was give the sign of the cross? He was no saint. He'd made a lot of mistakes in his life, and drinking away the last couple of years was one of them. He doubted God would be on his side, even in the most righteous of crusades.

"It was said that Saint Roch was born with the sign of the cross on his chest." Father Roberto's gaze dropped down toward Roc's chest.

Roc began walking back to St. Joseph's and Father Roberto matched him step for step. This change in conversation made Roc even more uncomfortable than discussing vampires on the loose. He'd rather focus on the case, on the perp, on tracking down this animal. Focus on the details. The details mattered.

And the detail that stuck with him the most was the Amish girl and the trick-or-treater. A coincidence? Even though Emma hadn't been dressed like an Amish woman, she'd been wearing plain blue scrubs the night she died. Was *plain* the connection? Pure simplicity? Or Amish plain? But if so, then the homeless man didn't fit the perplexing puzzle.

"That connection we were discussing…" Roc rubbed

a spot just beneath his left collarbone. "Could these Amish deaths—"

"I would say 'plain' deaths, as those dressed were plain but not necessarily Amish."

So the priest thought the same thing. Another thought occurred to Roc. "Could those murders have been attempts to change an Amish person into a vampire and it went bad?"

The priest stopped, the lines in his face furrowing and sagging, and he looked grief-stricken. "Then it might be worse than I thought. If this Akiva changes an Amish woman then it would be worse than death for her."

Roc watched their feet move in a cadence, the strides matching, the determination even. "For anyone I'd say."

"True. Very true."

Chapter Twenty-eight

Two days later, sitting in bed with Katie curled up beside her, Hannah stared out the upstairs window into the foreboding darkness. Deep in the night, Katie had crept into her room, saying she was cold, and Hannah had wrapped her arms around her little sister, holding her tightly along with all she'd ever loved, wishing she could hold it all even closer.

But her gaze drifted involuntarily toward the window in the direction of the spring house. The injured stranger—Akiva—had disappeared. But to where? Was he all right? Had he miraculously recovered? Or was he lying in a ravine somewhere needing help? Dying? She whispered a silent prayer for Akiva.

Her mind wandered down a dead-end road of questions about him: who was he, where did he come from, how was he injured…and where was he going? These questions took her nowhere and left her feeling lost and confused.

While he was here, she hadn't wanted to admit that some part of him reminded her of Jacob. Of course, he had dark hair, just like Jacob, but Akiva's was shorter than Jacob's bowl cut. His features were similar and yet not. He seemed unattached, unfazed by the world, curious and eager to wander new roads. That's how Jacob was.

Was.

And that same foolishness would be the end of Akiva. And her too.

Buggy wheels crunched gravel, and she knew it was Levi on his way home. He had stayed late to help Dat with a faulty compressor. He was a good man, conscientious, helpful, and kind. His heart, she was learning, was as wide as the heavens. She was foolish for putting him off, because he would make a good husband. And yet something kept her from making that step. Was it a simple need for her own running around time?

Jacob's *rumschpringe* had become a dead end, or so he'd prophesied about himself when he returned from his New Orleans journey. It might have been worth his money and her angst if it had brought him to a place of readiness to make his solemn vow to God and the church and the community, if it had brought him peace, but it hadn't. Now, her own eagerness to wander might bring her home again. If it did, then it might be too late for Levi. Then again, it might not.

She closed her eyes, squeezed them tight. *Don't think, Hannah, just sleep.*

That voice called to her. Confused her. Unbalanced her. Tilted her world. Where would it lead her? She shifted beneath the covers and covered her head with the pillow.

Hannah.

She fisted her hands, willed herself to stay in bed, and yet suddenly her feet were on the floor, the bed covers folded back over Katie. Resisting seemed impossible. She donned her clothes, gathered her wrap, and crept down the stairs, through the kitchen, and out the back door. This time she didn't bother taking the book, flashlight, or knife.

The air was still and cold, and she could almost smell the frost forming. The moon sat high and full, only a tiny slice had been shaved off, but it was bright and capable of lighting her path.

She entered the spring house, pausing, listening for any sounds, any visitors, but all was quiet. Peaceful. And yet, inside her was anything but tranquility. There was a rumbling, a stirring, a discontent. From where had it come? Or had it always been there?

In the back of the cramped space, past the machinery, cords, and tubing, she knelt at the place where Akiva had laid. Had she only dreamed he had been here? Was it some apparition born of her need for Jacob? Had she gone *narrishch*? Jacob told her only days before he had died that he felt crazy. Was her own death near?

She drew a slow, steadying breath. If she died, she was ready, for then she would see Jacob again.

She touched the cool, dirt floor, searching as if to be reminded that Akiva had been there. Somehow it made her feel closer to Jacob, and yet it made no sense to her. When her fingers nudged something hard, her hand faltered, then her fingers folded over a pointed corner of a book.

With her heart thumping, she moved back to the door, where moonlight slanted through the opening, and she turned the book over in her hands. Lovingly, she ran her hand over *her* book, the book Jacob had given her. How did it get here? Had she dropped it? Or had Akiva taken it? She dusted it off, opened the front cover, and read what Jacob had written: *To Hannah, With love, Jacob.*

A heaviness weighted her heart, but then whispers swirled through her head. That voice. That call acted like a steel hook piercing her heart and pulling her toward…*What?*

She hid the book inside her apron and pushed out into the night, closing the spring house door and latching it. Then a shadow fell across her. She startled and a tiny gasp emerged from her cold lips.

Akiva.

He leaned against the outside wall, his smile self-satisfied, but his gaze remained dark and intense. "Did I startle you, sweet Hannah?"

"I-I thought you'd left." Her stutter gave her away. "It's been days. I just now found…" She touched the book in her apron, but she decided to keep silent. Her gaze dropped to his chest where his leather jacket was unzipped as if the cold did not bother him, and he wore a clean, unblemished white T-shirt. "Are you better?"

"Much. Is that your book?"

She pulled it from her apron as if to remind herself what it was. Even though she knew. "Yes."

"I found it, Hannah. I didn't steal it." He spoke as if he had read her mind. But that was impossible.

"I wasn't accusing."

He straightened, standing tall before her, and took a step in her direction, his gaze intent on her. "I enjoyed reading it."

Her insides trembled, and she held the book out toward him, unsure what her intention was. Why would she offer the book, her most prized possession, to this stranger? Maybe it was a way to put a barrier between them. Or maybe it was a way to draw this man closer. "Would you like it?"

"You keep it. It's yours after all. Jacob gave it to you, no?" He moved around her, so close he could easily have brushed her clothes with his, touched her bare neck, bathed her skin with his breath, and yet he did not cross the invisible wall that stood between them. "I love words, the way they wash over my ears." He stopped before her, closed his eyes as if listening to the sounds of words in his head, then cocked his head sideways, and opened his eyes again.

She felt like she was falling into his gaze, losing herself, losing…

"Foolish, I suppose." His smooth forehead crinkled. "I apologize."

"Jacob," she whispered as if Akiva was her beloved, as if Jacob was standing before her. But it was impossible. This man wasn't Jacob. She shook her head, an attempt to shake loose her muddled thoughts. "Jacob…he loved words too." She gave an awkward laugh. "Will you be staying here tonight? I could bring the blankets back."

"Would that be a problem?"

"No, not at all. Can I get you anything? Something to eat?"

"I'm not hungry." But his heated gaze felt as if he devoured each curve of her frame.

She took a step backward, sensing something unusual, something dangerous. Glancing sideways, she looked for a route of escape.

"Hannah?"

Reluctantly, she met his gaze again, felt the same tilting sensation.

"Did you tell anyone about me?"

"I made a promise."

"And you are a woman who lives up to her promises, I see." She shifted from one foot to the next.

"Do I make you nervous, sweet Hannah?"

Heat bloomed along her neck and cheeks. "A little."

"Is it me? Or all men?"

His question unsettled her. "I'm engaged."

Her lie tasted sour in her mouth. What was she doing? It was as if she threw those words up as a protective mechanism against this man, but they turned out to be a feather against a powerful gale.

Akiva's face darkened. "Are you now?" He stepped toward her, his presence broad and dark and menacing. He was only inches from her, and she tried to avoid that gaze, the certainty of knowing her lie, but she could not. "Are you really?"

"No," she confessed. "Not yet." She comforted herself that her lie wasn't actually a lie. Levi was interested... *Wasn't he?*

"Who is it?" His voice sounded suddenly cold, and his gaze turned sharp. "This one who wants to marry you. Or is it the other way around?"

Her insides shifted. She should not have spoken in such a way. Levi might not want to marry her, especially because of the way she had treated him. And yet, why had his image bloomed in her mind? "You couldn't know him. He is Amish."

Suddenly, Akiva grabbed her arm, his grip unforgiving. "Have you been baptized already?"

Tears sprang to her eyes, and she twisted her arm, trying to loosen his grip, but still he held her tight. "Why do you care?"

Akiva's mouth distorted and as quickly as he'd grabbed her, he released her. "Why wouldn't I care?"

She touched her bruised wrist, her gaze shot toward the house, and her feet took two steps in that direction.

"*Hannah*." Something in the way he spoke her name, something familiar, kept her from running and somehow calmed her erratic heartbeat. "Hannah, look at me, please."

Slowly, hesitantly, she looked up and felt the impact of his gaze all the way down to the core of her being, parts of her she hadn't felt since Jacob had last kissed her, in that long, slow, sweet way of his that used to make her tremble.

"I am sorry." His voice gentled, stroked, appeased. "But I…" He shook his head, stepped back. "I feared…"

His confession startled her. "Feared what?"

"Feared you had made an irrevocable decision. One that would separate—"

"Separate what?"

He shook his head again and his lips rolled inward. "Why did you say you were not yet engaged? 'Not yet'?"

Looking into his dark gaze, she felt as if she could withhold nothing from him. "Levi is a good man. He will be a good husband."

"Levi." He tested out the name. But was that condescension or surprise in his tone? "There are a lot of good men in the world," he said. "Doesn't mean you love him."

She blinked. "Doesn't mean I won't."

"Touché."

His word puzzled her. "What does that mean?"

"A close touch." He reached forward with his pointer finger aimed right at her heart. Before he could make the final thrust forward, which would connect them, she backed away. "What are you afraid of, *sweet Hannah*?"

She lifted her chin a notch. "I'm not afraid."

"Then what keeps you from saying yes to this Amish boy?"

"He's not a boy. He's a man."

Akiva tilted his head as if giving in to her side of the argument, and yet it didn't feel like an argument. But whatever it was felt lopsided, weighted on Akiva's side. "Age isn't only a number but also life experiences and understanding of the world."

She gave a slight shrug. "*The Fear of the Lord is the beginning of wisdom.*"

He chuckled and rubbed his chin. "There is much to fear,

Hannah. But should we really fear the Lord? Love him? Yes. But fear Him? Hasn't he promised His love and mercy?" He stepped closer. "But what is it you fear?"

"Why do you care? You don't know me or my family or even Levi."

"You helped me, Hannah. I feel obligated to help you now. Is that wrong?"

She took a step away, which gave her the ability to breathe easier, and turned from him. "I guess not." She wrapped her arms over her middle. "But you're under no obligation. I only did my Christian duty. Anyone would—"

"No, not anyone."

She supposed he was right about that. Not everyone would have helped him. But did that mean he was right about the other things he'd said?

His hands settled on her shoulders and turned her back toward him. His gaze was gentle and kind. Maybe he would understand the fears she fought. Maybe…"What if I'm not a…good wife?"

"You? That seems highly unlikely. But I can understand how you might doubt your ability to…ah…"—a smile stretched his mouth—"to please him."

Grateful for the darkness, she felt her skin burn at his ability to see inside her mind or heart or both. "I should go."

"Or is it that you still want someone else?"

She brushed past this man she did not even know. She had already revealed too much; he had presumed too much. Nothing else would she reveal—to him or to anyone.

But his voice stopped her with, "Why have you not asked me about *him*?"

She lifted her chin a notch and pretended not to know whom he meant. "Who?"

"Jacob."

The few feet between them no longer provided a sense of security. She kept her back to him, as if that could hide her thoughts, her feelings. Even though she was wrapped in her cape with a scarf around her head, she felt unclothed, as if he could see right through her to the quick-flight beat of her heart.

She did not hear his footsteps, but suddenly he was there, next to her, peering over her shoulder to whisper, "You think of him. Don't you?"

Some days she thought of nothing *but*. Words jammed her throat. She swallowed and swallowed again, her throat convulsing with indecision. Then she felt Akiva's hand at the base of her neck, his touch gentle, and the pads of his fingers light yet insistent on an answer. Tears once again sprang to the surface. She didn't want or intend to, but she nodded nonetheless.

"You dream of him too."

She blinked, leaving her eyes closed, squeezing them shut, praying for control. Hot, vile tears stung the insides of her eyelids. His questions, his awareness, his probing, were unraveling her. Quaking. Trembling. Shaking loose. She was coming undone.

His hand folded about the ridge of her shoulders. His skin was hot against hers, burning into her like a brand. Was it her heartbeat she felt or his, the beat thud, thud, thudding into her? "Do not be afraid of love, my *sweet Hannah*. Embrace it. Hold on to it. Love deeply. For it is a miracle."

"It is impossible." Her voice cracked and tears fell.

"All things are possible…are they not?"

Her nod was slow and compliant. Was it her will or his? But then she whispered, "Will you tell me of him? Of Jacob?"

"Yes."

A constriction in her chest loosened and she could once again breathe.

"But you must come with me."

She swirled away from him, breaking the light hold he had on her.

He raised one eyebrow in a mocking question. "If you want to know more about Jacob, then you will come with me. Tomorrow night."

When she finally nodded her agreement, he smiled—a smile that carried a wallop, and she felt the repercussion deep, deep inside.

CHAPTER TWENTY-NINE

S HE WAS SCREAMING.

That's what Roc had heard over the cell phone—her screams. It was Emma's custom to call him as she headed out of the hospital after her late shift in the ER and walked toward her car in the parking garage.

"How's your night going?"

"Same ol', same ol'. You?"

"Slow actually. Ready to soak in the tub."

"Think of me."

Inane conversation. Nothing important. No way to know it would be the last time they'd ever speak to each other. How many times had he wondered: if they'd only known, what would they have said? What do you say to someone who holds your heart in the moments, seconds, before they vanish forever? And before your heart turns into a pillar of salt? Even now, he wasn't sure he had an answer. A moment was too short. So was a lifetime.

"Hold on," she'd told him.

He was on duty in another part of New Orleans, a good fifteen minutes away. He'd been typing into his squad car's computer about the traffic stop he'd just made. Over the cell phone, pressed between his shoulder and ear, he heard the murmurings of someone speaking to her.

"What?" Emma asked. "I'm sorry but—"

Then there was a clatter, a crunching noise. He realized later that Emma's cell phone hit the pavement.

"Stop!" Her voice came through muted but audible. "Let go!"

And then the screaming had started. And it continued rebounding in his head even now in his sleep.

He jerked straight up in bed, his arms flailing as if he could fight off her attacker, as if he could save her. His arm flailed wide, and he knocked a book he'd borrowed from the red-headed teen at the B&B onto the floor. The room was dark, the television flickering in the corner, the news scroll-ing along the bottom of the screen. Sweat poured off him. He shoved his fingers through his hair, clutched his skull, and squeezed—a poor attempt to stop the screams.

In reality, her screaming hadn't lasted long. He'd shouted into the phone for her and then radioed for an assault in progress at Children's Hospital. He was on the other side of Tulane University on Canal Street, but he spun his car in her direction and was there in less than ten.

Blue and red emergency vehicle lights were already slic-ing through the darkness, and doctors and nurses on duty at the hospital were standing around the parking garage. The police tried to hold him back, grabbing at his arms, restrain-ing him. But he fought through them. They couldn't hold him. He ran for the center of everyone's attention.

Emma.

She was lying with her back against a wall, feet splayed, one toe of a tennis shoe angled inward. Her head tilted at an odd angle. Her hand on the concrete floor was palm up. And Roc knew. Before he slid to his knees beside her, he knew.

Her eyes were open, the gaze blank. Empty. As if the levy

of all she had been, known, loved had broken, and everything drained out of her.

Blood splotched the front of her scrubs. Was it hers? A patient's? And then he saw the gaping hole at the side of her neck. Blood should be pouring out of her, pooling around her. He'd seen enough wounds in his life to know the major artery in her neck had been severed. But there wasn't much blood, even the tissue looked pale. Only the dark stains on her shirt gave vivid evidence of what should have been.

And her screams still resonating in his head became deeper, hoarse…his own.

CHAPTER THIRTY

Hannah watched Levi from the kitchen window as he hitched horse to buggy. She hadn't realized how accustomed she'd become to Levi's gaze brushing over her, settling on her like a gentle hand, until she felt the chill of his purposeful disinterest. In the days following her rejection of him, sending him away when he'd followed her to the cemetery, an unobservable and yet definite change had come over Levi.

A memory of Levi helping a barn cat deliver a kitten came back to her. The momma cat panted and strained, wedging herself between the wall and a milking can. Levi pulled her out, cradled her in his arms, and eased the kitten from her body with such a tenderness and awe that the moment had creased Hannah's heart. The tiny kitten mewed and the momma cat began licking her baby. Levi had grinned a mixture of happiness and relief, and Hannah smiled through tears at the miracle of life. But had there been more of a miracle in that moment than she'd been aware of?

Now, outside the window, Levi gave Mamm a hand as she climbed into the buggy, her scarf flapping in the stiff breeze, then he offered a smile to Katie who was accompanying Mamm on her trip to the Huffstetlers'. Mary was expecting a baby later in the month, and Levi handed Katie the basket of bread loaves and a cherry pie for the Huffstetlers' growing family. Seeing the creases in Levi's face, the warmth and kindness in his gestures toward her little sister, gave Hannah a pinch in her chest.

At the last Sunday service, she'd seen Naomi Zeller offering Levi more iced tea during the noon meal. Naomi had been baptized last year and had been baking pies for the available men in their district in hopes of getting one to pay attention to her. She was already twenty-two. Could Levi be interested in Naomi? Or someone else? The pinch in Hannah's chest compressed.

As Mamm flicked the reins and the buggy went off down the lane, Levi's gaze swerved sharply past the house where Hannah watched him and then cast sideways toward the barn. Was it purposeful in its hurry, not to seek her out, not to pursue her now? That concern for Levi pressed harder and tightened into a weighty nugget of guilt.

Even though Hannah stuck to the house all morning, busying herself with chores—both regular and invented—her mind wandered toward the barn. Finally, even though she could think of plenty of excuses not to go, she carried a thermos of coffee to warm the men working in the chilly, late November weather.

The air was crisp like a red, delicious apple. A cold, hard push by the wind tried to drive her back to the house, but she angled her head down and strove forward, feeling an icy bite on her cheeks. The sky was a pale gray, the threat of rain or even snow and ice sincere. The thermos warmed her hands as she traversed the hard-packed ground, a trail worn smooth by years and generations, from Dat and his father and his father's father going about their chores and responsibilities. There was a comfort and security in walking the same, solid path. What had made her so resistant to what she'd always longed for?

"Dat?" she called inside the doorway of the barn. The scent of hay was strong and made her nose twitch. It was warm and cozy with the shuffling and other movements of sheep and horses and milk cows. "I have coffee for you."

"Your father isn't here now." Levi appeared at the opening of a stall. With his coat off and sleeves rolled up to his elbows, he looked to be hard at work and not a bit chilled. Bits of hay and straw dotted his forearms and neck.

"Oh, he left?"

Levi's gaze, the intensity of those blue eyes, made her skin tingle.

When he didn't answer but just continued to watch her, Hannah lifted the thermos toward him. "Would you like some coffee then? Or I could bring something else?"

He nodded, set the rake against the stall door, and walked toward her, his ease of movements only emphasized her nervousness. Unscrewing the thermos cap, her hand trembled, and some of the dark liquid spilled onto the dirt floor. A tiny jab in the back of her leg startled her, and she jumped. Scalding coffee slopped onto the back of her hand, and she sucked in a breath. A gangly kitten, sharp claws now retracted, skittered away.

"Are you all right, Hannah?"

She nodded. The tears that sprang to her eyes were more of embarrassment than pain from the burn. But she knew she was not all right, and it had nothing to do with the rising red welt on the back of her hand.

Levi took the thermos and set it on a hay bale nearby, and his large hands cupped hers. Warmth spread through her, and she couldn't look up at him but stared at their joined hands. Slowly, he turned hers over and rubbed his thumb around the angry red welt.

"I'm sorry, Levi."

"You're the one hurt. Let me get some salve." When he started to move away, she clutched his hand tighter and met his solid, questioning gaze.

"I am sorry, Levi, about what I said the other night."

"*Ach.*" He stepped closer, his hands folding over hers in a comforting way that made her belly quiver. "It is all right, Hannah. It was my fault. I pressed too soon. You are not ready, and maybe you will never be."

Was that a statement or a question? She searched his solid gaze and wanted to lean her head against his broad shoulder and release the tears that clogged her throat. Did he really understand? Could he?

Then he patted her hand, careful not to touch her burned flesh. "You don't have to say anything, Hannah. I will wait."

"And if I'm never ready, Levi?"

He took a long, slow breath, and on its release he cupped her jaw and turned her face toward him when she would have avoided his probing gaze. But she could not. His blue eyes magnetized her gaze. "Grief is for a season, not a lifetime."

His gaze dipped to her mouth, and her lips parted, stirring a yearning deep inside. Was he thinking of kissing her? Even after her rejection of him? And yet, that was where her thoughts lingered. Her gaze fastened onto his squared chin, solid and sure, his mouth, and the sensuous curve of his lower lip. Her heart fluttered, and her breath sounded shallow.

"Come here." He tugged on her hand and led her to the hay bale where he had set the thermos, settling her on it like a chair. He poured a cup of coffee then placed it tenderly in her hands. "I'll get you some salve for that burn."

She knew in that instant that she would not go to meet Akiva.

Chapter Thirty-one

I was angry with my friend:
I told my wrath, my wrath did end.
I was angry with my foe:
I told it not, my wrath did grow.

Akiva watched Hannah and Levi, sharing a cup of coffee, and a burning sensation spread through his limbs, firing his blood, until it throbbed in his ears, blocking out the softness of their conversation.

Whirling away, he hid in the dark recesses of the shadows and nursed his wounds—not the physical one in his chest, which had easily healed. No, this one pierced his heart like a stake through the center of his chest.

He closed his eyes and concentrated on her thoughts, but a barrier had risen between them. He gritted his teeth and fought back the anger that surged inside him. Was it love that locked him out of her head…her heart? Or was it the anger throbbing inside him?

It didn't matter. He had been patient with her. He had waited too long. But no more.

And I water'd it in fears,
Night and morning with my tears;

And I sunned it with my smiles,
And with soft deceitful wiles.

William Blake must have loved and lost too, for he knew of what he wrote. Akiva fisted his hands and pressed them against the wall of the barn until he felt the wood begin to give, the fibers popping, the wood pulp pressing into his flesh. But no pain could overtake the sting in his heart at the sound of Hannah's laughter. She was laughing with *him*. Levi. For *him*.

And it grew both day and night,
Till it bore an apple bright.
And my foe beheld its shine,
And he knew that it was mine.

With a quick, hard thrust, Akiva punched the wall, splintering the wood. The horse behind him shied and whinnied. Akiva heard her laughter die.

"What was that?" Hannah whispered, fear etched in her voice.

"Rusty," came Levi's answer. No fear was detectable in his tone, but Akiva would see to it that fear saturated his voice soon enough. Very soon. "He's been restless all morning," Levi continued. "I'll go check on him."

Akiva moved back into the shadows and crumpled in on himself, fluttering up to the rafters where he peered down at Levi walking down the pathway between the stalls and entering the one where he had been. Levi spoke soothingly to the gelding, rubbed his hands along its flanks and down to its back hoof.

"What have you done?" Levi looked at the back wall and

the hole Akiva had made. "That's a good way to hurt your-self. And end up cold for the winter."

Akiva tensed, every muscle ready to spring into action. It would be easy, so easy, to swoop down and take a bite. And he would, if Hannah weren't so close. But soon.... Soon Levi would be dead, and Hannah would be his. Forever.

And into my garden stole,
When the night had veil'd the pole;
In the morning glad I see
My foe outstretched beneath the tree.

CHAPTER THIRTY-TWO

THE WARM SCENTS OF ginger and cinnamon swirled about the bakery, stirring a hunger in the customers the way Levi seemed to affect Hannah. She barely listened to Grace yammering away about a movie she'd seen at the picture show in Lancaster, her fingers not moving half as fast as her friend's mouth as she worked up a new batch of cinnamon rolls.

Grace scooped snickerdoodle batter onto the baking sheets and kept talking. "It was a silly movie really, but the men were hot."

"Hot?"

"Oh, *ja.*" Grace's head bobbed, making the ties of her bonnet dance. "Come with us next time. Please, Hannah."

She shook her head. "It is of no interest to me."

"Then come tonight. No movie. Just fun. There will be others from outside our district. It will be fun. I promise." Her eyes were alight with promise. "Really there's no harm."

Hannah turned away and began mixing the pie filling.

"Please come."

"I will see." It was a promise she regretted, one she would not live up to. But how could she tell her friend she was afraid? Afraid of going out in the dark? Or afraid of the darkness within herself?

"Hannah," Marnie Raber called, "Beth Ann needs help at the register."

She nodded, wiping her hands on her apron, and walked out of the kitchen area and into the store, which seemed crammed with customers already holiday shopping. She wove through the crowd and display cases of Amish crafts and candies toward the front.

A cold blast of air hit her as the door opened once again, but this tourist was different than the ones bundled up, fascinated with sampling Amish treats and buying Amish crafts. This one drew attention like a siren. Heads turned in her direction. The woman wore no coat, just a simple outfit that accentuated her large bosom, tiny waist, and slim boyish hips. But something else caught Hannah's eye: the woman's sleek, black hair, long and straight, which had a sheen to it that reflected the light and shimmered down the woman's back like a dark waterfall, her glory on display for all to see. The woman raised her sunglasses to the crown of her head. Her gaze had a worldly quality, and it wasn't the heavy eye make-up she wore, but something in the depths of those black eyes.

"Welcome," Beth Ann chirped without looking up as she punched the register keys. She told the customer standing before her the amount and took his credit card. When she finished the transaction, she folded the paper bag and handed the receipt to the man. "Thanks for coming in." Her gaze shifted to Hannah then. "Can you take over for a minute, Hannah?"

"Sure." She waited for Beth Ann to scoot around the end of the counter.

Before she could step behind the register, a cool hand touched Hannah's arm and stopped her. In that instant, the whispers assaulted her, spun her thoughts around, and disoriented her. The whispers she'd heard before, but these were somehow different, indistinguishable in their many voices;

they simply called her name, murmured softly in her ears, and yet she could not understand them.

She turned toward the lady with the dark, glistening hair, who stood so close her perfume blotted out the baking scents in the store. Hannah wrinkled her nose and glanced down at the hand on her arm. The woman's fingers formed a bracelet around Hannah's wrist, her touch so cold Hannah wanted to pull away, and yet something inside warned her against it. *Of course the woman was chilled; she had been out in the freezing weather without a coat. Didn't the woman have any sense?* "May I help you?"

"Hannah?" It was an odd pronunciation of her name, the emphasis on the last instead of the first. But even more odd was how this woman knew her name. "You are Hannah, am I right?"

"Yes."

"Tell me…" This strange woman leaned even closer, her peculiar scent wrapping around Hannah like tiny threads. Not a nose-holding or stomach-writhing smell, this aroma, but light and exotic, something Hannah had never experienced before, teased and lured her closer. "You work here, is this correct?"

"Were you looking for something?"

Those dark and intense eyes studied Hannah, her gaze scanning her features, clothes, and neck. Hannah's pulse leapt. She took an automatic step back.

Then the woman touched a delicate finger to her red-tinted lips. "Yes, I believe I am. And I may have found it."

Another blast of frigid air burst through the doorway, knocking the door against the wall. Someone gasped. Someone else squealed.

"Oh my! What was that?"

The shouts swirled around Hannah, like the frigid air, but she felt trapped by the woman, frozen in her gaze, unable and unwilling to move. The woman with the never-blinking eyes didn't move either, and Hannah lost track of time and space.

She began walking toward the open door, unsure why except she felt a need to go outside. There was something there for her. Something—

"Hannah!" Suddenly Grace was beside her. "Shut the door."

Hannah blinked and stared at her friend.

Grace brushed past her, their shoulders bumping, as her friend grabbed the door and closed it firmly, making the window next to it rattle in its frame.

Hannah felt the same rattling in her own bones, where a chill settled and made her shiver. She blinked and wrenched her arm free of the woman. "Excuse me." The wind had knocked a stack of advertisements off the counter and scattered them over the floor, and she bent to pick them up. "What could have caused this?"

"Someone"—Grace stepped past Hannah and behind the register to help the next customer—"must not have closed the door good and tight."

Hannah replaced the papers next to the register and glanced around for the strange woman. But she was gone. Hannah searched the faces throughout the shop. Maybe the woman had moved behind the turn-around display. She peered this way and that, searching, eager to avoid the woman with the cold hand and even colder eyes, but the tourist must have left.

"What's wrong?" Grace asked as she finished helping a customer.

"Nothing." But Hannah's forehead folded downward

like the crimped edges of a piecrust. "Nothing. I thought…" She rubbed her forehead and shook loose the peculiar feelings. "Nothing."

———————

Hannah. The still, quiet voice called to her.

She resisted, rolled over, and buried herself further under the quilt, but she could not block out the whispered invitation.

Come to me.

"No." Her voice sounded loud in the stillness of the house. She heard the bed downstairs squeak and Dat's snoring resume. She blinked against the darkness, squeezed her eyes closed, and prayed for sleep. But it didn't come.

I'm waiting.

She threw back the covers and lit the lamp, no longer fearing if her parents woke. She wanted them to wake up, to ask her what was wrong, to quiet the voice. She put on her prayer *kapp*, opened her Bible, and started reading: *In the beginning God created the heavens and the earth.*

By the time she'd read several chapters—from the forming of the world and Adam and then Eve, to the serpent twisting God's word, to the banishment from the Garden of Eden—she realized her mind had wandered to a place she didn't even recognize. She couldn't say what she was pondering as the words lost their meaning and significance. She went back and read again—*In the beginning*—but the same thing happened. She squeezed her eyes closed and prayed, pleaded with the Lord to help her, show her the way. Only the hum of the lamp filled the room and then…

Hannah.

The voice persisted and caused her hands to shake. She

closed her Bible and set it aside on the bedside table. This time when she crawled into bed, she covered even her ears with the quilt—a poor attempt to block the voice that pestered and prodded—until she finally threw off the covers. It wasn't a conscious decision to obey the voice. It simply called and suddenly her feet were on the floor. As if moving in a dream, she dressed, extinguished the lamp, and left her room.

A three-quarter moon cast pale light over the road, and an icy wind swirled around and bit into her. Clutching her wrap, Hannah buried her hands in the wool and walked toward the farm's entrance. To her left, a crunch of gravel and dirt alerted her. She stopped, her own shoes scuffing the tiny rocks covering the road. Slowly, she turned in the direction of the noise. Was Levi following her again? She searched the shadows, tried to ignore the way her heart quickened with anticipation, and whispered, "Levi?"

Silence throbbed around her. The stillness of winter hung as brittle as an icicle. *Oh, Levi, where are you?*

Hope expanded like blown glass, growing thinner until it shattered, shards of disappointment stabbing her. She shouldn't expect him to follow her. Shouldn't want him to do so. Shouldn't want him…shouldn't want him at all. But she did.

Silence filled her ears with her own heartbeat. She must have imagined the sounds because no one was there. Nothing stirred. She was alone, all alone, with only the whisper of the wind in the dry, dormant grass for companionship. Not even God was here with her anymore—or so it seemed.

A snap of a twig on her other side made her jerk, whip around.

Akiva stood beside her. Close. Close enough to touch. Close enough to smell a sweet scent on his pale skin. In the moonlight, his eyes were shadowed, the angles of his face pronounced.

"Did I startle you?" His voice was silken and soothing to her fatigued nerves.

"A little. What are you doing here?"

"Waiting for you. You said you would meet me here, yet you never came."

"I…" She cleared her throat. "I have been busy. And then I thought you might have left."

"Without saying good-bye?" He touched her cheek. "I would not do that to you, sweet Hannah. Not after all you have done for me."

Her skin warmed beneath his gaze. She shifted her foot, felt the heavy bump of the flashlight against her hip, then looked back toward the dark house. Dat and Mamm were sleeping, as was Katie, and Levi had long since left, leaving her alone—completely alone with this man, a man who was no longer wounded and in need of help, but a man apparently strong and capable and virile. Should she be afraid of him?

He'd known Jacob. Why should she fear him? She squared her shoulders toward the farm road and moved in that direction. Akiva kept in step with her.

"Are you going back to the cemetery? Back to Jacob's grave?"

His questions pricked her skin like a sharp quilting needle. "What does it matter to you?"

"Does he speak to you?"

His question startled her. How did he know? Did he hear Jacob's voice too? But she could not confess—not to herself and certainly not to this stranger—how she'd heard a voice on the wind. "Jacob is dead."

He tilted his head, slanting a questioning gaze at her. "You believe in the spirit world, do you not? That souls

move on from this life to another, to heaven? Some people…
I'm not saying you…but some…believe spirits can return to
the living."

A quivering began in her heart. "He's dead."

But was she trying to convince Akiva or herself?

"And you're sure of that?"

His question stopped her in the middle of the road
where she faced him. Everything about this man drew her
to him—his dark, good looks, his calm demeanor, his interest, his probing and prying. And everything about him
should send her running. And yet, she stayed. "Are you
saying Jacob *isn't* dead?"

He shrugged. "Are you open to possibilities, Hannah? Or
do you see things only as you have been taught? Only as you
are allowed?"

She wrestled with his questions and could not find an answer, so she began walking again. His footsteps stayed even
with hers and she wondered why he was here, why he was
walking beside her and hounding her with questions she
couldn't answer. "I'm quite fine on my own. You do not
need to accompany me."

"Maybe you need protection."

"From what?"

He leaned closer, his eyebrow rising, his mouth tugging
into an off-kilter smile that pulled at her. "From whatever
lurks in the night."

His eyebrows arched up and down, up and down, and she
laughed at his silliness, at the notion that there was something
here in her own yard to fear. "I am not afraid."

"Even of wild animals?"

"Deers and skunks?"

"Or worse."

The image of Snowflake wavered in the back of her mind, then surged to the foreground, and a tingle of uncertainty rippled down her spine. "Is that what happened to our lamb?"

He took a step in the direction she had been heading. "How would I know?"

She drew a slow, steadying breath, then resumed her walk, matching Akiva's slower pace and their steps aligned once more with each other.

"What do you think Jacob would say to you if he could return?"

One shoulder lifted reluctantly, regretfully. "I don't know."

But she did know and a smile played about her lips.

"What?" Akiva peered into her face as if he could read her thoughts. "What do you imagine?"

"He would probably quote some poem to me."

Akiva smiled and nodded. "Ah, yes, Jacob the bard."

"Bard?"

"Poet…writer. He had an ear for words, didn't he?"

She nodded, her throat thickening, and yet at the same time something inside loosened its hold. It felt good to speak with someone who knew Jacob. His name was so rarely mentioned by those in her district. Speaking of him with Akiva brought a sense of relief. Maybe if she'd been given the opportunity to speak of him openly then she would have been able to leave him in the grave. Maybe that's all she needed to be able to move beyond his death. Speaking of him would bring healing. And then she could return to her normal life, her regular activities…maybe then she could even turn to Levi.

Akiva had stopped walking, and she turned back. A dark scowl darkened his features or maybe it was only the slant of moonlight. "Is something wrong?"

His eyes narrowed on her. "Tell me of Jacob."

She shook her head, no longer smiling. "He always surprised me."

"And you like surprises?"

She nodded. He began walking again and she joined him. Companionable silence filled the spaces between them. Her thoughts wrapped around memories of Jacob, and she found comfort, a kind of peace she hadn't known in a long while.

When Akiva took the turn into the field that led over the rise toward the cemetery, he asked, "And what do you say to him?"

Suddenly her defenses rose sharply. "That's private."

"Of course, but let me give it a try." He cleared his throat and clasped his hands behind his back. "*How do I love thee? Let me count the ways.*"

Her footsteps slowed.

"You like poetry too, don't you?"

She purposefully turned and headed back the way they had come, suddenly not wanting Akiva to accompany her to Jacob's grave. "You should go. You're well now, I reckon. There's nothing keeping you here."

"I don't know about that."

Her arms pumped with each step, and her heart raced. "Please," she tossed over her shoulder, "leave me alone."

But suddenly he was in front of her, blocking her path. His hands bracketed her shoulders, his grip strong and painful. "You should go with me tonight."

"I do not wish to go anywhere with you. I want to be alone."

"To mourn? Yes, of course. I understand." He released her but his gaze held her in place. "But…"

"But?"

"Well"—he shrugged one casual shoulder and turned

slightly away—"you might enjoy it." Then he shook his head, looked toward the ground. "Nah, you probably wouldn't."

"Why?" She took a step toward him, but his face was shrouded in darkness.

"There is a party. Amish kids know how to party better than anyone. But you're not like them."

"It's true. I do not run around as others do."

"Because you're in mourning."

"I know what I want and it's not out here, not what they are seeking."

"But is it at home? What you want isn't there either, is it? Would Jacob be glad that you have stopped living because of him?" His hands slid down her arms and he clasped her hands for only a brief second, his warmth spreading through her. Then he released her. "Or would he encourage you to live life to its fullest, the way he did?" He paused long enough for his words to sink into her. "Come with me."

"I can't." Tears pricked her eyelids.

"Why?"

But she didn't have a reason.

"You probably know many at this party," he said calmly. "Kids from the area. Friends and family. Are they so wrong for living their lives?"

She thought of the seasons, how they bled from one to the other, and eventually even though the death of winter was inevitable, new life emerging in spring. It was how it should be. But death seemed to have taken hold of her heart.

"Come on then. Just this once."

She stared at his offered hand, and her tears receded. Then slowly, cautiously, she placed her palm against his, and Akiva folded his fingers over hers. His hand was warm, almost too warm. He began walking across the field in a new direction, away from the cemetery, leading her down a path she did not know.

CHAPTER THIRTY-THREE

LEVI STRODE ACROSS THE field, his fingertips skimming the tips of toppled cornstalks, now dried and withering from the cold temperatures. Most fields had already been cleared but this one had not yet been readied for winter. A part of him felt the same as these corn stalks, crumpling under the weighty demands of patience. With long days in the field over for the season, at night he felt restless and alone, and had taken to walking, sometimes with a purpose and destination, sometimes walking aimlessly.

A wispy, filmy cloud slid across the face of the moon and diffused its light, sprinkling bits about him and creating garish shapes out of the trees ahead of him, their limbs like arms reaching out and clawing at the air. Tonight, he needed to be away from the Huffstetlers and the crushing sounds of their joyous togetherness. A happy family, they were bursting at the seams, with little ones all around and another on the way. Blessings of God were good and should be celebrated, and yet these pained Levi, causing a deep ache inside him.

Forgive me, Lord. His prayers were short these days, more direct. If God heard, He wouldn't be more inclined to listen due to the sheer quantity of words, would He?

Levi had never doubted before that the Lord God Almighty heard each and every word of his prayers—until things had started to go so wrong. But now, maybe it was not Levi who wasn't being heard. Maybe *he* was not hearing the Lord.

Should he abandon his hopes, which centered on Hannah? Could there be someone else meant for him? Another Amish woman?

But no, he knew with certainty that she was the one for him. His assurance defied explanation or logic. No one touched his heart the way Hannah did. He didn't simply want a family; he wanted a family *with her*. He wanted to love her, sleep beside her, wake up to her soft smile, see her across the table during each meal. He wanted to raise a family with her and go through the seasons of life with her by his side.

And so he would wait. And walk. And walk some more.

The cold did not bother him even though he wore his coat open, the flaps slapping back against his arms in the stiff breeze. He ducked his head down, the brim of his hat blocking the wind from his head as he plowed across the field, intent only on pushing relentless and reckless thoughts out of his head and wearing his body out so maybe tonight when he crawled into his lonely bed he could sleep.

Rest was not his goal, only blissful, unconscious sleep.

But a noise over the stomping of his boots and crackle of dead leaves slowed his steps until he stood at the edge of the field listening to a throbbing, vibrating, and scraping against his eardrums. Even though weak, it grew stronger as he moved forward again and edged toward a tree break.

A shrieking voice accented the angry, repetitive beat. *English* music, or so they called it. Jacob used to listen to such.

Was Samuel, their youngest brother, doing the same now? Losing one brother felt like a part had been ripped out of him, but losing Samuel too…Even distance, which might as well have been halfway around the world, felt like a gaping hole in his chest. Levi's heart lurched as he thought of his family hundreds of miles away in Ohio. He stopped walking and blew out a low breath, trying to rein in his emotions.

"Ah, Jacob…" His brother's actions had changed everything.

His mother wrote occasionally from Ohio where his parents had moved with Samuel after Jacob's…well, after the burial, which was more of an emotional covering up than anything. But Levi had decided against moving. He'd stayed and hoped and now waited.

Would it all be for naught?

Hannah didn't know what she wanted. She was still grieving. Would time heal the pain? It hadn't eased the ache in his own chest. Yet, he did not have to relinquish the heartache in order to embrace love. While he waited for Hannah to move beyond her grief, Levi missed his mother's cooking, her encouraging smiles, how she let him swipe a glob of batter from the bowl of her peanut butter cookies. He missed talking with his father as they worked in the carpentry shop. Would his father tell him to give up on Hannah? Or encourage him to continue to wait? And he missed Samuel, arm wrestling and racing, teaching him how to use the saw and sander, how to hitch the horse and buggy. So much he hadn't been able to show his brother who was no longer a boy but a seventeen-year-old, teetering on the brink of manhood. So much of his brother's life Levi had missed. Was Samuel growing strong in his faith? Or running around like other Amish teens? Was he questioning tradition as Jacob had? Or was he finding faith a solid foundation in which to build his life?

Through the towering trees—just a twenty-foot span where the naked limbs of hackberries, elms, and oaks filtered

out the moon's beams and during the summer constructed a dense haven for creatures both large and small—Levi
walked, determined to put the regrets and pain behind him.
His heavy, black workman's boots crunched leaves and twigs
even though he moved slowly toward the jarring music.

Then from the shadows, he peered out at a humbled
jumbled group of cars and trucks and buggies, encircling a
blazing campfire. A teen poured something into the fire and
the flames swelled and leapt toward the black sky and moon.
Laughter emerged from the swirling smoke to be overtaken
again by the pounding music.

Levi recognized some of the Amish faces—Joshua, Luke,
Zachariah—kids just a few years younger than Levi, eager
to kick off the restraints of Amish life for a temporary (or
so their parents hoped) expedition into the *English* world.
Samuel might be hanging out with friends around a fire in
Ohio right this minute, and being here with these younger
men made Levi feel somehow closer to his brother, his family. Most of these kids would return to their families and
roots and traditions. But one or two…like Jacob….

Levi shook his head. Maybe he should go to Ohio, help
Samuel, convince him of the value of living for God and
that empty pursuits lacked meaning and purpose. But he'd
learned through his experiences with Jacob, when arguments
had been prevalent at the supper table over Jacob's radical
ideas, that there was no convincing someone who didn't
want to be convinced. The righteous path, narrow and sure,
had to be found by each individual.

"Aerosmith." The male voice, low and raspy, came out
of the dark.

Levi glanced left, his eyes squinting through the stinging
smoke. "What?"

"The music," the *Englisher* said, "it's a band called Aerosmith."

Levi shrugged as his gaze focused on the shape of a man, but he could not detect the face. "It's no concern of mine."

"Do you know them? The kids here?"

"Some, *ja*."

"Are they all Amish?"

"Some." Levi thought he'd seen this *Englisher* somewhere. "Do I know you?"

The man stepped out of the shadows into a slant of pale, shimmering moonlight. "Roc Girouard."

Levi clasped the man's hand. "Levi Fisher. The wedding, *ja*? You were at Josef and Rachel's wedding."

"Inadvertently."

Watching the *Englisher* with open curiosity, Levi asked, "What are you doing here? Are you a reporter?"

"No. No worries there."

"Are you writing a book or something? There are those who come here to search out our lifestyle."

"I'm guessing those things written aren't always positive." The *Englisher* shook his head. "I know how that feels. Thing is, my English teacher back in high school told me to stick to math. Funny"—he scratched his jaw—"my math teacher told me to stick to writing. I'm not a reporter, and I'm not writing a book or trying to bring harm to your community. In fact, you might say I'm doing the opposite."

Levi set his jaw firmly. "And what might that be?"

"Let's just say I'm like a guardian angel."

Levi crossed his arms over his chest. "What do you believe you are protecting us from?"

"Did you hear about the teen girl that went missing?"

Levi gave a grim nod. "Ruby Yoder."

"She was out partying like this group of numbskulls."

"Some say she went off with her *English* boyfriend."

"Her body was found."

A cold, spiky sensation crept down Levi's spine. "Too much to drink?" He'd heard of such happening. "Or a car wreck, I reckon."

"Nope."

The cold spikes jabbed at Levi. "Sometimes that happens."

"Not this time."

Levi looked at the kids around the fire, passing around a bottle of alcohol and handing a cigarette to each other. "Drugs then?"

Roc rubbed his jaw and met Levi's questioning gaze straight on. "She was murdered. The blood drained from her body."

Every ounce of blood drained from Levi's head, and the trees around him tilted and spun. He clenched his jaw hard, biting down, as if sheer will would keep him on his feet. *Not again. Not this time.* "A-and h-how do you know this?"

Roc maintained direct eye contact as if trying to read Levi or transfer some knowledge to him. "It's in the unofficial police report. They're not saying all of that, of course, publicly. Don't want to cause a panic. Some crazy killer on the loose. Might freak people out."

"Unofficial report? How would you see this? Are you the killer?"

"I'm hunting the killer. And when I find him, then I guess I'll be guilty of that charge myself."

Levi looked heavenward. The stars were few tonight, just a smattering of them overhead. Most were hidden behind the shifting clouds. He wasn't sure what made him speak. It was not the Amish way to speak much to outsiders, but the words came anyway. "We lost a lamb the other night."

Roc stepped toward him, his focus intent, his body taut as if ready to spring to action. "How?"

"Daniel believed it was a wild animal. It happens, *ja*? Not often but still…Daniel was convinced." But Levi had known. He'd tried to tell Daniel. He'd tried, but maybe not hard enough. He rubbed the back of his neck, his thoughts turned toward a night two years ago. A night he wanted to forget. A night that seemed permanently etched in his mind. It had split his family apart. And stolen his brother, both his brothers, from him forever. "But maybe it wasn't an animal."

"Not the four-legged kind," Roc said. "Was there a wound on your lamb?"

Levi pointed to his neck with two fingers and remembered the blood-stained wooly coat. He hadn't wanted to believe it was the same as he'd seen before. He'd wanted to believe what Daniel Schmidt had said about wild animals on the prowl—anything but what Levi had seen before. But instinctively he'd known there should have been more blood. It had made him frantic…worried…but he'd convinced himself it was something else…*anything* else.

What would he have done with such knowledge anyway? Could he have told someone? Convinced anyone? Worse, could he have saved someone? He looked to Roc, desperate to remove the guilt he bore. "You think the *animal* that did this is here in Promise?"

"No doubt about it."

If the animal was here, and if that animal was what he thought, then Levi knew the reason: Hannah. And he took off running, running like a wild animal was chasing and gaining on him, as if her life depended on him. Because it just might.

CHAPTER THIRTY-FOUR

A GROWLING NOISE BLARED FROM a car's open windows, and Hannah wanted to cover her ears, block out the noise, the pounding, pounding, pounding. "What is *that*?"

Akiva stared at her as if she'd grown a beard. "You're kidding, right?" Then he pretended to strum a guitar and said, "Rock. Rock and roll, baby. Haven't you ever—"

She shook her head and listened to the jumble of notes and the screeching voice. Jacob had told her so long ago about that type of music, but she'd imagined rocking-and-rolling to be gentler than the blaring sounds pulsing and vibrating the very air around her. "Rock and roll" sounded more like a lullaby, as one might rock a sleeping baby, the chair rolling forward and back in a lazy rhythm. But this rock and roll assaulted her ears. From Akiva's expression—a nodding smile—this "music" was to be enjoyed. She did not want to insult him, and the fact that Jacob had told her about it made her somewhat curious, even though she wanted to plug her ears.

She continued walking toward the grouping of cars, their headlights blasting beams of light into the darkness, which created a glow over a small field where young men and women, Amish from what she could see, which was confirmed by the occasional buggy, were having a party. Would she know kids here from her own district?

A horn blasted. She was yanked sideways against Akiva. A burst of hot air fanned her, and Akiva turned his body, tucking Hannah securely against his side.

A sudden numbness folded over her as she stared at the truck rumbling past them. As it bumped over the field, two teens stood in the truck's back end, their arms out to their sides as they balanced and swayed and laughed. Akiva joined in their laughter and loosened his grip on her arm.

"They're truck surfing," he told her, leaning close to her ear.

She nodded, remembering Jacob had told her about truck surfing once. It had been hard to imagine then but had sounded dangerous; now it looked even more so.

"Come on." His hand linked with hers. "This should be fun."

He tugged her toward a group of trucks and cars that formed a wide circle, even a couple of buggies were included, the horses looking uneasy and out of place. Inside the disorganized formation, a bonfire raged, the flames licking the darkness and sparks popping and spraying straight up toward the canopy of stars. Recognizable faces glowed warmly—Rosalie, Elmina, Sadie—some nodded toward her, calling her name in greeting, but others were too busy drinking from brown bottles or red plastic cups to even notice her. Her friends wore *English*-styled clothes—jeans and sweaters, rather than the Amish clothes she wore. Jonathan Yoder smoked a little cigarette, the smell a sickly sweet odor that embraced her momentarily until a breeze shifted it away. But then a wave of hickory smoke hit her full in the face, burned her eyes, made her cough.

As if she were a child in need of sheltering, Akiva moved her in a different direction, his hand at her elbow, guiding her. "You okay?"

She gave a nod as her eyes quit watering, and she drew in the clean night air. Then her gaze met a familiar one.

Grace hopped off a truck's tailgate and came to give her a quick hug. "Hannah! I can't believe you're here." She gave Akiva a long, curious glance, then leaned toward Hannah. "Where did you meet him? He's hot."

Hannah's face warmed and suddenly she was too aware of Akiva's fingers wrapped about hers. He was handsome, his features smooth and refined, but they also had strength and boldness.

Ethan Ebersol walked up behind Grace and hooked his arms around her shoulders, resting his forearms across her chest. "Hannah. About time you came out."

Grace wiggled her backside against Ethan's legs and laughed.

A deep burn spread through Hannah, and her gaze kept sliding toward Ethan's hand, which seemed so casual and yet so close to Grace's breast. Didn't her friend care? Did she even notice? Grace hadn't told her she was seeing Ethan, but then Hannah had been keeping her own secrets.

"If you want a beer," Ethan said, glancing at Hannah, his eyelids heavy, "there's some in the back of my truck. And punch"—he winked—"in the jug. Help yourself." Then he gave a nod to Akiva. "Hey, I'm Ethan."

"This is"—Hannah shifted back a step—"Akiva."

"Help yourself." Ethan didn't wait for a reply but pulled Grace away, and hand-in-hand they teetered and tottered toward the darkness, laughing and grinning at each other. Grace leaned against Ethan's shoulder and lifted her lips toward his just as they disappeared outside the circle of light.

It felt strange being here, seeing her friends as she had never seen them before. Distracted by a couple dancing, their bodies so close that their shadows melded together, their pelvises moving together as one, she lost track of everything for a moment. The pulsing music, the fiery heat, the smoky odor swirled around her, filled her head and made it spin.

Then something cold was placed in her hand, and she glanced down at a brown bottle, similar to the one she'd seen others drinking. Akiva stood next to her, holding one for himself. He tapped his against hers and said something but it was impossible to hear over the loud music.

"What?"

He leaned close, his chest grazing her shoulder, and whispered, his breath bathing her ear and causing a rippling sensation low in her belly, "To you."

"Me?"

"It's a toast." He shrugged. "Don't worry about it. Just try it."

She lifted the bottle to her lips, and the liquid bubbled into her mouth. Before she could swallow, her nose wrinkled, and the bitter taste had her handing the bottle back to Akiva.

He laughed and brushed his thumb against her bottom lip. "Don't worry. It's an acquired taste."

Shaking her head, she pursed her lips, and said, "I don't believe I will ever acquire a taste for that."

Akiva laughed.

Beth Ann walked past, glanced once then twice in Hannah's direction, and veered closer. "Hannah?" She touched her hand and smiled, then her gaze shifted toward Akiva, her smile vanishing, replaced by a tiny crease between her brows. "Where's Levi?"

She felt Akiva stiffen but his features remained the same: a stony, impenetrable hardness. "How should I know? Does he usually come to these things?"

"Not anymore." Beth Ann shook her head. Even though

she wore a sweater that embraced her neck and fitted snuggly over her curves, she also wore her prayer *kapp*. "Not since he was baptized anyway."

"Hello, Beth Ann." Akiva's voice was low and enticing.

Her frown deepened. "Do I know you?"

"I know of *you*."

Hannah tipped her head in Akiva's direction, not sure how he would know her friend, but she tried to explain. "He knew Jacob."

Beth Ann's eyebrows arced upward and her eyes widened.

Suddenly the music stopped, yet Hannah's eardrums still vibrated. The fire crackled, one of the logs breaking apart, and sparks burst into the sky. Then a long, vibrating note filled the night air, and throbbing music began again as couples moved together and began rocking and rolling to the female voice that soared and crackled from the speakers.

Akiva gave both drinks to Beth Ann, then turned toward Hannah with an outstretched hand. "May I have this dance?"

Hannah stared at his hand, not knowing what to do or say, but he clasped her hand and pulled her toward those dancing. She tugged back. "I don't know how."

"I will show you."

At first, Hannah felt frozen and stiff, unable to move the right way, the way the others were able to bend and sway their bodies in rhythm to the music. She didn't know what to do, how to act or if she should run for home. She stared at her friends as they touched and moved in ways she'd never imagined. They seemed carefree and without regard to how they appeared, their arms flailing about them carelessly, their bodies gyrating against one another in unseemly ways. Smiling and kissing, they rubbed their bodies against each other, both shocking and intriguing her.

What would Mamm and Dat think? What would Bishop Stoltzfus say? Was this kind of behavior expected of her now? Not that she was ignorant of the ways of men and women but she and Jacob had never been so demonstrative in public.

Watching her friends now stirred something inside her, awakened a need, as she hadn't been touched in such an intimate way since Jacob.

Four years ago, he had led her down to the creek, and they'd been surrounded by friends and family. Everyone had waded into the cool water, laughing and splashing each other, but when it was time for lunch, the others had wandered back to the picnic area. Jacob was too busy goofing around in the creek and still had his shoes off. At sixteen, he was bold and confident. He asked Hannah to stay and walk back with him. She was only fourteen, but already she loved him with all her heart.

After he had tied his shoes, which seemed to take much longer than necessary, he pulled her down to the grass beside him. It started out with him tickling her sides, making her laugh and squirm. "Stop, Jacob." She couldn't breathe for laughing so hard. "Jacob!"

He had stilled, and she realized he was lying beside her, his leg thrown over hers, his face inches from hers. His gaze dropped to her mouth, and then she couldn't breathe because of the anticipation building in her. With aching slowness, he had lowered his mouth to hers. His kiss was gentle, sweet, and then he playfully nipped at her bottom lip, making her gasp and laugh again.

Brushing a finger against her temple, he carefully picked bits of grass out of her hair, off her cheek, drawing a line along her jaw, and caressing the length of her neck. Laughter caught in the tightening of her throat, and she felt her insides contract and then melt beneath the heat of his touch. His gaze turned serious as he studied her.

"I've wanted to do that for a long time."

She felt her breath come in short, shallow gulps. "You have?"

"Haven't you?"

She'd felt shy and awkward. "Maybe once or twice."

"Oh, *ja*? Is that all?" He traced the neckline of her plain dress, his finger slipping just inside to skim her collarbone, electrifying her nerve endings. "I've dreamt of you and me…"

"Me?"

He smiled. "*Ja.* You and me. Together." He dipped his head again and tasted of her, his lips plucking at hers, and she felt her body hum with an inner vibration. "We will be one day, you know that, don't you, Hannah?"

His words sank into her, strengthening her, and she gave a shy smile as her heart beat faster.

"*Your lips are like a scarlet ribbon; your mouth is lovely.*" He followed the curve of her bottom lip with his finger.

Feeling jittery and nervous, she had asked, "Is that a poem? Something you wrote?"

"It's from the Bible."

Her eyes widened. "Really?" Then she slapped his shoulder playfully. "You're making fun."

"No, no. Really. Song of Solomon." His mouth pulled sideways in that mischievous smile of his that curled her insides.

She had dared to reach up and touch his jaw, and she could feel the fine hairs of his beard, which had begun and which he shaved like the other unmarried men. Because he *was* a man. Her thumb copied what his had done to her mouth, tracing the full curve. "Your mouth is lovely too."

He laughed, the sound shocking her.

Had she said something stupid? Wanting to impress him,

she lifted her mouth to his and kissed him back, but this time he surprised her by deepening the kiss. Stunned, she had pulled away from him. "Jacob Fisher!"

"Have you never kissed a boy like that before?"

"N-no!"

He chuckled, and his gaze flicked over her as if he could see all the way through her, beneath her plain clothes to her very plain soul. "I like being the first. And only."

"But—"

"Everyone kisses like that. Yes, even your sister, Rachel."

She jerked back. "How would you be knowing that?"

He watched her chest rise and fall, rise and fall. "I know."

She narrowed her gaze suspiciously, jealousy flaring inside her. "Have *you* kissed my sister?"

He pressed a finger to her lips. "Hannah, I only want to be with you. Only you."

He had traced her lips with his finger again, his gaze trailing along, followed by his tongue. This time, when his lips pressed harder, she opened to him, luxuriated in the textures and sensations, relishing Jacob's undivided attention. And yet, being his sole focus unsettled her. She touched his shoulder, applied pressure, and he looked at her, his eyes dilated, heavy-lidded, and she felt giddy that she'd made him look at her in such a way.

But being out there alone with Jacob, with his body nestled against hers, doubts and concerns had bobbed to the surface of her mind. "We should go back with the others."

"We will. I promise." He'd nudged her hand over his shoulder then, and her fingers combed his thick hair. He sighed like a contented barn cat. "That feels awful good."

And so she continued, enjoying his deep moans as she ran her hands along his neck, through his hair, feeling the heat of the sun on her arms, a rippling breeze through the trees, and his hand sliding along her shoulder and down to her waist, his thumb grazing the edge of her breast, causing her stomach to flip, the pleasure silencing the warning sound in some distant corner of her mind.

Then he kissed her again, slow and easy, soft and gentle as if they had all the time they could ever want or need. His hand skimmed her waist, pressed against her hip, and she felt an awakening inside her, like a flower blooming, opening for the first time, the petals softly unfolding.

"Hannah!"

She'd heard her name as if from a faraway place, and before she could pull out of Jacob's arms, Rachel had stood over them, hands on her hips.

"Hannah Schmidt! Wait until I tell Mamm what—"

But she hadn't told Mamm. Or Dat. Or anyone else. Because Jacob had whispered to her during lunch some of the things Rachel had been doing late at night with Josef Nussbaum. And so Rachel and Hannah began covering for each other when Josef came to call or when Jacob shined a light in their bedroom window.

Stolen kisses, forbidden touches, led to fabrications and deceptions about where she'd been. And yet, Jacob made Hannah feel alive in a way she never had before. Her skin tingled with anticipation of seeing him, being near him. But during church, guilt had crept into her heart.

"Maybe we shouldn't..." she'd ventured when Jacob cupped her breast as they lay in the barn's loft.

"Why?" His focus was on her chest, and his thumb skimmed over the peak. In spite of her clothes ultimately separating her from Jacob, her body flared to life like a struck match. "We're going to be married."

"I know but…"

Arguments and excuses were like a solitary thread holding a horse in check. And so Jacob probed her boundaries, made new ones, and stirred a fire within both of them, until Hannah thought the smoldering spark within might consume her like a stack of hay bales. But propriety and God's laws were not what put a halt to their experimentation and exploration.

She was lying against Jacob in an empty stall late one night, his coat beneath them, her head resting in the cleft of his shoulder. His shirt had come lose from his trousers, the fabric wrinkled and mussed in their groping and kissing. Her apron had been removed so the pins wouldn't prick him, and her skirt had scooched up over her knees.

He began to speak in a voice that resonated through her: "*And still as ever the world went round, my mouth on her pulsing neck was found, and my breast to her beating breast was bound.*"

The words tickled her ears and she marveled at his ability to speak in ways that made her heart flutter. "Did you write that?"

He chuckled. "I wish."

She sat up, rested her forearm against his chest. "Who then?"

"D. H. Lawrence."

She laid her cheek against his breast. "Tell me more."

His hand slid along her spine and rested momentarily at the narrow indentation before slipping further downward to cup her backside. "*But firm at the centre my heart was found; Her own to my perfect Heart-beat bound, like a magnet's keeper closing the round.*"

"Hmm," she sighed as her insides melted beneath his touch and words. "Is that all?"

"For now…" He kissed the top of her head, shifting until he could press kisses against her temples and eyelids.

"Why?"

"You're too much of a distraction. I have other things in mind."

She smiled and kissed the corner of his mouth. "Like what?"

He didn't answer but let his wandering hand turn her mind in the same direction.

A shiver passed through her as his explorations moved up the inside of her knee, and she clung to his shoulders. Jacob would be her husband soon. The summer was waning and at Sunday's service the bishop had mentioned classes for the coming baptism. If they both went through it together, even though she was still only fifteen, they could be married before Christmas. And soon their bodies would be one.

His tongue explored the delicate curves of her ear, and she felt his body shift, pulling her beneath him. When his hand reached her thigh, sending swirling sensations through her abdomen and lower regions, she whispered his name on a sigh, "Jacob."

"I know." He took her hand and slid it down his abdomen.

"Did you hear what was said today?"

"About?"

"Bishop Stoltzfus."

His hand stilled. "Are you kidding?" He glanced down at her exposed leg, his tanned, work-roughened hand against the delicate whiteness of her thigh. "I was thinking of you. Of this."

"But he was talking about the upcoming baptism." Her hand curled over his shoulder. "And I thought if we both were baptized together then—"

"Not yet."

Hannah straightened her elbow and pushed him back. "Why?"

"I'm going on that trip. I told you."

"But...I thought...when we started"—her gaze shifted sideways—"seeing each other that you wouldn't want to go."

"Not go?" He sat up, shoved a hand through his hair. "Are you serious? This is what I've been planning...saving for...for years. I'm going to Newark for the poetry festival in October then to New Orleans to visit where such amazing writers have lived—Tennessee Williams, Truman Capote—"

She'd heard that all before, and she slapped her skirt back into place, covering her exposed flesh and attempting the same with her hurt feelings. "Jacob Fisher—"

"What? You've known this."

Tears sprang to her eyes then, as they did even still. Maybe it was the smoke from the bonfire. Maybe it was seeing her friends enjoying themselves the way she once had, the hope of promise in each kiss and caress. Or maybe it was because once she'd felt so alive and now she simply felt dead.

She wasn't the only person to ever lose their heart's desire. There were widows in their district, parents who had lost children, all sorts of pain and loss embedded in the hardship of life. Others seemed to carry on. Why had she found it so difficult? And yet, she wanted to feel alive again, the way she once had when sheltered in Jacob's arms.

Akiva stepped toward her, his body blocking out all the other images, even those in her head. "Are you all right?"

Staring into those dark eyes, she heard the whispers circle her and nodded.

"Have you ever danced?"

"Never."

"I will teach you."

She stepped back, uncertain and scared, her heart thundering louder than the music. "I should go home."

"If that is what you want." His gaze seemed to pierce right through her as his hand settled at her waist. "But is it? Really?"

Her insides swayed and shifted. "I'm uncomfortable."

"You have nothing to fear. I will take you home if that is what you wish. But…"

She nodded but stopped abruptly. "But what?"

"Maybe Jacob would want you to dance. Just this once."

"This is not about Jacob." And yet she knew it was.

"Then your faith? How can you commit to your faith when you are blind to what else is in the world? Are they really doing something so wrong here? Or is it just that you have never experienced these things?"

"Drinking and smoking…it is not allowed."

"What does it say in the Bible? Does it say not to drink? It says not to get drunk. You have not experienced many things, sweet Hannah. Hidden things. Secret things. The mysteries of life." He touched her cheek, sliding his finger along her skin, leaving a trail of heat. "What would you have me do?"

Only one word came to mind, and it came out as a hoarse whisper. "Stay."

A hint of a smile teased the corner of his mouth and her heart gave an extra beat. "Good. Now"—he braced his hands on her shoulders and leaned down to look directly into her eyes. His were dark, black as rich soil, and flickered back and forth as they studied and tried to read her every thought— "close your eyes." At her hesitation, his smile broadened. "Do it."

She did, and her world went dark, awakening her other senses. The steady, thrumming beat pulsed around them. Warming one side of her, the fire crackled. The cold night air caressed her exposed cheeks and neck and wrists. She trembled, but not from cold or fear but from awareness… his closeness. His scent shrouded her, seeming to touch her, cover her, and yet not. It was like no other scent she'd ever known, overwhelming and alluring, just out of bounds and yet all around her—teasing, tempting, enticing.

Then he touched her, his hands warm on her shoulders. He placed a slight amount of pressure with one hand then the other, her body swayed right then left and back and forth, a wavelike action.

"Just relax," he spoke, his voice bathing her ear. "Feel the music flow over you. Let it tell you what to do, how to move." His hands slid slowly down her arms to her stiff fingers, and he gave them a gentle shake, loosening her limbs, and then he pulled her hands outward, lifting up her arms. She squeezed her eyes closed, unwilling to look at him or anyone else who might see her foolishness. Feeling exposed, she focused on the strength in his touch, the smell of the fire, the wide expanse of sky above them. Suddenly, she felt open and free.

Then his hands embraced her waist and her eyes automatically opened. She lowered her arms, only to have them rest on Akiva's shoulders because he was standing so close. So close, his breath washed over her. So close, his chest met hers. So close, his kiss was but a breath away.

She attempted a step back, but he held her fast, his arms folding around her, gentle yet solid. "Don't be afraid, sweet Hannah. I will not harm you. Let me guide you."

CHAPTER THIRTY-FIVE

ROC LEFT HIS CAR back on Straight Edge Road and ran, following after the quiet but anxious, and now obviously panicked, Amish man, Levi Fisher.

Something made the younger man take off like a croc out of the swamp, and Roc had to find out what spooked him.

This man, Levi, had stamina. Roc's side clamped down and his lungs burned but he kept going, keeping an eye on Levi who was a good twenty, okay fifty, feet ahead. The distance between them kept lengthening. Roc blamed it on the uneven ground, which seemed to reach out and grab at his feet, tripping and trapping him with snaking roots and deep ruts as they ran through a wooded area to an open field, then alongside a paved road to a dirt one, at the end of which they came to an open gate. Levi stopped and Roc limped up behind him. Beyond the gate in the stillness of the moonlight, a farmhouse loomed up out of the flat ground. All appeared dark and quiet. Was it an illusion?

Levi drew a couple of deep breaths, all the while training his gaze on that house, not seeming to care or notice that Roc had caught up to him. Then more cautiously, less recklessly, Levi moved forward, this time veering off the direct path, parallel to the road and yet set deep in the shadows, at a slower pace that gave Roc time to regain his breath and keep up. When they were opposite the side of the house,

Levi came to another stop. This time, his breathing was labored, his breath frosting the air in puffs like exhaust fumes. The place looked different at night, spookier, but Roc had been here.

"This the Schmidt farm?"

With his hat tilted far back on his head, Levi gave a quick nod.

"There someone here that you're worried about?"

He gave no response this time. Roc looked from Levi to the house and then back. "Look, man, if there is something going on here, you should tell me. Maybe I can help. Do you know something about the death of that Amish gal?"

"No." His word was merely a whisper.

Frustrated that he ran all this way for a lovesick fool, he grabbed Levi's shoulder and shoved him against the barn wall. Levi blinked as if coming out of a dream. "What do you know? Tell me about that animal of yours that died? Where is it?"

"I buried it."

"But where did it die?"

"The barn."

"Will you show me?"

His shoulders sagging slightly, Levi nodded and waited for Roc to release him, then walked toward the end of the barn. He unbolted the door and slid it sideways. The smell of hay and dung immediately hit Roc, and he heard the snuffling and shifting of animals inside, cozy and comfortable in the quiet warmth. Levi entered first, and Roc felt his Glock against his side, steady and solid.

A flair of light brought a warm glow. Levi held a lantern up, and without a word he walked down a passageway between two rows of stalls. Roc followed a few paces behind, peering over each doorway into the stalls, unsure if he was looking for something that might jump out at them or just curious about the different animals Schmidt kept. Slow, blinking eyes stared back at him—horses and cows, sheep and pigs. Some stood, others slept on their sides without a care.

It was at the end of the row that Levi stopped and held the lantern high to illuminate the stall. No animal was housed here. At least not anymore.

"This where you found it?"

Levi's face looked grim in the shifting light, the corners of his mouth pinched. "A young lamb."

Roc stepped into the stall and reached for the lantern. "Do you mind?"

Levi handed him the lantern and stepped back.

"Has the hay been changed?"

"*Ja.* Of course."

Roc frowned. "Did it look like there was a struggle?"

Levi's gaze shifted sideways as if he searched his mind for a picture of what he had found that day. Or was he uncomfortable with the topic? "Not at all. No struggle. At first, I thought the lamb had simply died in its sleep. But then I saw the blood on its neck."

"No other wound?"

"No."

Roc peered at the baseboards, shoved aside clumps of hay with the toe of his shoe. "The animal that killed your lamb didn't attempt to eat it?"

"No."

"Do you think you scared the animal away by coming into the barn?"

Again, Levi paused, thought back, and shook his head.

"No. I didn't hear any unusual sounds that morning. Other than Ash, one of the mares, was a bit skittish, is all. The lamb had been dead a while."

Roc turned back toward Levi. "So why would a wild animal kill and not eat its kill?"

Levi shrugged one shoulder, but it was his eyes that shifted again and told Roc what he needed to know.

Giving the man a bit of space, Roc knelt down and searched beneath some hay, but there was nothing to see or find but dirt beneath. What Roc needed was inside Levi. He knew something. He knew more than he wanted to tell.

"An Amish girl died a horrible death. I've only seen something like that back in New Orleans." He looked up at Levi who watched him. Slowly, Roc got to his feet, walked back to Levi, and handed him the lantern. "Maybe the wild animal got exactly what it wanted."

"What do you mean?"

"The animal that killed your lamb."

"Not mine. Daniel Schmidt's."

"Sure. Yeah. All right. Maybe what it wanted was its blood."

Levi blanched, his skin turning white in splotches, then the rest of the color drained from his face. But that stoic, strong face remained neutral.

"Maybe it's the kind of animal that feeds on blood. Have you heard of that?" Roc calculated the Amish man's facial muscles, noting each, measuring and gauging. Not one move, blink, or twitch; he was stony in his response. And yet his pale skin was a dead giveaway.

CHAPTER THIRTY-SIX

AKIVA STARED AT HANNAH'S luminous eyes, full of hope and possibilities, and traced the contours of her upturned face—beautiful, innocent, and trusting—following the delicate moonlight as it illuminated her tender skin. For so long he'd dreamt of this moment, to be close to her again, to hold her, to touch her. His hand shook with emotion and the willpower to control himself. *Not now. Not yet.*

He would not take her without her consent.

But she would be willing.

He would make sure of that.

Love, so said Emily Dickinson, *is anterior to life*. Akiva had loved Hannah for so long he couldn't remember when he had not felt his heart kick up a notch at her presence, had not searched her out in a crowd. It was always as if his heart echoed her beat. Or maybe the other way around. He was never quite sure.

It is all right, he whispered into her mind. *This is what you want. What you need.*

He lowered his mouth, aiming for hers, hovering, anticipating, and yet holding back. Her lips parted only a fraction but enough to prove her willingness, her acceptance, her hunger for what she too had been missing. But again, he hesitated, teasing her with his breath. She watched, waited… hoped? It was all there in her brown eyes. His hands at her waist pulled her toward him and he began to move his hips against hers, slowly in the rhythm of the music that pulsed the air around them.

As the poet extraordinaire wrote: *love is posterior to death*. And he could surely testify to that because his love had never abated, never dimmed, never faded. If anything, it burned more fiercely and threatened to overpower him.

> *Initial of creation, and*
> *The exponent of breath*.

With that one thought, he blocked out everything around them, covered her mouth with his, and kissed her the way he'd dreamt for years, their flesh melding, their breath mingling, their minds merging, and then he drew her breath right out of her, as if it contained her essence, and filled his lungs with her until his heart thudded and his resolve to wait swayed. She arched her neck, gave him access. Kissing along her jawline, he pressed his mouth to that sensitive flesh and felt her pulse fluttering beneath his lips. He could almost taste the sweet blood coursing through her veins, and his teeth glided over the surface of her skin, teasing her and himself, and she shuddered with a need that reflected his own.

It was then he pulled away, careful not to overindulge his senses and push beyond the extent of his restraint. He'd lost control before, with others who had meant nothing to him, others who had reminded him of Hannah but paled in comparison, but he would not take that chance with Hannah.

In New Orleans, he'd learned hospitals had what he needed—blood—in ample supply. But then he'd seen a woman one night…she'd looked so much like Hannah, with her hair pulled back, her features clean and pure, without all that stuff other women wore, and longing welled up inside him like a tsunami and overwhelmed him. He'd wanted to simply speak to her, hear her voice, be near her…but then another desire kicked in…overpowered him.

It had taken almost two years to gain a modicum of control, and then he'd seen an Amish woman walking along a deserted street. She'd twirled her prayer *kapp* carelessly as if it meant nothing. He'd attempted changing her, to see if he could, if it was truly possible, the way he would eventually change Hannah, but the woman had fought and a deeper instinct had clicked into full throttle.

But Hannah wouldn't fight. She would want this new life. She would want him.

Reaching for her hand, he twirled her beneath his arm, and her eyes widened with wonder and shock as he coaxed laughter out of her. The song on somebody's CD changer switched to something upbeat, but all he could see or hear was Hannah, twirling and dancing with him, moving her hips, her arms, her feet, her laughter ringing out into the night.

He showed her different dance moves, how they "got down" in New Orleans, some sleazy but exhilarating salsa and even a slow, unsteady waltz. He took her from fast to slow, smooth to frenzied, sensual to erotic. Her movements at first were stiff and jerky but endearing and sweet, and slowly, as the songs shifted from fast to slow again, she loosened up and began to relax, her body moving in a more womanly way.

When she became breathless, he led her away from the other dancers. He had taught her to follow him, and she did so effortlessly now. Akiva handed her a red plastic cup of punch and this time she drank more readily, thirstily gulping down the liquid, a sweeter concoction that made the alcohol more palatable but also more potent. Her eyes became dazed, and when she smiled at him, not as shy as before and now slightly lopsided, he became aware once more of everything around them, the glittering stars, the others dancing, some watching them, the swelling music, the scattered laughter.

"Come on." He clasped her hand in his and led her out of the circle of cars and light, passing other couples making out and groping in the back seats of cars and inside buggies, and into the darkness.

"Where are we going?" She clung to his hand as if it was the only thing she knew or trusted.

With a confident smile, he walked into the night with her by his side, swinging their joined hands between them. She giggled, and he laughed with her—the first carefree moment he'd had in ages. He kept walking beyond the beat of the music.

He should have come for her sooner. Actually, he never should have left. But regrets were useless. He would make the best of what they now had, with forever stretched out before them like a rainbow of possibilities.

When they reached a safe distance, far from the others, he pulled her against him and kissed her again, whispering into her mind, and tasting the sweet alcoholic brew on her tongue. She held on to him as if her world was spinning out from under her.

Eventually, she placed an unsteady hand against his chest, and he drew back immediately.

A frown settled between her brows. "Are you all right? Did I hurt your wound?"

"My…?" He tucked her hand in his and then flattened it against his chest. *So like her to be thinking of another's pain or need.* "No, sweet Hannah. I am fine. Come on."

"Don't you want to dance some more?"

"Later." He led her down a hill toward a forest, their hands linked, and her footsteps stayed close behind his. The music from the party had long since faded into the distance and the sounds of the woods took over, with the crackling of branches under foot and the fluttering and crunching of fallen leaves.

He took her to a secluded spot along a creek bank, near the spot where he had kissed her in another life. The water flowed in a concerto of rippling notes and trills, a composition no orchestra or maestro could emulate. The moon offered pale light to the sloping ground and wooded area, and seemed to safeguard them. Hannah held on to his hand as if reluctant to let go and gazed up at him.

"You don't have to be afraid," he said, feeling uncertain in their newfound relationship, wanting to tell her who he was and yet feeling fear hold him back. "I will always protect you." He looked deep into her glazed eyes. Maybe with her senses slightly dulled by the alcoholic punch he could tell her and she could more easily accept him. Maybe she would agree to be with him—tonight—and their forever could finally begin. Now. Tonight.

"I'm not afraid." She glanced down at the red cup in one hand, sipped from it, and then offered it to him. "Not with you here."

He placed it beside a nearby rock. When he turned back to her, she stared at him with an odd look, a mixture of timidity and boldness, her hands twisting together.

"Akiva," she bit her lip, "did I…" she hesitated, "do it wrong?"

Her question jarred him. He leaned toward her, thinking she meant the kiss and how he'd prove to her she was mistaken. "Do what?"

"Dancing. I just thought since maybe you didn't want others to see…"

He smiled. "Did you enjoy it?"

A blush brightened her cheeks. "Yes."

"Then you did it perfectly." He took her hand in his again. "And I brought you here because I didn't want to share you with anyone else."

She smiled back at him a bit crookedly and then glanced around as if just now taking in the sparse wintry scenery and seclusion of the place. "Where are we?"

"Does it matter?"

Looking at him, a sheen to her brown eyes, she shook her head, then moved toward the rock but tripped. Akiva lunged forward and caught her against his chest before she could fall.

"Are you okay?"

She laughed, twirled away from him, and plopped down on the ground with a solid *whump*. After a moment, she gathered her skirts around her, smoothed the material over her legs. "I'm fine. *Gut*." And she laughed again.

Akiva settled beside her and stretched out his legs toward the creek. "This is better. Quieter."

"I think I bruised my—" She leaned toward him and rubbed her backside.

Smiling, he asked, "Want me to check it for you?"

She jerked back the other way. "No!" But she was laughing then eyeing him warily. "You wouldn't, would you?"

"Not unless you wanted…or needed me to. I'll never do anything against your will, Hannah. There may be a lot of things you could say about me, but I will be true to my word. Understand?"

She nodded, searched his face as if looking for something…or someone. "You met Jacob in New Orleans?"

A mixture of emotions unsettled him. Was he jealous of himself? Or did he only want her to love this new creature he had become. But wasn't he one and the same? Sometimes he wasn't sure, and he leaned back into the shadows. "Yes."

"Does it hurt you when I talk about him?"

"It is one reason I am here." He wanted to tell her now that it was him—Jacob—in the flesh. But how? Did she already sense the connection? Could she accept the truth?

"Why were you there?" she asked before he could figure out how to tell her Jacob was alive and sitting beside her. "Were you on *rumschpringe* too?"

He chuckled and rubbed his jaw. "You might say that."

"You are Amish then." She seemed to like that about him.

"I was never baptized."

"But you were raised with the Amish?"

"One thing I've learned"—he stared into the dark waters rolling over stones—"our upbringing can't save us or protect us, Hannah."

She blinked as if taking his words into herself. "What did you two do in New Orleans? Party like this?"

He laughed outright. "The parties there make this"—he waved his arm behind them—"look tame. We drank until we were sick. We took crank. Smoked—"

"What's that? What did you say? Crank?"

"A drug."

"And were there…" She hesitated, suddenly looking vulnerable as she looked down at her fingers pinching together. "Were there girls with you?"

Ah jealousy, a byproduct of love. He approached the subject carefully. "Of course." He shrugged as if they were of no importance, because they had not been. Being with any other girl was not the same as being near Hannah. Sex was simply sex, a physical need to be satisfied, like hunger or sleep, nothing more, nothing less. He had a similar need now, a raw hunger, but he wouldn't satisfy it at Hannah's sacrifice. "Girls came to New Orleans with Jacob from this area. You may know some."

Shifting, Hannah straightened her skirt. "Yes, my sister, Rachel…"

"But that is not what you are asking, is it?

She looked at him then, fear and hope mingling in those large, round eyes. Moonlight shimmered in their depths as tears welled up.

"You want to know if Jacob was with another."

"Yes." Her reply was a mere breath. Was she more afraid to know or to hope?

"He loved you, Hannah. Only you."

Her shoulders sagged with relief and she gave him a watery smile. "Thank you."

"Never doubt that."

She tilted her head back, bracing her hands behind her, and one elbow dipped, then straightened abruptly, making her seem a bit unsteady. "Rachel was friends with Jacob. But they were just friends. Nothing more." Hannah rolled her lips inward then slowly relaxed again. "Rachel married a few weeks ago."

Had the doubt of Jacob and Rachel's relationship always stood between sisters? Akiva tilted his head back and studied the stars, picked out Andromeda and Cassiopeia. "Josef, right? Is that who she married?"

"Yes! How did you…?"

"She loved him even then."

Relief washed over Hannah's face, suffused color beneath her skin, brightening her eyes. "They're living with Josef's

family now, not far, but I miss her. I worried she might...
well, that she and Jacob might have...because she was older
than me." She blinked several times and tried to focus on
Akiva, but her gaze swayed as if he kept moving when he
was sitting still. "So you know Rachel...or she knows you.
Then I could—"

"Do you remember?" Akiva interrupted her, his gaze
now studying her rather than the heavenly bodies. To him,
she was heaven, her thick hair, her sparkling eyes—all the
promises of heaven wrapped in woman's body. But he didn't
want to talk about Rachel or anyone else.

"Remember what?"

He leaned close, and her wide eyes loomed before him.
His mouth was but a breath from hers when he whispered,
"When you first knew you loved Jacob?"

Emotions flashed over her features, easy to read, but it
was when they settled on despair that he struggled. At times
it was hard to remember that she was thinking of him, or
who he used to be. He felt eternally divided from that boy
that he once was. Her love for Jacob clouded his mind with
red rage and pulsing jealousy. Could she ever see Jacob inside
of him, find who he used to be and bring out that piece she
adored? Could she ever make the connection that he was
Jacob? Here? Now? In the flesh?

She swallowed hard, the muscles in her throat contracting
and drawing his attention to her pulse there, and then she
nodded. "Of course I remember."

Akiva laid back and rested his head in the cradle of his
arms. If his own despair was as telling as hers, he wanted to
hide it. Had he forgotten who he really was? What he was?
Somewhere over the past two years...too much had happened...he'd lost pieces of himself. But he was still the same

deep down inside. Wasn't he? He was. He knew it. *I am Jacob. I am Jacob. I am Jacob.*

Maybe she could help him find himself again. Maybe if he knew what it was she had loved about him, he could find that key part of himself, force it to the surface, and free himself, so she could see the truth and know that he really hadn't changed at all. And she would love him—Akiva. "What made you love Jacob so much?"

Hannah pulled her legs to her chest and rested her cheek on the tops of her knees. A wispy smile played about her lips. "Everything."

He made a face, rolling his eyes at the insincerity of that statement. No one loved everything about another. Not everything. It was not possible.

"Why that face?" she asked.

"*Everything*? Really?" So he tested his theory. "Did you know he snored?"

She giggled, hiding her face for a moment, then looking back at him, the corners of her mouth pinched in suppressing more laughter. "So does my father. Hearing his snores deep in the night makes me feel safe…protected."

"Did you know—"

"Jacob worked hard," she interrupted him. "But he could have fun too. He made even chores fun." Her gaze shifted away from Akiva. "He worked for my father, the way Levi does now. And there was a part of him that loved things not a part of our world."

Levi. The name conjured up dark emotions inside Akiva. When Hannah's head lifted and she looked back to him, he realized he had spoken the name aloud. With disdain.

The corners of her eyes tilted. "Do you know Levi?"

"We've met." His mouth tightened at the admission.

"He's a good man."

He narrowed his gaze and straightened. "Do you love him too?"

She looked away again, as if searching for an answer in the shadows and corners of her heart. Akiva cursed himself for asking the question. *Quit speaking of Levi!* His hands closed into fists and he braced them against the ground.

"Jacob and Levi are"—she hesitated, her voice small and uncertain—"were brothers."

It was not a denial, not the answer he wanted. Did their sibling relationship make it easier to love both or was it a stumbling block? His jaw pulsed with anger, jealousy, resentment. Someday soon, Levi would only be a distant memory. *Focus on Jacob. Keep her thoughts on Jacob. Only Jacob.* "You loved Jacob's curiosity?"

Her features rearranged immediately into a half-smile, and then she glanced around as if to see if anyone was near and listening. "Jacob loved language. Words. He loved poetry. He discovered Elizabeth Barrett Browning's writing and introduced it to me. I didn't understand all of the words but they sounded so beautiful. So achingly sweet. Especially when he read them to me."

Of course. Now he understood. She wanted to be wooed. And he was a master. Wasn't that what he did? Hunting. Stalking. Studying. Attracting. Courting. Alluring. Charming. Trapping. "So Jacob was a romantic, eh?"

"Oh yes." Her expression softened, but then she pressed her hand to her mouth.

Akiva tensed. Had he upset her? "What's wrong?"

A small belch escaped her lips, and a wry smile tugged at his. "I think I might be ill."

"It's the punch." He took a handkerchief from his pocket,

rinsed it in the cold creek water, and wrung it out. He helped her lie down, resting her head in his lap. As she closed her eyes, he smoothed the rag across her forehead. "I will care for you."

He caressed the side of her cheek, angling down to feel the smooth skin along her neck, and his hand rested there as he counted the beats, felt them pulse deep within himself. Serving as a distraction as much as a method of speaking to Hannah's heart, he spoke the words of the master, William Shakespeare:

> *"That time of year thou may'st in me behold*
> *When yellow leaves, or none, or few, do hang*
> *Upon those boughs which shake against the cold,*
> *Bare ruin'd choirs, where late the sweet birds sang:*

> *In me thou see'st the twilight of such day*
> *As after sunset fadeth in the west,*
> *Which by-and-by black night doth take away,*
> *Death's second self, that seals up all in rest:*

> *In me thou see'st the glowing of such fire*
> *That on the ashes of his youth doth lie,*
> *As the death-bed whereon it must expire,*
> *Consum'd with that which it was nourish'd by:*

> *—This thou perceiv'st, which makes thy love more*
> *strong,*
> *To love that well which thou must leave ere long."*

Chapter Thirty-seven

Levi paced the side of the barn, his gaze fastened on Hannah's window. He hadn't answered Roc Girouard's questions, and the man had finally left. But the peace Levi had hoped for did not come, and he suspected Roc would be back with more questions or answers Levi did not want. Uneasiness twisted his gut—not at the prospect of a return visit, but for the worry that he'd made a mistake. Should he have spoken of his suspicions about Jacob? His father had warned him to never tell anyone. But had his tight-lipped refusal to admit the truth put Hannah in jeopardy?

And where was she now? Sleeping in her bed? Or was she at the cemetery? He had no choice but to find out, to make sure she was safe.

Since he couldn't barge in and wake her entire family, he made the long walk to the cemetery, his concerns quickening his steps. When he reached the fence surrounding the graves, he stood as still as one of the grave markers and peered into the murky darkness. A watery light from the pale moon bathed the area, and he could see the field was empty of all but stones of remembrance. Many of these Amish folks he never knew, but some of the names were relatives or friends of his grandparents and parents. There was a small stone for a baby born to the Huffstetlers three years back. Ephraim's wife, Ruth, was in a far corner, a space beside her for her husband's eventual place. And just beyond was Jacob's grave.

With a weary heaviness from carrying this burden for so long, Levi climbed the fence as he'd seen Hannah do, and it wobbled beneath him. Then he stood at the foot of his brother's grave, read Jacob's name carved into the stone. Where once sadness occupied his heart at the loss of his brother, now fear took its place. Fear and anger.

"Jacob." His voice carried on the still night air. There was no wind. No sound. A deep silence pervaded the field, as if held in by the rickety fence surrounding the headstones. "Jacob!" Silence answered him. "Are you here now? Are *you*?"

A soft breeze stirred, brushed the hair back from Levi's forehead and pushed it up toward the brim of his hat. It was cold, deathly cold, and the chill crept into his bones as he stood there, waiting, watching, wondering. *Levi,* the wind seemed to whisper. He glared down at his brother's name and felt those emotions he'd tried so hard to pluck out of his heart pop up like bristly weeds.

His hands fisted. "Come face me, Jacob."

Levi was not afraid of his brother or of what he had become. His only fear was for Hannah. Because if Jacob were to return, it would be for the one thing he'd claimed to love.

Levi snorted. *What kind of love was that? Did Jacob really know what love was? Or how to love?* Levi doubted it. Jacob loved only himself. If he had truly loved Hannah, he never would have left her to chase after some nonsense.

Angry at himself for the toxic emotions cropping up and taking over his peace of mind, Levi turned away from the grave. How many times had Hannah come here? Should he have told her there wasn't a body in that grave? But how could he have explained what had happened when Levi couldn't fully understand it himself?

That long ago morning, when Levi and his father found Jacob crouched over a calf, his mouth on its neck, Jacob had looked up at them, blood covering his lips and teeth, his shirt and hands. But it was his eyes; his eyes had no longer been his brother's. They had become black as sin.

There had been a woman with Jacob, a woman with the same dark eyes. She had stalked toward Levi, a threatening gleam in her gaze that seemed to devour him, but Jacob had stepped between them. Together, they had vanished. Disappeared. In a blink. As if they had never existed.

Jonas Fisher's knees had buckled beneath him. He'd knelt on the ground and wept, unable to comprehend what had happened, unable to speak anything but one word over and over. With tears streaming down his rugged cheeks, he'd repeated: abomination.

Numb and pained at the same time, as if a fist had slammed into his gut, the shock stunning him and pushing through him, Levi had stood beside his father and stared at the bloody calf. Scripture verses he'd known all his life fractured apart, splintered, and pierced his heart. Everything he'd ever known and believed had been shattered. These things did not exist. Except they did. What was real? What wasn't?

When the red light of dawn first touched the horizon, his father pulled himself together. His face still wet and red, he clasped his hand on Levi's arm. "I need your help, son."

Levi nodded. This he knew how to do. This he could process. And he kept nodding as his father instructed him to go to the cemetery and begin digging a grave, even though that wasn't usually what happened when a family member died. Jonas Fisher's plan was simple though: they would *say*

Jacob had died. For he had in a way. Hadn't he? But the whole time his father had uttered instructions, Levi thought, *How can we lie? How can we lie to our family and friends, to the bishops, to the community that has been good and kind and trusting all these years?*

When his father finished speaking, Levi said, "I cannot lie, Pop."

"It is the only answer. It is the only way." His father's ravaged face, still tear streaked, still shocked from what they had seen, from the loss of his son and all he held dear, twisted Levi's insides.

He'd never gone against his father. How could he? So he had followed his father into a dark secret, the lie wrapping around Levi's heart and constricting it. After they had buried the calf in Jacob's grave and ordered a stone, his father had told the family to start packing. "I cannot stay here, buried in my grief. We will move to Ohio. We will start anew."

Levi had helped his mother and younger brother, Samuel. Neither of them understood or knew the truth. They believed the lie: that Jacob had an accident with the saw in the carpentry shop. They saw the devastation in Jonas's face, in his brokenness, and they believed. The ropes of deceit tightened around Levi, chafing him whether he spoke or not.

When the moving van arrived, Levi approached his father. "Pop, I'm not going."

"Not going where?"

"To Ohio. This is my home. This is where I will stay."

"If anyone suspects or if the truth is ever known about…" His father's face contorted as he wrestled with saying his middle son's name, but he finally offered a defeated shrug. "…then you will be shunned."

Levi shook his head. "That is not my sin. But is Jacob's worse than our lying?"

But he held back his other reasons for not leaving. Pop thought moving would make the lie easier, but Levi knew it would be worse because he'd face his mother and brother every day. The lie would consume them and rip their family apart. But the final piece of his reasoning, Levi kept buried inside his heart, because that reason had been Hannah. And he would guard and protect her from all of that ugliness and sin. He would keep her safe.

His father's jaw had set and his eyes had turned hard as flint. "Then stay. You are a man now. It is your decision. *But*"—his voice deepened—"I forbid you to speak of this."

Those were the last words his father spoke to him.

And so Levi had pretended and carried on the lie. It was easier than accepting the grief of a life gone wrong, a life lost. How could he have explained what happened to Jacob anyway? No one would have believed him.

Still, there had been rumors, questions whispered about the community. The bishops had come to visit with Levi, and he explained Pop's devastation at the loss of his son. The older men had solemnly nodded and gone away. For a while, the whispering had persisted but Levi's stoic silence calmed the questions, and life went on as it always had, the seasons fading one into another.

Now, two years since digging his brother's grave, Levi walked away from the cemetery as if he could distance himself from his own lies and deceit. He returned to the Schmidt farm some time after midnight and made a pallet on the floor in the barn. He tried to sleep for a short while, but he could not, tossing and turning on the hard ground. When Toby came into the barn with his thumping tail and peered at him with those sad, dark eyes, Levi finally rose and began the chores for the day.

And then he saw Hannah. She was alone as she walked the lane toward the house. Her footsteps were slow yet steady. She did not look afraid or even sad, but something about her countenance had changed. A smile curved her lips, and fear nettled into Levi's belly.

She disappeared into the house as if she glided over the path. Levi tried to wrestle his fear into submission. She was safe. That was *all* that mattered.

Yet her half smile haunted him. It was the kind of smile every man dreamed of giving to the woman of his choosing. Jealousy injected itself into his blood and infected him with an all-consuming illness. It was all Levi could think of. *Who had made her smile?*

CHAPTER THIRTY-EIGHT

I T WAS THE GIRL.

The vampire had come for the girl, Hannah. Roc figured it out from Levi's behavior, running from the party to the Schmidt farm, and from talking to the Amish teens once he'd plied them with liberal amounts of beer. Then they remembered how Levi's brother died under bizarre circumstances.

"They buried him." Joshua stretched out on the ground.

"Isn't that how it's usually done?" Roc had asked as the fire crackled behind him. "Bury the dead? Even in Promise?"

Luke shook his head. "Not before the community even knows."

"Or the body is embalmed," Zachariah finished.

Roc leaned forward and looked at each of the boys. "So when was this?"

Caleb yawned. "About a year ago."

Adam kicked Caleb's foot. "More like two."

"Were the cops...police called?" Roc asked.

The boys looked at him. Caleb shook his head and said, "Why would we do that?"

"Because, what if a crime had been committed?"

Adam crossed his arms over his chest. "No *English* crime. It was an accident. Still, very odd."

Zachariah nodded. "Lots of rumors went round the district."

"What did Levi say?"

"Nothin'." Luke swigged his beer. "Not even to the elders. My pop was one that went and spoke to Levi, questioned him. Because, see, Levi's family moved off right after Jacob died. Just up and moved."

"Which don't happen much 'round here," Joshua added.

Roc looked back to Luke. "And what did Levi say?"

"Just that there was an accident with one of the saws. Jacob died. And his folks were so torn up over it that they moved."

Roc did a few algebraic problems in his head, adding in a few variables, and came up with his best guess, which brought him back to the Schmidt farm.

From the road, he adjusted his binoculars and watched Hannah hang laundry on the line. She wasn't really a girl—by the looks of her, more woman than anything else—and still she struck Roc as not much more than a child. Maybe it was the innocence that seemed wrapped around these Amish that made them appear so young when they were fully grown.

She was pretty, though not in the worldly way Roc had become accustomed to in New Orleans. With her hair pulled back in that predictable bun, he could see the shape of her face, framed by her prayer *kapp*, both resembling a heart. Her eyes were large and luminous. Even beneath that shapeless dress and apron that looked like every other Amish woman, her womanly shape couldn't be hidden. Even from a distance, he could see that any man, Amish or *English*, would find her attractive.

It was easy to see Levi loved her in the same gut-wrenching, head-scrambling way that had tormented Roc since the day he'd met Emma, which felt like a lifetime removed from where he was today. He'd had eight years with her, and nearly two without—such a short time to live a lifetime in moments of tenderness and passion, and such a long time in agony. Emma's blue eyes could flash with irritation or soften with gentleness. "Roc," she'd say, then hum the Bob Seger tune, which always made him smile. But she'd been his rock, what he'd leaned on during their marriage, and he'd sunk hard and fast the day she died.

Watching Levi now, purpose and desperation in each of his steps as he walked from house to barn, Roc pitied him. Because the woman Levi loved was wanted, desired, craved by an animal. Because Levi might lose his woman before he ever had any time with her at all. Because his woman was going to force him to make a difficult choice.

Not a choice Roc would find difficult. But an Amish man? A man who believed in peace and love? Roc had learned killing was often necessary. Would Levi learn the same lesson? Or would he let Hannah go? And would Roc have to kill her too, to keep her from becoming one of *them*?

CHAPTER THIRTY-NINE

AKIVA USED TO STALK his prey late at night in a random, haphazard manner.

But now, as soon as the sun set, he began. During the day, he chose his prey, learned their habits and ways, their simple routines, so when he was ready to strike, it proved to be a simple, effortless kill.

When he first experienced the change, he fed himself infrequently, holding out, praying he wouldn't need to feed, but the hunger always overwhelmed him, and then he acted recklessly, foolishly. Then he went through a time when he toyed with his prey, stringing out a kill, enjoying the anticipation, like some sick game. Now, he performed it quickly and perfunctory, treating it more like a chore. In order to keep his hunger under control these days, he filled himself more often, so when he was with Hannah he wasn't overwhelmed or tempted beyond his endurance.

Hannah.

Controlling his hunger around her was painful. He wanted her. Needed her. Craved her. The very beat of her heart called to him.

But he had another in mind tonight. Another that would quench his thirst and solve his problem—Levi.

From shadows, Akiva watched the barn where Levi worked, and he planned his attack. On Levi's drive home, he would meet a stranger. A stranger he actually knew very well. Akiva had not yet decided if he would reveal himself to Levi or not; he'd learned no one he had known in his previous life recognized him in his changed state. He had the ability to conceal himself as a hunter camouflages himself. But it might be more satisfying if Levi were aware of his true identity. Even though much of Jacob had changed, including his name, he still felt much as he always had, still clung to bits of himself that other bloods no longer seemed to value, things like love, especially first love. Which gave him the answer. When there was nothing Levi could do to stop him, Akiva would tell Levi his plans for Hannah and feed on Levi's fear and jealousy. It would be most gratifying.

It was fully dark when Levi led a horse from the barn toward his buggy. But he was not alone. Another man walked beside him, watching as Levi settled the harness and hooked the horse to the buggy. The stranger, another Amish man, with the same plain clothes and bowl-shaped haircut, was not familiar to Akiva. The big burly fellow climbed onto the buggy seat next to Levi, and they sat there together in silence.

Who was he? Why was he there?

A wintry anger settled over Akiva. His temperature dropped almost instantly. He whirled away from the sight of Levi and stormed across the countryside ravaging any animal he could, growing stronger and warmer with each. And yet a coldness remained inside him.

Until he saw a man standing on the roadside, a backpack slung onto his back. He walked with his head downward, his gaze on his worn-out shoes.

Akiva joined him, matching his footsteps. "Hello."

The man glanced at Akiva, his drawn face full of

exhaustion and disappointment. He wore several days' growth of whiskers and smelled of sweat upon sweat. "What's it to you?"

"Mind if I join you? I could use a little company and it looks as if we're going in the same direction."

"You going nowhere too?"

"Maybe. I'm Akiva."

"Weird name."

"Some might think that."

"You Jewish or what?"

"No."

"Good. Don't like 'em. Don't like blacks neither. Or them Mexicans who are taking over."

"As you can see I'm not black or Mexican."

"Yeah. You're too pale, that's for sure. Fact is I don't like people. I'm a loner."

"Me too."

"Yeah? What's your beef?"

"I don't fit in. How about you?"

"Never have."

Akiva nodded his understanding. "What's your name?"

"Frank. Frank Robbins. I don't shake hands."

"All right by me."

Together they walked along in silence, just their footsteps carrying on a conversation as they traversed blacktop and the pebbly dirt that butted up against the road.

"You in a hurry?" Akiva asked.

"For what?"

"You keep moving forward when it looks like you'd rather get a good night's sleep."

"Yeah, and where's that gonna happen?"

"There's a motel up around the bend. I've got a few bucks

and I know the gal at the desk. She's got a soft heart. She lets me stay if they're not full up."

The older man eyed him. "You one of them fruitcakes?"

"What are you asking?"

"You a homo?"

Akiva chuckled. "No. I like women. One particular woman actually."

"Then why ain't you with her?"

Akiva shrugged. "Some things take time."

"What? Don't she love you back?"

Akiva's jaw hardened. "She will. I promise you that."

"Yeah, I heard that song before."

"So how about it?"

"Just as long as you know I got a switchblade and know how to use it if you get funny. I ain't no bitch for any dog cravings."

Akiva nodded. "I'll remember that."

When they reached the motel, he paid the woman at the desk in cash, looked deep into her blue-frosted eyes—*Forget me*—and then took the key.

No one was staying on either side of this lonely room at the back of the motel. It was an easy kill, fast and quick, the surprise in old Frank's eyes frozen for eternity.

CHAPTER FORTY

ROC WAITED AT THE end of the drive.

The headlights glared outward into the darkness, casting a haze around the Mustang. Roc popped the hood and bent over the engine, well aware of the buggy approaching from the direction of the Schmidt home, the clippity-clops slowing until it came to a stop. He heard the jangle of the harness and then, "Trouble?"

Roc straightened slowly, not too quickly or eagerly. He didn't want to overplay his hand. "You don't happen to have a spare battery, do you?"

Levi climbed out of the buggy, walked over, and studied the battery beneath the Mustang's hood. "Not that kind, no."

"Then you're right." Roc stared at his engine and frowned. "Trouble."

Levi studied Roc for a moment beneath the rim of his hat. "Can I give you a lift into town then?"

Roc glanced back at the buggy. "Hannah with you?"

Shaking his head, Levi thumbed over his shoulder toward his rig. "It carries more than just two."

Frowning, Roc crossed his arms over his chest, sure he'd seen another shape in the buggy. Could it have been Akiva? Would Levi hide his brother? Even if his brother was now an animal? He brought his focus back to the car and conversation, and walked the length of the buggy. "I haven't ever ridden in one of these rigs." He peered inside as far as he could, trying to see if someone was hiding behind the bench. But he didn't see anyone. Had it been a shadow? A figment of his imagination? He laid a hand on his Mustang. "Appreciate the offer but I hate to leave her."

"The car is well off the road. It will be safe for sure."

Roc propped a fist on one hip and glanced in either direction of the road. Levi's suggestion was not the one he was hoping for and he pulled his mouth sideways in an effort to conjure up a new plan. "You're a trusting fellow."

"I trust the good Lord." Levi's look told exactly whom he wasn't yet trusting, though: Roc.

The crunch of more footsteps reached them, and Levi turned back toward the house. Was it Hannah? Her father?

But an older man approached on foot, the Amish man Roc had first met when he arrived in Promise. He reached out to the gray-bearded fellow. "Ephraim, right?"

Ephraim Hershberger's eyes widened and then he shook Roc's hand. "Have we met? We have. *Ja*! I remember now— at my granddaughter's wedding."

Roc grinned. "You're right."

"Saw the lights. You having trouble with your car here? You helping him, Levi?"

"He was," Roc interjected before Levi could say anything. "I think it's the battery. Levi didn't think y'all had a spare."

"It's true. I could take you into town tomorrow." The older man leaned over the engine, eyeing it with unabashed curiosity. "I know where you can get it charged or else buy a new one."

"That would be terrific. Thanks." Roc clapped the older man on the back then pointed out the different parts of the engine to him.

"And where is he going to stay," Levi interrupted, "until morning?"

"In my house," Ephraim answered in a matter-of-fact tone. "I have a good sturdy sofa next to the fireplace. If that will suit you."

"It will suit me fine. I appreciate your help."

"Not a problem at all."

Roc grinned. Now he could keep a closer eye on Hannah and keep watch for anything that lurked in the night.

CHAPTER FORTY-ONE

Night was when she came alive.

Hannah's days were filled with mindless chores, her thoughts lingering on the evening she had spent with Akiva, reliving and anticipating the next.

Akiva came for her just after ten while her family slept peacefully in their beds. Even though the nights grew increasingly colder, his hand was always warm as toast and comforting to the touch. He took her to another party in another field with other Amish teens. Again they danced. They kissed. And they drank "juice," which she'd learned was a combination of liquors and fruit punch, but it tasted sweeter than beer.

"There is something I would show you." Akiva wrapped an arm around her waist.

She smiled up at him. "What is it?"

"Will you come with me?"

"I am with you now."

"Tomorrow, I mean."

She nodded, unable to say no. When she was with him, the world seemed to fade away and she was only aware of him. His eyes. His touch. His smile.

"I will meet you earlier than usual tomorrow. Can you be ready?"

"I will tell Mamm I'm staying at Beth Ann's."

"You do not have to lie."

"It will be easier that way, than to explain." For how could she explain Akiva? Mamm and Dat would not understand, especially because he was not Amish. She should not be seeing him like this, and yet she needed to be with him. Her need resisted logic or understanding. During the day, she reasoned it was because she needed to hear about Jacob, though Akiva never talked of Jacob, and she forgot to even ask about Akiva's time with him—until he left her.

"You know your family better than I." He lifted his chin and looked around, toward the spring house where he had once stayed. When his gaze narrowed, hers followed. "Someone is there."

"I can't imagine who." She shook her head, knowing it couldn't be Levi, for he had left hours before. She glanced toward the attached house where her grandfather lived and saw the lights were off, the shades drawn. It was way past his bedtime. He had become hard of hearing in the last year or so, and she doubted he was awake.

She scanned the barn, which held Akiva's attention, and could see nothing in the shadows. "There's no one there." But then she saw the glint of yellow, and she smiled. "It's Toby. Our dog. He won't bother us."

"Us." Akiva turned his attention back toward Hannah. "I like the sound of that."

With the crook of his finger, he lifted her chin toward the pale moonlight, cupped her jaw, and caressed her face with only his gaze, as if he was memorizing each contour. Her skin reacted with a tingling sensation. Slowly, he leaned toward her and kissed her, a soft kiss that made her insides curl. His kisses seemed more potent than any "juice." "I will see you tomorrow."

"Tomorrow," she repeated as if in a dream.

He stepped back, retreating down the back steps, and allowed her to climb the steps to her bedroom alone.

CHAPTER FORTY-TWO

THE GIRL WAS IN danger.

Roc had that same gut-clenching instinct when he knew, without evidence, without rhyme or reason. He simply knew. This was bad. Seriously bad.

When the door to the house closed quietly and he knew Hannah was safe for the night, Roc pulled his Glock from his holster and stepped past the yellow lab and away from the barn. At that moment, Akiva turned.

It was the same face. Those same dark eyes—soulless eyes, just as Father Roberto had described.

For a moment that seemed to stretch into eternity, Roc met the cold stare with solid intention. His thoughts spiraled down to one: *I'm going to kill you.*

But then a rumbling laugh filled his head, echoed around him.

And then the son of a bitch was gone.

Gone. Again. Without even a shot fired.

CHAPTER FORTY-THREE

EVERYTHING SEEMED NORMAL.
But it wasn't.

After Hannah's family bowed their heads for a silent prayer, the eggs, biscuits, bacon, and assortment of jams and honey were passed around the table. The silence made it feel like the ceiling might cave in any minute.

Hannah passed the *Englisher* the bowl of scrambled eggs across the table where he sat in Rachel's old place. Dat and Mamm had closed expressions, their gazes shuttered, their mouths thin lines. Levi too seemed excessively quiet, but Grandpa Ephraim and Katie wore big, enthusiastic grins.

Katie's eyes were alight with wonder. "What's it like in Louisiana?"

"Same as here, I guess," the man named Roc said. "But hotter. Swampier. Muggier. Which right about now, this time of year, sounds pretty good."

"Your blood is thin, not used to the cold." Grandpa Ephraim nodded as if agreeing with his own assessment. "You must eat. And over time you will become accustomed to the cold."

"I don't plan on being here that long."

Grandpa Ephraim heaped a pile of eggs onto his plate. "I've heard there is an Amish community in Louisiana."

Roc shrugged. "Wouldn't know. Haven't seen any."

"You've been here a few weeks," Dat said, "in Promise. Have you not had success in your endeavors?"

"I've made progress in finding the man I'm looking for."

"Oh? Who's that?" Katie asked, her eagerness catching a worried glance from Mamm.

Dat cleared his throat. "Katie, it is the man's business. Not ours."

"It's everyone's business." Roc rested his forearms against the edge of the table. "You all should be on the lookout for this man. Akiva is dangerous." He looked around the table at each one of them. Levi's features folded into a frown. Finally, Roc's gaze landed solidly on Hannah.

She felt her skin blanch and coldness settled over her.

"Akiva?" Grandpa Ephraim tested out the name. "Don't reckon I know anyone by that name."

"He's here. And—"

"Who are you?" The words came out of Hannah's mouth before she realized she'd spoken.

"Hannah," Mamm whispered a warning.

Hannah dropped her gaze toward her lap, stared at her tense fingers clutching each other, pinching the fabric of her apron. "I do not mean offense." Then she looked up, looked straight at Roc Girouard. "But we do not know who you are, what you are about. This man, Akiva, might say the same thing about you."

Then she stood on wobbly legs and retreated to the door, where she drew on first her sweater, then her cape and heavier bonnet.

"Shall I drive you to work today?" Grandpa Ephraim asked. "I can drop you at the bakery before I take Roc to the battery shop."

"The scooter will be fine." She offered her grandfather a grateful smile and avoided the solid gaze of the *Englisher*. And Levi's too.

CHAPTER FORTY-FOUR

So WHERE ARE YOU going?" Beth Ann swept the bakery's porch, where, in pleasant weather, customers liked to sit in the cane-backed rockers and enjoy the samplings they purchased. But this time of year, more leaves congregated on the porch than customers. "And who are you going with?"

Hannah sprayed the windows on the door with cleaner and then swiped it with a rag. "I can't say."

"Is it with Levi then? Or that man you were with the other night?"

The rag squeaked against the windowpane, and Hannah rubbed harder than needed.

"You're not doing anything crazy, are you?"

Hannah shook her head but still didn't look at her friend's inquiring gaze. "I'll tell you later, I promise. Just now…" She paused in rubbing the paned glass. "Please don't say anything."

The scuttling of leaves stopped and the broom stilled. Then a hand settled on Hannah's shoulder. "I promise."

Later that afternoon, after supper and cleaning the kitchen, Hannah took off her apron and wrapped herself again in her wool cape and bonnet. Mamm came to the back door and fussed with a thick, woolen scarf and wound it around Hannah's neck. "Do you want Dat to drive you over to Beth Ann's?"

"No. I'll be fine. It's not far."

Mamm nodded, smiled, and kissed her on the cheek. "Have a good time then."

When they were younger, Beth Ann, Grace, and Hannah would often sleep over at each other's homes, but it had been a while and Hannah sensed Mamm was glad she was returning to some normal activity after almost two years of self-imposed isolation.

"I'll see you tomorrow." Hannah pressed a kiss to Mamm's warm cheek.

"Remember, Rachel will be here early." For a moment Mamm held her close, her arms tightening around Hannah, and she had the sudden yearning to lean in and hold on to all that she held dear. "The good Lord keep you safe."

With a bundle of nightclothes in hand, she stepped out into the night. A few puffy clouds overhead looked like popcorn against the black sky, and the stars were scattered bits of salt. But the moon hung as if by a delicate thread and seemed weighted and closer to the horizon. Hannah watched the ground for potholes or rocks as she headed down the road. Night came early in December, but she felt no need of her flashlight. The clomp of hooves had her sidestepping into the dried grass.

The buggy slowed, and she recognized Levi, who had a firm grasp of the reins. "Where are you going, Hannah?"

"To Beth Ann's." The lies came so easily now. It should have made her feel ashamed but when she saw the man sitting next to Levi in the buggy—Roc Girouard—she had an urge to laugh smugly, but she refrained.

"I'll drive you then." Levi's serious gaze, his acceptance of her lie, caused guilt to loop around her heart.

"No, thank you, Levi. I will walk." She regretted disappointing him and saw his jaw tick with impatience, but he only sat there watching her with his *English* friend.

"I drive right past the Shetlers' place."

She wavered in her decision. If Levi had been alone, maybe then she would have ridden with him, but not with that man next to him. "I don't mind walking. What are you doing listening to that *Englisher*?"

"He makes sense, Hannah. You should know that."

She snorted. "It's perfectly safe."

"Is it?" Roc's voice although spoken softly had a shuddering impact on her.

"The good Lord tells us *let not your hearts faint, fear not, and do not tremble, neither be ye terrified because of them.*"

"Hannah," Levi said, "you should know—"

"Fear not, Levi." She clenched her teeth against a sudden chill, against so much more.

Then she began walking. When she was a few feet ahead of the buggy, she heard the crunch of the wheels along the gravel drive as it moved forward. At the corner, she should have taken a left to meet Akiva but with Levi watching she turned right, toward Beth Ann's house. She would have to double back later.

The buggy never passed her but kept at a slow, plodding pace behind. Its lantern gave off a hazy light that lit her path, as long as she didn't hurry her pace. The horse snorted its irritation at the slow speed. Finally, Hannah stepped to the side of the road and waited for the buggy to pull to a stop beside her.

"What are you doing, Levi Fisher?"

"Following, to make sure you get to Beth Ann's safely."

"And why wouldn't I?"

The two men just stared at her.

She shifted from foot to foot but held her ground. "And are you now taking the *Englisher* to stay with you?"

"Just helping him run an errand."

The skin between her brows tightened. "What is wrong with his car?"

"I don't know yet," Roc answered for himself. "It's not the battery but that's all we know."

Scowling at him, she huffed out a breath and continued walking. She heard the click of Levi's tongue and the jangle of the reins as horse and buggy followed.

With each footfall, her irritation built, growing taller and taller like the Tower of Babel. But was it her pride or theirs hammering the pieces into place? By the time she reached Beth Ann's front gate, it was too dark to see the house from the end of the lane. She gave a quick wave to Levi and headed down the dark path out of Levi's lantern light.

"Hannah."

She stopped and turned, only a few feet away from the buggy but Levi's face was set in shadows and she could not read his expression. "Yes?"

"Are you happy?"

His question stunned her and softened the crustiness around her heart. "Yes, Levi, I am."

"*Gut*. If you need anything…anything at all, you can come to me."

Her throat welled with unspoken words and tears intermingled with guilt for her deception. Levi deserved better than someone willing to lie to him. For that's what she was doing, and yet she couldn't seem to stop herself.

"Stay safe." His voice came to her once more.

Then the buggy creaked as it moved forward and disappeared into the night, taking the last remnants of yellow lantern light with it. She waited in the dark, hearing her breath and nothing else. After several minutes passed and the cold seeped beneath her cloak, she slid her hand into her apron and folded her stiff fingers around the flashlight's handle, not daring to turn it on and yet holding on to it somehow made her feel safer.

Counting off the minutes, trying to be patient and feeling the opposite, she finally deemed it safe to walk back the way she had come. But this time, she used the flashlight, aiming it at her feet so she could watch for sticks or ruts in the road. She quickened her steps, anxious to find Akiva before he gave up on her. After she passed her own driveway, she saw twin circles of light bore through the darkness.

She froze, pausing along the roadside, not knowing what to do, where to go. Her heart thudded heavily in her chest and Levi's warnings came back to her. *It's not safe, Hannah.*

And Roc's words: *I'm searching for a dangerous man. A man named Akiva.*

She stood completely still, like a deer frozen in fear. Her heart thumped loudly in her eardrums, and her breathing was harsh and ragged. The sound of a car engine rumbled, and she eased far off the road, but it never passed her.

Twin beams of light shot out of the dark and she shied away from the light. Then a car door closed. Someone walked in front of those headlights, and she could see the outline of legs, a male body. Her heart pounded out its uncertainty.

"Hannah." Akiva's voice was a welcome relief.

Moving toward him, she heard the whisperings, like sweet nothings, teasing her ears. Or was it her heart? "I'm here."

He held out a hand, the brilliant light behind him illuminating his skin, making it look iridescent, as if rays of light were shooting outward from his fingertips. She placed her hand in his, and his warmth folded around her. "Come. We don't want to be late."

He walked around to the passenger side of a two-door

car, and he opened it for her. A light came on inside and revealed buttons and knobs that she had no idea of the purpose of. Soft music floated outward from the interior, but she hesitated. "What's the matter, sweet Hannah?"

"I've never rode in a car before."

"Never?"

She shook her head.

"There's always a first for everything. Don't worry, I'll drive slow."

"But…"

"Are you afraid?"

Fear not, she reminded herself and answered, "Not of being hurt."

"Then of what? Losing your soul by riding in a modern convenience?" His tone mocked.

She bristled. "I would not lose my soul."

"Jacob tried to explain your ways to me, and I did not understand all those rules. They seem like a way to suppress the folks here."

"But there are reasons. Good reasons for—"

"I'm sure there are. But where we are going…well, you'd never get there by foot or scooter or even in a buggy. Don't you want to see what I have to show you?"

She hesitated.

"It was one of Jacob's favorite pastimes," he tempted her. "But it's your decision, Hannah. But if you're going we must hurry or we'll be late."

"Late?" She drew her lip between her teeth and glanced over her shoulder in the direction of her house, but she could not see the farm. It was dark. Completely dark.

Trust me. The words were not spoken aloud but pierced her heart.

Swallowing her reservations, she nodded. "Okay then. All right."

And she slid into the warm, comfortable seat and was surrounded by the soft instrumental music, which sounded as she'd always imagined heaven did.

CHAPTER FORTY-FIVE

D O YOU TRUST HER?" Roc's words were spoken carefully. But Levi felt a jolt right through him, and his grip on the reins tightened. "Why wouldn't I?"

"Because she's hanging out with a dangerous character."

"Not tonight she isn't."

"You're so sure of that, huh?"

Levi nodded, keeping his gaze on the road ahead. The lantern jiggled on the dash with the rhythm of the buggy and the light danced around them; his insides felt just as crazy and loose. "You're staying at the Benders', right?"

"It's not far."

"I know where it is."

That ended the conversation, and Levi focused on the cold air chaffing his hands and face, the movement of the horse, the sound of the iron shoes striking pavement. With every clip and clop, he doubted his earlier answer. Not so much about trusting Hannah, but Jacob. Because *if* his brother had returned, which Levi now suspected, then he was after one thing. Explaining that to himself was difficult enough, but to this *Englisher* sitting next to him seemed impossible. But were they chasing the same person? After all, Roc was looking for a man named Akiva. Could there be another like Jacob who committed abominations?

They reached the traffic light and Levi waited for the

signal before turning the buggy onto Lincoln Highway. The frosty bite in the air could mean snow by morning.

"You love her, don't you?"

The question came without preamble or warning and shocked Levi. It was not a topic discussed much between close friends and not at all with strangers. He glanced sideways at Roc, then back to the highway. His heart beat heavily in his chest, but he gave a perfunctory nod.

"So are you gonna marry her or what?"

"There is no 'or what' here in Promise."

Roc laughed. "Didn't mean to impugn the lady's reputation or anything. Or your own. Of course, your intentions are honorable. I just wondered if you were going to ask her to marry you or not." He shifted on the seat. "So how does all that work here?"

"What do you mean?"

"How does an Amish man make a lady aware of his intentions?"

Levi's throat worked overtime on a hard swallow. "Same as anywhere else, I reckon."

"Ah, no. I don't buy that. Where I come from, a fella might buy a lady a drink. Or pick up the phone and call her. But y'all don't drink or have phones."

"True. Do these things make it easier in your world?"

"Doubt it. Y'all seem to marry sooner than folks where I come from." He laughed, his gaze seeking out the low-slung moon. "Sounds like we're from different planets. So what do you do? Tell the gal you're interested in straight out? Ask her out on a date?"

Levi glanced at Roc again and rubbed his jaw.

"How do you say it...courtin'? Take a buggy ride?"

"There are ways."

Roc rolled his wrist, an encouraging gesture.

"Ways." Levi stretched a foot out and brought it back. "There are Sunday night sing-alongs."

"Ooh, that sounds like fun." The way Roc said it sounded like mucking out the stalls.

"Can be. Especially escorting her home."

Roc winked. "Gotcha. Okay, what else?"

"You can visit her in her home."

"With her folks there I imagine."

"Sure. Then at night, some of the kids in their running around years take a flashlight and shine a light in the girl's window."

"What's that mean?"

"Then the girl comes out—"

"Oh, yeah, well, I guess we have that custom too."

Levi glanced at Roc. "So why are you so curious? You do not have an Amish woman in mind for courting, do you?"

Roc gave a blustery cough. "Hell no. Oh, sorry, man. I just meant…I was married…once."

"Once?" Levi's lips flattened. "Divorced then?" But Roc didn't answer, and Levi regretted asking. It was not his business. From Roc's stony expression, Levi knew he was treading on treacherous terrain. "Do you still love her awful much?"

Roc leaned forward, braced his elbows against his knees, and cleared his throat. "Awful is a good word for it."

Levi nodded, fully understanding the pains one could feel in the heart. "With God, all things are possible."

For a few minutes, only the sound of the horse's hooves and the wheels against pavement accompanied their silence. Then a light flashed behind them, the light becoming brighter and filling the inside of the buggy.

"What's up with that?" Roc turned and peered out the

back window. "Can't you see we're driving here?" he yelled at the driver of the truck, as if he could be heard over the throbbing bass. "Go around." Then he waved his arm out the side of the buggy. "Go around!"

The roar of the truck's engine swallowed up the word Roc hollered at the driver.

"Do you have to put up with that all the time?"

Levi shrugged. "It's all right, I reckon. We slow them down, I'm sure. Everyone is in such a hurry."

"So you take everything slow, especially courting?"

Levi grinned. "You have a one-track mind, Roc Girouard."

"I've been accused of that."

"We marry sooner than those in the *English* world, remember?"

Roc nodded. "Okay, I give you that."

"Sometimes courting can be rather slow, and yet it doesn't necessarily take long to figure out the right one. Then if you are blessed, you have a lifetime together."

Roc's gaze drifted toward the road. "If you're blessed…" He rubbed his hands together. "So what about you and Hannah? When are you gonna take the bull by the horns?"

Levi's eyebrow shot upward. "I may be mistaken but Hannah is no bull."

Roc laughed. "That's just an expression. You're already there at her place all day, working for her father. You gotta do something to get the lady's attention."

Levi nodded. "I have spoken to her father."

"You did? Whoa. Now that's serious. Most guys don't do that anymore."

"Why not?"

"Too scared probably. Or maybe it's indifference."

"It's expected here. Did you talk to your wife's father?"

"Nah, he was dead. And she didn't live at home anyway. So, what did you say to Daniel Schmidt, who by the way looks formidable in his parental role?"

"He said it was up to Hannah and her preferences." Levi glanced downward and remembered how his own heart had pounded in his chest. "But he approved the idea."

Roc clapped him on the shoulder. "So...what have you been waiting for?"

Levi made a turn onto High Road and the buggy swung out and then straightened behind the gelding. "She has been in mourning."

"She a widow?"

"She was in love with my brother, Jacob, but they were never married. She is only just now eighteen." Levi stole a glance and saw recognition in Roc's eyes. Had he heard of Jacob? If so, then what else had he heard? Levi wiped a sweaty palm on his pant leg. "My brother has been dead"—his jaw compressed on the word—"two years."

"Do you think this Akiva fella is your brother?"

There it was: Levi's worst fear laid out like a splayed field-dressed deer. Not the question he had expected but one he'd been kicking around himself. "What makes you ask that?"

"A lot of things. I looked up the name Akiva. It's a derivative of the name Jacob. Coincidence?"

Levi shrugged, but his stomach folded into a hard knot.

"Jacob didn't die a normal death, did he?" Roc stared at him while they made a turn into the Benders' parking lot.

Levi braced his elbows on his thighs to keep his arms from shaking the way his insides were. He focused on guiding the horse to the back of the parking lot where he halted. The Benders' house was good-sized with multiple rooms and entrances. They were an older couple with only one teenager left at home; the rest of their large family had married or moved off. After setting the brake, Levi finally met Roc's probing gaze.

"I will wait for you while you get what you need."

Roc stared at him for a long moment, and in that moment Levi knew what Roc was doing, why he'd come to the Schmidt farm. All this that Levi had admitted Roc already knew. Then Roc jumped down from the buggy. "Right. Okay."

CHAPTER FORTY-SIX

AKIVA DROVE FOR A while, traveling down roads Hannah had never before seen. True to his word, he drove slowly and carefully, although she held one of his hands tightly. He grinned over at her, the corners of his eyes creasing. The streetlights and headlights crisscrossed his face with shadows, giving the planes of his cheeks a higher arch. His eyes were deep-set, shaded by the arc of his brow. His nose had a razor's edge, straight and sure. His driving was confident and capable, and she started to relax and gaze around at the other cars zipping past, stores on either side of the road, their signs glowing bright against the night sky.

A raw, earthy tone from the speakers drew her attention. "What kind of music is that?"

He tapped his thumb against the steering wheel and the volume soared, the music coming at her from all directions, vibrating in her soul. "It's jazz. Do you like it?"

She nodded, not quite sure of the rhythm, but it was pleasing to the ear.

"You like music?" he asked.

"I like singing in church." But she kept to herself that she'd missed singing with her friends on Sunday nights. A part of her died with Jacob, the part that recognized beauty and found joy in it. Could she maybe find that joy again?

"That's nothing compared to what you're going to hear tonight."

"What do you mean?"

"Just wait. It's hard to describe." His fingers flexed, then tightened on the steering wheel. "I grew up mostly without music and then when I discovered it…I couldn't get enough. It fed my soul. Still does."

She smiled, not exactly sure she understood, and yet the notes were soothing and made her want to sway and move to their slow, seductive rhythm. She forced her feet to be still on the floorboard.

"You heard of David from the Bible, right?" Akiva's mention of a biblical character grabbed her attention and made her wonder what his religious background was and if he truly believed God would never forgive him for whatever he'd done. After all, God had forgiven King David of adultery and murder.

"Of course," she said. "What about him?"

"King David wrote so many psalms, really just songs, and he played them on the harp. It's something I always wanted to pursue."

She studied his profile as the flicker of lights from a shopping center drifted across his features, highlighting the contours and edges, reminding her of Jacob. "Playing the harp?"

"For me, it is the piano." He flashed her another grin. "And I've been learning. Someday I hope to play for you."

"I'd like that."

Then he turned the wheel into a parking lot full of other automobiles. He parked, and she was glad to finally be sitting still. While she figured out how to unfasten the seatbelt, he came around the front of the car and opened the door for her. He held out a hand and helped her out of the low-slung car, then led her by the hand toward a building with a soaring roof made entirely of glass. The arch glimmered like diamonds against the night sky.

Akiva pulled her along, joining a tide of people dressed in fancy clothes and smelling of heavy perfume—a fast moving river of colors. Her stomach churned with uncertainty, and she pulled back on his hand. "Where are we going?"

"It's a surprise. You'll see."

But she planted her practical black tennis shoes against the pavement and refused to move forward while the crowd parted around them and continued on.

Akiva squared his body with hers and peered deep into her eyes. Whispering like little insects chattered in her ears, and she felt disoriented, and her hesitations seemed to fade, loosening their grip. "Do you trust me, Hannah?"

The noise of the crowd waned, the brilliant lights from the street and buildings dulled, even the cold lost its potency. Her fears paled, and she finally nodded.

"Good, then come."

He held the glass door for her as she entered the building. The ceiling arched heavenward and each light twinkled and sparkled with such clarity that she felt the need to shade her eyes. People crowded on either side of her like a surge of locusts, with all the talking bombarding her ears and making her skin recoil. The warmth of all those bodies and minted breaths made her cape feel as if it was strangling her. She started to remove it, but Akiva reached around her and plucked it off her shoulders then draped it over his bent arm.

Suddenly she sensed the stares of those around them, and she looked down at her plain blue dress, her bonnet ties, her simple black tennis shoes. Her stomach churned into a tight little knot. *Englishers* had been staring at her and her family for as long as she could remember, but usually it was easy to ignore. Usually *Englishers* were the visitors, not her, but now, out of her own environment, the intensity of their stares made her want to shrink into nothing.

Akiva seemed oblivious to the stares they were garnering. He put a hand to her elbow and led her through the crowd, which parted for them as if they were Moses incarnate, and those gawking eyes chased after them like the Egyptians. Hannah supposed they made an interesting pair in their conflicting clothes and obvious differences. Hushed whispers closed over her until Akiva swept her through a doorway and into a majestic auditorium that widened her eyes.

All the way down a long aisle, they walked toward the front, toward a wide, grand, and gleaming stage. She could only stare and take in the brightness, the cacophony of voices as the crowd gathering chatted like magpies. But it was the soaring ceiling and vast spaces that amazed her, as if she'd been swept up to the gates of heaven.

Akiva grinned at her and showed her to a plush-covered seat. The manufactured scent of flowers and musk tickled her nose. Men wore dark suits, the ladies sparkly dresses with plunging necklines, which showed off much of their bodies and bare shoulders and kept Hannah's gaze glued in her lap. What was she doing here? She didn't belong.

"Excuse me." A woman nudged Hannah's leg, then slid past her. The woman wore a dress like a second skin, black and sleek, the fabric shimmering beneath the overhead lights. Her hair was long, the color of a black waterfall, and Hannah recognized her as the woman who had come into the bakery. She wiggled her backside as she scooted past, then turned, bobbling in front of Akiva, and leaned down toward him. Her dress gaped open and revealed the full swell of her breasts and a necklace that undulated back and forth in a mesmerizing fashion, never even attempting to cover herself. Hannah felt her own face flush hot with embarrassment even though the woman didn't seem to suffer modesty.

Akiva stood so she could pass more easily, and his jaw tightened. But the woman didn't seem to be in a hurry or to notice his irritation…or was it attraction? Sweeping lashes accented her dark eyes, which were outlined with heavy lines and swaths of purple on the lids. She laughed and smiled, her shiny, white teeth flashing at him, her lips blood red. "Pardon me." Her voice was as thick and luxurious as the dark fur draped over her arm. "It's a tight squeeze in here. But I'm sure we'll all manage."

He stared back at her, not blinking, not moving, not responding in any way. Finally she moved on, scooting down a couple of seats and tossing her fur carelessly onto the seat next to Akiva. She made a production of sitting, crossing her long legs, then fussed and shifted in her seat, arching her back, her dress rising up her thigh. Men took notice, their gazes magnetized to her.

But Akiva angled his shoulders toward Hannah, blocking her view of the woman, and he stretched an arm along the back of her seat in a protective way. "Are you all right?"

"Maybe it would be best if…I'm not dressed for…" Her hand rested against her own covered neckline, the tie of her prayer *kapp* brushing her wrist. Not that she would ever wear something as revealing as the woman who kept glancing in their direction.

"You"—Akiva cupped her chin and lifted it so her gaze reluctantly met his—"are perfect." His eyes were as dark as coals. "And beautiful. Much more so than anyone else here. You don't need all that decoration to shine."

Her cheeks warmed even though she couldn't imagine

that a plain Amish girl was more beautiful than these women in their dazzling attire. Not that she wanted to dress like them or be like them, but they were dressed to attract men; she was dressed to please God. But she wasn't sure she was doing that anymore either.

Even though it seemed as if all the seats in the auditorium were filled, the seat next to Akiva and also next to Hannah remained empty. She whispered, "Did we not bathe? Do we smell funny?"

He tilted his head in question.

"No one is sitting around us," she explained, "but the auditorium is full. Are they afraid of us?"

He laughed. "I bought the extra seats, so we would not be disturbed. I wanted you to have a full view of the orchestra."

Surprised and thinking it was an unnecessary expense, she started to say so when something moved on stage, snagged her attention, distracted her from Akiva, and she watched as men and women all wearing shades of black and carrying a variety of instruments settled into chairs on the stage. Some of the instruments were shiny, like brass or silver, and others were made of gleaming wood.

"This is the Philadelphia Philharmonic. They're going to be playing Vivaldi."

"Vivaldi?"

"He was a composer from the late sixteen hundreds, known as the Red Priest."

"A religious man?"

"Yes. And he composed a piece called *The Four Seasons*."

Several of the instruments sounded out into the great hall, the notes random and disjointed.

"They're just warming up. The conductor will come out in a moment and it will begin."

Finally, the orchestra quieted and grew still, each musician seated, and a hush of expectancy fell over the audience as the lights dimmed. Only the stage lights remained bright. Then a man walked onto the stage, carrying his own instrument, and slid a long stick against the strings to make a sound like angel's wings. The long note continued and the orchestra echoed it with their different instruments, then all became still again. Anticipation hummed in the great hall, as if everyone waited as she did for what would happen next.

She felt Akiva's gaze on her, and she glanced in his direction and offered him a smile as she felt her own excitement build.

Finally, another man in a fancy suit like the one Akiva wore walked onto the stage and the audience erupted in applause. He smiled and acknowledged the audience with a slight bow, then turning away, he faced the orchestra. Everyone watched this man as if he was a savior of some kind.

Finally the man raised a thin stick, lifting both arms, and with a swoop of arm and stick, the violins came alive and the sweetest music Hannah had ever heard danced through the air. From the first note to the last, she sat spellbound, listening to each beat, note, and pause, imagining the seasons as they came and went, the budding spring to the full blossom of summer, the first frost of autumn to the chill of winter. She envisioned the crops growing and being cut back, the seasons of their lives, couples being wed, babies born, children raised, growing older until death arrived.

She thought of her grandmother, gone a year now, Jacob almost two. Grandma Ruth had lived a long, productive life. She married, had children, raised them to adulthood, and enjoyed her grandchildren and the fruits of her labors. But for Jacob, he was like a young, healthy tree snatched from the ground and tossed to the side, never allowed to fully bloom or produce anything of purpose or good.

To everything there is a season…birthing, dying…killing, healing…weeping, laughing…mourning, dancing…gaining and losing…keeping and casting away…rending and sewing…loving and hating…warring and peace-keeping. The words from Ecclesiastes poured over her, flowing with the music. *What profit hath he that worketh in that wherein he laboureth? I have seen the travail, which God hath given to the sons of men to be exercised in it. He hath made every thing beautiful in His time: also He hath set the world in their heart, so that no man can find out the work that God maketh from the beginning to the end.*

God's word promised trials, difficulties, and yet all was beautiful…in *his* time. Maybe she simply couldn't understand the beauty in Jacob's death, the reason or wherefore, but she trusted there was a reason…there would be a beauty. Someday. Somehow. Sadness crept into the music but then a joyfulness swept her from grief to promise.

She remembered the words of the psalmist: *When I consider thy heavens, the work of thy fingers, the moon and the stars, which thou hast ordained; What is man that thou art mindful of him? and the son of man, that thou visitest him?* Who was she to question the Almighty God?

When the music came to its climactic conclusion, all those around her applauded and the cacophony filled the hall. But she sat beside Akiva, whispering a prayer of forgiveness and praying for guidance. Maybe He had been guiding her all along, showing her a new way, a new path.

It was a glorious evening where understanding and discernment, which had eluded Hannah for so long, seemed to embrace her all at once. After the orchestra left the stage and the audience began to disperse, Akiva ushered her back to his car. They drove a long way in silence, the music still floating in her head, her heart keeping the steady beat, causing her toe to tap against the floorboard. Akiva drove to a secluded spot, surrounded by tree trunks and bare limbs that stretched skyward.

"Wait here." He climbed out of the car, moving easily in a smooth motion. The car jerked and she turned to see the back window blackened by the raised back end of the car. Then it closed, and she saw Akiva carrying something in his arms. He walked away from the car into the darkness.

Alone, she began to worry about being there...wherever "there" was, with this man. What future could they have together? Maybe he was simply a transition to help her move on from Jacob. Or maybe—

He opened the passenger door for her, taking her hand, and showing her toward a square cloth he had placed on the ground. A stand of candles illuminated the area with golden, flickering light.

"It's a bit cold for a picnic, but I couldn't resist. A restaurant or bar didn't seem right after *The Four Seasons*."

"This is perfect."

He helped her sit on the cloth and handed her a glass filled with a bubbly liquid from a green bottle. "Champagne."

She took a sniff, and it tickled her nose and made her smile.

Holding up his glass to hers, he grinned. "To great composers."

"And writers." She ducked her chin, embarrassed by her statement. "That's what Jacob would say."

"He would indeed."

The clink of their glasses rang out in the night with a lovely note of celebration. Although she wasn't sure what they were celebrating, she decided to celebrate her liberation from grief. This was a new beginning, a night of promise and hope.

He drank first, then she did, and the cool liquid tasted fruity and sparkly against her tongue.

"Jacob," Akiva said, rolling the stem of the glass between his forefinger and thumb, "appreciated Keats, maybe you will recognize this poem—

> *"Four Seasons fill the measure of the year;*
> *There are four seasons in the mind of man:*
> *He has his lusty Spring, when fancy clear*
> *Takes in all beauty with an easy span:*
> *He has his Summer, when luxuriously*
> *Spring's honey'd cud of youthful thought he loves*
> *To ruminate, and by such dreaming high*
> *Is nearest unto heaven: quiet coves*
> *His soul has in its Autumn, when his wings*
> *He furleth close; contented so to look*
> *On mists in idleness—to let fair things*
> *Pass by unheeded as a threshold brook:*
> *He has his Winter too of pale misfeature,*
> *Or else he would forego his mortal nature."*

The words seemed to drive out her worries and fears, and wrapped around her like a cocoon, sheltering her from even her doubts and questions.

"It's beautiful." She sipped again from the champagne glass. "Jacob had the ability to make words come alive. Or so it seemed." Her gaze dropped and shifted sideways. "And you do too."

He touched her chin and lifted it up so that her gaze met his. His smile was soft and tender; his touch gentle and warm. Her belly tilted and her head swayed beneath the potency of his gaze and caress. "You must try this," he said, reaching into a basket beside him and pulling out a red, ripe strawberry.

She straightened. "Where did you get such a thing this time of year?"

He smiled and held the tiny green stem as she took a bite from the plump fruit that tasted surprisingly sweet. He ate the rest then nodded toward the champagne. "Now try it with the taste of strawberry on your tongue."

Her mouth burst with flavor, and they ate several berries, some dipped in the champagne. Before she knew it the bottle of champagne was empty and her head felt light and wobbly. Even though the night air was below freezing, she didn't feel cold. She sniffed the air and it smelled of snow.

"Now," he said as he leaned back on his elbow and stared up at her, "what did you think of the concert?"

"The music was…oh…" Words failed her. How could she share all that was in her heart, which felt lighter and more carefree? "I'm not sure I have the words to say it." But it was as if her tongue had been loosened on its hinges and it waggled on and on about the different pieces, the joyfulness and sorrow found as the music dipped and soared, the words of Ecclesiastes stirring her, revealing her pride. With her cheeks warm and probably glowing, she quieted herself. "It's funny because it made me think of Grandma Ruth. I miss her."

"Grandma Ruth?"

"She was my grandmother on my mother's side, married to Grandpa Ephraim."

"What do you mean, 'miss her'?" Akiva's forehead folded downward into a frown.

"I used to catch her humming sometimes when she tended her garden. She would have loved the music tonight. I wonder if she is hearing music like that in heaven."

"She's dead?" His features tightened. "For how long?"

"Only a year." Hannah felt fresh tears, and looked away before saying, "Thank you for taking me tonight, Akiva. I will remember it forever."

"Forever is a long time." He inched closer and kissed her softly.

She felt drawn to this man, to his heat, to the taste of strawberries and champagne, to the very scent of him. She had felt this way with Jacob too, yet not exactly. This man made her feel things she had not felt before, and her melancholic mood made her want to cling to someone, hold on to them so the aloneness she had felt for so long would vanish. Her fingers sifted through the hair at his nape, and then he deepened the kiss. He pulled her into his arms, slanting her body across his lap and she felt the hard solidity of his frame. She opened to him as she had never imagined possible. Their breaths melded with their lips, the taste and touch making her mind spin. She clung to him and their generated heat wrapped around them.

He laid her back gently onto the blanket, his hands framing her face, caressing her skin. She felt her back arching toward him, and she was eager to lose herself in the moment, the night, this man. His mouth was hot and bold, and pulled even her breath from her as if he could possess her soul. His gaze smoldered, and she felt his heat through her cape and clothes. Then he dipped his head, drew a line along the column of her neck, and she looked heavenward to give him free access. A tiny snowflake fell out of the darkness.

But he shoved himself away and she lay there alone, shivering. Even with his back to her, she could see his breathing was labored too.

"Akiva, what—"

"Get in the car, Hannah."

"But—"

"Go. Now."

She scurried to get up, her legs feeling stiff and then wobbly. Without a backward glance, she ran for the car and, with the help of a sudden gust of wind, slammed the door closed. Chilled, she huddled inside her cape until finally Akiva followed, placed the basket and blanket in the back of the car, and joined her. He started the engine but didn't drive. He didn't look at her either.

"I thought I could control myself. I thought..." He clenched the steering wheel. "I'll take you home."

CHAPTER FORTY-SEVEN

DARK RIBBONS SWIRLED ABOUT Hannah, dancing and swiveling in a beguiling rhythm, and began one by one to wrap around her wrist and ankle and throat, the ribbon becoming thicker and twined along her limbs and around her middle. The bands snapped into strong lines. Then she felt herself falling, hurtling backward, yanked into a spiraling storm. She fought the bonds, but it was no use as she fell into a dark void where all she could hear was her own scream—far away and faint.

Her eyes opened. Her chest heaved with each ragged breath. She was lying in the dark, only a crease of light slipping inside and turning the black to gray. Shadows took shape, and she recognized the dresser, the pegs on the wall, her bedside table. Flinging off the sheets and quilt that entangled her legs, she sat upright.

Her head felt as if it had split open, exposing every nerve to the brightening light. Her stomach tilted uneasily, and she closed her aching eyes and lay back down, burrowing into the pillow.

But the clomp of horse's hooves and crunch of wagon wheels on the drive caused her to push up from the bed. She stumbled, a piercing ache in her temple, the weak light stabbing her eyes, but she made her way to the window and squinted out at the day, which had already begun without her.

Down below, a buggy came to a stop. She touched the neckline of her nightgown. How had she gotten home? The last she remembered she was with Akiva. Heat rose up inside her and scorched her cheeks. She placed a hand against her burning skin. What had she done?

As she watched the buggy below, Rachel climbed down and greeted Mamm with a hug and kiss. Embarrassment and shame fled beneath the onslaught of pure joy. It was good to see Rachel again. Hannah's hand pressed the cold glass. She must hurry.

How selfish of her, her thoughts focused on herself and not others, not even helping Mamm get ready. Hannah hurried to dress but felt her stomach lurch. She paused and put a hand against her belly until her insides settled again. Her fingers fumbled as she tried to remember undressing last night. Akiva must have brought her home as he'd promised. And left. Yes, of course he left. She would remember if he hadn't.

Before she could finish fastening the pin of her skirt, a knock on the door made her finger slip and she plunged the sharp pin into her thumb. Pressing the pad to her tongue and tasting the saltiness of her own blood, she said, "Come in."

The door opened and Rachel peeked around the edge. "Am I too early for even the birds?"

Rachel's gaze dropped to Hannah's bare feet, and Hannah curled her toes under. "I overslept."

"You, Hannah? Oversleeping?" Rachel tsked. "Shocking." She entered what used to be her room too and closed the door behind her. "Did you have a late night?" She smiled in a manner that suggested exactly what she was out doing and Hannah's skin prickled with an inner heat. Laughing, Rachel plopped onto the unmade bed. "How is Levi these days?"

Levi. Guilt stoked the fire inside her to burn hotter. She folded her nightgown, turning her back so Rachel could not see her face. There was so much Rachel didn't know, so much she had missed in the month since her wedding. "Fine. He's fine, I suppose. But I...uh"—she shrugged— "don't really know."

Rachel's eyebrows narrowed. "You didn't see him last night?"

Turning toward the window and the morning light streaming through it, Hannah shook her head and grabbed her brush, drawing out the strokes and trying to ignore the dull ache in her head.

Rachel came up behind her and smoothed out her hair, fashioning it in the traditional Amish bun. "You're pale. Are you sure you're feeling all right?"

Hannah kept a steady hand against her rebellious stomach. "I'm fine."

Then Rachel peered closer. "You aren't..." Her voice trailed off.

"Aren't what? I'm not ill."

Rachel's eyebrow arched. "What have you been doing... and who have you been doing it with?"

"No one. Nothing." She looked away and nudged Rachel's hand to continue fastening her hair in place.

"You're sure this isn't morning sickness?"

The words shocked Hannah. "No! Why would you think that?"

"I know the symptoms, and you don't look so good this morning."

"Must have been something I ate. Wait...You know the symptoms?" Hannah faced Rachel, who gave a slow nod and sheepish grin.

"Really? You're sure?"

Rachel nodded more vigorously, this time her cheeks flaming. "I think it happened on our wedding night."

Hannah hugged her sister and whispered congratulations. "Does Josef know?"

"Of course. But we haven't told anyone. So don't—"

"I can keep a secret."

"I know you can." She turned Hannah away and finished fixing her hair.

Afterward, Hannah hugged her again. It felt good to be with her sister. "I've missed you."

"And I you." Rachel fingered a wisp of hair near Hannah's temple. "Are you all right?"

"Yes, of course. But Rachel?" Hannah ventured, knowing this might be the only moment they had alone throughout the day. "If I asked you something…would you tell me?"

"Of course. What is it?"

"Tell me about the trip you took with Jacob?"

Rachel's face blanched. It wasn't the reaction Hannah expected. Rachel turned away and made the bed, folding the covers at the top neatly, then sat on the edge. Her hands trembled and she clasped them in her lap. "It was a foolish time. I only went to make Josef jealous."

"Will you tell me about it?"

"Hannah"—her mouth thinned into a prim line of disappointment—"Jacob is gone. You need to move on."

"I'm not asking about Jacob. I'm asking about you. And what you saw and did."

She stood and walked toward the door. "There's nothing to tell. Come, the other women will be wondering where we are."

Rachel and Mamm, along with several other ladies from the district, gathered around the quilt, needles at the ready and the chattering already at full steam, but the meek voices sounded like hammers pounding against Hannah's skull. They planned on finishing the quilt for Beth Ann's sister, Fern, who was getting married in two weeks. Hannah hoped it wouldn't take all day, as her eyes felt weak, and she pricked the edge of the cloth forming a straight if not quite even stitch. When Mamm peered over at her work, a frown marring her brow, Hannah gave herself a hard shake and concentrated on making each stitch tiny and even, with the same devotion she'd utilized when making the quilt she'd hoped to share with Jacob. But that quilt remained unfinished and buried in her hope chest.

Their hands moved quickly and efficiently, each stitch so like each of the many decisions they made each day, drawing together rather than unraveling the fabric of their lives, the seams solid and straight like their faith crisscrossing throughout their community, and the whole quilt reflected the love wrapping the couple in matrimony. Hannah looked across the stretched fabric pieces toward Rachel, who looked tired but also happy. And yet, her reaction to Hannah's question had unraveled her.

What piece was missing that Hannah couldn't see? Was it so vital that if yanked out into the open, it would strip all Rachel was trying to bind together? Or was it simply that Rachel had moved on? That looking back on a foolish journey only complicated her life? Was it simply a season of her life, now withered on the vine and forgotten?

A cooing sound made the women turn toward Katie, who tended Mae Troyer's six-month-old baby boy, Timothy, and Hannah stared at the blue-eyed youngster with a new wonder and awe that, in a few months' time, Rachel would have one of her own. Maybe it was that simple. Others had moved into the next season and were experiencing the blossoming of their summertime with marriages and babies, all while Hannah clung to the springtime of her youth, to a shriveling dream, a wilting hope, where the roots had died and could not sustain a full life.

"Your milk must be good," Mamm said to Mae, her fingers never slowing, "as your boy is growing strong."

Mae, only a year and a half older than Hannah, beamed. "*Ja.* He's always hungry, that one."

"Marriage seems to agree with you, Rachel." Edith Shetler, Beth Ann and Fern's mother, peered over the rim of her glasses.

Rachel blushed.

Beth Ann nudged her shoulder. "Josef treating you well?"

Rachel continued stitching, her blush deepening.

Mamm tsked. "We are embarrassing her."

"That's the lot of a young bride," Mae stated with a perfunctory nod. "A little teasing does no harm."

"Still," Mamm said, smiling at her oldest, "maybe we should change the subject."

Edith's hands stilled, and she rested one on the quilt as she glanced around the group. "Have any of you experienced the loss of livestock lately?"

Mamm nodded, her needle moving with lightning speed. "We lost a lamb not long ago."

"We lost a cow earlier this week," Mae said as she glanced toward her son, who rubbed his fist over his face. "He's getting tired, Katie. You might be able to rock him to sleep now."

Katie nodded, scooped the baby into her arms, snuggling

the chunky body against her chest, and settled into Mamm's wooden rocker, which had been used in their family to rock babies to sleep for over a century. The curved base rolled against the wood floor in a slow and steady rhythm.

"Josef says there is a wild animal loose." Rachel's needle snagged the material, and it took several jabs for her to correct her error in the quilt.

Mae glanced over her shoulder toward Katie and then hunched her shoulders, leaning over the quilt, and whispered, "A man came by our farm. An *Englisher*. He warned us about a stranger. A dangerous stranger in the area."

Mamm set down her needle and thread. "This is idle talk."

Silence descended as the women bowed their heads over the quilt and focused on their sewing, but concern came in through the back door like a cold, wintry wind and gave Hannah a chill that wouldn't go away.

Hannah walked arm-in-arm with Rachel toward the fields as the wind boasted and threatened to steal their scarves.

"Josef and I are going away for a while," Rachel said softly.

Hannah blinked back tears, whether from the wind or the emotions building inside her she wasn't sure. It was tradition for a newly married couple to go visiting. "You will enjoy that, I reckon."

"We'll most probably be gone for Christmas. Josef has an uncle and cousins in Ohio he wants to visit."

"It will be nice for you to meet them."

"A long journey for sure." Rachel patted Hannah's arm. There was something in her movement, in the way she kept patting, as if maybe she was trying to reassure herself and not Hannah. "But that's not why we're going." Her tone dipped low, and she stopped and took hold of Hannah's hands. Her eyes were suddenly bright. "It's the animal killings."

"There's no reason to fear. It's just a wild animal. That's what you said."

Fierceness hardened Rachel's blue eyes and stretched her skin tightly over the bones in her face. "You are naïve, Hannah. Promise me you will be careful."

Hannah searched her sister's face, trying to read her expression, but Rachel had never looked like this. "What are you afraid of?"

Rachel glanced over her shoulder as if someone might be listening, but there was no one to hear out past the laundry line, where the sheets billowed and snapped in the wind. The women had stayed in the house, Mae having already left, and the men were in the barn. Not even Toby, who was curled up in his shelter, would hear them. "You're not still going out at night, Hannah? Are you?"

"What's going on?"

Rachel licked her lips and stared down at their joined hands. "When I went with Jacob to New Orleans, there were"—she swallowed hard—"similar happenings."

A chill icicled down Hannah's spine. "Similar how?

Rachel pulled back, stepped toward the house. "I've said too much."

Hannah clutched Rachel's cape, held her in place. "Tell me. *Bitte*."

Tears welled up in her eyes and threatened to drown all the happiness she seemed to have in her new marriage and tucked deep inside her womb. "I cannot."

"This is all about Jacob?"

Rachel's eyes widened.

"He told me something happened," Hannah rushed on,

as memories crowded in on her. "He was confused...curious, drawn to something he said I couldn't understand. But maybe...maybe I need to know now."

"No. You must...stay close to Levi. He will protect you."

Hannah's jaw hardened with her resolve. "Jacob wasn't afraid. Fear not—"

"Yes, he was. Fear brought him home." Rachel looked down at the ground then back at the house, where Katie stepped out onto the porch, her hand shielding her eyes from the glare of the wintry sun as she searched the yard for them.

Hannah tugged on Rachel's arm and pulled her to the other side of the laundry line so the sheet would shield them from view. "What do you mean?"

A tear slipped down Rachel's cheek.

"Jacob didn't die in an accident at his father's carpentry shop, did he?"

"I don't know that for sure, but—"

"Hannah! Rachel!" Mamm's call shattered Hannah's chance. Rachel backed away, turned toward the house, and waved. "Coming, Mamm!"

Hannah trailed her sister's hastened steps, which she suspected were an eagerness to get away from telling more. "Tell me quick."

"It's getting late. Josef will be waiting."

"Meet me tonight."

Rachel paused. Fear made her eyes dark and intent. "I told you not to go out at night. Please, Hannah—"

"I have to know. Meet me."

"I cannot. Josef—"

"Wait until he goes to sleep." Hannah squeezed Rachel's fingers, placing in her hand all her hopes and dreams and fears. "Then—"

Rachel tugged free and raced ahead toward the porch steps.

Determined, Hannah called out, "I met the man from New Orleans too."

On the bottom step, Rachel turned back, her eyes pleading.

"Promise you'll meet me at the boarded-up mill on Slow Gait."

Rachel touched the tie of her prayer *kapp*. "If I can."

CHAPTER FORTY-EIGHT

Shoulders squared, broad-rimmed Amish hat angled, a man stood beside a horse and plow, backlit by a fiery setting sun that tinted the grass golden. For what seemed like ages, Hannah watched him, noticing each breath as if it were her own, precious and life giving. Her heart skipped past a beat then doubled its rhythm, and she walked toward him as if drawn by an invisible cord, her steps certain and unwavering.

Stored emotions bubbled up inside her as if the man stoked a fire inside her, and she whispered on a choking sob, "Oh, Jacob!"

He turned toward her, but the face wasn't the one she expected. Instead of Jacob, it was Akiva's bold black eyes that greeted her. His mouth curved in a now familiar jaunty slant.

Hannah jerked awake, blinked at the darkness, her face wet with tears, her nightgown damp with sweat. Her breath sounded harsh in the quiet of her room. Her heart thumped against her breastbone. What did it mean? Was this outsider taking Jacob's place in her heart? Could he ever fit into her world or did he simply remind her of Jacob? Nothing about him was Amish, so maybe it wasn't about him or even Jacob. Maybe it was really about Levi. Did she want Akiva to be more like Levi? Or the other way around?

Forcing her breathing to calm, her crazed heartbeat to

settle into a steady rhythm, she peeled off her nightgown and let the chilly night air cool her body. She stood in the center of her room, aware of every inch of her heated skin. Jacob had first awakened the woman inside her, and now Akiva had stoked that fire once again. Slowly, she pulled on first her undergarments, then the purple dress she'd worn earlier, and slid her feet into shoes. Still feeling as if her plumb line had tilted off center, she sat on the edge of her bed and pulled aside the dark green shade so she could watch the stars across the black canopy. As she leaned back into her covers, her hand bumped something hard and her fingers closed over a book. Jacob's book. She'd been reading a poem when she fell asleep. She splayed her hand against the leather cover. It seemed so long ago when Jacob had tossed that book in her lap.

"It's for you."

"Me?"

She'd touched it like she'd never held a book. The pages were crinkly and old and smelled musty. And she'd loved it instantly, because it was from him. Because he had touched it first. Because when he read it, he had thought of her.

Then he'd flopped onto the ground, stretching out his legs, placing his head in her lap, and looking up at her with those intense brown eyes. Had he known how much she had loved him? How she would do anything for him?

"Read something," he'd said.

Fingering his hair, letting it caress her skin, she felt a tingle all over and gave him a nervous smile that reflected the wavery sensation in her belly. "You know I'm not very good at—"

"Sure you are. Read."

So she opened the book, running her fingers over the words, her gaze over the pages. "I don't know where to start."

"Just pick one. It doesn't matter which."

The words had emerged in a halting and clumsy manner, clunking hard against her ears, but Jacob listened as she
came to the blessed end of one poem. Thank the Lord it had
been short, and she started to close the book but his voice
stopped her.

> *"I went to the Garden of Love,*
> *And saw what I never had seen;*
> *A Chapel was built in the midst,*
> *Where I used to play on the green.*

> *And the gates of this Chapel were shut*
> *And 'Thou shalt not,' writ over the door;*
> *So I turned to the Garden of Love*
> *That so many sweet flowers bore."*

The cadence of his voice, the deep timbre, and the way
his tongue stroked each word made her heart flutter like a
bird's wings until it took flight and a tear slid down her cheek
at the beauty of the words and sentiment behind them.

She tasted the tears even now, sitting, remembering, waiting. She reached over and took her flashlight, aiming it at
the book. The pages turned effortlessly until she came to the
poem by William Blake that he had so easily quoted on that
long ago day. It was longer than she remembered and she
read the words aloud, tasted each one, absorbed them into
her soul.

> *"I laid me down upon a bank,*
> *Where Love lay sleeping;*
> *I heard among the rushes dank*
> *Weeping, weeping.*

Then I went to the heath and the wild,
To the thistles and thorns of the waste;
And they told me how they were beguiled,
Driven out, and compelled to the chaste.

I went to the Garden of Love,
And saw what I never had seen;
A Chapel was built in the midst,
Where I used to play on the green.

And the gates of this Chapel were shut
And 'Thou shalt not,' writ over the door;
So I turned to the Garden of Love
That so many sweet flowers bore.

And I saw it was filled with graves,
And tombstones where flowers should be;
And priests in black gowns were walking their
*   rounds,*
And binding with briars my joys and desires."

Something inside her wilted at those final words, the meaning different than what she had thought or believed or the way Jacob had presented it. "Oh, Jacob. What happened to you?"

A rumbling from downstairs told her that Dat was sleeping soundly. It was time to go. She prayed Rachel would meet her…that she'd answer Hannah's questions, that the answers would bring resolution. She pressed the book to her chest and prayed for the Lord's will, but perhaps it was really her own she was seeking?

Rising, she left the book on the bed. In the hallway, she

glanced both ways before descending the stairs. Her hand
on the banister trembled as she eased one foot down a step,
then the next, knowing which steps to rely on and which to
avoid. Between Dat's snores, it was deathly quiet. The dark
created deep shadows, but she knew her way and felt no fear,
only hope that she would soon know the truth.

Her cape hung from a hook beside the door and she
pulled it around her, bracing for the cold. But as she put her
hand on the door latch, another hand came out of the dark
and covered hers.

She gasped, a scream clawing up her throat and lodging
there. She fell back a step, and her gaze collided with another.

"Mamm!"

Her mother's blue eyes crinkled at the corners from fatigue. "Who are you going to see? Do not lie and tell me
Beth Ann...or Levi. You were at a party without him."

Her resolve hardened as her mouth thinned. "How do
you know that?"

"Word gets around. Be careful, Hannah."

"It's not what you think. I'm meeting Rachel."

"Why?"

"She asked me to."

"Is there something wrong between Josef and her?"

"I don't know," she hedged and opened the door, the
cool air slapping her face.

Mamm's brow collapsed in worry lines.

"I don't want to keep her waiting."

Mamm nodded and released her. "Be careful, *ja*?"

She felt the weight of Mamm's concern upon her as she
hurried down the drive, her flashlight jerking crazily over
the hard ground. Glancing sideways and even back toward
the house, her nerves tangled into knots. Often Akiva joined

her here, but he did not show himself tonight. And she was alone. Even though it felt as if eyes were following her in the darkness.

CHAPTER FORTY-NINE

THE DEVIL WAS IN the details.

Or so "they" said, not that Roc was ever sure who "they" were, but looking at the pictures of the gruesome remains…well, he had to agree the devil, or something damn close, had to have ripped that neck open. Roc braced his hands on either side of the pictures scattered across Mike's cluttered desk. Anybody with a weaker stomach would have heaved up his Philly cheese steak at the sight of the body.

"Name's Frank Robbins," Mike said, his tone modular and seemingly unaffected by the pictures under the glare of the overhead lights.

"When did this happen?"

Mike flipped open a chart with the official autopsy report. Two hours ago, he'd called Roc and told him to come to Philly to take a look at some pictures. Roc had snuck out of Ephraim's cozy cottage and reattached the wires on the Mustang. He'd have to beat it back before daylight or his cover would be blown. As it was, he wasn't exactly thrilled that he was missing whatever might be happening on the farm tonight.

"The time of death was four nights ago. Between ten p.m. and two a.m. Too much of a time lapse to be more specific than that."

"Had Frank Robbins paid up front for all those nights in the motel?"

Mike shook his head. "Nah, and the manager wants the police department to pay the cost of those nights plus the fumigation service."

Roc laughed. "What took the hotel—"

"Motel," Mike corrected.

"—so long to discover the body then?"

"The maid hadn't been cleaning. Not sure the night clerk was much more dedicated to his job." Mike waggled his eyebrows. "Or maybe they were—"

"That's one theory." Roc straightened. "Could either of them be a suspect?"

"For what?"

Roc jabbed one of the pictures with his finger. "Murder 101, Mike. I'd think you guys up here in the big ol' city of Philadelphia would know these things. Dead body plus gaping neck wound equals homicide."

"Only if the coroner says it is."

That stopped Roc cold, and he stared at Mike a full minute, waiting for him to grin or make a joke. He couldn't be serious. Could he? "You gotta be kidding, right? This coroner a blind ol' fart who should've retired ten years ago? Or the stupidest new kid on the block?"

"Neither."

"So what then? He took a look at this"—Roc picked up one of the goriest straight-on pictures of the death wound and tossed it toward Mike—"and thought the guy did this to himself? His head's practically severed from the body."

"The coroner deemed it a suicide."

Roc paced in front of the desk. "Should we go pay this dumb ass a visit?"

"Won't do you any good."

"Why not?"

"He says the rope the dead guy hung himself on caused that damage, the body's weight dragging on it. Part of decomposition or some such bull—"

Roc kicked the chair and it toppled over and clamored against the tile floor. He glared at the pictures, noting the details…every detail. "This coroner…he wouldn't happen to have black eyes, would he?"

"Black eyes?" Mike rubbed his jaw. "Oh yes and new highlights in his hair. What, you looking for a date or something?"

"Just a crazy thought. But not any crazier than this guy killing himself."

CHAPTER FIFTY

THE CLOSED MILL, A mere shadow of its former self, had long been abandoned but had still seen many late-night parties by both *English* and Amish teens looking for a good time and zero parental control. A sliver of moonlight fell upon the two-story building, and even through the murky darkness Hannah could see that most all of the windowpanes were broken, the glass embedded in the dirt and overgrown grass that surrounded the mill. The paint was peeling, the roof sagging, the front door closed but the lock broken.

Clouds hung low and ominous, creating fog and keeping the temperature from dipping too low. Hannah waited outside, preferring the cold stillness, even with the creeping fingers of fog, as she paced along the side of the structure, waiting for Rachel and keeping an eye on the dense trees that formed a border along the side of the mill even as her mind turned inward. Was she a fool for coming here, for wanting to know, for suspecting something happened in New Orleans between Rachel and Jacob? For too long, she'd clung to the past, to what might have been, to a hope that she should have let die with Jacob, but maybe knowing the truth would help her let go.

A rustling in a nearby bush startled her. She jerked around. "Rachel?"

But the name died on her tongue as her gaze landed on

Levi. He stood on the edge of shadow and moonlight, his feet buried in fog, but beneath the brim of his hat his face was swathed in dark silhouette. "It's just me."

Exasperation sprang up inside her, and yet relief that she wasn't here alone eclipsed the former. "What are you doing here, Levi?"

He moved toward her, his footsteps slow but determined, his gaze hidden. "I could ask you the same. But I won't. Rachel told me you had questions about Jacob."

Her stomach knotted. "Where is Rachel?"

"I came in her stead."

"You can't help, Levi." She shook her head. "I need to know more about their trip to New Orleans, and you weren't there."

He stepped closer and stared down at her, his gaze as solemn and steady as his temperament. "I know you loved him, Hannah, but knowing about that time won't bring him back. It won't change anything."

"It might."

"How?"

"I'm trying to let him go."

"And will knowing something good or bad, something he did or didn't do, help your heart release his memory?"

"It will remove the questions."

He inched closer, settled his hands at her waist. He'd never touched her before so intimately, but his touch was solid and sure and demanded attention. She wanted to resist him. She'd come here to discuss Jacob, and once more Levi had injected himself into something that had nothing to do with him, that he knew nothing about. Even though prickly at his sudden appearance, she felt something else inside her— attraction, need, desire—flame to life.

"Hannah—"

"I know he's gone." The certainty in her voice surprised her, and for the first time she could speak those words without feeling as if she might fall apart. Was that because Levi held her? Was he holding her together? Or had her heart turned toward him?

"Is he?"

She cocked her head sideways. Levi's eyes were clouded and the emotion swirling in their depths indecipherable. "If you're asking has he left my heart…no, Jacob will always be a part of me." She placed a hand against Levi's chest and felt his heartbeat through his clothes, the steady cadence knocking against her palm. "Just as he is a part of yours."

"But there's more to it, Hannah." His hands tightened about her waist. They were strong, farmer hands, capable of hard work and yet able to care for even the tiniest creature born on the farm. "I can love my brother and you at the same time, without any conflict. Can you continue to love Jacob, to pine for him, and at the same time love someone else?"

"Levi—" She wasn't sure what she was going to say. Words and emotions swelled inside her as her hand followed the line of his shirt. She felt a light tremor pass through him. How different he was from Jacob, who never held back his thoughts or feelings from her. His ease at sharing the most intimate of feelings had impressed her, made her feel less alone. She'd always believed it took incredible bravery for him to be that open, particularly since no other man she'd ever known was like that. But maybe Levi had equal strength, or even more so, to restrain his emotions.

After all, an unbridled horse was a beautiful thing to behold, yet at the same time dangerous, capable of much destruction. With a simple leather strap, all that strength was controlled and reined in, the power put to good use. She realized in that moment, her hand still against his heart, that Levi's leather strap was his faith.

She peered up at him, and a pale shaft of moonlight made the deep pools of his eyes glimmer like a ripple across water. His jaw tensed, the muscle flexing, as he seemed to be struggling, resisting something, his very muscles trembling beneath the strain of something she could only imagine. She'd never seen him like that, teetering on the edge of control, and at that moment, it felt as if she could fall into the depths of those blue eyes and spend a lifetime learning what was really inside him.

"Levi." She tasted the surprising sweetness of his name, a new and welcome treat.

"If it's time you need, Hannah—"

She gave a tiny shake of her head. "That isn't it. Not really." Then the reason came to her, what had held her back for so long, what pushed Levi beyond her reach. "Levi, you don't really know me. You don't know what I've done… how flawed I am. And you're…"

"Just a man, Hannah. Like any other. I'm not perfect. I can't claim pure thoughts or always doing what's right. I want things I have no right to want." His thumb skimmed along her bottom rib and her insides trembled. "I sin," he said honestly and plainly. "I make mistakes. My worst mistake was how I dealt with Jacob."

She tilted her head sideways. "What do you mean?"

Levi looked down where her hand still remained over his heart, and his features constricted with what seemed to be self-condemnation. "Jacob was always spouting off, throwing out his crazy ideas, especially at supper. Sometimes he had a valid point about questioning something—I can't even recall what now—but I never acknowledged the soundness of his argument. I only sided with my pop, with our beliefs and standards…against Jacob. Maybe if I'd tried to be understanding, if I'd tried to listen to what he was saying, if I'd reached out to him…" The corners of Levi's mouth compressed and a glimmer of regret glinted in his eyes. "I was wrong. And that might have cost Jacob his life…and all of us."

She shook her head and smoothed her hand over the plain cloth of his coat. "It wasn't your fault, Levi." Her hand stilled and her gaze met his. "Jacob was who he was. Agreeing or disagreeing with him wouldn't have changed his ideas. Or him. I reckon we've all done things we're ashamed of, though, or wish we could go back and change."

A yearning dawned inside her and yet at the same time awakened feelings for Levi that ran deeper than she'd ever suspected. Had she simply needed to know he wasn't perfect, that he doubted himself too? Had she needed time to heal? Maybe the shield, which had once covered her heart, had fallen away. Or maybe Levi had simply broken through the barriers she'd erected.

How could she tell him another man, an *Englisher*, had eased into the place Jacob had once occupied inside her heart? Or maybe he hadn't. Maybe Akiva had shifted Jacob out of her heart, leaving a space yet to be occupied. She wasn't sure how she felt about Akiva. When she was with him, all doubts and questions vanished, but when she was alone, reason came back. Was he simply a temptation, something forbidden and seemingly irresistible, something she suspected might hurt her? Just because she was attracted to him didn't mean he was good for her or that he was God's will for her life.

With Levi though, it was different. He felt right suddenly. She was drawn to his heart, his faith, his purpose, as if he was

the hearth where she'd once found warmth and security before becoming lost and cold and afraid, and now she was set
on the path toward home again.

Levi stood close, and his heat drew her to him, yet it was
more than simply his warmth on a cold wintry night. He
aroused awe in her. He didn't cloud her thoughts the way
Jacob had…or the way Akiva did. Instead, her thoughts were
clear, and she became suddenly, acutely aware of his clean,
soap-and-water scent, his muscular chest, his chiseled jaw,
and his wide lower lip. What would it be like to kiss him, to
feel his arms tighten around her? Would holding her make
him lose control even momentarily?

She whispered his name again, not for any purpose other
than to sample it again, to feel it on her tongue and tease
her heart with its possibilities. Then Levi dipped his head
and brushed his lips against hers. His hands, already fastened
solidly on her waist, pulled her closer to fully embrace her.
As desire rose up inside of her, she fisted his shirt and stood
on tiptoe, looped her arms around his neck and kissed him
back. He tensed with surprise, then a smile emerged across
his mouth before quickly vanishing beneath a new force.
His arms were like solid bands, possessive and strong, and he
deepened the kiss. She gave into the moment, to the need,
to the promise.

CHAPTER FIFTY-ONE

Akiva melted into the darkness, his face hardening, his eyes narrowing, his heart burning with a hatred that fired his veins and radiated outward. It wouldn't take but a second to destroy Levi, and he would have, if not for Hannah standing between them. If she saw what he was capable of, she would be frightened and he would lose her.

Pushing away from the tree, he turned his back on Levi and Hannah, walked into the deepening fog, and felt his hopes dissolving, disintegrating, decomposing.

At one time, he'd wanted freedom to pursue his desires, other cultures, thoughts beyond the walls of this miniscule community, and the pursuit had stripped him of all he'd ever really wanted: Hannah. He'd come back for her, willing to give up everything—his desire to see the world and discover its secrets—all to be with her. But his chance had been thwarted.

It was all Camille's fault. She had chased him, stolen his hopes, his dreams; she'd taken his life, selfishly trading it for an eternal damnation. Even now, she had not given up in her pursuit of him, except she no longer had any real power over him, and she couldn't hurt him as she had before. She simply wanted him for a mate. She'd followed him all this way north once again, even sitting near him at the Vivaldi concert, boldly and daringly thrusting herself before him in an attempt to persuade and beguile him. He hated her—always had, always would.

When he had lived here in Promise during his previous life, he'd always felt like an outsider. Now he truly was, because he no longer belonged with the living nor with the dead. He found himself in a no man's land, gray like the burgeoning fog, that was neither sunshine nor dark, a world he still couldn't comprehend. The bloods he knew embraced their life of darkness, relished in it, thrived. But he could not. So once again he was alone.

Alone.

Being alone was the deepest, darkest pit, stretching beyond the realm of light, hopeless and forgotten. Loneliness was a raw ache never anesthetized by any drug or panacea, and the silence came upon him, isolating and shredding what was left of him.

When he thought of eternity—time stretching out to the far reaches of the heavens, the darkness, which never relented, the coldness, which never abated, and the silence, which never retreated—he knew a piece of him would shrivel and die each day. He wouldn't, couldn't survive that. If that was his future, he didn't want to survive.

But Hannah could change all of that. She could shun the darkness and banish the cold and destroy the silence with a smile, a touch, a laugh. Together, their love would insulate them for the harshness of his existence. They could escape love's mortal sting together, never apart, never forced to face a single moment alone. He could change Hannah the way Camille had changed him. But she had to be willing; it was his one stipulation. He wouldn't steal her life from her the way his had been stolen. She had to want *him*. More than life. More than death. More than heaven or the possibility of such.

One way or another, he wouldn't live without the one thing he'd ever loved, the one good thing he'd ever known—Hannah—the heartbeat of his desires. If she turned away from him, he could not go on, but she had to make the decision on the basis of her love for him, without competing suitors. He would not allow Levi to take away what was his. Not now. Not when he was so close.

His hands compressed into hard, fevered fists, and he turned back toward Hannah and Levi, watched them—body pressed against body, arms entangled, breath mingled—his hatred burrowing deep, stoking the fire, stirring the flames, burning inside his chest. Instantly, he knew the only thing that would satisfy. He sniffed the air and smelled blood.

CHAPTER FIFTY-TWO

H E COULDN'T GET ENOUGH of her.
Of her kiss, her sweet, apple-turnover scent, her soft, gentle curves pressed against him. All at once he felt weak and fierce at the same time—weak in his resolve, fierce in his raw need of her. If he didn't pull back, he wouldn't be able to.

Levi spun her around, laughing out loud, unable to contain the joy swelling inside him. When he pulled her against his chest, he gentled his embrace and kissed the top of her head, reveling in having her tucked close against his heart. Hannah fit against him perfectly, and he knew the Lord had made her just for him.

He wanted all of her, not just a part of her heart, not most of her attention. He wanted to banish the thought of any other man from her mind. He wanted to touch her, possess her with each kiss, see his child swell her belly, hear her breathe his name in the dark of night and call for him in the light of day.

But the time was not yet right, and Levi set her away from him, placing at least a few inches between them, and felt his arms tremble with suppressed desire and overwhelming passion such as he had never experienced. It was not as if he had never held or kissed a woman, just not the right woman. Of course, he'd been tempted during his running around time, but he had purposed in his heart not to violate the marriage bed before he was ever married. But soon, Hannah would be his wife.

He cupped her sweet face, brushed his thumb along the outer edge of her plump lip. For the first time he understood the impact of Jacob's loss on her, why she had floundered and mourned for so long, because if he ever lost Hannah, he would be crushed beneath the weight of grief.

His hands couldn't stop exploring the softness of her skin, as his fingers traced the slope of her jaw the curve of her ear. Even in the pale moonlight, she blushed as if he had lit a fire inside her, brightening her skin to an enchanting pink that warmed the caverns of his heart in ways he'd never imagined possible. She had a dazed look, a look he had given her, and his heart pounded so hard it shook him to the core.

She closed the space between them again, rested her cheek against his chest, trusting him, and his heart swelled and felt as if it might burst. He would never betray that trust or her love. He would guard her, protect her, and love her with every ounce that he possessed. Loving her fully, completely, would be his priority from this moment forward.

Ever since Jacob, and that whole ordeal, he'd felt frozen with indecision and fear, with confusion and disbelief. But now, maybe it was finally over. Maybe he didn't have to tell Hannah his terrible secret, the secret that had taken away his brother, then his family, and left him alone, forsaken in his grief and despair. Maybe now, Hannah and he could move forward toward a future together.

CHAPTER FIFTY-THREE

THE SHATTERING OF GLASS splintered the stillness. Hannah jerked upright, her eyes wide as she glanced around, then up at Levi for assurance. He looked as surprised as she felt, but fear did not darken his eyes. He pulled her sideways toward the mill and behind him, protecting her from anything that might harm her, as he searched the darkness.

"What happened?" she asked, clinging to his hand, seeking reassurance in his firm grip. Fear crawled up her spine, inch by inch, its talons digging deep in an effort to paralyze her.

Levi tugged on her hand, his gaze scanning the foggy surroundings, especially the copse of trees encircling the mill. "We should go."

She followed willingly, easily, both of her hands around his one, as he moved along the edge of the building. But then he stopped so suddenly that she bumped into his back. "What is it?"

"What do you want?" Levi spoke, not to her, but to someone else.

"I think you know, Levi."

The voice was familiar and stabbed at her from out of the darkness. She peered around Levi's broad shoulder and the sight of Akiva swept away the fear. "It's all right," she assured Levi, stepping out from behind him. "I know him."

But Levi braced an arm outward, which felt like an iron

bar across her middle, stopping her from moving forward. "No, you don't."

"Levi, he knew Jacob. His name is Akiva." She looked toward Akiva across the yard. He stood very still but seemed relaxed, his arms by his sides, his face cast in shadows. "Tell him—"

"Akiva?" Levi turned his head toward her, but his gaze remained on Akiva, his brows slanted downward in a distrusting glare. "Is that what you call yourself now?"

"He was hurt," she explained, feeling Levi's displeasure, and her nerves tangled at having to admit how she had hidden this stranger, which probably seemed worse than what actually happened. "I helped him while he was healing, while he—"

"*Mein Gott.*" Levi's voice ripped through her, and she felt a chill through her bones like a draft had opened in her soul. "Is that where...*who*...you've been seeing all this time?"

"What is it?" She searched his face, but he didn't look at her. He stared at Akiva as if he hated the man when he didn't even know him. "What is wrong?"

"Levi." Akiva spoke his name in a demanding way. But what was he demanding?

"You should have never come back." Levi's tone was hard, unrelenting. Hannah had never heard him speak in such a manner.

Akiva was back? What did he mean by that? Had he been here before? Hannah had believed he was new to the area, but he seemed to know Levi. And Levi knew him.

"Call it destiny." Akiva's gaze shifted to Hannah. "And I believe you know the reason why."

Levi's spine straightened and his shoulders squared. "I won't allow it, Jacob."

A jolt shook Hannah and she staggered back a step. "*Jacob?*"

She shoved Levi's arm aside, her gaze shifting between the two men—first on Akiva, then to Levi, and then back to the man standing a few feet away, watching her. How could it be Jacob? She would have known. She would have recognized him. As if dismissing the idea, the possibility, she shook her head. "His name is Akiva."

But the heavy clouds shifted overhead and revealed more of the moon, which offered more light. Yet with the fog, everything seemed coated with a haze. Whatever similarities Akiva had with Jacob were negated in those eyes that were so different. But could she have been wrong? Could she have not seen?

Then the whispers interceded, scattered her thoughts, her questions, like leaves skittering across the ground, chased by the wind. The fog seemed to penetrate her mind and obscure any clarity.

Slowly, he reached a hand toward Hannah, his palm up in a beseeching manner. "It's all right, my sweet Hannah." His voice resonated deep within her, as if it filled the very center of her bones. "Come to me now."

As if seeing him for the first time, she recognized him then, more than his face or his voice. It was as if his soul spoke to hers. Something pulled her toward him, and she took a step.

"Hannah." Levi grabbed her arm, held her back.

"Is it—" She stopped herself, unable or unwilling to speak Jacob's name as it snagged on the panic constricting her throat. She feared saying it, as if speaking it aloud might make her wake up from this dream.

Levi's hand tightened on her arm. "Stay away from him. Didn't you hear Roc—"

But she jerked loose and moved toward Jacob. "It's not possible, is it?"

"No!" The words burst out of Levi. He glared at Akiva. "Jacob, you will not—"

"She's mine, Levi."

Hannah stood between them, glancing back at Levi, not understanding what he was saying, why he was so angry, why for the first time she recognized fear in his eyes, and then her gaze shifted to Akiva...or Jacob. Was it really him? Could it be? She shook so hard she wasn't sure her legs would hold her up much less allow her to walk toward him.

"She has always been mine."

"I will not allow it."

"*Allow it?*" Jacob laughed. "You can do nothing to stop it."

"Things change." Levi's voice was firm with resolve.

"Do you think I would harm her?"

"I've seen what you can do. She is not yours. She is the Lord's." Levi came up behind her, braced her shoulders with his hands. "Hannah."

She stared straight at Jacob. This was a dream. This had to be a dream. And yet if it was, she didn't want to wake up from it. "H-how is this possible?"

"Oh, ye of little faith," Akiva...or Jacob said.

"She is not the one without faith, Jacob." Levi's tone was harsh, angry, and then he spun her around to face him. He bent down, his face inches from hers. "Go home. Do you hear me? Go now!"

But suddenly, Levi jerked back as if shoved. He shook his head, swatted the air, knocking his hat to the ground. "What is this?" He turned one way then the other, his body shifting sideways. "Jacob—" He ground the name out between clenched teeth as he wrestled with something that she couldn't see, couldn't imagine.

She looked toward Akiva, who was smiling, and her gaze locked with his again. It felt as if a giant magnet tugged at her, the whispers and murmurings pulling her toward him. She was already walking when Levi called to her again, said her name over and over, but his voice sounded far away... and fading into the distance.

"It is Jacob," she whispered.

"He's not Jacob." Levi's voice was faint. "Why then does he go by another name?"

Her footsteps faltered, and that one question penetrated the haze in her mind, followed by another. Why had he not told her he was Jacob? But the questions faded beneath the whispers, which grew louder and more insistent, shrouding any questions.

"Come with me, Hannah." His hand remained stretched out toward her. "I'll explain everything."

"What about..." she hesitated. "Levi?"

"Levi is jealous. My own brother doesn't want me back because he knows then he will lose you. Forever."

"But—"

"No!" Levi's voice rang out, echoed in the tree limbs above them, and this time resonating in her heart.

But her vision filled with only Jacob's face, her ears with his voice, murmuring to her, coaxing her, drawing her to him. "They said you died."

"You can see I'm alive."

"But—"

"Hannah!" Levi called to her again, sounding remote, the fog absorbing his voice.

"They lied?" her own voice quavered, as she thought of

all that Levi had told her, the grave where she had gone so often to be with Jacob. Was all of it a lie? But why?

"Jacob is lying to you now, Hannah." Levi's voice cut through the buzzing of whispers. Shaking her head, trying to clear it, she backed away from Levi...and from Jacob. "I don't understand. Why didn't you tell me that it was you weeks ago?" She remained caught between the two brothers, not moving in either direction. She kept shaking her head, unable to grasp what was happening.

"I didn't want to frighten you." Jacob spoke calmly, but there was an underlying current of something...something odd, something unsettling, something she did not understand.

Frightened, feeling betrayed by both Levi and Akiva...or Jacob, she bolted. Not toward home but through the dense forest. She didn't know whom she was running from or where she was going. She simply ran into the thick fog.

CHAPTER FIFTY-FOUR

THE MOMENT HANNAH BOLTED through the trees and disappeared, the invisible restraints holding Levi back released him and the voices buzzing and stabbing at his mind faded into nothing, like fog evaporating or a nightmare dying. He took two running steps after Hannah but stopped himself and turned back to glare at Jacob.

"What are you doing?"

Jacob gave a self-satisfied, half smile. "Whatever must be done."

With every ounce of self-control that he possessed, Levi held himself in check and didn't follow Hannah. She was safe. For the moment. Away from Jacob at least. If Levi followed, then Jacob might too, and he wouldn't take that chance. He kept his gaze trained on his brother and walked forward, blocking Hannah's path. "Go back to wherever you came from, Jacob. You're not wanted here. Leave her alone."

A low growl emanated from the back of Jacob's throat, and a slow, snarling smile spread across his face, the moonlight flashing against his white teeth.

"What will you do, Jacob? Kill me?" Levi's gaze dropped. "What is that on your hands?"

Jacob raised a hand, turned it palm up, and assessed it then shrugged as if unconcerned. "Blood." Then he laughed, wiping his palm on his pant legs. "I could so easily kill you too." He drew out the words as if he relished them. "You are as inconsequential as a dead twig." He stalked toward Levi, his hands fisted at his sides. "And would you hold to your faith so stoically and do nothing, brother, but allow me to kill you?"

"Will killing me win you Hannah's love?"

Jacob stopped, sniffed the air. "You've brought reinforcements. But you can't stop me."

"I wouldn't—" But the sentence died on Levi's tongue.

Because Akiva was gone. *Gone.*

Levi whipped around, turning in a circle, searching the shadows, the mill, the night sky. Fear overtook him, its teeth sharp and precise, like a lion overwhelming its prey, cutting it down, killing it, then ripping it apart. He ran a couple of feet and stopped. *Where do I go? What do I do now?*

"Do not hurt her, Jacob!" he yelled at the sky, the forest, the mill, his voice sounding hoarse and raw. "*Jacob!* Do you hear me?" His voice pulsed in the emptiness of the night.

CHAPTER FIFTY-FIVE

LIMBS AND BRANCHES CLAWED at Hannah's face, arms, and legs, shredding her tights, snagging her cloak, and scratching bare skin. She crashed through the forest, running without looking, without seeing, tripping over snaking roots and fallen branches hidden by the fog. Her foot landed in a rut, and she fell, her hands colliding with the ground, scraping her palms.

She lay there a moment amid the musty, dank smell of fallen, crusty leaves, her breath sounding harsh and labored. Her lungs burned, her side pinched, her heart pounded. Glancing over her shoulder, she gasped for air, for understanding, but her thoughts raced ahead, out of reach, while fear nipped at her heels.

Scrambling to her feet, she pushed forward, not knowing where she was going or whom she was running from, or which lie was pursuing her. She simply knew she had to get away. When she broke free of the bushes and came into a clearing, stumbling forward a couple of steps, she came to an abrupt halt.

Akiva—or was it Jacob?—stood in a shaft of pale moonlight, his skin like alabaster. Fog crept around the lower part of his legs. Her mind folded in on itself. Question upon question in rapid succession poked at her, not allowing time for any answers or thoughts. What was happening? How did he get here ahead of her? And yet, why hadn't he come to her sooner? Why hadn't he told her who he was instead of pretending to be someone else? And why hadn't Levi told her his brother was alive? Alive! And why hadn't she recognized him, known without him telling her? She should have known.

Across her skull, she felt a pressure pushing inward, and then the whispers started. She tried to block them out, remembered Levi battling them, remembered the fear in his eyes. She'd never seen him afraid. He always reacted calmly, quickly, easily. Was it fear of Jacob she'd seen in his blue eyes? Or fear of losing her?

The questions began to fade as she focused on Jacob. What was she running from when all she'd ever wanted was standing only a few feet away? With legs that felt disjointed, she walked toward this stranger that wasn't a stranger at all. "Jacob?"

"Yes."

"H-how is it possible?" Her voice cracked under the pressure of tears. She came before him, stopping only a foot or so away, yearning, yet disbelief held her back. It was his eyes that were different and that was all, the rest was the same. How could she have not seen it before? What could account for the change? "Are you a-a ghost?"

His throat muscles contracted. "No."

She reached out then, touched the solidness of his chest, the place where only a few weeks ago there had been a gaping wound. And blood. She'd seen the dark color staining his shirt. Ghosts didn't bleed, did they? Ghosts weren't solid. And Jacob was rock hard. Her hand remained against his chest, and a yearning welled up inside her as tears made the vision of him waver.

This was her answered prayer in the flesh. And yet, the only thing holding her back was his lie. Why had he lied? Why had everyone lied?

Then again, why did it matter? He was here! *He is alive!*

She tossed out all the questions torturing her mind, and her hand inched upward, touching the cool skin of his neck. It was when her fingers touched his hair at the base of his neck that something inside her snapped like a weak twig. Suddenly she was in his arms, solidly against his chest. Had she thrown herself at him? Or had he pulled her to him? The how no longer mattered, and neither did the how of his being there with her once again. The simple fact was: he lived. Gloriously. Amazingly. Thankfully.

That was all she cared about as she wrapped her arms around his neck, buried her face against the plane of his chest, a sob of relief and joy broke through her questions and disbelief. Frantically, her hands moved over him, touching, assuring herself it was Jacob. He was here. She bracketed his face with her hands and stared deeply into those impossibly dark eyes. "It is *you*."

Jacob kissed her then, an urgent, frenzied kiss that stole the chill of the night and banished any sense of time. When he pulled back only slightly, she felt disoriented, dizzy, confused.

"What's wrong, Jacob?" She marveled at speaking his name—to him and not a memory or a grave. And she had to say it again, as if that would make all of this seem more real. "Jacob."

"I am no longer the Jacob I once was. I am different. I'm Akiva now."

A disbelieving, irrational, joyful laugh bubbled out of her. "I don't understand. What does what you call yourself mat—"

"Hannah, you must know—"

"I don't care that you're changed or even why they said you were dead." She raised up on tiptoes, her mouth aiming for his, but his arm was sandwiched between them, his hand resting against the side of her neck.

"Hannah—"

Joy sparkled inside her, and a smile broke forth. "I can't believe you're really here." She touched his chest and shoulders and face, as if reassuring herself that this wasn't a dream. "You're really here. I know this sounds...*narrisch* but I knew you would come back. I knew it. You're here. That's all that matters now."

His grip eased, turned into a caress, his thumb grazing the side of her neck and settling at the pulse-point center. A tingling sensation traveled along her spine and she vibrated with need. As his thumb pressed against her pulse, the beat of their hearts joined in a new rhythm, steady, sure, strong.

"Come." He took her hand in his and led her to a fallen log. "You're trembling." He whisked off his leather jacket and slipped it around her shoulders, yet she didn't feel cold. Instead, she felt vibrant and alive and full of wonder.

He knelt beside her, stroked the side of her face. "Hannah, there are things you should know."

She kept his hand in hers, folding her other around his arm, not wanting to let him go for even a second. "All I need to know is that you're here with me now."

His gaze shifted sideways, and he stared at the ground.

"What is it?"

He gave a heavy sigh. "Hannah, Jacob...the Jacob you knew *is* dead. Just as they said." Suddenly the cold of the night made her bones ache. "I am Akiva now."

Shivering and trembling, she lifted his hand to her cheek, and when she pulled his hand back to her lap she saw a smear of something dark across the pad of his thumb. She moved to wipe it away, but Jacob sniffed, dipped downward, and licked it off his hand. The odd gesture unsettled her. She clasped his jacket over her chest to fend off the chill of the night but her hands were suddenly unsteady.

"I can call you Akiva if that is what you wish. All I know is that I've dreamed of this moment, prayed for it, and now…" Her jaw felt as if it was disconnected, her teeth chattering, because even though joyful, she also felt something was not quite as it should be. "I'm glad you're home."

He pushed to his feet, paced the length of the dead tree. His solemn face reflected some kind of inner turmoil.

"I missed you." Her voice cracked.

He stopped pacing and looked down at her, a smile played about his mouth. "I know, and I've missed you too. I've thought of nothing else but returning to you. I'm sorry I couldn't come sooner."

"But you're here now."

"For a while."

Fear struck at her heart. She tried to stand, to go to him, but her legs wobbled and felt suddenly weak. "You aren't staying then?"

"I cannot."

Forcing herself to stand, she swayed slightly as if she'd lost her center. But fear of Jacob leaving her again strengthened her, and desperation stiffened her resolve. "Then I will go with you."

His smile stretched wider though it did not seem to reach his eyes, but he reached for her, slipped his hand behind her neck, and pulled her against him.

"If you wish to come with me," he said, his gaze sliding down to her throat. "I will make it possible." He pressed his open mouth against her throat, and her body vibrated, then he whispered against her skin, "Do you trust me, Hannah?"

The word she imagined saying that spiraled through her mind caught in her throat. "Do you know when I first fell in love with you?"

He lifted his head, still holding her in his arms, and gazed down at her, as if amused. "Tell me."

"When you saved me from drowning." She traced the curve of his jaw. "I woke up in your arms. It was as if I awoke in more ways than just waking up. Suddenly I was aware of you as I had never been before." She'd never felt embarrassed telling him of her love before, but now she felt a constriction in her chest, as if he saw through her clothes and down to the real Hannah. "B-but," she stammered, "that really started much earlier. I remember you came in late for school one day."

"Not just once."

"No." She laughed, her chest heaving toward his. "Your cheeks were bright, your brow sweaty, your eyes glowing with mischief. After Miss Malinda scolded you, you took your seat and sent me a wink. That's when it began, I reckon. But you always made me so nervous. Until you breathed life back into me that day by the creek."

Slowly, he raised her back to a standing position, his arms still around her. "Have I told you of that day?"

"Some. But not everything."

"I will tell you now, because you must know. This is why I have come back to you." Gently, he moved her back and had her sit on the log, while he knelt before her. He rested one hand on her leg, his fingers threaded through hers. Her skin beneath her dress came to life like a flame from a match. "Many of us were at Hallelujah Creek, cooling off on that hot summer day. You were there, but I don't know what you were doing. Suddenly someone hollered out, and I saw a body lying face down in the water, the skirt billowing outward. The girl didn't move, didn't struggle, just laid face down. And I ran for the creek and jumped in without thought. I turned the body over and discovered it was you. Your clothes weighed you down, as did mine, and there was a cut on your forehead." He glanced at the back of his hand joined with hers. "There was some blood but not much."

She fingered her temple. "I had fallen. But I don't remember why or what I was doing."

His other hand cupped her face. "You were so cold. As if you were already dead. And I was so afraid. It felt like I was frozen, unable to move for my fear. But I pulled you onto the bank. I was so afraid that you were dead. And suddenly I feared I would never be with you, never have the lives we were meant to have together." He paused, his hand caressing her cheek. "But it doesn't have to be that way."

"It doesn't?"

"Not at all. That day when I thought you had died, I pressed against your chest and put my mouth to yours."

"You saved me."

"And I can save you now. If you will let me."

"Save me from what?"

"Death." He placed a finger against her lips when she started to question. "I will explain it all to you. That is why I am here. I do not want you to die. I want you to live. Really live. With me, Hannah. You and me together. Forever."

"But, Jacob—"

It was that moment, as she started to question, when she saw the change stealing across his features, the tightening of the skin around his eyes, the flaring of his nostrils, the clenching in his jaw. Jacob always wanted his way, but this irritation, this anger that seemed to radiate from him was beyond simplistic selfishness. The change in Jacob, she suspected, was not in his eye color, but deep within his heart.

CHAPTER FIFTY-SIX

LEVI CIRCLED AROUND THE empty space where Jacob had been standing only moments before. Hatred had burned in Jacob's eyes and told Levi he would have killed him without hesitation—without guilt or remorse.

Over the past couple of years, Levi had seen enough oddities not to begin questioning now that his brother had indeed thinned like smoke and vanished. He was gone. It was the same as the night Jacob had irrevocably changed. But where had he gone this time?

Was he with Hannah? Fear stripped Levi bare of all pretenses, for he knew why Jacob had returned and he knew Jacob would change Hannah if he could—and she would be lost to Levi forever.

Pain doubled him over, and he felt as if his heart would burst, but he fisted his hands and began walking, each step determined. He would save her. No matter what. No matter the cost. He would not let her become like Jacob. He would not lose her.

The *Ordnung* would say he had no choice. It was her choice to make. But was it? Would Jacob give her a choice? This wasn't a simple decision to leave their Amish district. This was something darker and more sinister that wouldn't lead to a life in the *English* world. It would lead to death beyond what he knew of those buried in the cemetery. Could she understand that? Would she be given the chance?

Or maybe the *Ordnung* would say it was God's will and Levi must wait and be patient. There was wisdom in that thought, and many scripture verses substantiated that kind of decision. But still, he kept walking.

He glanced heavenward and prayed for wisdom, for guidance, for help. Then a verse came to him from one of the parables in the Book of Matthew. *For the Son of man is come to save that which was lost. How think ye? If a man have an hundred sheep, and one of them be gone astray, doth he not leave the ninety and nine, and goeth into the mountains, and seeketh that which is gone astray?*

Many in their district might say, according to that verse, the Great Shepherd, and not Levi, should rescue Hannah. But if one of Daniel Schmidt's cows or sheep wandered off, would Levi wait and be patient for its return? Or would he go after it? Would he suffer snows and wind and rain in search of the lost one? Would he take that risk?

Fists tightening with the fear that each moment was precious and time was waning, he quickened his pace until he was running in the direction Hannah had gone. He ripped through the forest, shoving limbs aside, breaking branches that tore at his face and clothing. He ran until his lungs burned and still he kept on until he broke through a fog bank and stumbled into a clearing.

Moonlight poured down into the opening, which was surrounded by tall hickories and pines along with scrubby bushes. It was a wide space, pockmarked by fallen trees and the remains of a brick fireplace, which once had warmed the home of a settler. Nature had begun reclaiming the space once cleared. Seedlings and saplings sprang up from what was once a hard-packed floor, and weeds sprouted from the broken mortar of a chimney, proof of what became of things that went untended.

But the field was empty. No one was here. Not Jacob. Not Hannah.

Had they been there? Was he too late?

Desperation inched upward from heart to throat, and he searched the area, finding footprints pressed into the soft earth around a fallen log. But were they Hannah's? Jacob's? Levi wasn't sure. He searched the boundaries of the clearing for more broken branches or limbs, but he found no evidence that they had been here.

A crunching noise startled him and he whirled around, hoping it was Hannah, fearing it might be Jacob. But he saw nothing —nothing at all but the swirling vestiges of mist and fog.

Swollen clouds rolled across the moon. A blustery cold wind stirred up dead leaves, lifting them off the ground momentarily as if they might take flight but then catapulting them back down. The wind banished the fog and the temperature dropped considerably. Levi listened hard for a hint that Jacob might be near. Or Hannah. The voices in his head that had assaulted him earlier were no longer taunting and teasing him. As the wind died, the leaves settled once again. He searched the shadows along the edges, but the clearing was still and quiet, except for the clapping of his heartbeat.

He sniffed the air as he'd seen Jacob do. What had he meant by "reinforcements"? *What reinforcements?* Levi had brought no one. Maybe he should have.

Levi made a wide turn and backed toward the forest where he had come from. What now? Where should he go? Where would Jacob take her? Or where would she hide?

Then something cold and wet hit his cheek, and before he could react the sky opened and freezing rain poured down, stabbing at Levi. The sleet slanted downward at a hard angle and struck his exposed skin like sharp needles. With head tucked downward, he retraced his steps through the forest, hearing the clicking of the frozen rain against the leaves, and returned to the mill, where he scooped up his hat, but it did little to protect him and made him realize how little he was doing to protect Hannah.

By the time he reached the Schmidt farm, every post and shingle glistened with a light coating of ice. He felt his heart's full exposure more than his skin's. Heading straight for the back door, he pounded on it, his anxiety growing with each jarring sensation that rattled him as much as the door on its frame. Hannah's name burst out of him and he prayed she was home, prayed she was safe. "Hannah!"

The door finally opened, and a sleepy if not startled Daniel Schmidt stood there in his nightshirt and pants with his suspenders dangling at his sides. "Levi? What has happened? Is the barn ablaze?"

"Where is Hannah?"

From behind her husband, Marta Schmidt peered at Levi. "Why? What do you mean?"

"Hannah was with me...and then we were separated... and I need to find her. To talk with her. To make sure she is safe. Is she here?"

Alarm creased the older woman's brow. She turned toward the stairs and a pair of bare feet retreated. "Katie? Is Hannah upstairs with you?"

"She left a while ago."

"Something may have happened to her." Frantic now, Levi gripped the doorframe hard, the wood digging into his flesh, as his mind raced. What was he to do now? Where should he go? Where would Jacob take her?

A hand settled on his shoulder. Daniel Schmidt looked up at him, his face calmer than Levi felt. "She will come back."

Concern twisted Levi's insides. "We have to—"

"She is old enough to be of her own mind, Levi. It is her running around time. But I have faith—".

"But—"

Daniel raised a hand to stop Levi from saying anything else. "I know where your interest lies. If you had a disagreement with Hannah, she will come around. You will be able to discuss it in the morning after we've all had a good night's sleep."

"You don't understand."

"We must trust in the Lord."

But it was more than running around and doing things forbidden by the *Ordnung*, like smoking and drinking, and riding in cars. The danger Hannah faced was far worse than her father could imagine. But how could Levi explain? "Daniel—"

"I know how you feel, Levi, and I have been praying my stubborn daughter will have a change of heart. But first, she must test her faith." He patted Levi's shoulder. "We must be patient."

"You don't understand—"

"Most young folks think we old folks don't understand what goes on, but we were young too." He stepped outside and pulled the door closed behind him. "We faced temptations once. And you and I both know Hannah is a wise young woman. She will make the right decision in the end."

But would Jacob? It was a chance Levi was not willing to take. "Daniel—"

"And," the older man interrupted him again, "in the mean time, we must sleep. *Ja?*"

As Daniel turned back into his house and left Levi on the

porch with the tapping of sleet all around, Levi set his jaw. He would find her. He had no choice.

Chapter Fifty-seven

THE FREEZING RAIN DROVE most sane people inside. Roc had never been accused of that particular frame of mind but tonight he was content (if you could call it that) to lie on Mike's sofa and punch the remote control, not really paying attention to the images changing on the outdated television. The jumpy, incomplete conversations would drive most people insane. But not Roc. The random discussions blocked out the voices, the cries, the screams inside his head. Some only imagined. Some not.

It had been way past midnight when Mike and Roc left the police station in Philadelphia, braved the slick streets, and instead of driving back to Lancaster County in the sleet, Roc had agreed to bunk at Mike's. But sleep was proving as difficult as catching Akiva. He kept remembering what Father Roberto had said, how hard it was to kill a vampire.

It seemed damned near impossible.

Maybe he should pay Father Roberto another call. But what would that accomplish? Then again, maybe the priest knew something about the latest death or even the coroner. Why would a coroner lie? Or maybe Roc was beginning to see bogey men and sinister motives behind every dark eye and around every shady corner. That ability had once served him well as a detective—trust no one. Suspect everyone—but now, Roc was beginning to think it was making him jumpy and irrational. Really, *he* was believing in vampires! If that wasn't proof, he didn't know what was.

A pizza box lay open on the coffee table, the remaining slices now cold and the tomato sauce congealed. Just looking at it made his belly ache, and he remembered the fine, home-cooked breakfast at the Schmidt's, which only made him long for a time when life had seemed…calm and easy. When it was just Emma and he.

Not that she'd been much of a cook, but at least she'd forced him to eat healthier fare, buying packaged salads, granola bars, and fruit. He rarely thought of their days or nights together because it stirred things inside him that threatened to destroy him. Sleep had deserted him from the moment she died, and he'd turned to the bottle as much for the blessed unconsciousness as its temporary numbing effect. But now it had been weeks since he'd had a drink. And sleep still refused to befriend him.

For when it came, it wasn't gracious or kind. It only took a few minutes before the images assaulted him. The situations varied with him running, racing over and through and around obstacles, trying to reach Emma, trying to save her. Or he was holding her hand, trying to pull her up from dangling over the side of a cliff. Every time, he was too late or her fingers slipped from his grasp.

Pressing the heels of his hands against his eyes, he tried to smother the images, but they flashed across his mind like those on the television. Roc hurled the remote control across the room, and it bounced off the wall to the carpeted floor. The television screen remained on and a commercial for a floor cleaner morphed into a film about a glittery vampire that shimmered in the light like a rock star. Roc glared at the screen for a moment, then hit the floor with his bare feet. In two strides, he closed the gap and punched the button on the television. It went dark. Silence pulsed through the apartment until Mike's resonating snores rumbled from his bedroom.

Stalking toward the window, Roc pulled back the plastic blinds and stared out at the iced parking lot. Through the streetlights' glare, the sleet appeared silvery as it slashed downward and covered cars and sidewalks, rooftops and streets.

The jangle of his cell phone startled him. He stared at the phone beside the pizza box where he'd dropped his change and keys, but he didn't recognize the local number. Who would be calling at four in the morning?

He punched the button. "This is Roc."

There was a clearing of a throat.

"Who is it?" He didn't have time for nonsense. Or patience.

Again the throat clearing. "Um, Roc Girouard, this is Levi Fisher."

A hard knot formed in his belly. "What's up, Levi?"

"What we discussed the other night…in the field?"

"Yeah, yeah. The barn. The sheep." An Amish man with a secret. Roc's pulse began to vibrate.

"I am thinking I need your help."

CHAPTER FIFTY-EIGHT

S HE IS LOVELY." CAMILLE'S thick New Orleans accent had a melodious tenor and yet it carried an incisive bite.

Akiva did not bother to look in her direction but continued walking through Independence Hall. Outside the windows, trees glistened like diamonds. Not many tourists ventured out on a day like today, with ice coating the streets. For most of his life, he had lived an hour away from his nation's birthplace but had never visited the tourist areas, never understood the sacrifices represented here, the truth and freedom. Now that his own freedoms had been seized, he embraced these even more. After departing from Hannah at dawn, he'd sped here to think. "What do you want, Camille?"

Giving him a seductive look that only made him recoil, she ran a hand along his arm, grazed his hand with her cold touch. "I think you know."

"I'm not interested."

"What can that *haus frau* give you? Nothing. She will never understand you, but I can."

He ignored her.

"Do you believe she was stolen from you too?"

He had no answer for her, only a glowering stare. If looks could kill, then it would do the trick. But he knew it would take much more than that to destroy Camille. But one day...

"Does she have an appreciation for Vivaldi too? And all of that poetry you so love?"

"Do not follow me again."

She glanced around the hall at the sacred documents. "It is a free country, is it not? I too appreciate the finer things in life, Akiva." She trailed a long fingernail along his shoulder. "We could be so good together. You and me."

"I have loved *her* longer than you could understand."

"You know nothing of time. I have been alive for over a hundred years." She gazed at the display of the Constitution. She wore a silk top that revealed the soft mounds of her breasts in a way that Hannah never would, and her black slacks accentuated her long, slim legs and impossibly high heels. She didn't bother with the pretense of needing a coat in the winter; nothing penetrated her iciness. She would never understand his desire and need for Hannah.

Her eyes burned with hunger; she would feed today, as he would—but not together. He wouldn't give her that pleasure.

"Have you changed her already? Or would you like me to do so? It can be quite an erotic experience…even more so when shared."

Akiva wheeled around and through clenched teeth warned, "Don't you dare."

But Camille only laughed. "Oh, so you want the pleasure, is that it?"

"Stay away from her. I'm warning you."

She smiled, her lips closed and one corner of her mouth curling upward.

"I want…" He spoke low and threatening, but then changed course. "She will make the decision. Not me. And not you." He grabbed Camille's upper arm, squeezing in a steely grip, but she didn't even flinch. "Do you understand?"

"We will see." She gave him a half-lidded, unimpressed glance. "She is tempting, I must say."

Akiva loosened his grip, let his fingers glide down the inside of her arm. "There is another you might consider."

Chapter Fifty-nine

L EVI WAS WAITING FOR her. Standing inside the barn door, he kept vigil.

It was late the next morning when she appeared on the drive, walking toward the house, her shoes crunching the patchy ice.

"Hannah!" He ran toward her and skidded to a stop on the gravel. Most of the ice had melted with the rising sun and temperatures, but a deep chill saturated the morning air. He stared at her amber brown eyes, noting the color had not changed. "Where have you been? Are you all right?"

Hannah appeared as if she had survived, but her gaze was distant, distracted, and disturbing.

With a slow blink, she stared at Levi. "Of course. Why wouldn't I be?"

"Where have you been?"

"With Jacob."

Levi glanced past her, searching the road for a vehicle or some sign that his brother was nearby. "Where is he now?"

She gave a listless wave of her hand.

He frowned at her and held himself in check to keep from shaking her. What was wrong with her? What had Jacob done to her? "You do not know what you are getting into, Hannah."

She blinked, quickly this time, her eyelids fluttering slightly as if he'd taken a swing at her. Her shoulders squared against him, and she took a step away from him, her hands settling on her hips. "Who are you to tell me, Levi Fisher?"

Toby gave a bark, and both Hannah and Levi glanced in the dog's direction. He was staring out at the empty pasture, the hair on his back bristly, his tail pointing straight back. Levi leaned in toward Hannah. "I am only trying to warn you. You do not know who this is that—"

"He *is your* brother. Did he leave because of you?"

Levi flinched, felt the sting of her words. Maybe he deserved that, but he also knew it wasn't the whole truth. "Not *because* of me, Hannah." His heart heaved. How could he tell her the truth when he didn't fully understand it himself? "He is but a shadow of his former self. He has *changed*."

"I have seen the change. I am not foolish. But you have changed too, Levi." Her tone was soft yet steely. "You *are* jealous of him. Just as he said you were."

"Is jealousy bad? Even God is jealous of our affection."

She lifted an eyebrow. "Are you comparing yourself to God?"

He huffed out a breath. "I am trying to protect you, keep you from making an awful bad mistake."

"No one ever understood Jacob. Even you said so. And now—"

"Did he tell you what he is?" He paused and inched closer, hoping to crowd out whatever voice she was listening to. "Did he explain to you what he does?"

Her lips thinned.

"No, of course not. He lies. He deceives. He is the great pretender."

She shook her head, backing away, and Levi hesitated. He didn't want her to leave again. Her head was still shaking back and forth.

Levi advanced on her, grabbed her arm, not only to snag her attention but to assure himself that she wouldn't run or disappear. He had to make her listen, to understand, to see reality. "Who are you trying to convince, Hannah?" He hissed the words through his teeth. "Me? Or you?"

"But I loved him."

Loved. Not love. Her words pierced his heart. Had she changed? Had she seen the truth? "This isn't about love. About breaking your heart or his or even mine. This is about life and death. About Eternity."

She stared at his hand clamping onto her arm. Finger by finger, he forcefully released her. It went against every instinct, every fiber that wanted to hold her close and protect her. It was ultimately her decision. As everything else in this life, it was a choice. He had to let her make it. But could he release her if she chose Jacob?

"Levi, you must go. He is coming. I promised I would give him my answer."

"And what will it be?"

She looked at him, her eyes imploring. Was she asking him to understand? Or was she asking for his help? Her eyes filled with tears that reflected the myriad of emotions whirling through him.

For that one moment, all that had passed between them, the anger, grief, and longing, the deep kisses, the fresh hopes and dreams, pulled them once more together. She had felt something for him. She had loved him…if only briefly. If only for a moment. He had to remind her once more, and he pulled her to him, held her as if he'd never let her go. When she glanced up at him, questions churning in the depths of her eyes, he kissed her again.

He used every ounce of persuasion to convince her of

his love, of his tenderness, of his intensity, of the depth of his feelings. At first she felt stiff in his arms, but she began to relax and then melted against him. And finally she clung to him with equal fervor. The heartache and heartbreak pulsed between them, drew them together, bound their hearts as one. Could she find her answer here with him? Could she let Jacob go and find her future with him? Levi pulled back, breathless and hopeful, peering deep into her eyes.

"Hannah, do you trust me?"

In her eyes, he saw that she truly did. Behind the hurt over all she had lost, her love for him broke through like the sun's rays piercing rain-filled clouds.

"Oh, Levi…" She wrapped her arms around his waist, held him close, pressed her face against the beat of his heart. "You have to go, Levi. Jacob…Akiva will hurt you. And I can't bear to think about…anything happening to you."

"It's not me I'm worried about." He lifted her chin until she met his gaze. "Roc Girouard is coming here. He will help us."

"But how?"

CHAPTER SIXTY

"DID YOU SEE HIM?" Katie sat on the edge of Hannah's bed. She was dressed in her white nightclothes, her hair long and loose and flowing about her shoulders.

Hannah hung her prayer *kapp* on the wall peg, still feeling light and buoyant with love for Levi. "Who do you mean?"

"The *Englisher*. Roc. Think he'll be staying the night again?"

"How should I know? It isn't any of my concern." But Hannah knew why the *Englisher* had arrived: to tell her Jacob was evil, but she would not believe it. Yes, he had changed, but everyone changed. She had too. She wasn't the same wide-eyed innocent she once was. Neither was Jacob. If he'd left the Amish ways behind, the district wouldn't shun him because he had never been baptized. Living as the *English* did would not make him evil.

Still, she had agreed to meet with Roc and Levi tonight. Maybe then she would get the answers she needed. And when Jacob returned, she would tell him of her choice.

Now that her heart had opened to Levi, could things ever be as they were before? Or had life irrevocably changed? She could already see her life playing out with Levi, living a simple, plain life, working alongside him, building a home, a family, a future.

But they were not married yet, and he would not tell her what to do until that time.

You are being obstinate, Hannah. The whisper came to her and she wasn't sure if it was her conscience, the voice that had called to her, or maybe even God.

Tonight, she felt distracted and disoriented, impatient with Katie and her babbling. She must get Katie to go to sleep.

"He is very handsome." Katie hugged Hannah's pillow to her middle. "Do you think he would take me for a ride in his fancy car?"

"Don't go making yourself a nuisance. Leave the *Englisher* be." She gave her little sister a stern look, then yawned, stretching her jaws wide along with her arms, and hoped to spur a reaction in those wide, bright eyes of Katie's. "It's late, *ja*?"

"I'm not tired."

"Well, I am. And you should be." She gave Katie an affectionate chuck under the chin. "I will give you more chores tomorrow then."

Katie laughed and leaned back onto the bed, tucking the pillow beneath her head. "Can I sleep in here with you?"

"Not tonight."

"But I get lonely in my room." The mischievous smile that had been there only moments before disappeared under a haze of seriousness. "Do you believe in ghosts?"

Her question startled Hannah. "Why would you ask that?"

"What if I told you I thought I saw Grandma Ruth in my room? I woke up and she was sitting in the rocker beside my bed."

"Doesn't sound like you're lonely then," Hannah teased but stopped when she saw the fear in Katie's eyes. "You must have still been asleep. Fear not. There is nothing to fear. Remember: *For He shall give His angels charge over thee to keep thee in all thy ways.*"

Katie plucked at the sheet and considered the verse from Psalms for a moment before asking, "Are you going to sneak out tonight?"

"Why would you think that?"

"I've seen you before." Katie giggled. "Maybe I'm a better sneak than you."

Hannah crossed her arms over her chest. "Oh, you think so, eh?"

She nodded and grinned. "It's all right. I never tell. Are you going to see Levi?"

With a huff, Hannah grabbed her sister's hand and tugged her off the bed. "Come on, it's time for bed."

"Can I come with you?"

"You most certainly cannot."

"But I never get to go. I never have any fun."

"You should be in bed. Sleeping."

"Oh, all right." Katie hugged her, pressing her cheek against Hannah's stomach. "I like Levi. I can't wait till you marry him."

"Katie, no one has said…"

But the little girl grinned. "I can tell. And I like him better than Jacob."

That stopped Hannah as if a finger pressed against her heart. "You do? Why?"

"Levi includes me. Jacob always gave me things to make me skedaddle." With one last hug, Katie hurried off to her own room, saying, "I can't wait until I'm old enough to run around and have fun."

They were waiting for her.

With wariness, Hannah approached the two men standing just inside the barn entrance, her arms folded to keep her cape closed about her, and she gave a brief nod to Levi, who greeted her at the door. Roc, however, hung back in the shadows, leaning against the wall in an insolent manner. He had a dark look about him—dark hair, dark eyes—though not black as Jacob or Akiva's—and a perpetually dark expression.

"Come in, Hannah." Levi gestured toward a hay bale, his eyes deep, serious pools. "Would you like to sit?"

"No, *danke*. This shouldn't take long." She took one step inside the barn, where everything smelled normal with the hay and oats and animals scents but where everything seemed suddenly peculiar. Lantern light flickered along the walls, casting odd shapes and shadows about the stalls.

Levi closed the door behind her, the metal wheels sounding louder than normal as they slid the door along its track, then the bolt latched and jarred her. "You remember Roc?"

"Of course." She folded her hands together and stared at him across the way. "But why are you here?"

He didn't move, didn't straighten, but his voice came out sharp and straightforward. "I'm here to warn you."

She felt her jaw reflexively tighten, and her gaze shifted from Levi back to the *Englisher*. "About Jacob?"

"Akiva." His use of the other name startled her. "I don't know Jacob, the man you once knew, Levi's brother." Roc scuffed the bottom of his boot as he walked toward her, but he stopped still a few feet away and regarded her with a slow perusal. "He is the one that killed your lamb."

Her gaze swerved toward Levi for confirmation. He simply nodded, his expression grim. Her heart clamored inside her chest. "Snowflake? And why would he do such a thing? How do you know this?"

"I know. And it's not all he has done." Roc sat on a hay

bale and waved toward another that had been arranged for just this purpose. "Let me tell you a story."

She kept up her guard, but she already felt a trembling deep inside her and crossed her arms over her belly in an effort to hold herself together. Levi watched her beneath the brim of his hat, and, feeling nervous, she finally sat, the scratchy stalks poking into her cape and skirt like little warning signals.

"You can tell I am not from around here. I am not Amish. Where I come from, it is about as different from this place as hell from heaven. New Orleans is my home, where I grew up and became a cop...a police officer...right out of school. I loved it, but my wife...well, it's not easy being married to a cop. Bad hours. High stress. For the wife even more so. She always worried I wouldn't come home."

"I am sorry," Hannah interrupted, "but I do not know what this has to do with—"

"I'm trying to tell you that I didn't always live like this. I had a normal life. A home. And then Katrina happened."

"Katrina?"

"Summer of 2005. Hurricane Katrina swept through. Being a cop, well, I was there. Saw folks who should've left stay...and die. Saw things no one should ever see. The destruction of my home. My town. Everything I'd known." He rubbed his hand over his eyes. "There wasn't any law or order anymore. God had forsaken us. And I couldn't blame him. I saw dead folks. Killings. Rapes. Looting. You name it. But even that wasn't the worst of it."

His gaze remained on her, boring into her. "We found bodies, folks died in ways we couldn't explain. Even babies. At first, the captain said it was alligators coming into the city to feed. And we saw plenty of 'em among the floating caskets. But what we found was fresh bodies, their necks chewed and their bodies drained of blood. There wasn't a satisfactory explanation."

She plucked at her sleeve. Whatever she had expected Roc to say, it wasn't this. "What about your wife?"

His gaze shifted then, only slightly, but enough to convey his own struggle with emotions that obviously haunted him.

She sensed foreboding, a tension in Roc's body. She didn't want to care about this man or his problems, and though she tried to steel herself against any emotion, her heart skittered in response to his words.

"My wife…Emma…she died." The anguish in the *Englisher's* eyes spoke to her on some deeper level, and she recognized the pain as her own. "Not during Katrina. Later. Just over a year ago."

Her insides ached the second he spoke those words, and her heart turned toward him with sympathy and under-standing because she knew what it was like to hold love and lose it.

"And I became a drunk," he continued, his voice hoarse, "lost my job. Lost the will to live."

She hurt for this man, who so obviously grieved the way she had been grieving, but his story was different from hers. She clutched her hands in her lap, her nails biting into her palms. "What does this have to do with Jacob? With Snowflake?"

"My wife didn't just die. She was murdered." His eyes went flat as if all the emotion had been drained from them. "Just recently another young woman in New Orleans was murdered the same way. And then, up here, another murder. And another. And—"

"Seems to me, you are the only connection with these murders. Not Jacob."

He shook his head, and his look pierced her. "I'm hunting the animal that killed my wife."

"Animal?" Confused by all he had said and what he was trying to tell her, she wondered if she'd missed something.

"That is what *they* are. Animals. Without conscience. Without feeling. Without anything other than a selfish need driving them. That is your Jacob. Akiva."

His words punched Hannah in the stomach. The shock of it radiated outward, along her nerve endings, rattling her as hard as if he were to grab her arms and give her a hard shake. "But Jacob would never—"

"He's *not* the Jacob you knew. He's Akiva now. And he's a killer."

"How do you know all of this?" She stood, her legs more wobbly than she anticipated. She wanted to run out of the barn but fear and the need to know more kept her rooted in place.

Roc stood too but didn't step toward her, his movements appeared jerky, awkward. "Look here, I know you don't want to face this about your"—he glanced at Levi as if groping for the right word and settled on—"friend. You loved him. I get that, know how it feels. But in a sense, Jacob did die. He was changed, maybe even by that woman who is with him."

"What woman?" She glanced from Roc to Levi and back.

"She's one of *them*. They kill without thought. Without care. They kill because they have to have the blood to live. It's survival. Them or us. And I'm gonna make sure it's them this time."

A trembling rocked through Hannah and she reached out to grab something, anything, but her hand found only air—until Levi reached for her, held her, lifting and supporting when her legs threatened to give in to the pressure. Her head was shaking in denial. She stared at the *Englisher* and saw the darkness of grief well up in his eyes. "I'm sorry you lost your wife. Really I am. But that doesn't have anything to do with me. It doesn't."

A tick in his jaw pulsed. His gaze flattened, like a shield going up between them. He'd given her one tiny glimpse of his pain, an attempt to convince her, but she was as resistant as he had been at first.

"Tell her, Levi."

Levi's lips compressed, dimpling his cheeks. "Hannah, I saw him...I saw Jacob..." He shook his head as if reconsidering what he was about to say. "I saw the change, the way he became." Abruptly, he released her hand, and she teetered again, shaken and unsteady, while he looked helplessly at Roc. "She sees and hears what used to be, not what is."

"Levi," she spoke, sounding steadier than she felt, "you're talking about Jacob! Your own brother." She shook her head decisively. "I will go to Jacob and speak to him. He will tell me the truth."

"You are naïve." Roc's statement sounded cold.

Levi approached her but this time he didn't reach out to her, didn't touch her. "I will go with you. Protect you. I saved you once, and I will do so again."

"What do you mean? *You* saved me."

"When you almost drowned in the creek."

She shook her head. "But that was Jacob."

"*I* found you, Hannah. *I* pulled you from the creek. *I* forced air into your lungs again."

"But Jacob—"

"You are not remembering it right. Think back, Hannah. I am telling you the truth. Only the truth."

CHAPTER SIXTY-ONE

LEVI WALKED HANNAH BACK to the house. Even though he was physically beside her, he seemed distant, as if his thoughts were far away and his emotions locked inside his chest. Had he locked her out? Was he disappointed in her? Angry? Her steps harmonized to his pace, but he didn't offer her his arm or even a hand. And she realized she wanted that connection, needed it more than she had ever imagined.

Their footsteps clomped loudly against the porch steps, and she hoped they wouldn't awaken her grandfather. At the door, he faced her, his eyes dark and serious, his jaw tight. "I will be here all night if you need me."

"Levi, it isn't necessary." Her hand lifted as if to reach out to him, to assure him, but she held back. "Jacob will not hurt me."

"His intentions are not pure. I will be here."

His tone ignited a spark of fear inside her. Fear for Levi. Fear for Jacob. "What will you do?"

"What I must."

"But—"

"Hannah"—the timbre of his voice resonated through her—"it is no secret, my feelings for you. I love you. I want to marry you."

Her heart beat in a heady rhythm, but her throat tightened,

closing down on the words she would say, wanted to say, and that Levi was waiting to hear.

"But this thing with Jacob," he continued, "it must be decided once and for all. I do not understand what he has become and I'm not sure I want to. But a line has been drawn and decisions have to be made. Do you understand?"

She nodded, her throat convulsing with all the emotions bombarding her, and she laid a hand directly over his heart and felt the rhythm of it matching her own. "You know my choice. You cannot doubt it. But I must be the one to tell Jacob. I must speak to him."

"It's more dangerous than you know, Hannah. It is not our way to fight, and yet, I feel that is what we are in: a fight for our lives…for *your* life. It is too late to save Jacob or I would fight for him too." He ran a hand through his hair and settled his hat firmly back in place. "I always thought the armor of God was more symbolic but now…" He glanced downward. "Maybe it's not. The Old Testament is filled with battles waged." His gaze returned to hers, imploring in their slant. "I wish you could understand the danger you are in."

"Jacob will not hurt me. This I know."

Levi grabbed her by the arms, pulled her toward him so that their hearts were but a beat apart. She raised up on her tiptoes. His gaze bore into her. "Didn't you hear what Roc said? Jacob is not who you believe he is. How can you know how he will react? He is an animal."

"You don't know that!" She jerked back until his fingers released her.

He pulled away then, stared at his hands as if surprised by his own actions, and then he rubbed them against his chest. "Hannah, we're talking about *my* brother. Do you think I would make that claim lightly? Without much prayer and thought?" His tortured features compressed. "He is my *bruder*." His voice cracked, revealing his heart, the pain and struggle he'd been through. "And yet he is not. Not anymore."

A long silence separated them and yet at the same time pulled them closer. Finally, she drew a ragged breath. "I will go to him. He will listen to me. He told me it is my choice."

"But he has ways of convincing you."

"I understand he"—her voice cracked into shards of brokenness—"he deceived me. He lied to me. Jacob would never have lied."

"I am not so sure about that." Levi's statement made Hannah wonder if he had experienced a different side of Jacob than she had. "But you are right, this Akiva has deceived you. And he might yet again."

She inched closer to him, touched his hand, and felt his fingers fold over hers possessively. "It is as much my fault as Jacob's. I opened my heart...my mind...to him. I missed him so and wanted his return. I allowed this to happen."

"No," he whispered, "I allowed this to happen. I should have told you long ago about Jacob. But I didn't think anyone would believe me. This is my fault. My father ran from the truth, but I should have owned up to it. I should have warned the bishops, the district, you. But I promised..."

"What would you have told them or me?"

"I don't know. I don't know if they would have believed me either. My father was probably right about that."

She slid her hand along his arm and shoulder, noting the slope and strength beneath the cloth and understanding finally the fibers of strength embedded in Levi's character that they needed now to get through this.

"We cannot allow fear to rule our lives." Levi slid his

hands around her waist, holding her next to him in a no-compromise manner. "But that is exactly what I've been do-ing. I have feared living, loving, losing."

Tears sprang to her eyes at the truth in his words. "Me too, Levi." Her fingers tangled with the hair along his neck-line. "I too kept my feelings inside out of fear that no one would understand. It kept me isolated. And alone. And vul-nerable. But no more. Now we have each other."

He cupped her face, his thumb brushing over her skin in a light caress. "It's a tool used by a predator, getting a weak animal off from the herd where it is defenseless and more eas-ily killed. *Be sober, be vigilant; because your adversary the devil, as a roaring lion, walketh about, seeking whom he may devour.*"

Hannah shivered at the implications that Jacob would harm her in such a way.

"Are you all right?" His hands squeezed her waist and she leaned into him, needing his warmth, and yet needing more…needing him.

The seconds pulsed as she relied on his strength, his warmth, and his steadiness. She thought back to that day, so long ago, when she awoke in Jacob's arms. Many times Dat had asked what happened when she almost drowned and she never could remember. It was as if her memory had been wiped away like the chalkboards in school, the images smudged and smeared, blurry and unrecognizable. "Levi?"

His arms tightened around her, as if he refused to release her.

"What happened…that day I almost drowned?"

He smoothed a hand along the side of her face and lift-ed her chin until her gaze met his. His fingers followed the curve of her cheek, along her neck, and settled at her shoul-der where he fiddled with the tie of her prayer *kapp*. "What do you remember?"

"Nothing. I don't even remember going to the creek that day. I've tried. Really I have."

He nodded. "All we could figure out was that you slipped on the rocks and hit your head. Jacob and I had gone there to fish, because it was a beautiful day, perfect for catching fish. As I crested the hill I saw you floating face down. Of course I didn't know it was you.

"I hollered out for Jacob to get help." His jaw tightened and his gaze drifted away, as if seeing it in his mind's eye again. "I ran down to the creek and jumped in. I should have taken off my coat or shoes first because they weighed me down, but I reckon I wasn't thinking clearly. And of course the water filled my shoes, tugged on my coat, and made pulling you out twice as hard. I got you to the bank but the mud pulled at me, trapped my feet. Jacob took you from my arms." His voice stretched and cracked on those words as if he feared the same thing would happen again.

He drew a slow, shuddering breath. "It took me a few minutes to strip off my coat and shoes and join Jacob on the bank. You were lying on the grass. Not breathing."

She felt her breath trapped in her lungs then, as she listened to Levi's side of the story and imagined it so differently than the way Jacob had described it. "And Jacob," she ventured, "what was he doing?"

"Panicking. He didn't know what to do. Finding a girl in the creek, unconscious and not breathing is not something we came across every day. He feared you were already dead. And I have to admit, you looked that way—all pale and still."

She sensed Levi was trying to protect Jacob in a way. Even with all they were facing, turning his back on his brother, divulging the truth, was not easy. "But you didn't think so?"

"I wasn't sure."

When he grew silent, Hannah pushed him with, "What did you do, Levi?"

He rubbed the back of his neck. "If you were alive still, then I knew time was critical. But Jacob was…"

She waited, watched Levi's lips twist as if trying to figure out the best way to say it. Finally she offered a suggestion. "Not helping?"

"More in the way," he rephrased her words. "I shoved him aside. Sent him to get help, but I'm not sure he did. He was frozen, unable to move, but I wasn't aware of anything but you. And trying to get you breathing. I was terrified. Scared I would cause you more harm than good, frightened I didn't really know what to do. But I remembered when my father helped birth a colt and it wasn't breathing, and he had to take action to help it. So I turned you on your side, pounded your back, pushed against your chest, tipped your head back, and gave you my breath."

His words made her tremble.

His blue eyes darkened to the color of the sky at dusk. "All the while I was praying. Praying God would save you."

Those words told her what she needed to know. Jacob had never said that in his tale of her rescue; he'd always given himself the credit. But Levi was different; Levi could be trusted. She rested a hand against his heart, felt the rapid beat pumping hard against her palm. "And the good Lord did. You did.

"When you coughed and spit out water, I fell away, exhausted, trying to catch my own breath. And Jacob scooped you up and cradled you in his arms."

"And that's my first memory." *Jacob.* But as she peered into that long ago moment and examined it, she remembered Jacob's hair was dry, as were most of his clothes. How then could he have pulled her from the creek? "All this time…I believed…" She lifted her chin toward Levi. "I wish I had known the truth."

"So do I."

But it wasn't in Levi to brag about his actions, and so he hadn't said anything. Hannah raised up on tiptoes, angled her mouth toward Levi's, and whispered, "Thank you, Levi."

He closed the gap, pressed his lips to hers. The textures brushed and blended, folded over each other, and swept away any doubts. It was Levi: Levi who loved her, Levi who held her, protected her, cherished her. He could be counted on. He was dependable. And she clung to him now.

When he pulled back, only an inch away, his breath and her own still mingling and crystallizing in the cold night air, he whispered, "I love you, Hannah Schmidt. I have for a long while now."

"I know." Her heart fluttered and raced, the beats growing stronger and more sure. "And I love you, Levi Fisher."

His eyes contracted. "Do you love me because I saved you?"

"I love you because you are the best man I have ever known. I love you because you never gave up on me. I love you because that's all I know to do. Because you are willing to risk everything. To save me from the creek. And to save me now." She smoothed her hand along his chest and shoulder, luxuriating in the solidness of him, the sturdiness of him, his faith.

And he kissed her again, his arms tightening, banding around her waist, holding her as if he would not let go. Breathless and full of hope, she felt herself respond to his kiss in ways she'd only imagined.

But before anything went further than it should, he set her firmly back on her own feet, inching them apart, his pupils dilated, his breath harsh, his chest hot to the touch, and she knew what she must do. No longer were there shadows of doubt or dark areas of resistance in her heart. Her path was clear, a light of truth leading the way. She didn't believe Jacob would harm her. But would he hurt Levi? She'd seen the way Akiva had responded when she'd spoken Levi's name. She hadn't understood then but she did now.

"Let me take you away from here, Hannah."

"And go where, Levi? How far would we have to run? Would *he* follow?" She shook her head. "No. We must face this fear. We cannot outrun it."

His nostrils flared slightly and his jaw set. "Then I will go. I will tell Jacob—"

"No." Her tone was stronger than she felt. "You do not have to risk anything else, Levi. I will go to Jacob—Akiva—and tell him I have chosen another. *You.* This life. Not his."

"You can't go alone."

"But it is my problem—"

"Our problem," he corrected.

"I allowed it, and I must stop it now."

A frown tugged his brows downward. "How will Jacob react?"

"He will not be happy but he will go away. He's given me a choice and he will honor it."

"I am not so sure."

"I am." She smoothed her hand over Levi's chest in an effort to calm his heart, his questions, his doubts. "Jacob will accept my choice since he never had one. He cannot help what he is, or what he has become. It was not his choice."

"It is always a choice, Hannah. Always."

She stared at her hand, solidly against his chest, and he covered it with his own. He was right. She'd made small, seemingly inconsequential choices, choices in the dark of night and secrecy of her own bedroom, choices that had allowed this problem. Maybe Jacob had invited the trouble too. What did Mamm always say? "Don't go looking for trouble or you'll surely find it." Jacob had found trouble. As she had. And he had brought that trouble to Promise. "This," she said firmly, "is my choice now.

"I could not bear it if something happened to you. Jacob will not hurt me. But you—" She couldn't tell him of the hate she'd seen in Akiva's eyes when aimed at Levi.

"Roc believes—"

"Roc is but an *Englisher*. What does he know of this? Of us?"

"He understands what Jacob has become better than we do." Levi bracketed her shoulders. "Jacob must be destroyed. And Roc will help us."

Shocked, she stared at Levi. "How can you say that? About your own brother?"

"Don't you think it's killing me to do so?"

And she knew it was. "I will not let you harm Jacob. Just let him go, Levi."

"Not if he's going to harm others. How could I live with myself then? I have to make a stand and end it once and for all. Don't you see I can't protect you both? Not anymore. It's you or Jacob, and since he's no longer really Jacob, then the choice is easy."

"It is not a choice for you to make."

CHAPTER SIXTY-TWO

RACHEL LAY DOWN ON the bed, carefully, gently, fearfully, and lifted her feet onto a pillow, all the while breathing in and out, slow and steady. Her hand rested on her lower belly. Not much had changed yet, not much rounding with the baby, as it was still early yet. She'd only skipped one of her times of the month.

She felt no pain, which she figured was a good sign. Yes, of course, nothing unusual, except the gas bubbles she'd been experiencing for the past few days. She should go to sleep and in the morning it would all be better. But that small amount of blood frightened her. That's all she'd seen in her underpants, just a smear. Could she have been wrong about being pregnant? But Mamm had agreed with her, assessing her symptoms and confirming she was indeed expecting. She closed her eyes and prayed for her unborn child, her lips barely moving, but tears dampened her lashes and trailed down her cheeks, pooling along her neck.

Time seemed to pass slowly or quickly; she wasn't sure which. She lost count of how many breaths she drew in and out until the back door opened. The small cottage they shared was attached to the back of Josef's parents house, where his grandparents had lived. Hearing Josef usually gave her heart a happy jolt as she anticipated the evenings when their chores were finished and they changed into their night clothes and snuggled under the blankets, his hands eager, his body warm, hers responding.

But her heart reacted with uncertainty. What would she tell her husband? Should she share her fears? How could he help her? Would he be disappointed? Anxious? Would he blame her?

The pop and whoosh heralded the pale yellow glow from the gas lamp in the kitchen as he rummaged around for something to eat. He'd stayed in the barn later than usual, tending a horse with the colic. She should get up and greet him, but a still, quiet voice whispered in her heart to stay put. *Rest. Relax. Pray.*

"Rachel?" Josef called to her. He came to a halt in the doorway, his shoulders filling up the space as he stood there a moment while his eyes adjusted to the darkness of the room. "Rachel." His tone was gentle, unsure.

"I'm here."

"Are you all right?"

"Yes." Her voice dipped lower than normal in an attempt to fight back tears. She squeezed her eyes closed. If she looked at him, if she looked into those concerned blue eyes, she would shake apart. Her hands clutched each other in an effort to suppress the fear pulsing through her.

His boots clomped against the wooden floor, creating a hollow sound, and then she felt his weight dipping into the edge of the bed. His leg pressed against her arm. It was not until that moment she felt the chill in the room and scooted closer to his warmth. He covered her hands with his larger one. "Are you sick?"

"Just awful tired." She had been tired a lot lately, but Mamm had said that was normal while carrying a babe.

"It's the baby, *ja*?"

She opened her eyes, raising her gaze to meet his, and his features changed, wavered as tears filled her eyes again.

His hand tightened on hers. With his other, he wiped away the tears wetting her cheeks. "What is it, Rachel? What is wrong?"

"I should rest." She patted his hand and prayed harder. "That is all."

"Are you unhappy then?"

She shook her head, biting her lip to still the trembling. "I've never been happier."

He studied her for a moment. "Should I get your mamm then? Would she be a comfort to you?"

Mamm. Yes. She would know if the baby was in trouble. She would advise her what to do. And if she said to go to an *English* doctor then she would without question. She would. Whatever it took. "Yes. That would be awful good."

He nodded, traced the curve of her cheek. "I will be back shortly. You will be all right, *ja*?"

"I will be fine."

He stood, hesitating, then bent back down and pressed his lips to hers. His beard was filling out and growing, showing he was now a married man. The kiss warmed her and she lifted her arms around his neck, pulled him back toward her. But he braced a hand against the bed and pulled back. "I will be back quick. No dancing till then."

She laughed at his attempt at humor, and the tension in the room scattered, banished to the corners by hope, faith, and love.

CHAPTER SIXTY-THREE

How sweet the moonlight sleeps upon this bank!
Here we will sit, and let the sound of music
Creep in our ears: soft stillness, and the night,
Become the touches of sweet harmony.

AKIVA SAT ON THE bank of the creek and listened to the burbling water moving over the smooth rocks, which somehow reminded him of Shakespeare and the musical quality of his words. The moon's hazy light made the fog shimmer and distort the trees into giants with arms stretched out wide, as if offering up prayers to the stars. His prayer had been to be with Hannah again…forever, and he was so close to that reality that he could taste the sweetness of the moment.

He stretched out his mind and called to her. *Hannah. Come to me.*

Rising, he began the walk toward the cemetery where he knew she would meet him. She would decide tonight. He sensed it the same way he could smell the thick flow of blood. He needed no light, as his eyes were those of a predator's, sharper in the dark than in the light. Fleeing from his approaching footsteps, rabbits and tiny critters moved through the dry grass under brush or into holes.

He imagined Hannah lifting her arms to him, tilting her neck to give him free access, and that first sweet taste of warm, pulsing blood. He had to be careful, he had to draw the life from her slowly, leaving only enough to keep her heart beating, and then he would offer her a taste of forever. Which meant he needed to feed first, to have a sacrifice ready for her, so she could draw life from it and feel the surge of power, the strength forming deep within her, the change overtaking her.

It would come quickly, this strength. Her eyes would darken, maybe even widen with surprise at the rush. And it was a rush, better than any drug he'd ever taken. Then they would be together. Forever.

From far away, he heard the clippity-clop of horse's hooves on the pavement. Akiva went very still. The metallic sound of horseshoes against blacktop came closer; the jingle of the halter sounds were loud in the stillness beneath the solid moon. Someone was out late, probably some young man courting his love. The steady rhythm of the hoof beats echoed through the cold night air as fog floated above the ground, curling about his ankles. The clip-clop, clip-clop began to recede, and Akiva veered toward the sound, an answer to his need for curbing his appetite. He would feast only enough to render his prey helpless and then he'd give Hannah the rest for her first meal.

Taking his place in the middle of the road, he waited and watched for the yellow lantern light on the buggy. It grew larger as it approached, the horse's hooves striking the pavement louder too, then the clippity-clops slowed. "Whoa."

Akiva stood still, not approaching. Not yet. Patience was as much a part of the hunt as the chase.

"Hello?" came the voice from the buggy. A male voice.

Making his voice panicked and weak, Akiva called back. "Can you help?"

"*Ja*, sure. Let me pull off the road." A click of a tongue and slap of reins encouraged the horse to the side of the roadway.

Akiva moved forward then, and the horse began bobbing its head.

"Easy," the man in the buggy said. He swung down from his seat. "Did you have a car wreck or car trouble?"

"Something like that," Akiva answered.

"It was an accident," a feminine voice came out of the dark, and then Camille stepped into the circle of golden lantern light.

A cold sense of dread washed over Akiva. What did she want? To ruin his plans? To destroy his future?

Her eyes glowed darkly, and her long black hair hung about her shoulders like a mini cape. She was dressed for New Orleans' weather, not Pennsylvania cold, but of course Akiva knew the biting chill disturbed her as little as it did him. But he could see the Amish man giving her an odd look, as if he considered her a foolish *Englisher*.

"We were just driving along and the car died." Camille gestured behind her toward the Miller Cemetery, then walked toward Akiva, her mouth pulling sideways in a confident smile. "I can't imagine what could be wrong with it."

"I don't know anything about car engines," the Amish man said, "but I was headed toward my wife's parents' house. Their neighbors are Mennonite and have a phone. You could call someone from there."

"Oh, how perfect. I'm Camille. And you are?"

"Josef. Josef Nussbaum."

Camille slipped her arm through Akiva's and she snuggled against him, smiling up at him. "Isn't Josef just the nicest to help us out this way? That's what I've written my friends about Promise. We've discovered just the nicest folks here. Haven't we, *ma cherie*?"

A low guttural growl emanated from Akiva's throat, an instinctive response to her encroachment. "What are you doing here?"

Camille touched his chest. "Helping you."

Why did he doubt that?

The Amish man took a step back, bumping into the horse, which snorted.

Camille snapped her attention toward him, dipped her chin low and cooed. "Where do you think you're going?"

CHAPTER SIXTY-FOUR

THE WIND HOWLED THROUGH the trees, a lonely, forlorn sound that caused a shiver down Hannah's spine. The long branches of a willow whipped and waved, and leaves fluttered to the ground, skittering and twirling in utter surrender to the elements. Hannah's hands and limbs trembled, but not from the cold. Fear shook her from the inside out.

After Levi left to return to the barn, she'd entered her father's house but had not gone to her bedroom. She'd crept to the other side of the house, lifted the side window in the sitting room where she wouldn't be seen by Levi or Roc, and left the house, her family, and Levi behind.

Only she could end this. Only she could make Akiva understand.

Where was he? How could she find Jacob? Or Akiva? Or could she? Was it even possible? All the times she'd spent with Akiva had been when he sought her out, found her, came to her. On the road. In the barn. The cemetery. He always found her somehow, as if he had an ability to see where she was. She had no idea where he stayed, slept, or spent his time. Maybe she should have asked those questions. So many maybes led her backwards instead of forwards, and she was ready to move ahead now and leave the past in the past. Shouting for him would do no good. But in her mind, she called out to him. "*Jacob! Akiva? Come to me. Please.*"

But there was no response. On the road only her footsteps were accompaniment to the steady swish of the wind and beat of her heart, where she should have heard his voice, felt his presence, but now she sensed only a vacancy.

Her flashlight wove back and forth and jiggled ahead of her as she followed the asphalt that led to the cemetery. When she arrived among the silent stones, she climbed the fence and traversed the uneven ground, moving through rows of graves to the one place she hoped Akiva would come.

But a noise stopped her, and she strained her ears. The snuffling, burrowing sound came from up ahead. She swept the light over the tops of the leaning granite stones, and it slid past a large lump. She jerked the light back until the round glow illuminated a dark shaped object. Fear welled up within her. What was it? Should she have brought Levi? Even Roc? What if there was a wounded deer? Or some other wild animal? After all, it was hunting season.

But then the dark mass shifted, turned, and a pale face with dark, glinting eyes turned and stared at her. Those eyes fixated on her, bore into her.

Jacob.

No, not Jacob.

Akiva.

She took three steps toward him, relief pulsing through her, until she heard a growl rumbling from deep in his throat. His mouth was wet and gleaming. Behind him, something twitched and moved. A leg. But not a spindly deer's leg. This was a man's leg, covered in dark cloth, the shoe plain and tilted far to the side. Once more, she stopped, her legs suddenly wooden. Her heart lurched in her chest.

Akiva rose from his position on the ground, his shoulders hunched slightly until he straightened fully. His movements were slow and sure as he took one step and then another in her direction. His path, however, was not straight but curving outward, as if to come at her from a different angle or to turn her from the sight of the man lying on the ground. Was he hurt? Wounded? Dead?

Akiva licked his lips and swiped his arm over the lower portion of his face, smearing what she now saw was blood.

A trembling took hold of her and shook her from the inside out until she thought she would fall to the ground, unable to stand. "What are you doing here?" Her voice sounded distant, odd, as if it was not really her speaking. She gestured toward the man. "What's wrong with him?"

"You wanted me here, didn't you? You called to me."

So he had heard her.

"Yes, but…This is…" Her voice faltered, trembled, and the words wouldn't come, and she took a step back. "Should I get help?"

"No." His voice was firm, commanding.

Her gaze shifted toward the man, and the leg twitched again, kicked out in a weak impotent way. "What are you doing?"

"This is how I survive." He emphasized the last word.

"But it's—"

"Is killing a cow so different? Or a pig or goat? You must eat too." He took another step closer.

"This is a man…a person…someone's…" She stared as the man struggled to sit up. The flashlight struck him in the face but he was too dazed to even flinch, and she almost dropped it. *Josef.* A gash in his neck bloodied his white shirt, which matched the paleness of his face. "…someone's husband…father."

Jacob cut her off, angled her away from Josef. "You don't want *me* to die, do you, Hannah?"

She shook her head.

"You prayed for whatever it would take to bring me back. Well this is what it took. Your prayer has been answered. Now are you going to reject the very thing that gives me strength? That gives us the ability to be together?" He walked past her, turning her toward him, like the moon trailing the earth. "There is power in the blood. Power that I need." He came to a stop and stared down at her, moonlight flooding one side of his face and slanting shadows across the other side, revealing distortions in his features, in his soul. "And I know the secret of that power."

"Secret?"

"It will give *us*, you and me, a life together. *Forever.* Isn't that what you want too, Hannah? Isn't that what you have prayed for? Yearned for?"

Fear trapped her in its steely jaws and held her frozen in this place when all she wanted was to run. *Run for help for Josef. Run for Levi.* "What have you become?"

"A vampire." His tone was as if that was the most obvious thing in the world. "It is not some crazy notion in fantasy novels or the movies, Hannah. It's real. I'm real. The old, old stories and myths are true." He leaned toward her, his voice only a whisper. "Everyone has always wanted to find the fountain of youth. Well, I have. It pumps within each human."

She took a step backward, her head still shaking, her body trembling, but he stayed her retreat with a hand on her arm, a solid band of resistance. "This isn't right, Jacob...Akiva." Her voice cracked on the name. "I don't even know what to call you anymore."

He bracketed her arms, and she felt the strength in his hands rattle her bones. It was useless to run, fight, or attempt escape. Would he hurt her? Jacob would not have. But this truly was no longer Jacob. Her Jacob was dead. Now, this Akiva lived.

"Where am I?" Josef spoke behind her, his voice weak as a mewling kitten. "Rachel?"

Hannah tried to turn but Akiva held her firmly. "It's okay, Josef. I will help you."

Akiva laughed. "Will you now? Or will you help yourself to him so that you can really live? This is how we can live together, Hannah. Forever. Just imagine. We can go anywhere. We can be together, as you and I have always dreamed."

She stared into Akiva's black eyes. "You must let him go. It's Rachel's husband. You know Rachel! She needs Josef. They're going to have a baby. Please…Jacob, for me…."

"It is *for* you, sweet Hannah." One hand held her upper arm, but the other snaked up over her shoulder and cupped the side of her neck. "*He* is for you." His gaze shifted downward, studied her neck, and his lips parted. "This will not be difficult. Trust me. Soon, you will feel the strength of a thousand." He took in a deep breath, his nostrils flaring. "You will see as you never have before. You will feel so much more." His thumb slid along the length of her windpipe, caressing or threatening she wasn't sure. "It is all for us."

CHAPTER SIXTY-FIVE

Roc watched Levi pace along the side of the Schmidt farmhouse. All of the animals had been secured in the barn. The Schmidt family was in their house. Only Roc and Levi were out here freezing their butts off. What was the blasted man waiting for? He tried to wrap his brain around the man's thinking...that Amish thinking.

It is God's will.

We must trust in the Almighty.

It will all work according to His will.

But faith and trust had never come easily to Roc. What was he supposed to trust in as a kid? That Daddy wouldn't lick him with a belt? That the old man wouldn't push his mom around? That she would finally stand up to her husband?

She had prayed. The beads on her rosary were worn, the paint on the wooden beads long since rubbed away. She would sit in her chair and stare out the front window of their run-down house, all the while clicking those beads, her lips moving in the rhythm of the prayers. Obviously the saints weren't listening because nothing ever changed. She gave Roc a St. Christopher medal to wear around his neck when he was just a kid, then a St. Michael medal when he became a cop. But he didn't believe in superstitions and hocus pocus, Hail Mary and holy water.

He didn't believe in anything. Not anymore.

But then he had seen evil, not like from one of those slasher movies, not kids dressed in goth style or whatever they called it these days. No, he'd seen pure, undiluted evil, minus all the façades and illusions. He'd looked into its black heart.

Evil existed. But what about the yin of that yang? Was there a polar opposite, a good to counter the bad, a holy to the unholy? Imagining that there was some benevolent all-good creator was much more difficult for Roc to comprehend. *That* God had never rescued or saved his mother. And God certainly hadn't saved Emma.

Once more he clamped down on the emotions that rose up inside him, hot and fierce with volcanic intensity. His jaw tightened. But he couldn't hold back the explosion of emotion, and his fist smacked a post. Again and again. Then he grabbed the post and held on to it as he punched his emotions back down. He focused on his stinging knuckles, the grains of wood, the solidness of the post. It took every bit of focus to restrain the emotions. He wouldn't succumb to them. He couldn't. He had something more important to do.

He pushed away from the barn and stalked toward Levi. "What are you doing?"

The Amish man whirled around, his gaze peaceful and calm. Unrattled. But he should be rattled. He should be scared. Roc wanted to shake him, shake some sense or fear into him.

"What are you doing?" Roc's tone sharpened.

"Praying. Thinking. Waiting."

"All the praying in the world isn't gonna stop this show-down. Get the girl. We'll follow her, keep her in sight, and then when Akiva approaches, we'll at least have a chance."

"I will not put her in harm's way. How can you stop Jacob from harming her?"

"I have a theory."

"A theory?" Levi crossed his arms over his chest. "I am supposed to put her life on the line for a theory?"

"Okay, look, the bloodsuckers can disappear. Have you noticed?"

Levi glanced sideways, as if remembering, and gave a slight nod. "When Jacob first changed…when I found him…that's what happened. He just vanished. I couldn't understand or—"

"Exactly." Roc nodded. "I don't know how they do it, but I do know that they can't vanish if something has a hold on them. So if you're touching them, they can't do their disappearing act. If they're bound, chained, even by a rope, they can't disappear."

"Roc," Levi's voice dipped low as he said, "I do not want Jacob harmed."

Roc cursed. "Of course you don't. But then you haven't seen what he's done. Maybe then you'd change your mind."

"I have seen plenty, but I won't—"

"It's not your choice. You don't have to do anything. I'll take care of him. So get the girl. Where is she?"

"Sleeping. Tonight is not the night for this…showdown. Go on home, Roc, or to wherever you are staying. At the boarding house? I will watch for anything."

"And then what? What would you do?"

"Whatever I have to do."

"Would you really?" Roc stood less than a foot away from Levi, the heat of his breath frosting the air between them. "We should set a trap for Akiva. It's the only way."

"I will not use Hannah as bait."

"Who would you use then? Who else…who else would he come for?" Roc placed a hand on the younger man's shoulder. "This is our one chance, our only opportunity. We will protect her, I promise you that. But it is the only way. We must lure Akiva to us, then we can make sure he doesn't bother Hannah or anyone else again."

"I will not set my brother up to be murdered."

"*He* is the murderer." The words hissed through Roc's teeth. "Don't you get it?"

Levi stepped away from Roc, rubbed a hand along his neck. Without looking at Roc, he gave a confirming nod. "I will help you."

"It's the only way, my man. The only way."

CHAPTER SIXTY-SIX

AKIVA HELD OUT A hand toward Hannah.

It was a compulsion that she couldn't seem to resist. Trembling, she laid her palm against his. Slowly, his fingers folded over hers. "Hannah, you can call me Jacob if that feels more comfortable."

"Wh-why did you change your name?"

He stared down at their fingers pressed against each other. "Because I changed. Irrevocably. And yet, a part of Jacob still lives here." He touched the back of her hand to his chest. "That's the love Jacob had for you. And that I have now."

"Jacob…" She tasted the name on her tongue, a name that she had loved for so long, and yet what was once sweet had turned sour.

She stared at his chest and wondered if there really was a part of Jacob inside him, buried deep. She couldn't imagine the boy she'd known and loved killing someone or doing any of the things Roc accused him of. But then there was the wound he'd had when he first came to her in the cemetery, a serious wound. She locked gazes with the man who had deceived her, a man she no longer recognized, knew, or trusted. "How did you get hurt?"

He shrugged. "It was nothing. It is gone."

"But—"

"Do you know how people stared at us in our plain

clothes? Staring at the Amish with curiosity? Some even made fun of us."

She nodded, knowing the looks like they were caged animals in a zoo, as visitors filed by, trying to peer into their lives. Thankfully most of her encounters with the *English* had been pleasant, but she had heard stories of far worse encounters. She didn't understand the fascination *Englishers* had about their plain lives. They were simply plain. What was interesting about that? Was it that the *Englishers* were so dissatisfied with their own busy lives? Or was it just a passing fancy for most? "But," she said, "what does that have to do with your wound? Did some tourist hurt you?"

"No, sweet Hannah. There are some who hate you, just because you are Amish, just because you stand for what you believe and live it out each day. Your ancestors were tortured and killed because of their beliefs. Outsiders did not understand your faith. Even today, there are those out there who would harm you if given the chance. They fear you, what you stand for, what you are, because it might cause them to make some sacrifice that is normal in your life.

"And it is the same for me now. Because I am different." His hand smoothed over the leather jacket covering his chest. "And there are some who hate me because of that. Some fear me. Some would cause me harm."

"And that's what happened? Someone tried to hurt you?"

He nodded. "But it is not easy to fatally wound me." He chuckled. "And you will be strong like me too. You do not have to worry. I will protect you."

"That is not—"

"Come with me." His voice took on a more commanding tone. "Now."

She felt the tension in his hand, the way it tightened

possessively on hers, and she resisted, tired to pull out of his grasp. "What about Josef? He's hurt. I helped you when you were injured, now we must help him."

His grip tightened, pinching down on her fingers, clamping down hard on her hand. Pain shot up her arm. There was no escape.

She glanced over her shoulder; there was no one there to help her. For the first time, she realized he might not let her go. Ever.

"Josef is here to help you." He tucked her hand against his chest and pulled her closer. "The change is not so painful. I will be gentle and help you through it. Do you trust me, Hannah?"

But it was not Jacob she saw anymore. It was Akiva. A bloodsucker, as Roc called him. A vampire. A killer. The evidence was in the blood smeared across his cheek and spotting the collar of his shirt.

A trembling rocked through her, unforgiveable and unrelenting. Roc had been right. She had been naïve. And Levi…How could she ever pit brother against brother? And yet, had she already? She would die if harm came to Levi, or anyone else, because of her poor decisions. She had opened herself to all of this, to Akiva's…and even Jacob's influence. It was her fault. And she would pay the price, even if it was with her life.

Alone and now grateful for that, she would have to end it herself, or at least put a wall between brothers so that Levi would never be harmed.

"W-why," she asked, "did you lie to me?"

His features remained unchanged, and yet there was a subtle shift, a tightening about the eyes and mouth. "About what?"

"About what happened the day I almost drowned."

He laughed. "What did Levi tell you? Some fabrication?"

Her brow furrowed. "Levi was the only one who was there. Wasn't he?"

Akiva's mouth twisted. "Hannah, you're going to believe Levi? How do you know that what Levi told you is the truth?"

"He *never* lied to me."

"Levi told you I was dead."

A sudden rush of tears filled her eyes, and the bottled emotions from so long ago bubbled up inside of her, tightening her throat. "You promised...before you left for New Orleans that nothing would change between us. But it did." Her voice cracked, then grew stronger. "You changed. Even before all of this. I knew it then. There was something different about you."

He smiled. "It's that difference you always loved. And you can love the new change too."

She shook her head, trying to deny the truth of his words, but she couldn't escape it. She'd loved Jacob because he wasn't like all the other boys. He wasn't plain. And yet, it was the solidity of plainness that drew her to Levi now, made her love him, and want to be with him forever. "It was a darkness that I didn't understand at the time. But I see it now. I see this darkness in you."

His top lip flirted with a sneer. "So you have chosen Levi?"

She met his gaze with her own challenge. "You said *you* found me in the creek. Alone. You pulled me from the water. You breathed life back into me. Yet, I remember you holding me, that your clothes were dry. Why? Because you lied. Again."

His face twisted and knotted into something as solid and

hard as anger. Suddenly she was flying back through the air, shoved backward by Akiva with only a second to feel the rush of air beneath her before she slammed into a gravestone and darkness caught her in its arms.

CHAPTER SIXTY-SEVEN

THE PEBBLE HIT THE window squarely and pinged off of it, falling back and crashing into the dogwood bush. Leaves crunched, tracking the pebble's fall until it lay silent in the dirt. Levi waited, staring up at the window. The green shade didn't lift or move. He counted slowly to ten, then bent, picked up another pebble off the ground, and aimed again. This time the collision of rock and glass sounded louder. *That should do it. That should wake Hannah. Or the dead.*

He had to speak to her. He had to convince her of Roc's plan. She had to see that it was the only way for any peace or security.

After another count of ten, he picked up another pebble, but this time he caught movement at the upstairs window. The shade rippled as the corner pulled upward. Only a black triangle came into view. It was too dark to see Hannah but she must have seen him. He tossed the pebble and caught it against his palm. She would come to the back door now and meet him.

Tossing the pebble into the bushes, he walked up the back steps and waited. The minutes seemed to pass very slowly. Very slowly indeed. He paced a few steps along the porch, turned and retraced his steps.

Then the back door squeaked and the door opened. Levi whirled around but Hannah wasn't the one standing in the doorway. It was Katie. The young girl was wearing her nightclothes and a sleepy expression. Her long hair had been hastily pulled up and covered by her *kapp*. "Levi Fisher! What are you doing here? I thought—"

"Katie, go wake Hannah. I must speak to her."

"That's what I'm trying to tell you. I thought she was already with you. She left a while ago."

"She left?" His heart missed a beat. "Where'd she go?"

"Now how should I know that?"

Panic sliced through whatever resolve Levi had.

Katie stepped out onto the porch, curling her bare toes under and shivering. "What's wrong, Levi?"

"Nothing. Go on back to bed. I'll find Hannah and make sure she gets home safely."

If it was the last thing he ever did.

CHAPTER SIXTY-EIGHT

AKIVA STOOD OVER HANNAH. She was not dead, yet she wasn't awake either. He fisted his hands in a poor attempt to curtail his anger. He hadn't meant to harm her. And yet, he'd had enough. "You are not leaving me. I cannot...*will not* live without you."

He whirled away from her. It was time for this foolishness to end. *Enough!* His patience snapped like a winter twig. She would adjust to her new life the way he had.

When she awoke, he would make the transition. But she needed to be awake. He scooped her up into his arms and carried her over to the half-dead Amish man. Camille was beside him, her mouth wet from sampling Josef's blood.

"Get away from him," Akiva growled at her. "I don't want him dead yet."

"There is still plenty. For you. For her." Camille licked her lips suggestively, her gaze shifting toward Hannah's face. "Having trouble with your lover, Akiva?" Her Caribbean accent, melodic and antiquated, was thick with memories of her ancestors and their rituals.

Akiva had watched her lure in unsuspecting victims and felt the tug of her allure himself. In ancient times, stories of old, the siren song of mermaids attempted to distract men from their missions, and Camille's soothing voice attempted to distract him now.

"Nothing I cannot handle."

"Oh, but I know how to handle the reluctant ones. You were once reluctant if you remember. I could help you with her." She leapt forward and landed on the ground so softly no animal could have heard it. She had the stealth of a seasoned predator. "If you want, I could hold her for you. Tilt her head just so. Of course, I would not dare interfere with your—"

"I don't need your help." He knelt and set Hannah on the ground, her body curling instinctively inward from the cold, but still her features were relaxed. With the tip of his finger, he brushed a loose hair from her forehead. Having Camille here was not in his plan and aggravation shifted inside him because he didn't know how to make her leave.

"You are more than capable." Camille brushed her hair off her shoulder, revealing her sleek neck. "I have watched you, Akiva." Her laughter had a seductive lilt. "You have grown strong in your new life. You have not languished and suffered as some do. You are more than capable of so many things." Her gaze dipped low. "But the giving of life...well, this is a fragile matter, no?"

"You should know about that."

Her smile spread as her fingers traced her own neck and rested along her plunging neckline, toying with the voodoo charm she always wore. "Do you simply want nourishment? Or to transform her?"

His gaze shifted toward Hannah's softly parted lips, then he jerked his focus back to Camille. Trust, if it existed between them, was fragile at best. "It is none of your business."

"Oh, but it is, *ma cherie*. You have spent so much of your time running, hiding, staying off by yourself, that you have not learned there are rules." She moved a step closer, her body like liquid silver. "Do you think I alone changed you? I had to ask permission."

"Of whom?"

"Of the leaders." She walked over to a grave marker and sat on it, crossing her legs seductively. "You come from a life of rules, do you not? The Amish have rules. They are under a law. What is it called?"

"The *Ordnung*."

"Yes, precisely. Rules must be followed, no? We chose you, Akiva. You must—"

"I don't want any part of your group."

"You've always been an outsider, a rebel, haven't you?" She clasped her hands together. She wore rings on almost every finger. "And what has it done for you? You are alone still. Isolated. No wonder you are seeking a mate of your own choosing. But there are many of us to choose from. Many." She stroked her own hand. "If you are not happy—"

"I know what I want, whom I want."

He carefully angled his body between Hannah and Camille, not giving the other vampire an opportunity.

"There are consequences for going outside of the law," she warned.

"There is no law. We make our own rules."

Camille shook her head, causing her long hair to dance about her shoulders. "Do you think we can have new vampires running around all over the place? There would soon be no humans left. How would we survive then? These things must be regulated. It is the only way." Slowly, she stood and moved toward him. She drew a finger along his shoulder. "But do not despair. I can take care of this problem for you." She dipped her chin low, and her dark eyes grew large. "Is this what you wish, Akiva?"

"I don't know!" His voice boomed, carrying the force of his frustration and regret. He'd lost his temper with Hannah, and he'd hurt her. He regretted his reaction but he also wouldn't be thwarted; he wouldn't lose her. Not again. But now, she'd never choose him. Not if she had the choice. But if he changed her, then she would come to understand and eventually forgive him. But doubts clawed at him. "I don't know what to do."

"Of course not." Camille sidled up to him. "Let me help you. It is my job as your guardian."

"Why didn't I know about any rule or a governing body?"

"You never asked. You have hidden yourself from us. If you had quit running, if you had become a part of us, you would have been trained properly."

"By you?" His words snaked outward with a sneer.

"Yes, of course." She looped an arm around his neck, toyed with the hair at his nape. "I will help you the way I have always helped you."

CHAPTER SIXTY-NINE

SAVAGE SOUNDS AWAKENED HANNAH, like a predator killing a defenseless animal. She pried her eyes open, blinked against the darkness. Her vision was blurred and she tried to focus on a blade of dried grass, her hand. Slowly the images came into focus. But her head throbbed. She dared not raise her head. She was slumped over, grass and dirt pressed into her cheek. The sounds penetrated her confusion and she glanced beyond her own hand.

Only a few feet away, she saw a woman with long black hair straddling Josef's waist, her mouth at his neck. Josef was defenseless, lying on his back, his arms splayed outward as if he had no strength or will to defend himself. Maybe he was already dead. Hannah could hear the crunching of bone, the chomping of teeth, ripping of flesh.

Hannah squeezed her eyes shut, so tight the muscles twitched with fatigue, and she tried to block the sounds. The top of her head rested against something hard and rough, and peering outward through barely slit eyelids, she guessed it was the edge of a grave marker.

Without moving, she listened and squinted through eyelashes until she located Akiva who stood nearby, not watching but not flinching at the grotesque sounds. He looked bored, his gaze scanning the cemetery, his features placid, his stance relaxed. Hannah remained still, pretending to be dead…or something similar, praying she wasn't going to be next.

Rising up from Josef, Camille gave a bloody smile. "Want more for yourself, Akiva?"

"Save the rest. Do you have a vessel?"

"In my bag."

Akiva walked a few steps over to a leather bag, tossed back the flap, and dug inside until he pulled out a round flat object. With a flick of his wrist, a cup emerged, and he handed it to Camille.

"Would you like me to do the honor?"

"She's mine. I will take care of Hannah." Then he turned in her direction, closing the steps without seeming to even take a step.

She snapped her eyes closed and held her breath, listening to his footsteps move toward her. Her heart felt like it would burst through her chest and take off running. But she waited, remembering once watching a rabbit, still and quiet, its eyes blinking as she approached, and just as she got close, it bolted.

That was her plan now. And so she waited, keeping her eyes closed, her body as relaxed as possible.

Akiva knelt beside her. He was quiet. If he could see her heart, which bounded inside her chest like a frightened rabbit on the run, he would know the truth, but she prayed he could not. She prayed, *Lord, help me. Help me.*

"Is she awake yet?" the woman's voice came to her.

Then a warm hand touched her arm and something caressed her face in such a loving, gentle way she began to shake. "Hannah?"

She jerked upright, shoved Akiva backwards, and scrambled to her feet. Her vision wavered, the world around her tilted. But she ran, stumbling, scuttling across the frozen ground. It felt as if she ran through thick mud, her legs stiff, her feet dragging. She tossed a look over her shoulder, but Akiva was not there. Camille stood over Josef. Hannah's stride stretched longer until she plowed right into a solid wall: Akiva's chest.

"Let me go!" She backed away.

But his hand clamped on her arms. "Not this time, Hannah."

She let her legs collapse under her, tried to fall out of his grasp, but he held her steady. "No! This isn't what I want. You said—"

"It's no longer your choice." With one hand he held her in place as if his hand was an iron band. With his other, he cupped her face in a gentling, soothing caress, following the curve down toward her neck. "Why should your choice affect me, decide my fate? So I will make the choice for you, the way it was made for me. You will understand then."

She bucked, but his hand on her throat tightened. She felt her muscles contract, and her bones trembled. She stilled, afraid to move.

Then the woman was there, standing beside her, stroking her *kapp*, her shoulders, her back. It was the woman with the long black hair, who had been to the bakery and the orchestra. "Easy, love. Be still for Camille now. Akiva has been practicing. He will not go too far. He will not let his hunger get out of control. He will stop before it is too late."

Akiva glared at her, then softened his features as he focused again on Hannah. "Easy now, breathe easy. I will not hurt you. And soon it will be over. You will only feel a bit of discomfort. I will be gentle and go easy. I must draw out your blood. Then when I tell you to drink, you must—"

"No!" she spat the word in his face. "No."

"Hannah, you can make this easy or difficult. Please—"

"I reckon," a male voice came out of the dark, "she chooses to make it more difficult."

"Levi!" Hannah recognized his voice. Her gaze went wild searching and straining until settling on him.

He was standing just inside the fence line of the cemetery, standing there bold and confident and unafraid.

Her heart tripped over itself in relief. He'd come for her. But then fear raised its ugly head. *How could Levi fight Akiva and win?*

Something flapped in the corner of her eye, and Hannah turned to see Roc wrapping a leather strap tight around his fist, the other end secured around Camille's wrist. Camille hissed and lunged at Roc, but as he stepped out of her reach another strap looped over her head and caught about her slim throat. Levi held that end, and the two men pulled the straps taut, trapping Camille between them. Her beautiful face contorted, transformed, as she snarled and hissed, tugging and wrenching her arm sideways to get loose, but the tautness of the strap restrained her. Roc moved in a slow circle, guiding Camille away from Hannah, but his gaze, along with a handgun, remained aimed at Akiva. "Let go of her."

But Akiva's arm looped over Hannah's head, and he spun her around, pulled her back against his torso, his arm braced across her chest. She stared at Levi and Roc. She felt calmer than she ever would have imagined. She knew what she had to do. And she spoke directly to Levi, hoping he could see what was in her heart.

"You must go, Levi. It is too late for me. I have made my choice." She turned toward Akiva and wrapped her arms around his neck.

But she heard Levi holler, "No. I'm not leaving you, Hannah. He won't take you."

Looking deeply into Akiva's dark eyes, she whispered, "Let Levi live, and I will go with you. I will do anything you ask. Just please…" Her voice broke. "Let him live."

The warmth that she had once seen in the depths of Akiva's eyes was now cold and barren of emotion. He sneered. "That's all it took then? What if I no longer want you?"

"You can't lie to yourself, Jacob. This is what you came for. And I will be yours for eternity."

Akiva laughed an exultant crowing sound. He grabbed Hannah's arm and spun her around to face Levi and all she was about to lose one last time. "You heard her, Levi. She is mine. I have won. You can take Camille." He jerked his chin toward the struggling vampire who bucked and fought the straps. It took all of Levi's and Roc's strength to hold on to her and keep her solidly between them. "You can have her."

Then all at once there was a movement from Roc, his arm whipped outward, throwing something, which spun through the air. It smacked Camille in the center of her chest and sunk deep, only a thick knobby end of a stake protruded. Camille's black eyes went wide, then her gaze dropped toward her chest. Her arms lifted an inch or two but then fell back to her sides and her knees gave way. "Akiva," she spoke slowly, her gaze seeking him in a frenzied search, "help me."

Akiva backed away, tugging and dragging Hannah along with him.

"Akiva?" Panic arced Camille's voice.

"Now, for you…" Still holding the leather strap, which restrained Camille, Roc stepped toward Akiva. "You cannot disappear while holding onto Hannah. So I will let you go if you will release her now."

"I don't believe you."

"Know this though." Roc's gaze was hard and intense. "No matter where you go, I *will* come after you. I will not rest until you are destroyed."

A soft, unconcerned chuckle rumbled out of Akiva as Camille seemed to be sinking and crumpling on the ground, losing strength. Nearby, Josef lay face up, neck ravaged, a gaping hole in the side. His gaze stared blankly up toward the dark sky.

"She is mine," Akiva said, and he pulled her back against him, keeping a firm hold of her, making her a shield in front of him. "You heard her. Nothing will change that."

"Her choice changes everything, Jacob." Levi stepped toward what once was his brother. "She has a choice. Just as you did."

"I had no choice!"

"Levi," Hannah begged, "go." Sadness welled up in her throat. She couldn't speak the words but mouthed, "I love you."

"You love me." Akiva whipped her around to face him again. His gaze flicked from her to Levi and Roc then back again. "Kiss me."

"Hannah!" Levi yelled.

But without hesitation, she raised up on tiptoe and pressed her cold lips to Akiva's. She squeezed her eyes closed, trying to block out the image of Josef's blood on Akiva's mouth. She kissed Akiva, trying to remember him as he once was and knowing that this kiss might determine Levi's fate. She would kiss Akiva and go on kissing him to protect her beloved.

Suddenly, Akiva jerked her away from himself, glared at her, searching her face. She was breathing hard. Fear made her heart skitter. But she met his stare with her own determination. "Do you love me?"

"Yes, Akiva. Whatever you want. Whatever—"

"You lie!" He shouted the words.

And she flinched and braced herself to be flung aside again or ravaged like Josef had been. Whatever happened, she deserved it.

He yanked her against his chest, his breath hot against her neck. "I will always love you, Hannah. Always." Then he pressed his open mouth against her neck. She felt him draw her flesh into his mouth as he sucked hard, then the grazing of his tooth against her skin. She squeezed her eyes closed and waited.

"Take her!"

Her eyelids burst open at Akiva's scream. He shoved her forward and she spun around, stumbling and falling forward until Levi caught her in his arms. Her face pressed against his chest, she clung to the solidness of him.

A shot rang out, the sound reverberating off the stars. But when she turned to see if Akiva was falling to the ground as Camille had done, she blinked, because Akiva, Jacob, was gone. And this time, she knew she would never see him again.

A bullet was buried in a grave marker three rows behind where he had stood.

CHAPTER SEVENTY

LEVI HELD HANNAH AS if he would never let her go. He ran his hands over her, convincing himself that she was in one piece and safe. Her arms embraced him. He felt her shaking and he chafed her arms, trying to warm her. But she stilled his movements and looked up at him with tear-filled eyes.

But a noise behind her brought Levi back to the situation at hand, and his gaze shifted from Hannah to Roc, who stood over the female vampire. She laid flat on her back, one leg twisted beneath her. She wasn't dead yet. But she didn't look far from it.

"Take Hannah home." Roc gave a nod in the direction of the road, the direction he hoped Levi would take. "Really go now."

The vampire's breathing shallowed, her limbs awry as if she no longer cared or no longer could straighten them. Moonlight fell across her pale features. She kicked out with one foot but without force, without strength.

"I can't leave you alone with this," Levi said. "What must we do now?"

"What will you do with her?" Hannah asked, still safely inside the circle of Levi's arms.

Roc knelt beside the woman vampire, just out of her reach, and she attempted to grab hold of him, to claw at him, but her movement was pathetically slow. "The old priest was right," Roc said, his voice slow, just as his acceptance had been. The wooden stake stood straight up, emerging out of her chest like an angry fist. "The myth is true."

She snarled, revealing a tooth still stained with Josef's blood. "You are a fool. You cannot stop us."

"Maybe we can. We'll take it one vampire at a time."

"Some myths are true, some aren't." Her words sounded disjointed, breathy. "Why should we make it easy?"

"It might take time to sort through the myths, but we will." He glanced over his shoulder at Levi. "Go, Levi. Get out of here. Neither you nor Hannah needs to see this. I will wait for a buddy of mine to come. We will dispose of her."

"What about Akiva?" Levi asked.

"He will get a few hours start. But then I will continue the chase." He rubbed his tired face. "This is now my duty."

"Your destiny." Levi voiced what Roc couldn't seem to consider. "Will Akiva come for…?"

Roc shook his head. "No, I do not think he will. He will run and hide."

Levi moved a few steps away, still holding on to Hannah, and knelt beside Josef. His chest constricted at the sight of his friend's pale, still face. He laid a hand on Josef's chest. It was silent. No heartbeat, no breath. Levi couldn't speak for a long moment. "What about Josef? What should I do?"

"I will get the body taken care of for burial," Roc said. "No one has to know how he died. We will say it was a buggy accident."

"Another lie," Levi whispered.

At Hannah's soft sob, Levi stood and wrapped an arm about her shoulders. She buried her face against his chest. He looked at the *Englisher*. "He was married to Hannah's sister."

"I'm sorry." Roc's mouth compressed into a thin line. "Really I am. I was too late." He looked down at the ground and rolled a rock over with the sole of his boot. "Too late in a lot of ways."

"We will tell Rachel." Levi squeezed Hannah's shoulder. "We will go there now. I don't know why he was out so late at night. It is not like Josef."

"Bad timing all around."

"How can I face Rachel?" Hannah pressed her hand to her mouth. Her whole body shook and trembled like a leaf in the wind, but she was anchored securely against Levi. "How can I tell her…?"

"This isn't your fault," Roc said, but his words fell flat.

Levi knew both he and Hannah would carry the burden of guilt for the rest of their lives. "I will take you home first, Hannah," Levi spoke solemnly. "I will get your father, then we will go to Rachel."

"No. I must be with her. I must help her…if I can."

Roc stood again and tossed aside a twig, which landed on Camille's leg. She attempted to move it off but acted as if it weighed as much as a log. Then Roc stepped away from the vampire, easing Levi and Hannah away from the area. "You will not see me again. But I want to thank you for your help."

Levi shook Roc's hand, packing his own thanks into his grip. "You be careful, my friend. We will pray for you."

"I need all the prayers I can get." He pulled a knife from a sheath at his waist. "And a few of these should do the trick."

Headlights cut through the darkness.

"Your friend?" Levi asked.

"Father Roberto." Roc glanced at Hannah. "Stay safe."

Levi helped Hannah into the buggy, feeling as weak and ill as she looked. He climbed in beside her, took the reins in hand, and released the brake, but he kept one arm around her shoulders, pressing her against his side. He wasn't sure where her trembling ended and his began. "It's over now, Hannah. It is all over."

"I don't know, Levi. I don't know anything anymore."

He rested the reins on his thigh. Her pale skin looked even paler in the soft moonlight. Still she was the most beautiful woman he had ever seen. He longed to hold her, to comfort her, but he knew he must wait, because now was not the time. Because when the moment came, they might both fall apart...until they could help piece each other back together. "Then tell me what you do know?"

"What do you mean?"

"I mean there are things you know for certain. Things you can hold on to through times like this." He looked deep into her brown eyes and could see the shock she was in. "You know that the good Lord is lord of all heaven and earth. Even though we have seen evil this night, we know that it is the Lord that reigns over it all. It is written: *And he had in his right hand seven stars: and out of his mouth went a sharp two-edged sword: and his countenance was as the sun shineth in his strength. And when I saw him, I fell at his feet as dead. And he laid his right hand upon me, saying unto me, Fear not; I am the first and the last; I am he that liveth and was dead; and behold, I am alive for evermore, Amen; and have the keys of hell and of death.*"

With each word of scripture that Levi spoke, his voice grew stronger and his own countenance flushed with immense feeling. Hannah felt her heart begin to pound, thrilling to the sound of his voice and confidence. She clung to his hand and pressed it against her cheek.

"And what is it that you know, Hannah?" he asked.

She gazed up into the watery blue depths of his eyes. "I know I love you." Her voice gained strength as did her heart. But did he believe her? Did he take comfort in her love the way his love sheltered and protected her? She felt ashamed at what she had said to Akiva, what she had promised him. Could Levi ever understand her reasons? "Levi," she said, holding his hand between both of her own. "I didn't mean what I said back there. I lied to Akiva." She squeezed his hand. "Do you know that?"

His gaze intensified. "I know you risked your life for me. You said what you thought you must to protect me."

"I did no more than you risked coming after me."

He cupped her face with his hand. She tilted her head, leaning into his touch, his caress, and closing her eyes. "You know that I love you. *Ja?*"

Tears rushed to the surface at his words, which resonated deep in her soul. "Still, Levi?" Her voice cracked. Her lips trembled. "Even now? After all of this…after you know what all I—"

He pressed a finger to her lips and then silenced her completely with a soft, reverent kiss. "Even always."

His next kiss was filled with all the passion and hope that she too shared. It would have gone on and on except Levi's horse snorted and stamped its hoof. Levi pulled away only slightly, his face alight with a smile. Then he tucked her against his side, covered her lap with a blanket, and she felt the sheltering of his love wrap around her.

She leaned her head against his shoulder, her *kapp* askew, the long tie falling across his arm, and she knew there were stronger bonds that would hold them together forever, bonds from the past, and bonds that they would one day vow to each other. But there was a precipice between this moment and their future, and it would take a leap to reach the point where they could love each other without reminders or hindrances from this night. "How will we get beyond this?"

"It will not be easy. But we will." He lifted the reins with one hand, tugging them to the left, and clicked his tongue for the horse to turn around on the narrow road. "Together." He squeezed her hand. "For scripture says, *He that loveth not knoweth not God, for God is love. In this was manifested the love of God toward us, because that God sent his only begotten Son into the world, that we might live through him. Herein is love, not that we loved God, but that he loved us and sent his Son—*"

"*—to be the propitiation for our sins,*" she spoke the ancient words with Levi. "*Beloved, if God so loved us, we ought also to love one another.*"

"For we have both sinned, Hannah, you and I. But God's sacrifice covers our sins, and through His love, through the love we will share, we will get through this."

"Together," she whispered, squeezing his hand in return and smiling at him through tears.

Snowflakes began to fall, lightly covering the fields and road. The clippity-clop of hooves echoed in the stillness, reminding them of where they had come from and where they were going, and the faith that had carried them through together. Their love, a real love, a sacrificial love, would see them through, because love always triumphed.

ACKNOWLEDGMENTS

A novel is one part inspiration and the rest is all perspiration, never simply an individual project but requiring the help of many, and I am grateful for all the help I had with this project. This book was particularly difficult because of the subject matter and maybe even seen as controversial because I utilized the Amish way of life to showcase this story. I did not want to bring harm to or disparage the Amish in anyway. I greatly admire the Amish for their convictions and staunch beliefs. They make daily sacrifices for God and for the sake of their families. Any discrepancy about the way the Amish live and make decisions is my error, but please note that sometimes I tinted things slightly in order for the story to work.

For those who didn't laugh when I mentioned the idea for this book: Dorothy, Julie, Shelley, Cathy, Rachel, Beth, and countless others who not only didn't laugh but encouraged me (or was it pushing me off a cliff?), offered help with research, and pointed me in the right direction. Thank you so much!

For my agent, Natasha Kern, who laughed *enthusiastically* when I told her about this project. Thank you for embracing my ideas, even my crazy ones, and for working overtime and way beyond the call of duty to find this project the right home. I am so grateful for your help and expertise! You are simply fabulous!

For my editor, Peter Lynch, thank you for loving this project, pushing for it, and loving the book even more! I am grateful for your insights in making this the best book it could be. I am also grateful to Sourcebooks for giving this story a chance.

For Julie Whitby, my valiant critique partner, thank you for reading and reading and reading again and offering advice and encouragement. Thanks to you and Alex for touring Amish country with me. What fun we had in Intercourse, PA! We must do that again!

For the countless folks who helped me with research or brainstorming: Shelley, Beth, B (you know who you are!), Rachel Hauck (with my pitch!), Betty Seaman, and my sweet cousin John Wilson (who wants to be a vampire in my novel—watch for book two!), thank you so much for your help! Thanks also to those amazing Amish writers who encouraged and welcomed me even though my story wasn't as traditional. I am grateful for your support. Also, to some amazing prayer warriors: Rachel Hauck, Lisa Buffalo, Jerri Phillips, Margo Carmichael, Maria Jerke, Leslie Morris, and so many Facebook friends who so willingly pray; I can do nothing without your prayers and God's help.

For Dorothy Love, can you believe we've been writing this long? I would not have missed the journey or your friendship. Writing would be half as much fun without our brainstorming sessions! Love you!

For my sweet family, my husband and my children, who never complain about doing laundry or eating pizza (again) when I am on deadline. I am so grateful for each of you, for your enthusiasm and delight when I start a new book. I love you.

ABOUT THE AUTHOR

LEANNA ELLIS IS THE winner of the National Readers' Choice Award and Romance Writers of America's Golden Heart Award. She has written numerous books in the romance genre as well as the inspirational market. With her husband, two children, and wide assortment of pets, she makes her home in Texas.